Marianna Morgan, Private Investigator

Udder Confusion
The case of
Choreographed Cows
and Alien Experiments

Janet Christian

Plum Creek Publishing
P. O. Box 29
Lockhart, TX 78644
www.PlumCreekPublishing.com

This is a work of fiction. All of the characters and incidents are products of the author's imagination or are used fictitiously. Any resemblance to actual events or people is purely coincidental, unless the person begged to be included, in which case they're stuck with the author's depiction. No cows were harmed in the writing of this book. All knowledge of aliens will be summarily disavowed by the author.

Please visit Janet's author's page at: www.JanetChristian.com
Follow Janet on Facebook at: www.facebook.com/JanetChristianAuthor/
Connect with Janet on LinkedIn at: www.linkedin.com/in/janet-christian

ISBN-10: 0692837124
ISBN-13: 978-0692837122

BUBBA'S BLUES

*He that climbs the tall tree has won right to
the fruit. ~Sir Walter Scott (1771-1832)*

I eased my butt onto the makeshift deer hunter's perch—a metal tractor seat bolted twenty feet up in the fork of a centuries-old live oak. I told myself it was fine and would hold, since I'm a medium-sized female and most hunters, at least around here in central Texas, are well-fed men.

In the darkness, I could barely see the twenty-something head of horned, red-with-white-face cattle grazing below me. *How'd I get to this?* I thought. As a private investigator, I've taken some pretty funky jobs, but cow-sitting ranked at the top of the list.

At least the weather was nice. The moon was a mere sliver, and the sky was crystal clear and filled with ten times the stars I'd ever see where I live, in the well-lit town of Cedar Park, northwest of Austin, Texas. The early October air was cool, but not cold.

My weekend had been normal enough. I'd gone on my usual Saturday morning motorcycle ride on Pancho Villa, my Suzuki 1200 Bandit motorcycle. Every Saturday that I could, I joined other members of the Hill Country Cruisers motorcycle club for breakfast at the Blue Bonnet Cafe in Marble Falls, followed by a group ride through the rolling hills and winding roads of the Texas Hill Country. I looked forward to my weekends for this reason more than any other. My own family was small and scattered, so my fellow riders were my family.

I'd awakened to a gorgeous, cool Sunday morning and decided to blow off household chores and take another ride. Instead of heading west again, I'd opted to go south. Austin straddles the Balcones Fault, so while there are hills to the northwest, the southeast quickly flattens to gently rolling plains and, ultimately board-flat coastal grasslands and scrub.

After a pleasant, hundred-mile circuit through half a dozen small towns, I'd found myself eating barbecue in Lockhart, the *Official BBQ Capital of Texas*. I bravely fought the usual crush of visitors who hit the famous barbecue joints every weekend.

Hundreds willingly stand in line outside, even in the summer heat, baking in the sun for a couple hours, just to get a bundle of ribs, brisket, or sausage wrapped in butcher paper. No forks here— this is Texas finger food. At least the October weather didn't leave me with a sunburn as I waited for my turn to order.

I'd planned to start for home after lunch, then saw a sign for the Lone Star Gun Range. Since I had my Sig 380 semi-automatic handgun with me, I figured it was a good time to check out a new range. I'd never had to shoot anyone, although I'd surely wanted to in my last case. But for a variety of reasons, I was glad I'd ended up not doing that. Still, like most PIs, I needed to be prepared. So, like all *smart* PIs, I hauled myself to the gun range at least once a month.

Eagle Peak, my usual shooting gallery a few miles west of Cedar Park, was closing soon, another victim of the rampant growth in my once-sleepy town, now just another bedroom community being swallowed by Austin. I would miss Dee Day, the crusty, but sweet owner of Eagle Peak. Even if I never ran across her again, her name would always make me giggle like a schoolgirl.

I paid Lone Star's range fee, filled out an ID card, and bought some paper targets. The firing area was clean, and the shooting stations were a comfortable couple of yards apart. I waited for a break in the shooting, then headed downrange and stapled my first target in place.

I fired six rounds, reloaded, and popped off six more. It was hard to see my bullet spread clearly, so I set my Sig on the bench, stepped back, and held up my hand to signal to the other shooters I wanted to collect my target. Within a couple minutes, everyone had stepped back and together we headed downrange across the firing field so we could inspect or replace the stapled paper targets off our respective plywood backboards.

All but one of my shots was in the center circle. I was removing my target when the guy next to me said, "Not bad for a girl."

I spun his direction, feminist assault-tongue fully loaded, but stopped short. He looked to be in his seventies. He wore faded, worn denim overalls with a ragged tear in the bib pocket. His face had the weathered, boot-leather look of a man who's worked hard most of his life in the Texas sun.

I snapped my mouth shut, biting my tongue in the process. After swallowing the coppery-tasting blood, I smiled at him. "Thanks. My grandfather taught me. Now I'm a private investigator, and I need to keep my skills in good shape."

"A PI, huh?" He shook his head. "Ain't even that many men PIs, let alone a gal. What pushed you in that direction?"

I shrugged. "I'm pretty good at getting to the bottom of things." With a smile I added, "And I like helping people out of bad situations that aren't their fault."

He stared at me for several seconds, then stepped close and whispered, "Ma'am can I buy you a cuppa coffee? I do believe I am in need of help getting to the bottom of something."

"Sure." I finished tearing my target off its corner staples, rolled it up, and tucked it under my arm so I could extend my hand. "By the way, my name's Marianna Morgan."

His grip was firm but not crushing, his fingers calloused and thick. "I'm William Taylor Sutton Livasee" His voice rang with the unmistakable tone of family pride, although the string of names meant nothing to me. "But all my friends call me Bubba."

Of course they do. Half the men in south Texas are nicknamed Bubba. The rest are Sonny or Junior. "It's nice to meet you, Bubba."

Fifteen minutes later, we were sitting at Harvey's Cafe, sipping steaming coffee and eating some of the best pecan pie I'd ever had. "Tell me how I can help you."

He hesitated, then leaned toward me. "It's about my cattle."

I blinked. "Cattle. As in…cows?"

"Yes'm. I'm afraid they're goin' crazy."

"Shouldn't you be talking to a vet?" *Or an animal shrink? Or maybe a human shrink?*

He shook his head. "Can't do that. Even if the gubment just suspects mad cow disease, they can destroy a whole herd."

"But what if it is mad cow? Wouldn't that be dangerous, not just for you, but for all the other ranchers in this area?"

"Yes, it would." Bubba nodded. "But I honestly don't think that's it. They ain't crazy all the time. And their behavior don't look like the news reports I've seen of those infected European cows. But something is still very wrong."

"Can you describe their symptoms?"

"Ma'am, you wouldn't believe me if I tried. I think you need to see it for yourself."

I'd followed him to his ranch two miles east of Lockhart. We took his Gator Utility Vehicle, which looked like the offspring of a mini-pickup and a golf cart, to the back field where the cows were lounging.

"Gonna rain." Bubba pointed toward the cows.

"How do you know?"

"Cows are laying down."

Never having studied bovine meteorology, I didn't know how to respond to that, so I said, "They just look calm and peaceful to me."

He nodded. "They are right now. But they won't stay this way. Always happens at night."

As much as I wasn't looking to investigate cows, I was intrigued. "Tell me what happened. What you saw."

"I can't." Bubba frowned. "You'd think I was the crazy one. Please take on the job, and I'll get you set up to see for yourself."

We agreed on my fee, then I headed home to swap my bike for Pickle Toy—my red Mustang GT.

For years, I'd made up acronyms and phrases to help me remember important license plates. I'd started the habit when I was still a technical writer in California's Silicon Valley area, so when I was late to work, I could tell which bosses were already there. Back then, it was a hide-and-seek aid. These days, it came in handy in my private investigation work. I didn't have to create an acronym for my own license plate, but I did anyway. My PKL-20Y license plate became Pickle Toy.

Besides wanting the car, I needed the supply case in the trunk. My Trusty Spy Kit contained binoculars, a whistle, pepper spray, 9 mm Kahr P9 semi-automatic handgun, blanket, first aid kit, and a change of clothes, in case I ended up covered in blood, mud, or other unsavory filth. I also joked the clothes might come in handy if things got really scary and I didn't react well.

Even without swapping vehicles, I had to feed my furry horde of five cats—Boggle, Polly, Cooper, Mayfly, and Deke. Until recently, I'd had six cats. Georgie was now buried in my backyard. The means of his demise still woke me up some nights.

As soon as I wheeled into the garage and shut off Pancho's engine, I could hear the cats meowing at the door. They were expressing their usual discontent that I'd gone a whole day without feeding them their beloved canned food.

They had dry food in multiple bowls around the clock, but they clamored like starving vagrants when twice a day I gave them each a tablespoon of canned food as a treat. I portioned out their evening snack then showered, changed into my usual all-black, Stealthy-PI-Mode clothes, and ate a tuna sandwich, washed down with strong coffee so I'd be ready for whatever lay ahead.

Before leaving home, I'd called Judy, my best friend since high school, to tell her about my new case.

"You're heading to Lockhart to babysit *cows*?" It took Judy several minutes to stop laughing. "Girlfriend, you've had some weird cases, but…cows?" She broke into another fit of laughter before calming down again.

I promised to keep her up to date on anything I saw, heard, or smelled while staking out the cows.

I'd pulled into Bubba's ranch just before dark. He'd given me directions to the back field where we'd gone that afternoon and handed me the keys to the Gator.

I'd trundled down the rutted gravel road to the location of the deer blind and stashed the Gator among some ash junipers, or cedars, as we called them in Texas. Comfortable that the Gator was reasonably hidden, although against what I couldn't guess, but being discreet was a sensible habit for a PI, I'd climbed the tree I now sat in and settled in to wait. It'd now been dark for over an hour. *How long will I have to wait?*

Not long, apparently. A low hum snapped me back to my present situation. Someone—or something—was heading my direction.

MUTILATED MEMORIES

This was more than just a cow—this was an
entire career I was looking at.
~Gary Larson (1950-)

I gripped the cold edges of the tractor seat and shifted to a more secure position. Squinting into the darkness, I saw nothing, but the hum grew louder. Out of the blue—black?—a bright light suddenly shone straight down from overhead.

I blinked against the intense onslaught to my eyes. The beam lit up the ground like a nighttime construction site. All I could tell for sure was that the source came from above my twenty-foot perch.

I was glad I'd worn dark clothing to disguise my presence. My brown hair wouldn't show, but my white-girl skin would be easy to see. I pulled my black T-shirt up high over my nose, brushed my shoulder-length, brown hair forward across my cheeks, and squinted to hide the whites of my eyes.

The humming sounded like a swarm of killer bees were headed my way.

What the hell is going on?

I looked down. Shock almost caused me to slide off the tractor seat. All of the cows were facing the nearby creek, standing shoulder to shoulder at full, silent attention. As one, they stomped their right hooves three times. Then with equal precision, they stomped their left hooves. They mooed together several times as if following some invisible conductor's wand. Their final bit of synchronous performance art was to take two steps backward while remaining perfectly shoulder to shoulder. It was all I could do to keep from yelping.

I stared with rapt attention, gripping the tractor seat so hard my knuckles cramped. The cow-show went on for another minute, then one cow near the middle shuddered and collapsed. A split second later, the light went out and the humming faded away.

Blinking rapidly, trying to adjust my eyes to the sudden darkness, I could do nothing but listen. The soft, random lowing of the cows returned. After a few more minutes, I could just make out their white faces in the dark. They were wandering around beneath my tree, nibbling on grass, seeming either unaware or unconcerned of what had just happened. I was neither of those things.

I sat for a long time, afraid to move in case the—whatever the hell that was—came back. Finally, I stepped onto the top board nailed into the trunk of the tree and eased down the make-shift ladder.

I stood still, listening and watching, before nervously picking my way between the grazing cows, to stand beside the fallen one. Fishing my penlight from my pocket, I examined the poor thing. She appeared dead, at least to my bovine-untrained eye. Her eyes were open, but her side was not going up and down. If she was breathing, it was slow and faint.

My hand shook as I reached out to touch her neck. I felt around, unsure where one would find a cow's pulse. I found none in the neck, so moved to her chest area. Her heart no longer beat. She was definitely dead.

What killed her? She dropped like a stone, with no hint of what happened.

I'd watched the whole thing and still had no clue. I hurried to the Gator and headed to Bubba's house as fast as the utility vehicle could go. I didn't care how late it was. Bubba and I were going to have a talk.

"Bubba! Wake up!" I pounded on his back door.

The porch light flipped on and Bubba opened the door, then pushed open the screen.

"I can tell by the look on your face you saw what I couldn't describe to you earlier." Bubba stepped back. "Come on in. I'll make coffee."

Shivering from nerves, I sat at the man's simple wooden kitchen table and watched him prepare the coffee. I don't know why I was surprised to see he had a fancy, new coffee machine. Just because his house—and he—looked country and a bit run-down on the outside, didn't mean he wasn't a modern man on the inside.

Bubba set a large mug of black coffee in front of me and sat in the opposite chair. He didn't offer me sugar or milk, and I didn't feel like asking. I took a sip and nearly choked. He might use a modern coffee machine, but he'd managed to make it taste like strong, bitter campfire coffee. I probably could have stood a spoon straight up in the mug.

"Tell me what you saw," Bubba said.

I shook my head to clear it. "Now I know why you wouldn't tell me earlier. I really would've thought you were crazy."

Bubba grinned. "Maybe I am. But that's got nothing to do with the cows." He sobered and looked me in the eyes. "Go on. Tell me."

"Nothing happened for a while. I just sat in the tree and watched them graze, at least as much as I could see in the dark. Then I heard a hum and..." I told Bubba everything that had happened, including checking on the fallen cow.

"Damn." He shook his head. "That's three cows in just two weeks. Whatever the hell's going on is gonna cost me a fortune."

"You lost two more cows before this? The same way? Did you see what happened?"

"Stumbled on the first cow. Didn't see the second cow fall at the time. Found her a few days later."

"Wait, I'm confused. What did you see? When?"

"Found the first cow a week and a half ago. I was walking the fence, checking for breaks and climbovers, when I ran across her in a dry ditch."

"Climbovers?"

Bubba nodded. "When someone comes poachin' on your land, they cut or climb over your barbed wire fence. Cuts are easiest to spot, of course, but climbovers leave a telltale droop in the wire."

"Okay." I filed that tidbit away in the Useless Trivia section of my brain. "Did you look the cow over?"

"Sure did. She was still fresh, probably died the night before. Didn't see nothin' obvious. No sign of wild animal attack or disease. She was just…dead." Bubba shrugged. "Cows die sometimes."

"I never thought about it, but yeah, I can see that. Even people sometimes just die. What did you do?"

"Didn't think no more about it or say anything to anyone. Did a headcount on the rest of the herd, and they was all there and seemed fine. Left the dead one for the coyotes."

"You just left it there?" It may only be a cow, but it was hard to imagine not burying it.

"Can't afford to have the vet come with his backhoe to bury a cow. Always do for my horses, though." Bubba shook his head. "Horse is more like family. Gotta remember, cows are my livelihood. I can't get attached to them."

I nodded. "I understand. What about the second cow that died?"

Bubba stared at his coffee. "I was huntin' wild hogs. It's always open season on 'em, because they're an invasive species. They wreak havoc on crops, dams, fences, and pretty much anything they can get near to. And they can kill a calf without breakin' a sweat. Not that hogs sweat. Anyway, ranching don't bring the money it used to, and my Social Security ain't that much. I get five dollars from the county for every wild hog tail I turn in, plus the meat helps keep my freezer full. My belly, too." He paused, probably to see how I'd react.

"Sounds smart. You've got to protect your land." I wasn't sure I'd eat wild hog, but my answer must have been what he wanted to hear, because he continued.

"Late last week, I was in a box blind not far from the tree blind you was in tonight. I heard and saw pretty much the same thing, including watchin' a cow drop dead. Just the bright light from above and the weird way the cows acted. Like soldiers. Or circus performers."

I wouldn't have thought of those descriptions, but both worked. "Box blind?"

"Looks like a outhouse, 'cept instead of a crescent moon on the door, it's got small openings on all sides where you can watch for deer and shoot 'em from inside."

"Oh." I sat back and exhaled a big breath. "So you're pretty sure it's happening fairly often, but no idea how often? Or why?"

"Or who's doing it." Bubba nodded. "That's why you're here. You've got to figure this out before all my cows end up dead."

"I'll do my best." And I would, too. I just hoped it was enough. "Let me ask a question. You said you found the first cow in a ditch. Where'd it happen the second time? And how far were both of those from the deer blind where the one died tonight?"

"Ditch is by the back fence, maybe a hundred yards from the tree blind. Second cow was more or less between those two spots. Why?"

I frowned. "I'm trying to get a sense of geography. Sounds like it's only happening at the back of your ranch, far from the house."

"Yep, that's right." Bubba chewed his lip. "Sometimes I can't sleep and I'm up in the wee hours. Never seen no light or heard noises coming from the nearby fields, even when the cows are in 'em."

"How about neighbors? Are there any houses near the far end of your property?"

Bubba shook his head. "No nearby neighbors. No one around to see what's goin' on. Maybe it's Colorado all over again."

"Colorado?" I cocked my head in confusion. "I don't remember anything in the news."

Bubba barked a harsh laugh. "Happened long 'fore you was born. Late sixties. A horse, a bunch of cows, and even some sheep were found mutilated on ranches in southern Colorado."

"Mutilated? Like an animal attack?"

"Nope. Like surgery. Or dissection."

That gave me pause, and caused my stomach to flutter. I shook my head. "But who was doing it? Who *would* do it?"

"No one was ever sure, but folks was sayin' it was some government black project. Or aliens. Or both workin' together."

"Oh come on. You can't be serious." *Aliens? Black projects? Should I return Bubba's retainer and get out of this case before I get sucked into his delusions? Have I ended up with yet another nut for a client?*

"I'm serious as a heart attack. And I ain't crazy, dammit."

Crazy was exactly what I feared, but I wasn't going to admit that. "I can't believe that's what folks thought. You're sure?"

"I just said so, didn't I?" Bubba frowned. "Are you gonna believe me or not?"

"It's not that I don't believe you…"

Bubba's eyes narrowed.

"Okay, it's hard to believe, I admit. But I'm willing to listen. Really. Please go on."

After several seconds of silence, Bubba *hrmphed* and continued. "Anyways, all the animals looked like they'd been cut on real careful. Hide stripped off. Neat and clean, like with a scalpel. Internal organs all missing. Not tore out, but cut out. No blood around the bodies. No footprints, neither. And flies and coyotes wouldn't touch the bodies."

"I've never heard about that. How long did this go on?"

"Don't remember no more. Weeks. Months. A while. Then it all just stopped."

"And no one ever found out what'd happened?"

Bubba shook his head. "No ma'am. Some folks claimed to have seen UFOs. Others said they saw gubment helicopters. Painted all black. But there was never proof. No evidence of either. Didn't have no cell phone cameras back then."

As much as I didn't want to give any credence to Bubba's story, it would certainly help explain the bright light and hum. Just how quiet were those government black helicopters? Weren't they almost silent except for a low hum? I was troubled by the whole idea, but one thing especially bothered me.

"You said those animals looked surgically cut on, or dissected. But there wasn't a mark on the cow I watched die tonight. And didn't you say the cows you found were clean, too?"

"Yes'm, that's right. Not a scratch on either one." Bubba stared into the distance for a moment, then continued. "Course, these days they have laser surgery and micro surgery. Stuff they didn't have back then."

He seemed to be presuming a lot as far as alien capabilities went, but I decided not to bring that up. Instead, I stood. "Tell you what. I'll do some research on the Colorado case. And I'll see if other incidents have happened since then. Might be a long shot, but may as well rule it in or out right from the get-go." *I need to see if you're nuts or how true what you're telling me really is.*

"Thanks for not blowing me off. I almost didn't say nothin' for fear you'd react just like you ended up doing."

I blushed. "I'm sorry. It all just sounds so...far-fetched."

"May be, but the gubment's done worse."

"You're right." I nodded and sighed. "Let me get some sleep, and I'll get started on my research."

Bubba stood and held out his hand. I gave it a firm shake before heading to my car and then home.

I didn't doubt that Bubba remembered the sixties incident. But was his recollection of the story accurate? And were the mutilations really never solved? And more importantly, was it happening again?

I was halfway home when another thought occurred to me. He said he'd left the cow in the ditch for the coyotes. Had they touched it? Knowing whether they had would tell me a lot. Or not. But I needed to know. I'd have to head back to Bubba's ranch soon to see for myself.

RUSTLED CATTLE

*They move in stealthy secrecy. They are
unidentified, alien, extra-terrestrial, UFO.
~Michael Dorn (1952-), Narrator,
Where are all the UFOs? (1996)*

I didn't get home until after two and immediately undressed and crawled under the covers. As tired as I was, though, my brain refused to turn itself off. I ended up flopping around like a fish, much to the consternation of the four cats that wanted to snuggle next to me. Mayfly wisely chose to curl up on the chair in the corner, on top of my still-warm clothes.

The ringing of my cell phone woke me at 6:45 Monday morning, an hour after I'd finally drifted off into exhausted sleep. I grabbed the phone from the nightstand, resisting the urge to throw it against the wall. "What?" It was the best I could manage.

"Good morning, sunshine!" Larry Morrow's baritone voice boomed in my ear.

"Says you." I sat up and rubbed my eyes.

"You sound like crap." Larry knew me better than even my own family. We'd been best friends since we were five. We'd tried dating in our teens but decided that was a bad idea. We'd returned to best friends status and had remained that way through thick and thin.

"Yeah, well, you deal with lights from the sky and dead cows at midnight."

"For this story, I'll bring tacos." He hung up before I could protest. Not that I would. I'm a sucker for brisket and scrambled egg breakfast tacos, and Larry knew the best place to get them.

I took a quick shower and fed the cats. I was brewing coffee when Larry's car pulled into my driveway. I'd already unlocked the front door, and shortly he waltzed into the kitchen, waving a paper bag that sported grease spots on the bottom. I poured coffee as he piled the tacos on plates. We sat at the table and dug in.

"Tell me about your new case." For the last five years, Larry had been a detective with the Austin Police Department. Not only was he interested in my cases out of professional curiosity, he'd bailed my butt out more than once. I was always happy to update him, in case my butt needed bailing in the future.

When I finished my story, Larry whistled. "You sure get some weirdo clients. Government conspiracies? Aliens?"

I laughed. "The weird cases are always the most fun." I glanced at the visible part of the scar on my right leg, which extended from my upper thigh to below my shorts. "Most of the time."

"Any case can have problems." Larry got up, refilled his coffee, then sat down again. "Since each of your cases pretty much pay you the same, you may as well have a good time while you're working."

"I hope I'm not as clueless with this case as with the last one. I felt like an idiot by the time I figured out what was going on. And I don't even know where to begin with this new case."

"Go searching for aliens." Larry laughed so hard he snorted.

"You're close." I shrugged. "I'm going to research the Colorado incident and see if there are others. Look for similarities. If nothing else, I can eliminate that hypothesis from Bubba's mind.

"Sounds like a good idea. I don't believe one bit of that crap, but some folks do. Might as well settle it right off the bat." Larry stood and stretched his six foot frame. "Gotta go. Working with a trainee today. Wish me luck that he doesn't get us both shot."

I stood and gave him a hug. My head barely reached his chin. "Luck to both of us."

After he was gone, I cleaned up the kitchen, changed into jeans, and headed for my office. I could easily have worked at home, since I mostly use a laptop, but I'd decided long ago to discipline myself to keep work at work and home as a sanctuary. I can be compulsive, or is it obsessive? Whatever. I just know if I let myself work at home, I'd end up working all the time.

Plus, I like to have a neutral location to meet clients. Sometimes clients turn out to have issues they failed to disclose for one reason or another. I've learned to keep those issues far from my house.

I drove to my small office on the second floor of the Winchester Office Center, a nondescript, borderline-ugly building north of downtown Austin. I didn't care how it looked on the outside. The WOC was affordable, well-lit, and safe. I gave up on my previous office—which met only the *affordable* criteria—after being burgled one too many times for my insurance's comfort level.

Another reason to make regular visits to my office was the large palm plant in the corner. I'd recently nearly killed it, not on purpose, but through unfortunate neglect while I recuperated from a nasty accident. I figured I owed the plant my TLC for having held on through my recovery time.

It was just after nine when I parked in the small, shady lot and entered the two-story building. I took the stairs instead of the elevator, and strolled past the office of Jason R. Storga, Attorney at Law. Jason often hired me for research and stakeouts. His jobs were usually boring, but also usually lucrative, thanks to his clients' willingness to pay handsomely to accumulate evidence before going to court.

There was an envelope from Jason taped to my office door's frosted glass window. Since my hours were irregular, he often left notes about services he wanted me to provide. I pulled the envelope off, unlocked the door, and entered, flipping on the flourescent lights. I glanced at the potted palm, which looked pretty healthy today. I glugged some water from the Ozarka cooler behind my desk and dumped it into the plant's clay pot.

I glanced at my answering machine as I sat at my desk. No messages today. Good and bad. Good, because I was already busy enough. Bad, of course, because like any self-respecting, self-employed person, I worried that *busy enough* might not last.

Before starting my cattle mutilation research, I opened the envelope from Jason. He needed some property records research. I hated the basement archives at the county courthouse, but I'd go there for Jason. *I just hope the clerk doesn't remember what happened last time I was there. I wonder how long it took to recover all those ancient computers I managed to lock up?*

I could try searching ERAS, the Electronic Records Archival Service I subscribe to, but they charged a per-search fee in addition to their monthly minimum. I could find the property information for free at the courthouse, another good reason to go.

I opened my laptop and checked my business email. I had a few requests for casework, none of which would take long. I loved and hated these quickie one or two day jobs. They were easy, making them lucrative. They were also boring, making them a drag. I preferred getting into the meat of a case and really having a chance to dig into things. Still, the short-term cases helped keep the lights on. The longer cases didn't come around every day, and I couldn't count on them for steady income. I sent a polite response to each person, confirming I'd be happy to talk to them.

I brewed a cup of coffee from my single-cup maker, then got up and circled my desk to straighten the magazines on the small, wood table between my two leather guest chairs, purchased dirt cheap from Jason when he'd recently redecorated his office. My crappy vinyl chairs had gone out to the curb, scooped up within minutes by a bunch of young men in a battered van.

Picking up the magazines, I used the palm of my hand to dust off the table. I replaced the magazines, fussing briefly over aligning them perfectly straight. I stood and pondered moving the cheap landscape prints around on the walls when I froze.

What the hell am I doing? Why am I dragging my feet?

Researching possible alien visits or government conspiracies should have me salivating on my keyboard. *What's wrong?* I returned to my desk and stared out the window toward the haze over downtown Austin. *What am I afraid of? That Bubba might be a nutjob and I'm wasting my time? That he's right, and I might be in the middle of something really big and scary?* I sighed, turned to my computer, and started searching.

It took some doing to wade past all the woo-woo, crazy conspiracy sites, but I found plenty of juicy facts. The first case, back in 1897, was reported by Alexander Hamilton. I was excited until I read further and realized it wasn't *that* Hamilton, it was a farmer of the same name. *That* Hamilton died in 1804, so unless time travel goes along with cattle mutilations, they were different Hamiltons.

Farmer Hamilton's story was still pretty woo-woo. It was long before TV talk shows and book deals, so I hoped that meant he had less reason to lie. Hamilton claimed he was awakened at night by loud humming noises coming from his cattle yard. He and two other men went outside and saw a three-hundred foot long, cigar-shaped airship hovering over the yard. The beings inside, whom he could see through windows encircling the ship, had already fastened a cable around one of his cows' middles. But the cow had managed to get its head tangled in the barbed wire fence.

To keep the distraught cow from choking, Hamilton first tried to remove the cable, then gave up and cut the barbed wire. Last he saw, the space ship, struggling cow dangling beneath it, rose into the sky and disappeared. A neighbor found the cow's hide, legs, and head in his field the next day. Of course, there were no tracks—animal or human—near the carcass. Hamilton insisted he'd found weird metal triangles at the scene, but if that was true, they'd disappeared somewhere along the way.

The first modern case was the one Bubba must have remembered. The year was 1967, and the location was the San Luis Valley in southern Colorado. A family's pet horse, Lady, and several other livestock animals, were found with stripped flesh and missing organs, all removed with precise, surgical-quality incisions.

Oddly, all of the animals left out in the field remained untouched by scavengers or insects. They slowly rotted away in the sun.

Some witnesses claimed seeing UFOs and strange lights when the alleged mutilations occurred. Others claimed seeing black, unmarked helicopters. No conclusions were ever reached. Once again, metal triangles were left at the scene. This report included a couple of photos of one triangle, next to a ruler to show size. The item was shaped like a slice of pie, about five inches by three inches. The report described the metal as *unknown*.

I sat back and shook my head. This stuff was reported more often than I would have guessed. Of course, I'm a city girl, so cow news wouldn't generally float my way. But in just two years, between 1975 and 1977, nearly two thousand cattle mutilations in twenty-two states were reported to authorities.

I was stunned at the amount of information I was learning about something I'd never heard of before. Could it be happening again? Bubba's cows weren't mutilated, just dead. Could whoever was doing this be changing methods? There had to be another explanation. It was time to check back on Bubba's cows.

I called Bubba as I was closing up the office. He answered with a drawled-out, two-syllable, "Yup?"

"Good afternoon, Bubba. I'd like to run back down, if you don't mind, to have a look at those three dead cows."

"Come on. I'm here."

I debated swapping my car for Pancho Villa, because a motorcycle ride would be more fun, but I was already halfway through Austin. I sighed, climbed into Pickle Toy, and headed south.

Less than a quarter mile after I left the Austin city limits, and the laws preventing cell phone use while driving, my phone rang. I should've known by the perfect timing who it was.

"Hello, Luv," Aunt Louise chirped.

"Hi, Aunt Louise." I smiled. Aunt Louise is really my Uncle Louie. He's been cross-dressing for so many years that everyone calls him Aunt Louise. When he learned that's what people called him behind his back, he said not to worry, that he loved the name. Thereafter, everyone said it to his face. He's never expressed any interest in surgery — he simply prefered women's clothes.

Uncle Louie'd dressed in silk and frills since before I was born, so to me his clothing choice was as natural for him as his curly black hair. Even the hair that peeked out above his lace collars. And I'd never called him anything other than Aunt Louise. It could get confusing when having conversations, but the family had come to accept the variation on names and constant switching between pronouns. I just stuck with *she*, no matter who I was talking to.

Aunt Louise is somewhat of a clairvoyant. I'd received more than one call after she'd been gazing into her crystal ball or reading her Tarot cards. I probably wouldn't have the scar on my leg if I'd listened to her warning a couple of months ago.

"What's up?" I inwardly cringed, hoping it was just a call to touch base and say hi and not another vision of doom or danger.

"I see lights. And twisted, confused minds. And flying pebbles."

Bummer. It was a warning. *She sure has the lights right. But twisted minds? Is she seeing mine? Bubba's? The cows'? The aliens'? And what in the hell are flying pebbles?* As usual, I didn't want to encourage her, in case that might lead her to try reading my future even more often than she already did.

"Well, I am on a new case that involves some mysterious lights." Even though I always remained somewhat vague, I'd learned as a child not to lie to her. She had ways of knowing when you were. And she got very clingy when she took it upon herself to protect you from your own denial.

"What kind of mysterious lights? They're from above, aren't they?"

That gave me pause. *How would she know that?* "Yes they are. I'm working right now to figure out what's causing them."

"That's good, child. But beware of confused minds. There's danger there."

Before I could stop myself, I asked, "Whose minds are confused?"

"I cannot see. That part of the vision was obscured, almost as if deliberately blocked. I'm sorry."

"It's okay. I'll be extra alert and make sure no one is trying to confuse me. And I'll be careful not to believe anyone who appears confused themselves." It was a pretty good, albeit generic, promise. I figured I could keep it without too much trouble.

"And watch for the flying pebbles. They're coming for you."

I stifled a laugh. "I will keep a close watch. I promise."

"That's all I ask. I share what I see to protect those I love."

"I know you do, Auntie, and I love you for it. I'll let you know if I learn who's confused. Or if I encounter those flying pebbles."

By the time I hung up, I was just north of Lockhart. I took Ranch Road 672, which led to Bubba's place. When I drove up his driveway five minutes later, I found him standing on his porch.

"Howdy," he said as soon as I stepped out of the car. "You do that research you talked about?"

I nodded and smiled. "I sure did. And I learned a lot. That's why I'd like to borrow your Gator again. I'd like to see how those dead cows are looking now."

"Tell ya' what. I'll go with you. You don't know where the first two carcasses are layin'. And I'd like to see for myself."

We climbed onto the Gator's sun-cracked, vinyl seats and headed for the back field. We started with the oldest incident, the cow in the dry ditch. Except there was no cow. No bones. No nothing.

"Aw, hell." Bubba shook his head and frowned.

"What happened?" I circled the ditch, as if changing perspective would cause the animal carcass to suddenly reappear. There was some matted grass in the ditch and near the fence. Had something dragged the animal away?

"How much does a cow weigh?" I asked.

"This was a young 'un, so not much. Probably six hundred pounds or so."

"Six hundred pounds is considered not much?"

Bubba nodded. "Them gals weigh around eight hundred at maturity. Mr. T's now over twenty-six-hundred."

"Mr. T?" I cocked my head.

"My one bull."

"I had no idea." I leaned in for a closer look at the barbed wire fence that marked Bubba's property line. One of the barbs had a tuft of hair on it. I pointed to it. "Could this be from the cow?"

Bubba squinted at it. "Maybe. But lots of animals go through these fences at night. Coyotes, hogs, deer, coons, even the occasional stray dog. Might just be coincidence."

"But what about this drag mark? Could someone have poached the cow for food?"

"This cow died two weeks ago. Most people like aged beef, but not that old." Bubba spat in the dirt and shook his head.

"Well, then where'd the cow go, and who or what took it?"

"Probly hogs or coyotes. Drug it off into the woods. Or maybe into the field over yonder." He waved toward the neighbor's land. "Could be anywhere by now."

"Why wouldn't they just eat it here?"

"No idea." Bubba shrugged. "Scavengers don't usually bother movin' a dead animal, but they're unpredictable. Maybe there were other scavengers in the area."

I wasn't convinced, even though I knew less about wild scavengers than I'd known this morning about aliens and cattle mutilations. "Let's check the second one."

The second cow was still there. At least most of it. The head was gone. No animal had created the nice, clean cut that had separated the head from the body. The rest of the cow was bloated, but appeared untouched. The ground was too covered with leaves to see any prints — animal, human, or alien.

This time it was my turn. "Aw, hell."

"Damn," Bubba added. "I don't wanna be the next Colorado."

I didn't want that either, but things weren't looking good. "One more. Let's see what's there. She just died last night."

It was obvious as we approached the cow I'd watch collapse that she, too, was missing her head. And with just as fine a precision cut.

A cold dread washed over me. I didn't mind quirky cases, but I really didn't want them to go so far as to include little green men. Or grays. Or whatever the hell aliens were called these days.

"Looka here." Bubba pointed at the ground a few feet from the cow's body. Right in the middle of a cow pie was the unmistakable impression of a boot print, probably a man's, judging by the size.

"That's good, I guess." Whatever was happening wasn't being done by aliens. Humans were behind it. I wasn't sure secret government experiments were any better than alien ones, but at least if I got caught and hauled off, my feet would still be on terra firma. I hoped.

HIPPY SECRETS

You can be a good neighbor only if you
have good neighbors.
~Howard E. Koch (1901-1995)

We returned to Bubba's house to continue our discussion of what we'd just seen. I again sat at Bubba's table. This time, instead of making coffee, he poured us each a highball glass of Bourbon.

"Bourbon okay?" Bubba asked as he set the full glass in front of me. "Or do you want somethin' else?"

"This is great. Perfect, in fact." I tossed back a mouthful. Bubba smiled, probably because I didn't choke or cough from the hard stuff.

"So what'd you learn this morning?" Bubba took a long drink from his own glass and waited.

I filled him in on my research.

"You think that's what's happening here?" Bubba asked.

"I honestly don't have a clue. Unfortunately, I also don't have any other ideas at the moment." I shook my head. "You said you had no neighbors near your property. What's on the land around you? How close are other houses?"

"No nearby houses. The ranch to the east is three-thousand acres. The house is on the far side, a good mile or more as the crow flies from my fence line. He runs several hundred head of mostly Charolais. The ranch on the other side is almost as big. The owner lives in town. No house on that land at all. Just a big herd of Brangus and some Longhorns."

"I don't know one cow from another." I shrugged. "Except Longhorns."

"Can't miss them horns." Bubba laughed. "You've probably seen the others. Charolais are white or cream. They're the oldest breed in France. Good beef producers. Brangus are a crossbreed of Angus and Brahman—the ones with the big hump on the back of the neck. First Brangus were in South Texas. They're either black or dark red. Hardy and have great maternal instincts."

"What are your cows?"

"White faced Hereford. Most popular breed in the world. Originally came from Herefordshire, England in the 1800s. Thrive in almost any climate. Mine aren't polled, as you probably noticed."

"Um…can't say I noticed, since I don't know the difference between polled and not-polled." I grinned.

"Polled have no horns. Been bred out of that variant. I like the traditionals. Horns and all. Better temperament if ya ask me."

"How many do you have?"

"Not countin' the three them aliens killed, twenty-seven. Twenty-six heifers and Mr. T." Bubba shook his head. "Had almost a hundred, but sold 'em during the worst of the drought. Was plannin' on goin' to the auction and building my herd back up, but not until we figger out what's goin' on."

The cow lesson was interesting, but I needed to get us back on topic. "Have you talked to the other ranchers? Anyone else losing cows? Or anyone see or hear anything?"

"I didn't want to sound like a kook. Ain't talked to no one but you."

"I understand." I nodded and smiled. "But do you mind if I do some asking around?"

Bubba blanched. "I'd rather... Aw, hell, I guess you're gonna have to."

"Thanks. I promise I'll be as discreet as possible." I cocked my head. "By the way, you mentioned the ranches to the east and west. What about behind you?"

"No cows on that land. It's leased to a buncha weirdos."

That piqued my interest. "Weirdos? How so?"

"Hippies, or witches, or Satanists, or some such nonsense. They live on the far side of that land, so they ain't close to my property either."

I sat back, momentarily speechless. Maybe I was thinking about this wrong. Maybe I didn't need to worry about nearby houses, or even cows. I needed to consider proximity of land to land. "Whose land is across your back fence where the cow in the ditch disappeared?"

Bubba made a disgusted face. "That'd be the weirdos. You think maybe they're doin' it?"

"I wouldn't want to guess. Can you think why they'd be killing your cows? And how would they create a spotlight up in the sky?"

"Dunno about the light." Bubba shrugged. "But if they're witches or Satanists, maybe they're using my cows in their rituals."

I strongly doubted that was the case. Living so close to Austin, and previously living in Silicon Valley, I'd met both witches and Satanists. The witches were mostly earth-mamas and papas. Tree huggers. Friendly. Harmless. The Satanists, at least the ones I'd met, were all about decadence and having fun. They might be doing long-term harm to their own bodies, but they didn't pay much attention to the outside world. Still, I wasn't going to ignore any possibilities for now. It wasn't any more farfetched than aliens.

"I guess I'll talk to them first." I chewed my lip in thought. *Whoever they are, Bubba believes they're out of place, so it's as good a starting point as any.*

I checked my phone. It was only two, still early in the afternoon. Plenty of time to to visit the hippies. Or witches. Or whatever. I also saw I had a couple of texts from Judy, probably asking about my stake-out. *Or maybe that should be steak-out. Sometimes I crack myself up.*

I stifled a giggle so I didn't have to explain my mental pun to Bubba. He might not find it funny.

I took another swallow of Bourbon to fortify myself and stood. "I'm going to get back to work." *I also want to see what Judy had to say.* "Tell me how to get to your…unusual neighbors."

"I don't know exactly how to get to their place, but my best guess is to take the first gravel driveway off Dry Creek Road." Bubba grabbed a pad and pen from a cluttered desk in the corner of the kitchen and drew a simple map.

I promised to keep him updated and left. While turning my car around, I glanced at the license plate of Bubba's ancient-looking white, Chevy pickup. His J40-BKH became: *Just For Nothing, But Keep Hoping* for me. Sounded like a good idea to me.

When I reached the road at the end of Bubba's long driveway, I stopped and pulled out my phone. There were three texts from Judy. The first simply said a concise *Well?* The next was the equivalent question with lengthier wording. The last was an adamant. *CALL ME DAMMIT. I WANT TO KNOW WHAT HAPPENED.*

I called and she answered before the end of the first ring.

"Was it fun? Creepy? What happened? Did you see anything? Tell me!" Judy's questions came out in one long string with no pauses.

I laughed and told her everything I'd experienced and learned.

"What now?" she asked.

"Heading to the hippies. I'll keep you posted."

"You be careful. No telling what a crazy group like that is up to."

"I only have Bubba's opinion that they're weird, but I promise I'll be careful. Just in case, though, if you don't hear from me in three hours, call Larry."

I hung up and turned back toward Lockhart on the Ranch Road, then as Bubba'd drawn on the map, I turned right onto Dry Creek and stopped at the first crushed, white caliche-limestone driveway, also on the right.

A simple metal pipe gate and two posts blocked the driveway. A NO TRESPASSING sign hung on the gate, held in place with wire. I've never been one to pay much attention to rules, so I unlatched and swung the gate open, drove through, then closed and re-latched it. I was chancing it by entering in the first place, I didn't want to get in trouble for someone's livestock getting out. This might not be the weirdo's place, or Bubba might be wrong about them having no cattle.

The rutted, caliche road wound among live oaks and mesquites. A hundred yards up, it bulged out on the left into a large, round clearing. Three single-wide trailers bordered the far side of the circle. The continuation of the road past the trailers and parking area was rough and weed-choked, indicating much less use.

I glanced around. I didn't see any signs of what these people might be. No hippy peace signs, no witchy hats or brooms, no Satanic upside down crosses. Looked like a normal place where poor country people lived.

I parked and got out. Immediately, two men and one woman appeared, one from each trailer. One man, tall and slim with a buzzcut hairstyle, held a rifle. From this distance I couldn't be sure, but it looked like it had a folding buttstock, which would make it an M1 Carbine rifle. My grandfather had owned one. He'd left it to my father, and now it was mine. I'd shot it a few times, but mostly it stayed in its case. For me, it was more sentimental than useful. I preferred handguns.

Maybe the guy holding this rifle, or his dad, had been a paratrooper in the military. He certainly had a military style haircut. The M1 was commonly used by those brave souls in World War II. That's how my grandfather had gotten his. At least the guy across from where I stood was casually pointing it at the ground. I took that as a good sign.

"Good afternoon!" I used my best Friendly-Visitor-Voice and smiled so wide my cheeks hurt.

"Can I help you?" The woman stepped off her trailer's small stoop and walked toward me, stopping about twenty feet away. She had shoulder-length, curly brown hair and wore baggy cotton pants and a T-shirt with a picture of Stevie Nicks on the front. I judged the woman's expression as wary, but not dangerous.

"I hope so." I stepped forward a half dozen paces and nodded toward the south, where Bubba's ranch was located. "I'm trying to help Mr…" My brain struggled to remember his string of names. "…Mr. Taylor Sutton—"

"—You mean Bubba?" The man with the rifle crossed the scrubby grass and stood on the parking circle near the woman. He wore jeans and an ancient-looking, white cotton shirt with a Nehru collar. I'd only ever seen those in vintage ads.

"Yes." I nodded. "I couldn't remember his whole name since he asked me to call him Bubba."

"What's that old man got you doing?" The woman squinted at me.

I hesitated, not sure how much to divulge, wondering what they thought of Bubba. I decided for cautious honesty. "My name's Marianna Morgan. I'm a private investigator. He hired me to help solve a problem. He's had some trouble with his cattle. Strange behavior and even a few deaths. He's wondering—"

"We got nothin' to do with anything happening on his ranch." The woman's tone was petulant.

The unarmed man, who'd remained on his wood deck, finally stepped forward, joining RifleMan at the edge of the driveway. He also wore jeans, but he'd topped his off with a tie-dyed T-shirt. He looked scruffier than the other two, with stringy, dirty blond hair. He remained silent, but I noticed his face showed keen interest.

Now that all three were closer, I could see they looked older than I'd expected. Probably mid or late fifties. Maybe these *were* aging hippies, leftovers from a time now past.

I shook my head in response to the woman. "That's not why I'm here." It was, but I wasn't going to admit that. "I spent last night monitoring Bubba's cows. Saw a strange light and heard a weird noise. Watched a cow drop dead right in front of me."

"What kind of light? What kind of noise?" NotRifleMan asked.

"I was sitting in a deer blind in a tree. The light came from above my head. The noise was a buzzing or humming, like a huge swarm of bees. I'm hoping y'all have seen or heard it, too. I have no idea what it was, and talking to neighbors seemed a good place to start."

"I've never seen or heard anything like that." The woman shook her head. She looked me up and down again, then finally smiled. "I'm Bengy. Sorry I can't help."

"Me, neither." RifleMan said. "Name's Earl."

"I…" NotRifleMan hesitated. "I have. I'm G.J. and I seen 'em."

"You what?" Bengy jerked her head toward G.J.

"When?" Earl added.

"A week ago. Didn't say nothin' cuz I figured y'all'd just laugh at me and tell me I've been in the crop again."

Bengy darted a quick look at me. I shrugged and grinned.

"What'd you see?" Earl asked G.J.

"I was walkin' the back field, lookin' for Bruiser. Damn dog got out of his pen again. Anyways, it was prolly around eleven. Moon was new, so I had a hard time seein' while walkin' that rutted road. We really need to get Darren over here to drag it again. It's rained, and I know he's busy, but maybe we could—"

"G.J.!" Earl snapped. "What about the light?"

"Oh, yeah. Anyways, I was all the ways to the back corner when it all of a sudden got real bright. I knew it weren't the moon. Couldn't see where the light was comin' from, but I could tell it was from Bubba's direction."

"Did you hear anything?" I asked.

"Nothin' but Bubba's cows mooing. Sounded like they was all mooin' at the same time. Like they was singing or somethin'."

"Singing cows." Bengy raised an eyebrow at G.J.

Earl snorted, but said nothing.

"I dunno. But it sure sounded weird." G.J. dropped his head and shuffled his feet, clearly embarrassed. "I knew y'all'd make fun of me."

"Thanks, G.J." He looked up, and I smiled at him. "It's sure nice to know I'm not the only one who experienced the light and odd cow behavior. I really appreciate your telling me. I wonder if Bubba's cows are the only ones affected by whatever's going on."

"We ain't got no cows," G.J. said. "We grow—"

"We're an organic farm." Earl glared at G.J. "So we don't have to worry about any critters dying on us."

"Sounds like whatever's going on at Bubba's is just there," Bengy said.

"Maybe his cows have gotten into our crops." G.J. hooted, then winced and blushed tomato red when Earl elbowed him in the side.

"Thanks for your help." I turned to leave, then paused. "Have y'all been to the back of your property today? One of Bubba's dead cows disappeared. I saw hair on the barbed wire fence and what looked like a drag mark. Bubba thought maybe coyotes or hogs had dragged the cow off, maybe onto your land."

Earl shrugged. "Could be. None of us have been back there."

"Would one of you be willing to take me?"

"I will." Bengy nodded. "We'll take the truck."

Bengy walked to a truck that was more rust than metal and climbed in. I followed, hoping like heck I could trust these odd people.

LAYERS OF LIES

*Truly, to tell lies is not honorable; but when
the truth entails tremendous ruin, to speak
dishonorably is pardonable. ~Sophocles
(496 BC-406 BC), Creusa*

Bengy had to crank the noisy diesel engine three times before it started. Soon, we bounced down the overgrown, rutted road for what felt like miles, but it was probably less than one. It hadn't rained for a couple of weeks, but gumbo-clay soil, as it's called around here, can stay gummy for weeks when not in direct sun. I felt the truck occasionally slip sideways when we passed under heavy tree cover along the road.

Bengy stopped and waved toward a barbed wire fence. "That's the fence that separates us from Bubba's place."

"Mind if I take a look?"

"Nope."

We both climbed out and approached the fence. I pointed to the other side. "There's the ditch where the dead cow was laying. And here's the bit of hair I saw from the other side." I bent over and examined the ground. "Hard to tell if this slick area is from rain washing out part of the dirt next to the ditch or from something being dragged across it."

Bengy walked over and bent beside me. "Could be either." She shrugged and stood. "Hair could be any animal, too. No way to tell if it's from a cow."

"Bubba said the same thing." I straightened and looked around. There was no sign of a cow, or any part of one. I walked up and down the fence line for a dozen paces, looking for animal—or human—tracks. Or any other sign of what happened to the cow, but along the bare, sun-baked fence line the ground had already dried hard and was too packed to show any footprints.

I was returning to the truck when something caught my eye.

"Wow, look at this." Around forty feet past where we'd parked was the clear impression of a large truck or van's tire tracks. Someone had driven in and parked beneath a live oak tree. The tracks made a large Y, indicating where they'd angled back to turn around.

"Well, shit." Bengy joined me. She was staring at the ground, hands on her hips.

"Y'all own a vehicle big enough to make these?" I asked.

Bengy waggled her head toward the truck. "You're looking at our only vehicle. Except for Earl's Harley."

Whoever had driven onto their property stopped where we stood. "Anything back here someone would be interested in?"

Bengy's body stiffened. "What do you mean by that?" She briefly glanced toward the center of their property. Past a bunch of scrubby mesquites was a thick, straight line of cedars.

I shrugged. "Whoever it was, chose to park way back here. Just wondered if there was any other reason someone would. Creeps me out that they came onto your property just to steal a dead cow."

Bengy's body relaxed and she smiled. "Yeah, that'd be creepy. But now I remember. Bluebonnet Electric was back here after that big storm a couple week's ago. Power was out all over the county. Nothing creepy about it."

I glanced around again. There wasn't a power line or pole in sight.

Bengy was lying.

I'd bet money these folks were growing more than organic vegetables on the other side of those cedars. I was lucky I hadn't been shot on sight for violating their no trespassing sign. But I wasn't about to say anything to make her suspicious.

"Yeah, I remember that storm." I nodded. "It was huge. Even lost power in Cedar Park, although the radar showed it was much worse down here." I gave her my most innocent, trusting smile. "Bet those Bluebonnet guys were crazy-busy."

"Yeah." Bengy waved toward the truck. "You ready to go? Satisfied Bubba's cow isn't here?"

No, I'm not satisfied at all. I really wanted to look around more, but that wasn't going to happen under Bengy's watchful eye. I'd figure something out. There was definitely something hinky going on on this land. But I turned to Bengy and smiled. "Sure thing. Guess whatever critters got ahold of Bubba's cow must have already polished it off."

Bengy nodded. "Some of those feral hog herds include dozens of animals, and the boars can get to seven hundred pounds. Even the sows are five hundred or so. They'd have no trouble eating a whole cow."

"Sure, I can see that." Bengy was lying again. Even if two dozen feral hogs descended on a dead cow, there'd still be bones, bits of hide, maybe even scraps of meat. Again, I kept my mouth shut.

We returned to the truck and Bengy drove us back to the trailers and my car. The two men sat on the middle trailer's stoop.

I nodded to Bengy and waved to the men. "Thanks for your help. I appreciate your time."

"You're welcome. Sorry you didn't find your cow," Bengy said.

The men nodded in unison and said nothing. As soon as I was back on the Ranch Road, I called Judy so we could chat while I headed for home. She always let me think aloud to her, and she often had great insight and suggestions.

"What's up? How were the hippies?"

"Older than I'd expected."

"So what'd you learn?"

"I'm not sure." I updated her on my encounter with Bengy, Earl, and G.J. "Today left me with a lot of questions. First, Bubba and I weren't imagining things, not that I'd ever believed that. Still, it was nice to get confirmation from an outside source, even if it was G.J., who seems a few beers short of a six pack."

"I've found that many times the simple-minded folks are the most honest. They don't scheme and plot like the sharper minds often do."

"You're right. Bengy lied to me several times. I don't know why, yet, but eventually I'll find out."

"So let's say you assume G.J.'s story is true," Judy said. "Can you also assume that, since the lights stayed over Bubba's ranch, whatever is happening is isolated to him?"

"Makes sense." I nodded as I drove.

"What else can you conclude?"

"Well..." I drummed my fingers on the steering wheel. "What about the truck or van that left deep tracks? Was it involved? Or was it there for whatever's on the other side of the cedars Bengy glanced at? The tracks were a distance from the line of cedars, but maybe the driver didn't want to cross the scrubby mesquites for fear of getting a thorn in a tire, so he or she stayed on the rutted road."

"Could be. But are you sure they weren't there for the cow?" Judy asked.

"No. In fact, those tracks make me extra suspicious. For one, why'd Bengy lie about the source of the tire tracks? Does she know who it was, or was she worried someone had been there without their knowing about it? But then why lie, instead of just admitting she had no idea?"

There was a pause before Judy responded. "Well, fear of *the feds* can make drug dealers do and say strange things."

"That's true. So would the fear of being caught while involved in something illegal."

"Now what?" Judy asked.

I sighed. "Much as I hate the thought, I'm going to have to do more night reconnoissance. This time, I'm going to investigate Bubba's back field more closely. Then I'll cross the fence into Bengy, G.J., and Earl's field to check that area, too. I'll be alone and not under Bengy's watchful eye. Or Bubba's. I'm not telling him my plans. Both investigations are going to have to be soon, if I want to figure out what's going on before Bubba loses more cows."

"You be careful!"

"I promise. Besides, in the middle of the night, those folks won't know I'm even there. Since I'll have crossed from Bubba's property, I won't be on their road. And that fence line is on the opposite side of their land from their trailers."

"I expect to hear from you bright and early tomorrow."

"Deal. Gotta go. I'm hitting Austin city limits." The last thing I needed was a ticket for talking on the phone while driving. My car was too old to support Bluetooth. Guess I needed to invest in a wireless earbud.

I drove the rest of the way home loudly singing along with the radio, doing my best to avoid thinking about spending another dark night outside, with just me and the cows. Oh, yeah, and also with whatever was stalking — and killing — them.

FLYING PEBBLES

*It is as hard to do your duty when men are
sneering at you as when they are shooting at
you. ~Woodrow Wilson (1856-1924)*

I was giving the cats their dinner when my phone rang. I smiled when I saw Patrick's name on the Caller ID.

"Hi, Heinz " I grinned into the phone.

I'd first met Deputy Patrick O'Meara a couple of months earlier, when he responded to an accident I'd been in. After we'd been dating a few weeks, I told him about how I made up ways to remember license plates. His, H57-SDT, became *Heinz 57 Super Duper Trooper*. He thought my habit was hilarious, and liked what I came up with for his license, so I started calling him Heinz.

"Hey, Crash," he said. "How's things going? Any new cases?"

I always winced at his choice of nickname, but I'd learned to accept he chose it because it was how we'd met. I smiled to myself. "A doozy. Just got home, in fact."

"How about dinner? You can tell me about it over Thai food."

An hour later Patrick and I sat in Tham's Thai, Cedar Park's only ethnic restaurant other than a half-dozen or so Mexican places of varying quality. We were both enjoying Thai iced coffee and Pad Thai noodles.

"Why would someone want cow heads?" Patrick shook his head for the dozenth time as I filled him in.

"Before I can figure that out, I've got to discover who took the two heads and one whole cow. Guess I'll go back tomorrow night."

"Do me a favor and take your gun." Patrick squeezed my hand. "Your case may sound silly, but you don't know who you're really dealing with."

"I *always* take my gun. This time, I'm taking both my gun *and* a high-powered flashlight. If that flying saucer—or whatever the hell it is—comes back, I'm going to see it this time."

After dinner, we returned to my place and spent the rest of the evening in *assault with a friendly weapon*. Patrick left just after midnight.

I slept like a baby until eight thirty. Late for me. I could've slept longer, except the cats decided I'd delayed their breakfast long enough.

I spent the rest of Tuesday morning in the basement at the Travis County Courthouse, researching the property records Jason had requested. I managed to only lock up two computers this time. I went over the notes I'd made as I ate a loaded baked potato at a wooden picnic table in front of Potayto-Potahto, one of the hordes of food trailers that had popped up all over Austin.

Someone had hired Jason to determine who actually owned a contested piece of property in one of the older neighborhoods. With Austin's recent boom, property was selling in days, sometimes hours, and often for far more than the already-exorbitant asking price. In the case of the property I'd researched, a distant uncle had popped up claiming ownership and demanding the profits. Based on the details I found in property records, the uncle was going to be sorely disappointed. The nephew, on the other hand, was about to be thrilled. I'd have to ask Jason how it went.

The rest of the day was a blur of errands and chores. Two hours before dark, I changed into my Stealthy-PI-Mode clothes and headed once again to Lockhart. When I called to say I was on my way, Bubba said he had a lodge meeting, but to take the Gator and do whatever I needed to do. He'd left the key in the ignition.

I parked Pickle Toy near his house, then drove the four-wheeler to the back of Bubba's ranch, searching for his cows. I found them mostly bedded down not far from where the second cow had died. They seemed unconcerned that one of their own lay—headless— less than fifty feet from where they lounged.

I parked the Gator and made a quick survey of the area. As I headed for the cow carcass, I coughed and gagged on the smell. On a hike several years ago, I'd run across a decomposing, partially eaten dead possum. That was a fragrant meadow compared to this. I guess the cows were unconcerned about the smell, too. They watched me and chewed their cud with no sign of distress.

I hadn't wanted to do too close an examination under Bubba's watchful eyes, but I was alone now. I'd have loved some menthol to put under my nose, a trick I'd learned from a mortician friend, but didn't have any with me. Instead, I held my breath as I bent closer to examine the cow's neck. I'd forgotten rubber gloves, so didn't want to touch the poor thing.

Other than the missing head, there wasn't another mark on the cow's body. Whatever, or whoever, had removed the head, had done so with surgical—or Samurai—precision. Cutting through cow hide, not to mention muscle and bone, also took some serious strength, no matter how sharp the tool.

The mere thought sent waves of ice through my body and my stomach lurched. For a minute, I was afraid I was going to lose the tuna sandwich I'd scarfed down before leaving home.

I swallowed several times, walked away from the reeking cow, and stood with my eyes closed. Slowly, my stomach settled down, and the chill in my body subsided. I took a few deep breaths, then turned my flashlight toward the other cows. Their white faces stood out clear against their dark red hides and the surrounding scrub. Twenty or so pairs of eyes glowed green in the flashlight beam.

A few cows lowed softly. None acted nervous or concerned. *How aware are cows? When a cow dies, does it just become part of the landscape to the other cows? Do they realize they're helpless in this world, so decide not to worry when death touches one of their own?*

I know nothing about cows, but even I knew I was probably over-analyzing a cow's thoughts. I shook my head. It was time to get ready for my stake-out. I walked the area, staying far enough from the herd that I could run if one of them, especially the towering bull Mr. T, stood and headed my way.

I intended to check out the hippies' property before settling in to a night of cow-patrol and watching for aliens, but wanted to first figure out where I'd plant myself when I was ready.

There was the nearby hunter's box blind, but it would severely limit my view. There were few trees—the area was mostly cleared for grazing. I wasn't comfortable crouching among the one cluster of thorny mesquites, for fear I'd get tangled up. A large pile of dead tree limbs and stumps was nearby, but I blanched at the thought of sharing a hidey-hole with snakes, scorpions, or other critters.

A single, squatty cedar twenty yards from the cows looked promising. I circled the tree and realized there was a small gap in its center, where a limb had split and fallen. It wouldn't afford a very good view of the cows, but I was interested in looking up. The gap left by the broken limb in the tree's low canopy was great for that.

Nodding with satisfaction, I fired up the Gator and headed for the ditch and fence across from which Bengy and I had seen the tire tracks. I'd get back to the cows after checking out the neighbor's secret garden.

I parked the four-wheeler beside some bushy cedars, then stretched across the seats on my stomach, fetching my flashlight from where it had rolled around the passenger side. At least it hadn't fallen out the doorless opening.

First, I looked over the ditch once more. There definitely was no sign of the missing cow, but when I squatted down and looked closely at the flattened area in the grass, it was clear something large had been dragged across it. Plus, there were bits of hair stuck to several thorny weeds and sharp rocks.

Whatever had taken the cow had definitely been headed for the adjacent property. I bent over and carefully wiggled through the barbed wire fence, briefly catching one barb on my shirt. I crouched and duck-walked along the drag mark, retracing the progress of the dead-cow thief. The drag stopped at the deep ruts made by the truck or van.

There were two possibilities. Either the tire tracks obscured where an animal had taken the cow, or the cow had been loaded into the vehicle that'd made the tracks. I didn't like the idea of the second possibility at all. Why would someone steal a dead cow?

Of course, someone had also taken the heads off the other two cows. The carcass I'd just examined was not beheaded by any animal other than a human—or alien—one. Another chill ran through my body, but I wasn't going to let it get to me again. I stomped my feet and shook my head, forcing my brain's attention to my physical actions.

If the occupants of the heavy vehicle had stolen the cow carcass, they probably weren't there for whatever was growing on the other side of the line of cedars Bengy had glanced at. But there was still the chance—*yeah, right*—that some animal had dragged the cow farther onto the property, and the tire tracks had simply obscured that fact.

I crossed the rutted road and made my way through the scrubby mesquites on the far side, catching my jeans half a dozen times on the damn thorns before reaching the line of cedars. Good thing I wore my old jeans. The mesquites were leaving small tears all over them.

What I found on the other side of the cedars was more than aging hippies trying to earn a little snack money. An area of at least an acre was thickly planted with marijuana plants. To hide them from aerial surveys by drug-enforcement, Bengy, Earl, and G.J. had installed tall poles every eight or so feet. Tied to the tops of the poles, and stretching across the entire pot field, was camouflage mesh netting.

I had to give those three credit. Not only had they hidden their entire crop beneath the same netting used by the military to disguise encampments and ammunition caches, they'd woven leafy cedar stems into the mesh. And they'd spray-painted the leaves and stems green so they wouldn't turn brown when they dried out.

Ingenious. Definitely illegal, but probably quite lucrative. There was no reason to move deeper into the pot field. There were cows waiting to be observed. I found a less dense route back toward Bubba's fence through the dreaded mesquites.

I'd gone less than a dozen yards when a loud crack broke the silence. Searing pain in my butt and the back of my thighs knocked me to my knees. My flashlight flew several feet away, landing at the base of a prickly pear cactus. I grunted and struggled to stand. Another noise made me pause. *Oh crap, a vehicle's headed my way!*

I lunged for the flashlight and clicked it off. Bolting for the fence, I ignored the screaming pain in the back half of my body. It was pretty much impossible to run through mesquites, especially in the dark. The needles clawed at my thighs like a wild animal, ripping holes in both the jeans and me.

I'd just reached the far side of the tire tracks when headlights beamed my way from the direction of Bengy, Earl, and G.J.'s trailers. Remembering the M1 rifle Earl had held, and knowing it was legal in Texas to use deadly force at night to protect property, sent a wave of fear through me. I tripped, going down hard on my palms. Small rocks sliced a dozen cuts into the soft flesh. Before I could get up, the noise grew more distinct.

A diesel pickup was coming directly toward me.

I had to get away. Fast. I wasn't about to stand and let them see me, so I scuttled on my stomach, GI Joe-style, the last few feet to the barbed wire fence and wiggled under the lowest strand. I yelped once as a barb pierced my shoulder, but I kept crawling. I clenched my mouth shut against a second yelp. My life might depend on it.

I rolled into the ditch and froze seconds before the truck reached where I'd tripped. The doors opened and slammed. Hushed voices volleyed back and forth, too distant to make out. A flashlight beam passed through the trees and weeds above me. It was all I could do to keep from screaming.

Instead, I focused my attention on listening, doing my best to ignore the pain in my thighs, butt, shoulder, and hands. The voices got louder, as whoever it was approached me. Even though I'd only met him a couple days before, I recognized Earl's voice.

"Go see if you can tell what set off the booby trap. And check on the pot."

"Coulda been a deer or some other animal." That was G.J.

"Maybe. If so, then we'll have fresh meat ready and waiting, won't we." Earl's voice dripped with sarcasm. "Check the damn trap. And reset it and the alarm."

"Okay, okay."

I heard shuffling, followed by several yelps. In spite of everything, I had to smile. G.J. was fighting his way through those same damn mesquites.

Footsteps crunched toward me and I ducked my head and tucked my hands under my body. I hoped the men hadn't seen me running. My tripping and falling could have saved my life.

Unless Earl pointed his flashlight down into the ditch, he wouldn't see me now, either. I badly wanted to look to see if he was shining the light around where I lay, but I was too afraid to move.

After several minutes, G.J.'s voice broke the silence. "I reset the trap and alarm, just like you said. Couldn't tell what set it off. Pot's fine. Don't look like any plants is missing."

"Really? You counted every plant?"

G.J.'s voice turned whiney. "Aw, Earl, you know I cain't do that in the dark. But I didn't see no big holes or nothin'."

"All right. Let's go back. If it was someone, he's gone now. Besides, they'll be here soon. Just as soon avoid them."

My pulse quickened at Earl's words. *They? Who were they?*

I didn't move for several minutes after Earl and G.J. drove off. When I finally tried, searing pain shot through me. I didn't think I could get myself into a standing position. *Am I stuck in this damn ditch?*

I was sure I'd been shot, although I didn't know with what. I reached as far around my backside as I could and felt the warmth of my own blood on my jeans. At least it didn't seem too extensive, so probably no major veins or arteries had been hit. In my self-exploration, my fingers found several small holes in my pants. I guessed either buckshot or birdshot.

Oh shit! Aunt Louise was right. I was chased by flying pebbles. I really needed to learn to listen to her. So far, her track record was pretty much one hundred percent accurate, even when her vision was rather obscure.

I reached into my pocket for my cell phone, but it wasn't there. *Oh god, I hope I didn't lose it in the hippies' field. I'd never find it, certainly not in my present condition. And if they found it...*

Rolling onto my side, I felt around the area, looking for the flashlight. Wherever it was, it was out of my reach.

What now? Surely Bubba will come looking for me after he gets home and sees me and the Gator are still gone. Then a horrible thought screamed at me. *Maybe he won't. He might not look for me until dawn. He'll expect me to sit out here late, waiting for the lights.*

A second horrible thought followed the first. *How will he get back here without his utility vehicle? The sheer quantity of mesquite thorns and the badly rutted trail make it unsafe for a truck or car.*

Panic welled up inside me, threatening to take over. I fought it down with everything I had. My survival depended on keeping my wits about me, and thinking of what to do next.

I slowed my breathing and thought about my cats. Focusing on their funny antics when I gave them catnip calmed me down. I listened to the sounds of the night. In the distance, the cows mooed at random intervals. *What do cows say to each other? Is their mooing about the food they're eating? Are they commenting on the sounds they hear?*

Speaking of sounds, I suddenly heard noises close by. I froze. The rustling became loud and I started shaking. After a couple of minutes, a mother raccoon and five kits wandered by just feet from my head. She stopped and stared directly at me. Sniffing the air, probably pungent from my sweat and blood, she bared her teeth and started to approach.

I reached for my gun, which was thankfully still snapped in its holster on my belt. I didn't want to shoot a mother animal, but I would if she got any closer. I didn't want rabies, or extensive facial reconstruction, either.

One of her kits trotted to the edge of the ditch. I waved the gun and growled as fiercely as I could. The kit bolted and ran, so the mother abandoned her inspection and ran after her baby, followed by the other four.

I sighed and reholstered the gun. The movement caused the pain in my thighs and butt to grow worse. I felt light-headed, and I was getting cold. It was a mild night, for October, but I was hurt and laying on damp soil.

I tried shifting in the ditch, but that only made it hurt more. I sucked in a breath and gritted my teeth. I was going to have to get myself out of the ditch, but every time I moved, my head swam and what little night vision I had threatened to fade completely.

To keep from passing out, I strained even harder to hear the night sounds around me. No more animals came my way, but I heard something scarier. Another vehicle was approaching from the pot farmers' field.

I froze, again. The vehicle stopped. From my position I couldn't tell how far away. The engine switched off, followed by the sound of doors opening and closing. It was too far to hear voices. *Are these the people Earl had mentioned? What are they doing? Are they doing something with the pot? Maybe they maintain the camouflage netting.* I snorted. That sounded lame even to me.

After what felt like an hour, but was probably only ten minutes or so, I heard what at first I thought was yet another vehicle. I couldn't tell what direction it came from. It was a lower noise. Could Bubba have a second utility vehicle?

I wanted badly to yell Bubba's name, hoping it was him, but whoever had driven up in the neighbor's field was still there. The second sound continued, somewhere off to my right, in the direction of the cows.

Horror shot through me when I realized what I was hearing. It was the Thing From the Sky. Sure enough, the bright light switched on. I couldn't see exactly where it was, but I'd bet money it was above the cows.

I could do nothing but listen as the cows began mooing in perfect harmony. *G.J. was right. They do sound like they're singing.* The last thing I remembered before passing out was the distinct sound of many hooves simultaneously stomping the ground three times.

MY SORRY ASS

*Isn't it a bit unnerving that doctors call
what they do "practice?"*
~George Carlin (1937-2008)

When I came to, it was still dark. Even the mysterious bright light was gone. I had no idea how long I'd been out. Was it still before midnight, or was it already the wee hours of Wednesday? While unconscious, my butt and thighs, and even my torn-up hands, had stiffened, making it hard to move. Plus, I was shivering—it felt more like shock than a response to the chilly night.

I reached around and explored my wounded backside again. The bleeding had stopped. My pants were sticky, but not wet. Still, I couldn't lay in this ditch and wait for Bubba to show up. I had to get out of here. If nothing else, the smell of blood might attract something much worse than a raccoon. I was probably lucky it hadn't already. Feral hogs and coyotes were plentiful in this part of the country. Even my citified-self knew that from reading local news articles.

I dug my fingers into the hard-packed dirt at the edge of the ditch, trying to pull myself out. After just a few minutes, I was panting like I'd run a marathon. Maybe I'd lost more blood than I thought. Or maybe shock and pain limited my abilities.

I rested a bit and tried again. Slowly, and straining hard, I crawled my sorry ass across the ground. Every movement sent hot pokers of pain through my nether regions. I grew dizzy and paused, taking a few deep breaths before continuing. The Gator seemed a hundred yards away, but I knew it was less than a hundred feet. It still took close to an hour for me to cross the distance.

When I managed to reach the vehicle, it took another ten minutes to pull myself onto the seat. I couldn't sit up, so I laid across both seats on my stomach.

Now what? The Gator didn't have a horn. I couldn't drive it while laying across the seats. It was then that I noticed my cell phone on the passenger floor. *Yes! It must have fallen out of my pocket when I was rooting around for the flashlight.*

Things were looking up. I checked the time. *Shit! Two in the morning?* I'd been passed out for three or four hours.

I dialed Bubba's number. It went to voicemail after four rings. I hung up and dialed again, hoping the repeated rings would wake him up. The phone went to voicemail a second time. I repeated the process. I redialed six times before Bubba finally answered.

"Yeah." His voice was slurred from sleep.

"Bubba it's me. I've been shot."

He reacted as if I'd just shot him. "What? When? Where are you? How bad?"

"I don't know exactly when. I passed out. But sometime around ten or so."

"Oh hell." Panic was evident in his voice. "Where are you?" he repeated.

"I'm by the ditch where your first cow died. But I have your Gator. How can you get back here?"

"I'll get there. Just hang on. Try not to pass out again."

Twenty minutes later, the rumble of a vehicle sounded in the distance. Another five minutes, and Bubba pulled up beside me on his John Deere riding mower. He jumped off and hurried to my side.

"Boy, I'm sure glad to see you." I grinned in spite of my pain.

Bubba nodded and shined a flashlight over my backside. "Holes in your jeans are small. Looks like maybe buckshot or birdshot."

"That's what I guessed, too."

"There's a bunch of 'em, though. Probably close to thirty pellets."

"Feels like a hundred." I moaned and shook my head.

"Who shot you?"

"Nobody. I was in the neighbor's field and tripped some kind of booby trap."

"What the hell are they doing with a booby trap? What's over there?"

"Later, Bubba. Right now I need a doctor." My head started swimming again. "How are you going to get me out of here? I can't sit up."

Bubba stroked his chin and squinted in thought. "If ya' don't mind my pawing on ya' a bit, I can wiggle under your legs. You can keep 'em laying across me while I drive the Gator back."

"Paw away." I grimaced and gritted my teeth. "I hurt bad. Can't take much more."

Bubba grabbed me around my knees and lifted. A searing pain greyed my vision and I passed out again. I didn't come to until he stopped in front of his house and killed the Gator engine.

He slid from beneath my legs and stood. "Not sure what to do now. If I call nine-one-one, it'll take 'em at least twenty minutes to get here. I'm in a Volunteer Fire Department district, not city limits. Response can be slow."

I also worried that an all-volunteer VFD might not be as well-trained as a city EMS. "What's our other option?"

"If I can get you into my truck, I can drive you to the ER in Kyle or San Marcos. Those are closest."

I nodded. "You decide where. Whichever's closer. Just get me to a hospital."

Bubba helped me wiggle and maneuver into a position where he could pick me up and carry me to his truck. I hung across his arms like a wet towel.

When we reached the truck, I opened the door, since Bubba's arms were busy holding me. One thing was immediately obvious. I wasn't going to fit on my stomach across the bucket seats and stick shift of his truck.

"Sorry, Marianna. I'm afraid I gotta put you in the bed."

"I understand, Bubba." *I just hope he hasn't recently hauled any animals or manure fertilizer back there.*

Once at the back of the truck, I unlatched the tailgate, but couldn't hold it. It fell with a bang. "Sorry."

"S'okay." Bubba grunted as he shifted me from his arms onto the tailgate. "Ain't the first time this gate's been dropped."

I shimmied off the gate and into the truck bed. It was surprisingly pristine for a farm truck. "Thanks for keeping your truck clean." I smiled as Bubba slammed the gate closed.

"You shoulda seen it last week. I hauled a mangled sheep to my back field for a friend who lives in town. Sheep was a pet. Got out and was hit by a truck. No place to bury it at her place. Truck went to the car wash after that."

I closed my eyes and said a quick thanks to the Gods of Clean Trucks for Bubba's wisdom in visiting the carwash.

"You gonna be okay back here?"

"I'll be fine. Just try not to go over too many bumps."

"County road will be the toughest. I'll go slow. Oh, I got an idea. Hang on a sec." I heard Bubba running toward his house. He quickly returned and tossed a blanket into the bed next to me. "This should help."

"Thanks!" I wiggled and squirmed until the blanket was mostly underneath me.

I passed out and woke up several times as Bubba drove. By the time we turned into the Emergency Room at the hospital in Kyle, my hip bones were sore from bouncing on the metal truck bed. The blanket had helped, but not much. I'd probably have matching bruises in a few days, one on each hip.

Bubba stopped outside the ER entrance. He exited the truck and leaned over the side. "You stay here. I'm goin' inside to tell those folks to come get you."

"Don't think I'll be going anywhere." I tried to shift to see him better, but the pain made me wince.

"I better hurry!" Bubba's voice trailed behind him as he ran for the door.

Within a couple of minutes, three ER nurses—two men and one woman—came to my rescue. One of the men pushed a gurney. They lowered the tail gate, much more quietly than I had. One of the two male nurses climbed in with me and started helping ease me toward the other nurses, who waited with the gurney at the edge of the tailgate.

"I'm Hector. Mr. Livasee here says you were shot. Tell me what happened."

I nodded. What could I say? I wasn't about to admit I'd set off a booby trap while trespassing. But I had to be careful, since I didn't know exactly what I'd been shot with.

"I was hunting on Bubba's land. I needed to pee, so I leaned my gun against a tree. Damn thing fell over and shot me in the ass."

"You didn't flip the safety on?" the second male nurse asked.

I grinned as innocently as I could under the circumstances. "I forgot to. When a girls gotta go, she's gotta go."

The third nurse, a hefty blonde woman, chortled. "Sorry for laughing, but I totally get it." She patted my shoulder. "Looks like minimal blood loss and no big gaping holes. You'll be fine. I'm Chris. And the guy who doesn't seem to understand female urgency is Paul."

"Thanks, Chris."

Through all the process of getting me from the truck bed onto the gurney, Bubba hovered at the edge of the tailgate, wringing his hands and mumbling. He looked more worried than my own grandma would've been. He also looked as if he felt completely responsible—guilty, even. But it was entirely my fault.

"Can I come with her?" he asked when they started to wheel me away.

"Are you family?" Nurse Chris asked.

"I'm—"

I was afraid they'd say no if he told the truth, and I didn't want to leave him alone in such an upset state, so I cut him off. "He's my uncle."

Bubba grinned and nodded.

"Come on, then." Nurse Hector nodded toward the sliding doors.

I've been in emergency rooms more times than I care to remember. This was the speediest I'd ever made it from check-in through the double doors into triage.

They made Bubba wait on a row of ugly, orange plastic chairs while they rushed me to x-ray. I was back within minutes and wheeled into one of a half-dozen curtained cubbies. Nurse Hector called to Bubba, who joined me and the three nurses in the cramped space.

The nurses moved briskly around me, hooking me up to monitors, drawing blood, sticking an oxygen cannula tube in my nostrils, and inserting a saline IV drip. Bubba stood off to the side, eyes as big as saucers.

Hector pulled surgical scissors from his pocket, then hesitated. "Sir, you may want to step outside the curtains while we prepare the injured area for the doctor's examination."

For a moment, Bubba looked confused. I decided I'd save him from embarrassment. "They're going to cut off the back of my jeans."

"Oh!" Bubba's face turned tomato red. "I'll be right out here if you need me." He hustled through the curtain as if the rest of us had just burst into flames.

Hector paused again. "Sorry about your jeans."

"They're old anyway." I shrugged. "Besides, far as I could tell by reaching back, these are pretty ventilated at this point."

All three nurses snorted with laughter. A minute later, my backside clenched at the sudden chill from the cold emergency room air.

Nurse Paul whistled. "That's quite a peppering you have there. Looks like you have" — he paused — "twenty-seven pellets embedded in you."

"Could've been worse," Nurse Hector said. "This looks like birdshot. About as small a pellet as it gets."

Aha! So that's which of the two possibilities it was. I added that fact to the statement I'd made to the nurses. "Yeah, I was hunting…" What the hell could I be hunting with birdshot at night? My brain whirled. I finally came up with what I hoped sounded plausible. "I was hunting rabbits."

"Well, we still have to write up a police report. That's required for all gunshot wounds," Nurse Chris said.

Oh crap. I'll have to be sure Bubba backs up my story. "Sure. No problem."

I felt something cold and wet cover my skin. I uttered a short yelp. Nurse Paul said, "Sorry. It's just Betadine. Gotta disinfect the area before the doctor gets here."

"You're not going to like this next step." Nurse Chris leaned down so she could look me in the eye. "But you'll thank me afterward. I'm going to numb the area up with Lidocaine injections."

I felt a sharp sting, followed by more in quick succession. Right after I moved back to Texas, I sat on top of a fire ant mound while I was wearing a bathing suit. This felt about the same. I lost count of the sharp stings of the needle after half a dozen.

I tried hard to stay calm, but I panted from stress and pain. The heart monitor I was hooked to beeped like a telegraph. Within another minute, though, my butt felt like it had disappeared. I sighed with relief and my breathing returned to normal. So did the monitor.

Nurse Hector draped a sheet over my bare backside. "Doc can move it when he gets here. No need to keep you exposed."

"And your uncle can come back in." Nurse Paul stepped out and returned almost immediately, followed by a still-visibly-shaken *Uncle* Bubba.

"Doctor will be by soon. After he looks at the x-rays." Nurse Hector lowered the height of the bed, and all three nurses left.

Bubba stepped close and patted my arm. "I ain't never been in an emergency room before. You okay?" He waved toward the beeping and humming monitors. "Looks scary as hell. "

"Living on a ranch and working with cattle and you've never been hurt enough to need ER care? I'm impressed."

"Oh, I've been hurt plenty a' times. But I just taped it up, wrapped it up, or stitched it up and kept workin'."

Seeing Bubba's overall healthy, but weathered look, his comment didn't surprise me. I hoped to be in such good shape when I reached my seventies. If I survived my chosen line of work and actually lived that long.

I took the opportunity of our being alone to fill Bubba in on my story, and to stress the importance of synchronizing his with mine. He had to lean in to hear my whisper, but I didn't want anyone else to hear.

"You can count on me." Bubba's volume was more a stage whisper than an actual whisper. I was glad the meaning of his words could be taken in a caregiver sort of way. In a slightly softer voice, he asked the same question he'd asked back by the ditch, "What's so important on the hippies' land they gotta protect it with a booby trap?"

I hesitated. I wasn't ready to have the authorities descend on the neighbor's ranch. Based on Earl's comment about the mysterious *they* arriving soon, I wasn't sure how involved those three were with what was going on with Bubba's cows. But I hated to lie to my own client. I opted for the middle ground.

"Looks like they have something hidden. I set off the trap while I was trying to investigate."

"Dammit. I knew those people were nuthin' but trouble."

"Maybe, but don't do anything." I shifted onto my side far enough that I could look directly at Bubba. "Let me finish my investigation first."

"Why? Are they involved?"

I hesitated again. "I don't know. And I'd rather find out before cops show up over there."

"Okay." Bubba sighed. "But I don't want no illegal crap goin' on right next to me."

"Fair enough. When we figure out what's happening with your cows, we'll contact the authorities." To dissuade further questions, I changed the subject. "How'd you get that riding mower through all the mesquites?"

Bubba shrugged. "Tires ain't suited to mesquite thorns, but it got me there. That's all that mattered."

We returned our voices to normal volume and chatted about rabbit recipes while waiting for the doctor. He blustered in ten minutes later.

"So, I hear you shot yourself!" The doctor crossed his arms over his chest, and raised one eyebrow. He looked about fifteen. Either he was a fresh grad, or I was just getting old, or both.

I blushed. "Not exactly. It was an accident. Happened when my gun fell over from where I'd leaned it on a tree."

"Cops have to come anyway, but sounds like nothing to worry about. Now, let's have a look."

The doctor whipped the sheet off of me, exposing my entire backside to the cold air, and to Bubba, who promptly fainted in a heap on the floor.

POLICE REPORT

You gotta love livin', baby, 'cause dyin' is a
pain in the ass. ~Frank Sinatra (1915-1998)

Attention immediately shifted from the pellets in my butt to Bubba on the floor. The doctor yelled for help, and Nurse Hector came flying through the curtain. The two men lifted Bubba onto the hard plastic chair next to the head of my gurney.

Bubba came to almost immediately and seemed none the worse for wear, except for being visibly mortified. He rubbed his forehead and wrung his hands. "I'm so sorry. Nuthin' like that's ever happened to me before. Heck, I've slaughtered and gutted animals, and even sewn my own stitches."

"It's okay Uncle Bubba. You were just worried about me." I smiled.

Nurse Hector nodded. "Happens sometimes. It's more about stress and worry than fear."

The doctor shrugged. "Nurse, check his vitals. I need to get back to this young lady's lovely derrière."

Based on the doctor's demeanor, and the fact that he hadn't even bothered to tell me his name, either they still weren't teaching bedside manners in medical school, or he'd skipped that class.

I didn't want to affect the quality of my care, though, so I gritted my teeth and said nothing about my *lovely derrière*. At least the male nurses were professional. I smirked when I caught Hector's eye. He winked and gave me a barely visible nod. *Yep, he knows exactly what I'm thinking.*

I couldn't see what was going on behind me, since I was on my stomach facing the wall. I couldn't feel it either, thanks to the Lidocaine, but I was able to follow the doctor's orders to Hector.

The first was to start a morphine drip in my IV. The second was to put a metal basin on the bed next to me. It would hold the pellets as they were extracted. The last things I heard as I drifted off, was the first plink into the basin and Bubba saying he'd be waiting on the orange chairs outside my cubby.

When I woke, I was still on my stomach, but I was no longer in a cubby. I was staring at a wall instead of a curtain. Bubba sat next to me, his face inches from mine.

"You're awake!" He sat back and nodded. "I been scared to death for the last hour."

I blinked several times to clear my head. I must have still been getting a morphine drip. I was woozy and my head swam. "Where am I?"

"Room four-twenty-nine. They said you needed to stay for observation."

"What time is it?"

Bubba looked at the saucer-sized watch on his wrist. "Coming right up on ten."

I glanced at the window. The sun streamed through the curtains. Morning, then. I tried to roll over, but Bubba grabbed my arm.

"Nurse said to be sure you stayed on your stomach." He released his grip. "What's wrong?"

"My cats! I've been gone since yesterday afternoon. Where's my cell phone? Do you have it?"

"Sure do. Can I call someone for you?"

"Yes, please." Morphine had me slur-tongued. "Please call Larry Morrow."

"That your husband?" Bubba asked.

"Nope. Best friend. Since fifth grade. I trust him more than anyone." Plus, I didn't want to worry Patrick. Our relationship had started over my injured body. No need to remind him how often this type of thing happened to me. Might not be good for a long-term romance. And I didn't want to have Judy come to my rescue — again. She'd mothered me the last couple of times. I'd hate to ruin our friendship over my frequent need for *care and feeding*.

I tried to listen to Bubba's end of the conversation, but drifted off again. When I woke up the second time, Larry was the one inches from my face.

"Hey there, Cutie. Always knew you were a pain in the ass."

I stuck out my tongue. "You wait until I'm up and around. I'll whup your ass."

Larry's face briefly crumpled with distress, but he quickly caught himself, smiled, and stroked my hair. "You worry me, you know. You can't go before me. Ever. You hear me? Friends don't do that."

"I'll do my best."

"That's all I ask." He sat back and nodded toward Bubba. "Bubba filled me in on the latest details. You honestly think it could be aliens? Another Colorado?"

I shifted so I could see a bit better. "Not aliens. Least I'm pretty sure it's not aliens. Especially after seeing the large footprint in the cow pie. People are involved. Apparently some not-very-nice people. No one ever knew who did Colorado. Probably people in those cases too, not aliens."

"Gubment, probably," Bubba grumbled. "Military tests."

Larry laughed, but immediately caught himself. Even out of the corner of my eye, I saw how red he blushed. "Sorry, Bubba," he said. "I know the government has done some pretty horrific things over the years. This just doesn't seem like a government job."

"Yeah, why not?" Bubba's voice was sharp.

Larry shrugged. "They could buy their own cows. And no one would ever find a shred of evidence."

After a minute's silence, Bubba sighed. "You're right. So what is it? Who's killin' my cows?" His voice cracked with emotion.

"And making them sing and dance." I giggled and wiggled my hands behind me. I was immediately mortified by my flippant response. "I'm sorry. It's gotta be the drugs."

At least my comment broke the tension. Both men laughed. I drifted off into deep sleep. When I woke, I found Larry sitting beside me on one side and a large male nurse I didn't recognize standing on the other. The nurse was taking my pulse.

When the nurse was done, I wiggled and shifted and managed to roll onto my back. I raised the head of my bed so I wasn't flat anymore. I grinned. "Hey, there's no pain."

"It's the drugs." Larry smirked and wiggled his eyebrows. "Wait until they wear off. Gonna hurt like hell to sit."

"How would you know?" I asked.

"Kuwait. Got hit in the ass by flying debris from an IED. Ate a lot of meals standing up for a while."

Bubba returned around four, looking less haggard than the night before. Larry stood and shook the rancher's hand.

"Thought I'd see how you're doin'." Bubba motioned at me. "I see you're sittin' up and not on your stomach. Guess that's a good sign."

"I'm not too bad." I smiled at his thoughtfulness and concern. "Were you able to recover your lawnmower? How're the cows?"

"Made a sled out of a big ol' sheet of plywood tied behind the Gator. Towed the mower back. Needs new tires, thanks to mesquite thorns, but that's okay."

"I'll take the tire cost out of my fee. I'm the reason they're all ruined."

"Aw, ya' don't have to do that."

"Yes, I do." I smiled, then cocked my head. "But what about your cows?"

Bubba stared at his feet. "Found another. She might've been early pregnant, too. Not sure. Didn't want to cut into her to check."

My stomach lurched. "I'm so sorry, Bubba. I'll get back on your case as soon as I can. I promise."

The older man nodded, but said nothing. Larry squeezed Bubba's shoulder. "Marianna's as good as they come. She'll figure this out for you."

"Thanks." Bubba looked up and met my eyes. "Sure am tired of losin' cows."

A knock on my room door interrupted our chat. I looked up. A police officer strode in, holding what I assumed was the report on my gunshot incident.

He crossed the room and introduced himself. "I'm Deputy Taylor Miller with the Caldwell County Sheriff's office." He sat on the chair so I didn't have to look up at him. "Tell me what happened."

I repeated my story about hunting rabbits and needing to pee, and about forgetting to put my shotgun on safety when I leaned it on a tree. It was a good thing Larry was standing behind Deputy Miller, because the smirk on Larry's face would've ruined everything.

Deputy Miller turned to Bubba. To Larry's credit, he wiped the look off his face before Miller's head finished moving. "This was on your land?" the officer asked Bubba.

"Yes, sir." Bubba nodded vigorously. "Ms. Morgan is helping me with…a potential cattle rustlin' problem, and I told her she could get her some rabbits to take home for dinner. I ain't rich, so she cut her fee in exchange."

"You got anything you can add?" Miller nodded to Larry.

Larry glanced briefly at me. "Nope. I didn't get here until around noon today."

Deputy Miller stood. "No one else was involved. Nothing but some birdshot recovered. I see no reason to pursue any further investigation. Thanks for your time." He folded the report, put it in his pocket, and left.

I sighed with relief. "I was afraid you might blow it, since you didn't know the cover story."

Bubba chuckled. "Sure, he did."

"Bubba filled me in while you were sleeping." Larry shrugged. "Good a story as any, I guess. Of course, I know you wouldn't be so careless, but Miller doesn't. He'll chalk it up to girly stupidity."

"Damn. Oh well. Better than trying to tell him I was investigating an illegal—" I froze. Not only did Bubba not know about the pot farm, I sure didn't want to tell Larry. Best friend or not, he was an upstanding detective with the Austin Police Department. He might feel obligated to take official action. "I was illegally on neighbor's land when I tripped the booby trap."

Larry narrowed his eyes at me, but said nothing.

"How long they gonna keep you?" Bubba asked.

"I'm hoping to get out of here today. Just waiting on the doctor. Soon as he says I can drive, I'll be headed your way again." Then I remembered. "Oh crap, my car's at your place."

"No it ain't." Bubba grinned. "It's out front. Got a friend to follow me here. The one who had the pet sheep. Owed me a favor. She's down in the cafeteria gettin' coffee." He placed my car keys next to the remote on a small table.

"Thanks!" I returned Bubba's grin. "This'll help a lot. At least as soon as the doc says I can drive."

"I'll be goin' now. Got another calf due any time now, and I wanna be there. I moved the heifer up to the sortin' pen by the house. Hope she'll be safer there."

"Sounds like a good idea." Larry nodded.

"I'll call you as soon as I know my timeline." I motioned Bubba over and squeezed his hands. "And thank you for everything. I won't let you down."

Bubba's eyes were glistening as he turned and left.

"That's a tall promise." Larry sat again beside me.

"I have to keep it. Bubba's a sweet old man. He really went out of his way to help me. And I hate that he's losing cows. Hate it for the cows, too."

The doctor finally showed up at six in the evening. "I'm Dr. Green. How are we today?"

I grinned and shrugged. "You tell me. Not like I can see back there. Or feel it, either, at the moment."

Dr. Green nodded, remaining serious in spite of my lame joke. "Dr. Lazlo removed twenty-seven birdshot pellets. None were deep, and there appears to be no long term damage, but you'll be sore for a while. He injected a strong antibiotic, so you should be safe from infection."

I said nothing. I assumed Dr. Lazlo was the *your lovely derrière* doctor in the ER.

"How long since you've had a tetanus shot?" Dr. Green asked.

"I keep up with those," I answered. "Had one a couple months ago, after an accident."

Dr. Green raised his eyebrows before continuing, "Dr. Lazlo stitched a few of the wounds, so avoid squatting for a week. They'll dissolve on their own in a couple of weeks. And you'll do yourself a favor if you make sure to keep a soft pillow with you to sit on at all times."

I nodded again. "When can I leave? And can I drive?"

"We generally don't discharge patients at night." Dr. Green frowned. "I can sign you off for tomorrow morning."

"Can't I get out? I have Larry here to help me get home. And I'm sure my insurance will be happy to avoid another overnight charge." I flashed the doctor my most endearing smile. I glanced at Larry and saw he, too, was smiling broadly at the doctor.

After a pause, the doctor sighed. "I'll see if a discharge nurse is available." He left without another word.

Five minutes later, a tall, painfully thin brunette, pushing a rolling computer station, entered the room, followed by a tiny redhead who looked about twelve.

"Hi. I'm Brenda," the brunette nurse said. "I hear you're going home tonight."

"I am? Oh, yes, I *am!*" I nodded with the enthusiasm of a kid at a carnival. "The sooner the better."

Nurse Brenda asked questions while the petite nurse moved around me, taking final readings and removing the medical devices attached to me. By the time Nurse Brenda stepped away from the keyboard, I was attachment-free.

"You're all set," Nurse Brenda said. "Dr. Green wants to see you back here in seventy-two hours to check there's no sign of infection. No getting your stitches wet before you come back. And no driving for twenty-four hours. Let the morphine dissipate from your system."

I nodded. *Damn. Of course, they don't know my car is here. How would they know if I drive myself home?* I lifted the sheet in preparation to getting up, but immediately hugged it back to my chest. "I have no clothes. They ruined my jeans in the ER. Well, I guess they were already ruined, anyway." I turned to Larry. "What am I going to do? You've got to help me out here."

He winked. "You know good and well I always keep a spare change of clothes in my car. Be right back."

I donned the clothes Larry retrieved. "I feel like a clown." I looked down at the baggy jeans, extra-large plaid shirt, and belt cinched into a hole Larry had to punch with his pocket knife. "All that's missing are big, floppy shoes."

Larry put his hands on his hips and grinned. "At least you don't have to worry about the pants rubbing on your butt."

I laughed. "There's always a silver lining. I'll take this one."

The petite nurse returned with a wheelchair. "Ready?"

As soon as the nurse helped me from the wheelchair into the front seat of Larry's car and left, I turned to Larry. "You can drop me at my car. Follow me home, if it makes you feel better."

"Not a chance. Your car stays here. I'll bring you back in twenty-four hours and we can get it then."

"But what about Bubba? I can't wait a whole day to get back to his place!"

"You'll figure something out. Let's just get you home first. By the way, you going to tell me what you were really messing with when you triggered that booby trap?"

I sighed. "Will you feel an obligation to uphold the law?"

"Maybe."

"Then, no. At least not yet. Give me a few days. Please."

"A few days. No more."

I stared out the window as we drove north. *Speaking of no more, I hope no more cows die because I'm not there.*

EAVESDROPPING

I knew it, you're all in cahoots!
~Hollis P. Wood, 1941 (1979)

The cats knew the minute I stepped through my front door that something was wrong. They circled, sniffing and even hissing, until Larry shooed them away.

"I'll feed the little…darlings. You settle on the sofa." Larry tossed pillows from side chairs onto the sofa as he headed to the kitchen.

"Hey, where's my phone?" I snuggled under the fluffy afghan I kept draped over the sofa's back.

"In my pocket. Be right there." Larry returned, carrying two Bourbon and water cocktails. He handed me a glass, then fished out my phone and handed it over, too.

"It's *off*." I glared at Larry. "No wonder no one called." I pressed the power button and took a big swig from the drink while I waited.

He shrugged. "Bubba said he was going to turn it off after he got off the phone with me. Didn't want you to be disturbed."

I scowled, but inside I knew Bubba'd probably done the right thing. "By the way, can I drink this while on pain medication?"

"I notice you waited until after you downed half of it before asking." Larry grinned. "But yeah, don't worry about it. It's half water. Just don't have a second one. The morphine that's left in your system won't last much longer. Figured even a weak drink would help you sleep."

I gulped the rest of the smooth liquid. "Sure will. At least I'm a side sleeper, but it's still going to be an uncomfortable few nights."

The phone blinked on and displayed that I had six missed calls and four messages. *Great. I hope these aren't angry clients.*

Two messages were from Patrick. The other two were from Judy. Both their first messages reminded me of plans we'd made. Both their second messages were considerably more agitated, wondering where I was, why I hadn't called back, and if I was okay.

Damn, I promised to call Judy back. No wonder she's worried. Tomorrow's Thursday. We're supposed to do our regular happy hour at the Oasis. That's not gonna happen. At least my date with Patrick isn't until Saturday. Hopefully, I'll be up to going out.

Neither return call was going to be pleasant. I wasn't sure who'd be more angry at my not calling from the hospital. My money was on Judy. She'd been my best friend for more years than I liked to count. Patrick and I were a fairly new couple—we'd only been dating a few months.

Larry took our glasses to the kitchen, then returned and kissed me on the top of the head. "See you, Cutie. Get some rest. I'll call you in the morning."

After he left, the cats slowly came over to check me out. I was sure I had all kinds of scary smells on me: medicine, antiseptic, strange people, and even residual sweat from when I lay shaking with fear in the ditch. Come to think of it, I might even have some eau de dead cow on me, too.

I spent ten minutes cooing and talking softly to the cats, who still kept their distance. I didn't like to think of myself as a budding Crazy Cat Lady, but my critters meant a lot to me, and their company was a big comfort. After fifteen minutes, I was covered with cats. I sighed and snuggled deeper into the pillows.

I woke up confused and stiff. It took a minute to remember where I was and why I hurt. Grabbing my phone off the coffee table, I was surprised to see it was four Thursday morning. *Should I go get in my actual bed, or just finish out the night on the sofa?*

My logical brain won out over my comfiness, plus I needed to pee. I wiggled out from under the cats and shuffled stiffly down the hall. I stared at the toilet. Sitting wasn't an option. I opted to pee while standing astraddle over the bowl, then crawled into bed.

When I finally woke up, it was after nine. Bless the cats' hearts, they'd let me sleep five more hours. Moving with the grace of the Mummy, I fed the cats and did my morning ablutions. I was brushing my teeth when my phone rang. I hurried as best I could to the coffee table, toothbrush sticking out of my mouth. A quick wave of dread washed over me when I glanced at the caller ID. It was Judy.

"Hng on minit," I mumbled as I hurried back to the bathroom sink, phone in hand. Moments later, I continued, "Good morning."

"Where have *you* been?" Judy's voice was understandably accusatory. It was also filled with worry.

"Don't be mad." I winced, knowing the reaction my next statement would get. "I was in the hospital."

"What!"

"It wasn't that bad." I filled her in on everything that had happened, including the pot farm. Judy wouldn't care, and she sure wouldn't report it to anyone.

"I knew something was wrong when you didn't call back. I should have called Larry. Next time, I will."

"Speaking of Larry. He doesn't know about the pot farm."

Judy laughed. "Got it. Isn't he going to really be pissed when you tell him?"

"He'll be okay. He knows I'm trying to solve a tricky case."

"Can't wait for an update on how it's going. You're probably not up for drinks tonight, though."

"Sure, just not at the Oasis this time. Don't think I can manage the steps." We'd met at the Oasis the third Thursday of every month for years. But tonight wasn't going to work.

The Oasis Restaurant jutted forth on the side of a 450-foot, nearly-vertical cliff on the east side of Lake Travis, twenty miles northwest of Austin. Its thirty open-air, wooden balconies connected to the one above and below by steep stairs. I didn't want to deal with all that climbing. Then I had a moment of brilliance. "I have a great idea."

"Uh-oh. I know that tone, and it usually isn't good. It's your equivalent of the *Hey y'all watch this* said by some Bubba about to do something stupid."

"That's not true! Okay, maybe it is. But hear me out."

Judy laughed. "Sure. What's this big idea?"

"I can't drive for twenty-four hours, well, make that twelve hours as of now. But I really need to go back to Lockhart. Take me down there. We can have lunch, see Bubba, then stop somewhere there or on the way home for our customary margarita."

"That's actually a pretty good idea. And it doesn't even sound stupid or dangerous. Deal. I'll be there in two hours."

In deference to my sore bottom, I opted to wear a skirt, which I topped with a simple sweater. I was usually more comfortable in jeans, but even the *thought* of denim-against-butt-cheeks-and-thighs made me cringe.

While I waited for Judy, I called Patrick. He was distressed to hear about my incident, but not really surprised. He'd come to accept that accidents were a part of being a private investigator, or at least a part of *my* being a private investigator. I assured him I'd be ready for our dinner date Saturday, but we'd need to raincheck on dancing at the Broken Spoke Dance Hall.

I opened the door when Judy rang. She immediately put her hands on her hips and grinned. "Aren't you Little Miss Fancy."

"Shut up. Pants are not gonna happen for a few days."

"Guess I can understand that. Okay, show me the damage."

I rolled my eyes, but still turned and lifted my skirt, revealing my wounded bottom, at least through my cotton undies."

"Ouch! You okay to sit in the car?"

I lowered my skirt and grinned as I held up a feather pillow. "I'm all set."

We chatted during the hour drive to Lockhart. Mostly, Judy talked about the latest scuba-diving group trip she was organizing, this time to Roatan, Honduras, location of the second longest barrier reef in the world.

Judy ran the Bubbles Below scuba shop near Lake Travis. Lake Travis wasn't ever going to match the beauty of Monterey Bay in California, where I'd learned to dive, but it was fun to get wet, and once a year Judy organized a group trip to the Caribbean, which was just as clear as Monterey plus about thirty degrees warmer.

"Where should we eat?" I asked when we reached Lockhart's city limits. "Do you want barbecue?"

"Not today. How about something lighter and healthier?"

We found a small cafe on the courthouse square. The inside of the Market Street Eatery was a charming combination of 1800s architecture and modern furnishings and art. A tall, attractive black woman greeted us the minute we entered.

Perusing the menu, I discovered they offered casual gourmet and specialty tea. I ordered a panini and Judy got a chicken wrap. We both ordered tea. Judy opted for peach and ginger. I was intrigued by the one labeled RARE on the menu.

"What's this one?" I asked our server. "Puerh tea?" I struggled with the pronunciation, choosing to say it like a cat's purr.

"Pooh-air." Our server smiled. "It's a fermented and aged dark tea from the Yunnan province in China. It's quite exotic."

"Exotic sounds good. I could use some exotic in my mundane life." I smiled and nodded.

Judy leaned in when the young woman walked away. "Mundane life? You just got shot in the ass while escaping from a pot farm during your investigation of cow deaths by possible aliens."

I shrugged. "Fine. Maybe it's not a mundane life, but it isn't what I'd pictured for myself, either."

"Now that I understand." Judy patted my arm. "You're worried about the case. I can tell. It'll be okay."

"I just don't want more of Bubba's cows to die before I figure this out."

The server returned with our tea and food. As soon as my tea had steeped a few minutes, I sniffed and wrinkled my nose, then poured a cup and took a sip. At least it didn't taste like it smelled. I held it out to Judy. "Sniff this."

"Why?"

"Just do it."

She leaned in and sniffed. "It smells like a barn. Does it taste like that?"

"It's not bad, just tastes earthy. But it smells like cow pies. A week ago I wouldn't have recognized the smell, but I sure do now." I pushed the tea to the side. We spent a few minutes eating and not talking much. It was then that the conversation between two middle-aged women at the next table caught my attention.

"You're just messin' with me, Sarah Ann. There's no such thing as aliens."

"I swear I'm telling the truth. Lucas saw their ship. Came right down from the sky and just hovered. Scared him to death."

"When was this?" the first woman asked.

"Several nights ago. But he said it's not the first time he's seen it."

"Maybe Lucas is yankin' your chain."

"He is not! He turned white as a sheet while he was telling me."

"Where'd this happen? Here in Lockhart?"

The woman named Sarah Ann nodded. "Just east of town. Lucas was hunting feral hogs."

I caught Judy's eye and raised my eyebrows, mouthing "What the hell?"

She quirked her mouth sideways and made an almost-imperceptible shrug.

I leaned toward the women and smiled. "Excuse me. I didn't mean to eavesdrop, but I couldn't help overhear. I may have seen the same UFO as your friend Lucas. Can you tell me anything else?"

Both women stared at me, mouths agape. After almost a minute, Sarah Ann said, "I don't know anymore than what I just told Becky."

"Do you know where he was hunting?" I asked.

Sarah Ann shook her head. "Just that it was east of town. Sometimes he's paid to hunt. Sometimes he finds hog tracks and, um…climbs a few fences while following them. Don't know which it was this time."

"Well, thanks." I smiled again. "You can at least tell Lucas you met someone else who's seen lights come down from the sky."

Becky narrowed her eyes at me, clearly not believing me any more than she'd believed Lucas's story. But Sarah Ann returned my smile. "I'll surely tell him that. Might make him feel better."

Judy and I scarfed the rest of our lunch, I paid our tab, and we hurried to the car.

CONFIRMATION FROM G.J.

*Whenever people agree with me I always feel I
must be wrong. ~Oscar Wilde (1854-1900)*

"What the hell?" I repeated aloud what I'd mouthed to Judy in the
cafe.

"You got me. Did they see your client's UFO, or is there another
ranch being invaded?"

"That's a good question. Bubba is just east of town. If Lucas
climbed a few fences, as she put it, he could've easily been trespassing
on Bubba's land, so maybe he saw the same lights I've seen." I
frowned. "Otherwise, there's something super creepy going on
around here."

"What you're investigating isn't super creepy enough?"

"Yeah, but at least it's isolated to one ranch. Or I thought it was.
And I did see some man's footprint, so I know that somehow or
other actual humans are involved."

"What if it isn't happening only on Bubba's ranch? What'll you
do then?"

"Well *I* won't be doing anything. I'm just hired to help Bubba. I
have no desire to become part of some Alien Investigation Bureau

or whatever. Speaking of which, let's go check on Bubba and his pregnant cow."

I directed Judy to Bubba's ranch. I knew as soon as we pulled up he wasn't home. His truck was gone. His riding mower, minus the flat tires caused during my rescue, was up on blocks.

"Guess I should've called. I wasn't thinking straight. I blame my sore ass."

"No worries. Lunch was great, and it's fun spending time together." Judy grinned. "Guess we can head back."

"Let me check on that cow first. He said he brought her up by the house" I eased out of the car and followed Bubba's driveway around the far side of his house. Sure enough, I found the loading pen. Inside was one large white-faced cow and one tiny replica. I couldn't help it. I squealed like a little girl.

"What? What's wrong?" Judy hurried up behind me. Then she squealed, too. "Oh! How adorable."

The mother cow stepped protectively between us and her new baby, who was standing on visibly wobbly legs.

"Looks like it was just born." I wiggled my fingers at the baby.

"I think you're right. It's still wet." Judy nodded. "At least these two are safe."

I sighed. "I sure hope so. I'd hate to see something happen to such a sweet baby. Or its mama."

We mooed and cooed at the baby for a few minutes then returned to the car.

I fiddled with my seatbelt. "Long as we've come this far, do you mind if we make one more stop?"

"Nope. This is fun. Where to?"

"Let's go talk to the pot people."

"The ones who shot you?" Judy's eyes grew big.

"Yeah, but they don't know they shot me. It was their booby trap. I can say I sprained my ankle or something. I'm walking funny, but the reason why isn't obvious."

Judy shrugged. "Why not. I'd like to see those old hippies for myself. And maybe pick up a baggie."

"Judy!"

"Kidding! I'll behave. Promise."

I climbed out when we reached the hippies' gate, opened it so Judy could drive through, then closed it behind us. We pulled into the cul-de-sac, parked, and waited for someone to come out of one of the trailers.

"Should I honk?" Just asked.

"Don't bother. Their truck is gone." I pointed to where it'd previously been parked.

"Guess no one's home here, either." Judy started the car and was just backing up to turn around when the door on the right trailer opened and G.J.'s head poked out.

"Stop the car! This is perfect. He's here alone." I got out and waved. "Hi, G.J., remember me? Marianna Morgan from the other day?"

He squinted in thought before breaking into a big grin. "Yeah, sure, I 'member you. Ain't you a detective?"

"Private investigator. Helping Bubba with his cows."

"That's right. Watcha doin' here again?"

I motioned for Judy, who got out and stood beside me. "This is my friend, Judy. We were hoping to talk to you. You're the only one of y'all three who's seen the mysterious lights and heard the cows singing. Can you tell me more?"

G.J. nodded with enthusiasm. He stepped off his porch and walked over to join us. "Earl and Bengy never want me ta talk about it. They call me an idjit."

I smiled. "If you're an idiot, then so am I. Remember I've seen the lights and heard the cows, too."

G.J. spent the next fifteen minutes pouring his heart out about aliens, abductions, cattle mutilations, and anal probes and other unpleasant experiments on humans. G.J. didn't strike me as a big reader. He'd probably watched every alien-oriented television show from *The X-Files* to *Battlestar Galactica*.

I glanced at Judy. Her expression was a cross between creeped out and total disbelief. I didn't know what my own face looked like, but my thoughts were probably similar to hers.

G.J.'s beliefs were such a convoluted mish-mash it was hard to follow any logic at all, but it was clear he believed every word. It was also clear he'd seen the lights over Bubba's place on several occasions.

"Have you ever noticed any kind of pattern? Do the lights always show up on Tuesdays and Thursdays, or only on the full moon, or anything else like that?" I was half joking, but G.J. took my question seriously.

He frowned and shook his head. "Ain't seen 'em enough to really get a handle on that." His eyes grew big. "You think that's important? You think the aliens are on some kind of weird schedule?"

Judy started coughing. I glanced sideways and could tell from years of experience with her that she was covering up a laugh. Good thing. Laughing at G.J. would have shut him down like Bengy and Earl's behavior toward him did.

G.J. stepped toward Judy. "You okay? Need me to whup you on the back?"

Judy shook her head and turned away, coughing harder. I decided to divert his attention away from my flustered friend.

"She'll be okay. Probably allergies. You've really studied this alien stuff, haven't you? I'm impressed."

"Aw, thanks." G.J. shuffled his feet in the white caliche. "No one's ever been 'pressed by me before."

"I am, too." Judy cleared her throat and turned back to face G.J. She waved toward the sky. "I haven't seen what you and Marianna have, but y'all are both very…educational."

It was time to bait the hook for a bigger fish. "Do you think the aliens are working alone? I suspect there are humans helping them. What do you think?"

G.J. glanced around as if afraid of eavesdropping. "There's these men. They come here late at night. I dunno what they're doing, but I know they're part of it. Bengy 'n Earl won't answer any of my questions. They say it's better I don't know. But it scares me."

So the people who arrived while I lay in the ditch *were* part of the picture. I'd suspected so, but to hear G.J. more or less confirm it convinced me I was on the right track.

"Do you think they're the ones who stole Bubba's dead cow?" I decided not to mention the cow heads. It wouldn't change G.J's answer.

"Dunno what they'd do with no dead cow, but I did see —"

Before G.J. could finish, Bengy wheeled her truck up beside me and slammed on the brakes, spraying the side of Judy's car with small rocks and white dust. Bengy and Earl leaped out as if their truck seats both just caught fire.

"What's going on?" Earl's voice dripped venom.

"What are you doing back here?" Bengy's voice was equally vile.

"I… We… " I didn't know what to say.

G.J. took the opportunity of having Bengy and Earl's attention directed at me to scuttle away and slip back into his trailer.

Judy saved the day. "Marianna and I came down here for lunch. She was telling me about her case and how she'd heard Bubba's cows sing. I told her she was crazy, so she brought me here because G.J. said he'd heard the same thing."

"That's right." I nodded vigorously. "I didn't want my best friend to think I was nuts. I hoped G.J. would back me up."

Bengy and Earl finally both noticed G.J.'s absence from the scene. "Y'all are both nuts." Earl stomped off to G.J's trailer, entering and slamming the door behind him. I didn't envy the tongue-lashing G.J. was likely going to get.

"Get the hell out of here and don't come back." Bengy pointed down their driveway. "Next time we won't be so friendly."

"Sorry." I wanted to shrug but held my posture still. "Didn't mean to cause any trouble. We'll leave. Won't be back."

Judy and I didn't speak until we were safely on the other side of the pot farm's gate.

"What the hell were they so angry about?" Judy asked.

"I don't know, but I'd bet it has something to do with the mysterious men G.J. mentioned. The same ones who showed up the other night after I'd been shot. Now I'm sure that to figure out what's going on at Bubba's, I have to find out who these men are."

"And if they're in cahoots with the aliens." Judy grinned.

By the time Judy dropped me at my car in the Seton parking lot, I was exhausted, and my butt was on fire. As much as I wanted to go to the office and do more research on aliens and UFO sightings, common sense prevailed, and I headed home.

I'm missing something. There's gotta be one key to this whole thing, but so far it's just out of my reach. I will find it, dammit. I'll get an early start on Friday.

A SHOT IN THE DARK

Most of their lives, people are just waiting to
be ambushed. ~Brandon Hull (1974-)
Undressed To The Nines: A Thriller Novel

I awoke Friday morning still sore and stiff but feeling much better. I couldn't wait to get back to work on Bubba's case. I called him to say I'd be down later in the day.

"You sure you're ready?" Bubba asked.

"Sure, I'm sure. I have some more research to do, but I'll be there before dark. Can I borrow the Gator again?"

There was a pause before Bubba responded, "You up to that?"

"I'll bring my feather pillow. I'll be fine." *I hope I'll be fine.* I remembered how rough the ride across Bubba's property was under the best of circumstances.

"Okay, then." Another pause. "I guess."

My first stop was my office. I knocked and poked my head in Jason's door before heading down the hall. Rebecca, his admin, looked up and smiled. "Hi Marianna. How're you doing?"

"Much better, thanks. He here today?"

She jerked her head. "In his office. Go on back."

I crossed and stopped at the door, which was open. "How's your case going?"

Jason grinned. "The uncle backed down. Turns out he was a step-uncle by a third marriage, so the court didn't put much stock in his claim to the property. Thanks for your help."

"Any time."

"I'll drop a check by to you next week. And I'll probably have a new job for you. Something trickier I'm still researching on my own."

"Sounds great. And perfect timing for the check. That's when my motorcycle payment is due." I grinned and waved before heading to my office. I watered my palm plant before sitting at my desk.

My answering machine blinked that I had two messages. The first informed me I was eligible for cheap insurance. A young woman left the second. She wanted to hire me to find out if her boyfriend was cheating on her with her best friend. Not usually my kind of case, but I jotted down her name and number. I'd call her back later.

I sat back and stared out the window, wishing I knew Bengy, Earl, or G.J's last names. A search through ERAS might be enlightening. I'd have to see if I could come up with those. I'm a firm believer that there's always a way to find something out. I doubted Bubba knew, but *someone* did. Or maybe I could catch G.J. alone again. I'd just have to be very discreet to keep him out of trouble with Bengy and Earl.

Maybe I can go about this through the property owner.

I didn't know the address, but a search of the county's appraisal district records at the courthouse in Lockhart would provide that. I'd start with the plat maps and go from there.

I opened my laptop and spent half an hour searching for any reported alien sightings in the Austin/Lockhart area but had no luck. My heart wasn't really in it, anyway, and I wasn't surprised when I found nothing. Besides, I was anxious to get to the Caldwell

County Courthouse and search for the owner of the pot farm property. It was already after noon, and I wanted time to delve through the tax office records.

I shut down the computer and headed south, stopping briefly at the That's Messed Up food trailer for one of their noodle-based Messy Bowls.

The big-haired lady at the Caldwell County Appraisal District office was courteous and helpful. She directed me to a back room where the large plat maps were stored.

"You don't have an address, honey? Sure would make it easier." She tsked and shook her head.

"The address is what I'm hoping to find through the plat maps." I smiled and shrugged.

It took me an hour of shuffling through drawers and flipping through plats to find the right location. The total property was a mere three-hundred-forty-three acres, small by Texas standards, and was somewhat pie shaped, almost as narrow as the gate and driveway at the front, much wider at the back. It paralleled Bubba's ranch along his entire back fence.

Bubba's property, I noted, was one-thousand-twenty-three acres and almost a perfect rectangle. I'd never asked how big his ranch was. In Texas, asking's considered a breach of etiquette. Plus, it hadn't seemed to matter. But now, looking at the two even larger ranches on either side, I could get a sense of his ranch's isolation. Only the hippies' ranch was smaller. It made sense that the strange men were using it as an access to Bubba's.

I jotted down the address—001 County Road 182—and wrestled the plat plans back into their drawer. I returned to the front area, caught the employee's eye, and waved to the two antiquated computer monitors on a shelf at the end of the counter.

"I got the address. Can I use one of these to look up the property records?"

The employee nodded "Sure can. Let me know if you need help."

The program interface was clunky and confusing, but I managed to navigate to the Property Search section. I keyed in the address and clicked the Search button. It was hard not to squeal with excitement when the actual record displayed on the screen. Finally achieving real progress after fighting obstacles always made me giddy.

The owner was a woman named Linda Favoccia. The Owner Mailing Address was listed as a post office box at the Lockhart post office. *Damn. I was hoping for a physical location.*

This was definitely a speed bump, but not an insurmountable one. At least I had a name. Maybe Bubba could help. Depended on how well he knew the post office employees.

"Can I get a print of something?" I asked.

"Sure thing, hon. Ten cents a page."

I printed the entire record, which cost me a whopping sixty cents. It was just after three. Earlier than I'd planned to go to Bubba's. It was too far to drive home, so I decided to do a bit of reconnaissance in town. Maybe someone in one of the local shops knew Linda.

I left my car on the Courthouse Square and circled the large block on foot, entering every store that was open and chatting with the employees and owners as I browsed their wares. In each store, I made sure I found some way to mention Linda Favoccia's name.

I got a response in only one store, a sprawling antique shop called Chisholm Trail Stables Antiques. The owner, Katherine Fields, was a feisty but knowledgable resource. And an excellent salesperson.

Not only did she tell me about Linda, she convinced me to buy several items. Some would go in my office, a couple would decorate my home, and two would be put aside for future Christmas gifts. I especially liked the antique brass, deep sea scuba helmet I got for Judy. It was way more than I'd normally spend, but Judy'd been so much more than a friend—especially since I seemed to be a somewhat accident-prone private investigator — she deserved a special gift.

As for Katherine's comments about Linda, they were both enlightening and baffling.

"She comes in here pretty regular, looking for vintage jewelry. She especially likes rings with semi-precious stones." Katherine waved toward her extensive jewelry collection as she spoke. "But she hasn't been in for over a month. Makes me wonder, since she's usually by every week."

I doubted her absence had anything to do with aliens or hippies, but at this point I wasn't ruling it out. "It's kind of important that I find her. Can you point me to where she lives?"

Katherine narrowed her eyes. "Now why would I do that? I don't know you."

"You're right." I nodded. I debated how honest to be and decided to go for broke. Katherine's personality was a bit brusque, but also upfront and straightforward. She'd likely appreciate, and more likely accept, my honesty. I took a deep breath and told her my story, leaving out mention of the one acre of pot.

By the time I was done, Katherine was doubled over with laughter. She straightened and wiped her eyes. "I'm sorry. I'm not laughing at your being shot. But this whole idea of aliens and cows is preposterous."

"That's what I think, too. I think it's people, although for the life of me I can't figure out what they're doing. That's one reason I need to find Linda. Somehow, her land is involved. At the very least, it's being used as access. I think she'd want to know."

Katherine nodded. "You're right about that. Linda's an all-business type." She stared at me for a full minute. "Okay, I'll tell you what I'll do. Give me your information, and I'll call her. If she wants to talk to you, she'll let you know. And you're going to come back as soon as you know more and fill me in. Deal?"

"Deal!" I fished one of my business cards out of my purse and wrote my home address and cell phone on the back. "Here's both of my addresses and phone numbers. Have her call my cell."

Katherine handed me one of her own cards. "I can't promise how fast she'll respond. She doesn't always answer her phone and never checks her voicemail. She's got a bit of a Luddite thing going on."

"Thanks. I'll do my best to be patient, but it's kind of important. I appreciate anything you can do to encourage her to call me." I picked up my packages. "I can't thank you enough. I promise I'll keep you posted. Besides, your shop is too cool not to visit again."

Katherine nodded and pointed her finger at my face. "You be careful. No matter what's really going on, it doesn't sound good. There's lots of worse things that go on out in the country than aliens messing with cows."

By the time I lugged my purchases back to my car, it was almost six. Now it was later than I'd planned to get to Bubba's. At least it was still light. The sun wouldn't set for another hour or so.

Bubba stepped out on his porch the minute I drove up. He was fidgety and wore a big frown. "Wondered when you'd get here." His frown deepened. "I'm not sure I like you going back there again after dark, 'specially after what happened last time."

I joined him on the porch. "I'll be okay. I've got my big flashlight, my gun, my whistle, and my cell phone. I'll be sure to keep all of them with me at all times. And I won't climb your fence again. I'll stay on your property."

Bubba nodded slowly and chewed the inside of his lip. "I'll let ya' go, but yer gonna call me ever hour and let me know you're still okay."

"Calling might be overheard, so how about I text instead?"

"I ain't big on texting, and I'm slow as they come thanks to fat fingers, but I reckon that'll do."

I smiled and patted his arm. "That'll actually make me less stressed, too, knowing you're up here keeping an eye on me."

I collected my evening's tools—including my feather pillow—from the trunk of my car. I tucked my phone and whistle into jean pockets, shoved the big flashlight in my waistband, and clipped my 380 semi-automatic handgun's holster to my belt. Thanks to the long, wrist-thick flashlight handle and my recently bird-shot-peppered butt, I waddled to the Gator and clambered on.

I wiggled the pillow into a comfortable position. Before firing up the noisy vehicle, I checked my phone. "It's a quarter to seven. I'll text at seven, when I get settled in my hiding place, then on the hour after that."

"Good luck." Worry lines etched Bubba's forehead.

This time—thank goodness—the cows were nowhere near any of the carcasses. I could only imagine how they smelled at this point. I realized I didn't know where the dead cow Bubba told me about in the hospital was located. I rode around until I finally found the small herd, gathered in one corner of Bubba's property.

It took me a minute to figure out exactly where I was. In the dimming light, I could see a couple of Longhorns in the distance across the fence. That meant we were next to the property to the west, the one with no house on the land. The land on the other side of the corner was Linda's, although I couldn't see the rutted road Bengy and I had driven down.

After parking the Gator under a large live oak, I texted Bubba:

Back corner by the Longhorns. Everything is fine.

Bubba's response was short but still included a typo:

Okya

I resisted the urge to surf social media while I waited. I only had so much battery, and if I ran out and couldn't text Bubba, he'd think something bad had happened. Instead, I spent time staring at each cow, trying to see if I could tell them apart.

A few weeks ago, I'd have believed all Hereford cows look alike. I was surprised to see just how different their markings were. Almost all of them had red ears and solid white faces, but the patterns on their necks, where white met red, varied wildly. A few also had red circles around their eyes. Only one had a red splotch on her face, just above her pink nose. The splotch was shaped like Florida, at least to me. I decided to name her Mooami.

The cows occasionally stared at me. I wondered if they were assessing my overall size and pattern, too.

Shortly before nine, I drifted off and didn't snap awake until my phone vibrated. It was Bubba:

You there?

It was after nine. I'd forgotten to text. Poor Bubba was probably a nervous wreck, considering my track record on his ranch:

Fine. Took a short nap. Awake now.

I could almost picture Bubba shaking his head when I read his response:

Nap? There?

Giggling, I typed my response:

Nothing happening. Crickets and frogs made me sleepy.

I set my phone on the seat beside me and clicked on my flashlight. The cows had mostly bedded down. A few still grazed. Their eyes glowed as they stared toward the sudden bright onslaught. I clicked off my flashlight and blinked until my eyes readjusted. After a couple of minutes, I found I could see pretty good by the light of the full moon. Nothing to do but wait. And wait.

I'd just texted Bubba my ten pm check-in when I heard the now-familiar faint hum. Within a few seconds, overhead lights flooded the area. I grabbed my flashlight, clicked it on again, and pointed it toward the lights, but they were just on the other side of some tall oaks.

Dammit. I am going to see where those lights are coming from if it's the last thing I do.

Climbing off the Gator, I hurried through the scrubby mesquite and cactus, heedless of the brush thorns and cactus needles raking my jeans. I cleared the last tree and looked up, pointing my light.

Before my brain could register, I felt a sharp sting in my right shoulder and a wave of dizziness swept through me.

I dropped the light and lost my balance. I grabbed for the closest tree trunk, but my arm and hand wouldn't behave. My fingers clawed at air. I went down hard. My face erupted in stings. Either I'd landed on a cactus or a fire ant mound. I tried to roll over but everything in my body had turned to molasses and refused to respond.

My eyes watered from pain. My heart pounded in fear. I felt my consciousness slipping and fought hard against it. It was no use. Just before I passed out, I heard voices approaching from behind me. Chills swept my body. *It's going to be almost an hour before Bubba misses my check-in and knows something is wrong.*

CAPTIVE

*The true worth of an experimenter consists in
his pursuing not only what he seeks in his
experiment, but also what he did not seek.*
~Claude Bernard (1813-1878)

I woke to find myself lying on my side on something cold and hard. Still heavily drugged, my mind was sluggish, my body slow to respond. It felt like I was scuba diving in deep water and suffering the effects of the pressure and nitrogen narcosis.

How long was I unconscious? Where am I? Who brought me here?

A scratchy blindfold covered my eyes. My mouth was taped. My hands were bound behind me. My ankles were also bound. I tried wiggling forward and almost fell off the edge of something. Shifting back, my hands encountered an edge on that side, too.

I explored behind me as much as my confined wrists would allow and concluded my perch was a narrow, metal table. The kind in my doctor's office. Panic washed over me.

Why am I on an exam table? Visions of G.J.'s alien experiments flooded my brain. If my mouth wasn't taped, I'd have screamed. My nether regions puckered at the thought of an anal probe.

Stop it right now. Get a grip. Think this out. I closed my eyes and consciously slowed my breathing. Panic wasn't going to help me. I needed as clear a head as I could manage in my drugged condition. After several minutes, I'd calmed down enough to do a more thorough exploration of my surroundings.

Realizing the blindfold still left gaps on either side of my nose, I moved my head around, peeking through the tiny openings. I was definitely in some type of a room. A searingly bright light shone overhead. The rest of the room was dim, so I couldn't tell how big it was. Against the wall I faced were the vague outlines of tall, metal cabinets. All the doors were closed, so I had no clue what they might hold.

Alien anal-probe tools? I shook my head, causing a wave of dizziness. *STOP IT! I have to keep focused.*

I wanted to turn over, but the table was narrow, and in my bound and druggy state, I was afraid I'd fall off. Since I couldn't see anything else, I focused on my other senses. The first thing I noticed was that my cheek stung. I wished I could reach up to see if it was covered in the tiny festers left by fire ant stings. At least my butt wasn't hurting too bad.

Switching my focus to the sounds around me, I heard faint voices, but couldn't understand a single word. Other noises were more baffling. I heard the low thrum-thrum of some type of appliance like a refrigerator or freezer. I could hear no traffic or outside noises, so I guessed I was in a central room in a larger facility.

Maybe I'm inside the UFO. I really wished my internal voice would shut up. I didn't need it feeding my fear and paranoia about where I was and why I was there.

I heard no more unusual noises, so turned my attention to the olfactory. The room smelled like a doctor's office—the acrid disinfectant clearly evident. Then I noticed another smell and cringed—urine. I wiggled my butt and felt wetness between my legs.

At some point, I'd peed myself. As humiliating as the idea was, I could also understand. I'd been drugged. I'd possibly been out for hours. Besides, it was the least of my problems. Still, I felt my face grow hot with embarrassment.

Even if I could have called out, who would hear besides those responsible for my abduction? And if I really was inside a UFO…

My mind wanted to drift back to sleep. I fought hard, blinking rapidly, squeezing and releasing my hands into fists, and chewing on my tongue and inside of my cheek. But it was no use. Whatever they'd shot me with was either still surging through my system, or they'd given me something else after putting me on the table. Against every ounce of my strength, I fell back into oblivion.

When I woke the next time, I was no longer on the table. I was also no longer bound, gagged, or blindfolded. It didn't do me any good. I was on the floor of a small, dimly-lit, windowless room. The single door had no inside doorknob. The only furnishing was a simple metal stool in the center of the room, directly beneath a single ceiling light.

I felt my cheek, which no longer burned. The skin was slightly irritated and rough, but I found no festers. I must have landed on a cactus rather than fire ants. Whoever was responsible for my current predicament had at least removed the cactus needles.

I tried to sit up but was still groggy and dizzy. My movements brought to my attention that I was no longer in my jeans and shirt. They'd been replaced by a baggy shift of some type. My stomach lurched in fear. At least I was still wearing my thick socks and athletic shoes, not that they'd do me any good.

I reached behind me. There was no gap, so it wasn't a hospital gown. *Maybe aliens don't need a back gap to do what they do.* My stomach lurched again. Then growled. I had no idea how long since I'd been abducted, but it'd been long enough to make me hungry and thirsty. And I needed to pee again. I tried to speak, but my throat was parched, my lips cracked.

I cleared my throat. "Hello? Anyone there?"

Only silence responded. I realized I no longer even heard any of the previous mechanical sounds. Was I deeper in the building—or ship—or was this room soundproofed? *Why would they need to soundproof a room, unless they do…*

My stomach lurched for the third time. If I'd had any food left in me, I'd've lost it right then and there. I closed my eyes and tried to think, but my brain was simply still too drugged. When I moved my head, my vision tracked a fraction behind, giving me a strange double-vision, slow-mo-replay effect. This time, bile rose in my throat. I swallowed the acid, but the burning in my throat remained.

"Hello? I need water. And I need to use the toilet. Anyone there?"

I heard a noise and looked toward the door. A smaller panel near the floor I hadn't previously noticed slid open. The exterior of the opening was dark. I couldn't tell if the door was automatic or if someone—or something—was on the opposite side.

A flat cart, like an auto mechanic's creeper without the little rubber pillow, trundled through the opening. On it was a large glass of clear liquid, which I presumed was water. Next to the glass was a bucket and a roll of toilet paper.

"Oh. Hell. No." I shook my head at the opening, even though it was already closing. "I am not going to squat over a bucket."

There was no reply. The rapid delivery of the water and the bucket indicated they—whoever *they* might be—were at minimum listening to me. Scanning the corners and ceiling of the small room, I saw no sign of cameras, which wasn't proof they couldn't see me.

I crawled to the cart, picked up the glass, and sniffed. There was no smell, so I dipped in my finger and touched it to my tongue. It was water. I wanted to gulp the whole glass, but after years of watching old westerns, where the cowboy who's rescued from the desert throws up because he chugged water, I opted to sip my own supply.

The water not only eased my burning throat, it perked me up a bit. If I was dehydrated enough to be disoriented, I'd been out for at least a day.

What's Bubba doing? I'll bet he's panicked. Did he call Larry? Did he have Larry's number? I hoped Larry was smart enough back at the hospital to give his number to Bubba. I closed my eyes and said a silent prayer they'd thought of that. If Larry knew I was missing, lots of things would be happening right now to ensure I was found.

And what about my cats? More panic rose. I fought it down. I had to trust that someone was taking care of my fur babies. Worrying about them right now would do me no good.

I tried shifting from my hands and knees to sitting on my bottom, but quickly realized my twenty-seven pellet holes didn't much like the hard floor. I eased again onto my side and uttered a long, frustrated sigh.

Damn, I'm going to miss my follow up with Dr. Green. The absurdity of being concerned about that made me giggle.

I raised up long enough to down the last of the water and lay back on my side. I stared longingly at the bucket, but I couldn't bring myself to squat on it, knowing that I was probably being watched as well as listened to. My bladder's urgency argued with me. I had to do something.

"What do you want? Why am I here? Let me go. I've done nothing to you."

This time the response was a sharp pain at the back of my neck. I immediately grew dizzy and felt consciousness fading. *Did they just shoot me again?*

The third time I awakened, the metal stool was gone. So was the bucket and cart. I suddenly noticed my urgent need to pee was gone, too. *What the hell did they do to me while I was out?* I started to shake. The hairs on my arm stood out. Sweat beaded my forehead.

I scrambled to my feet, my fists clenched, my temples pounding. "What the hell are you doing to me? LET ME GO NOW!"

In response, the small opening in the door slid open and the creeper once again rolled in. This time it held a plate with some type of sandwich and another glass of water. The opening slid shut.

I didn't want their food. I wasn't even sure it was safe to eat. But my stomach growled in response to the proximity of food. If I'd received any nourishment since arriving, it had been while I was unconscious.

I bent over the creeper, picked up the sandwich, and peeled back one slice of the slightly dry, brown bread. I snorted with sarcasm. "You kidnap me and hold me for who knows how long and you finally offer me a peanut butter and jelly sandwich?"

Still, it was better than nothing. I took a large bite, washing it down with a big swig of water. I'd barely finished eating when I again felt the sharp sting in my neck.

Oh no, not aga…

This waking and being drugged went on for half a dozen more times. I'd lost all track of time. It could have been one day or a week. I had no clue what they were doing while I was out. Every time I woke up, I patted down my body and took mental stock of my innards. I could find no bruises, cuts, or unexplained pains.

I was given a large glass of water after each *session* — or whatever it was they were doing. After the third time being out, I was given another peanut butter and jelly sandwich.

After the sixth episode, I burst into tears. "How much longer are you going to keep me? Please just let me go. I have cats to take care of. I haven't done anything to you. Please."

When the sting in my neck hit me for the seventh time, it was almost a relief. At least while unconscious, I didn't realize where I was or what was going on.

I woke feeling completely disoriented. It was dark. I was not lying on the cold, hard floor of my prison-exam room.

I'm on dirt! I'm outside somewhere. But where? I peered into the darkness and patted my hand on the ground in front of me. I pushed myself up and froze.

Someone — or something — was behind me.

I slowly turned my head, yelping when a large white face loomed into view. Then I giggled. It was a Hereford cow. I glanced around and saw a dozen in a loose semicircle around me. All were staring. None seemed threatening.

I thought some of their red and white patterns looked familiar. "Are y'all Bubba's cows?"

Several cows mooed in response. One approached to within a few feet and mooed again. I noticed she had a red, Florida-shaped patch above her nose.

"Mooami? Is that you?"

She stepped closer and lowered her head. After a few seconds of staring at me with her huge brown eyes, she lowed softly.

It is Mooami! And the rest of Bubba's cows. I'm home. Well, sort of.

I stood, albeit a bit unsteadily, and brushed leaves and bits of gravel off of me. I was still wearing the gown I'd been dressed in by my captors. I'd never been more thankful for plain cotton socks and clunky athletic shoes.

I had no possessions. I'd dropped my flashlight when I was first drugged, however long ago that was. Bubba probably had it by now. My phone had been in my jeans pockets. My gun had been clipped to my belt.

Was I close to where I'd been taken? I glanced around in the dim light and realized I knew exactly where I was. *I was in the cow-carcass ditch – the same place I'd hidden after I was shot.*

For whatever reason, my captors had returned me to Bubba's property, and chosen the same place where they — I presumed it was them—had taken the whole dead cow. At least I knew where I was, but how would I get back to Bubba's, or let him know I was back?

I could try walking to where I'd left the Gator, but it was even farther than I already was from Bubba's house. Besides, it was likely Bubba had taken the Gator back home. He had no reason to believe I'd end up here again.

Maybe I can walk to Bubba's. I shook my head, knowing that was a stupid idea. It was a couple miles, at least. I had no flashlight and I wasn't exactly wearing clothes that would protect me from thorns. I wasn't completely sturdy yet, either.

I shivered in the October night air. I sure couldn't stay where I was. Who knew how long it would be before anyone came. They certainly wouldn't be looking for me back here.

There really was only one choice. The hippies were less than a half mile down the rutted road on the other side of the barbed wire fence. In spite of my most recent reception, that was where I had to head.

I opted not to wiggle between strands of barbed wire while wearing a glorified hospital gown. Instead I grabbed a nearby tree branch for stability, then used the wire strands as ladder rungs. I glanced back from the other side. *Bubba won't be happy that I created a sagging crossover on his fence wires.*

Trudging my way down the road, I hoped at least one of the hippies was home. *Just please don't shoot me on sight.*

HIPPIES TO THE RESCUE

*The best way to escape from a problem is to
solve it. ~Alan Saporta*

I stopped as soon as I was within site of the three trailers. "Hello?
Anyone home? I need help! Please. This is Marianna Morgan, the
private investigator. Earl? Bengy? G.J.? Please, help me!"

I waited in the shadows for several minutes, then cupped my
hands around my mouth and called again, much louder. This time,
all three trailer lights flicked on. I stepped out of the shadows and
raised my hands.

"Please, help me. I was abducted, then returned to Bubba's up by
your fence. I need help."

The three trailer doors banged open and Bengy, Earl, and G.J.
each stepped onto their porches.

"What the hell are you talking about?" Bengy's voice was not
welcoming. I noted that Earl was again holding the M1 rifle, but this
time it was pointed straight at me, instead of safely at the ground.

I lowered my hands, but remained where I was. "I don't even
know what day it is. I was back at Bubba's again Friday, trying to
help solve his cow mystery, when I was drugged and abducted. I

was kept in some kind of cell. I have no idea how long I've been gone."

"You was abducted?" G.J.'s voice was filled with fear. "That's why they came lookin' for ya."

"Who? When?" I cocked my head in confusion.

"Bubba and some other man stopped by here on Saturday morning, asking if we'd seen you," Bengy answered.

"And of course, we hadn't," Earl added.

"Saturday? What's today?"

Earl whistled. "Lady, it's four am Tuesday. You say you just got back? You've been gone three days."

"Oh no, my cats!" The realization that I'd been held for three days, having who-knows-what done to me, was just too much. My head swooned and my vision turned grey. I faintly heard Bengy say, "Aw, hell."

I woke up lying on a bed, with G.J. sitting beside me. As soon as I opened my eyes, he patted my arm. "I was sure worried about you! Glad you're awake."

I smiled. "Me, too."

"Was it the aliens?" G.J.'s eyes were big as saucers.

"I honestly don't know, G.J. I never saw. For all I know, I was inside a UFO somewhere."

G.J. sat back and exhaled hard. "Holy moley. Did they do bad stuff? Did they do them 'speriments on ya?"

I shook my head. "I don't know that either. They kept me drugged a lot. I'm pretty sure they did things while I was out."

G.J. looked about to cry. I decided to change the subject. "Where are Bengy and Earl?"

"They done gone to get Bubba. Should be back soon."

"Can I have some water?" I sat up slowly, so as not to cause another blackout.

"Bengy got some ready for ya." G.J. handed me a glass from a bedside table stacked with romance novels. I presumed I was in Bengy's bed. "Thanks." I took several large swallows and handed the glass back.

"Can you tell me anything else about the men in the vehicle who've been coming here? I think they had something to do with this."

"They ain't been here for several days. Least I ain't seen or heard 'em. I figured they—" Before he could finish, headlights played across the bedroom curtains and tires ground to a rapid stop on the caliche driveway.

I swung around so my legs dangled off the bed, just as Bubba burst into the room. He ran over and hugged me like a long-lost daughter. For a few seconds, all I could hear was his sniffling.

He released me and pulled back. Tears glistened at the corners of his eyes. "I been so worried. Sheriff's been hunting for you. Larry's about plum crazy. I called him on the way here. He's probably already on his way down." He swiped his shirt sleeve across his nose. "You sure you're okay? What happened?"

I glanced at Bengy and Earl, who stood just inside the bedroom door. How much could I say in front of them? Would guilt cause Bengy and Earl to be less accommodating to the men who were using their property? What did these two know about those men? Were the men even involved in my abduction? Probably, but I couldn't be absolutely sure. Then again, maybe not only were they involved, but so were Bengy and Earl. Considering everything I'd been through, I decided to err on the side of caution.

"I was kidnapped. I have no idea why. I don't know who did it. I was kept drugged most of the time. When I did wake up, I was kept pretty groggy and disoriented."

"Why the hell would someone kidnap you? All you was doin' was watchin' my cows. They may be all I got that's even worth a plug nickel, but they ain't worth kidnapping for."

I shook my head. "I don't know. For all I know, it's someone I sent to jail getting even with me."

That sounded lame even to me. I wasn't surprised when four sets of eyes stared back at me with skepticism. I noticed that after a brief look of disbelief in my direction, Bengy and Earl exchanged a quick, but very worried look.

"Bubba, I promise, if I had any idea who or why, I'd be more than happy to tell you." *At least that much is true. I'd be telling everybody.*

"I gotta get you back to my place. Larry'll be there soon. He was gonna call Patrick and Judy, too. They may all be showin' up soon."

"I hope one of them brings me some clothes." I glanced down at the ugly cotton gown I still wore, now filthy from lying on the ground, not to mention three days worth of my own body oils and sweat.

"I can help you out." Bengy crossed to her closet and fished around. She tossed an old pair of jeans and a faded green *Earth Day Every Day* shirt on the bed. "Don't even need them back."

"Thanks." I flashed a smile. "These will work great."

Before I could ask she pointed to a door. "Bathroom's in there."

"Thanks again." I scurried in and changed. I started to leave the gown behind, but decided it might be evidence. I left the bathroom with the gown tucked under my arm.

Bubba put a protective arm around my shoulders as he turned to Bengy, Earl, and G.J. "Thank y'all for helpin' Marianna. And for comin' for me. We been worried sick, and tearin' up half the county lookin' for her." He shook each of their hands.

Stress and relief prevailed, and I gave them each a hug. Bengy and Earl looked surprised, but G.J.'s return hug felt sincere.

"Will you let me know if you find those aliens?" He whispered in my ear.

"You bet," I whispered back.

Larry's car was just pulling up next to mine when we reached Bubba's house. The minute we stopped, Judy, Patrick, and Larry all piled out and hurried my way. They gathered around me, each of them expressing how worried they'd been. Judy burst into tears.

"I'm okay. I think. It was scary, mostly because I have no idea what really happened."

"Let's go inside and you can fill us in." Bubba led the little troop into his kitchen. We crowded around his kitchen table, and he brewed a pot of coffee. "I'd offer ya' somethin' stronger, but if ya been drugged, it ain't a good idea."

"Coffee's great." I smiled. "I'd rather stay awake and alert." *And your coffee's plenty strong.*

The others sat with rapt attention while I recounted everything I could remember. There were lots of gaps, but I did my best. No one even asked any questions until I ended my story with my walking to the hippies' trailers.

"Do you think the hippies had anything to do with it?" Judy asked. "Bengy and Earl weren't exactly neighborly that day we stopped there."

"I wondered about that. They know more than G.J., that's for sure. But I just can't believe they were involved. I didn't sense any guilt in them."

"I agree." Bubba nodded. "They may be weirdos, but they seemed honestly worried when they showed up to tell me you was there."

"So what now?" Larry asked.

"I have to finish this case."

"No, you don't." Patrick's voice had the authoritative air of a cop talking to a suspect.

I narrowed my eyes. "Yes. I. do. I make my living as a private investigator. I can't turn tail when something bad happens. And I'm not about to give up now." I smiled. "Plus, I don't want any more cows to die. I have to solve this."

"Then I'll take time off and help you," Patrick said.

"No." I shook my head. "I appreciate your concern, I really do, but I have to do this. It's *my* case." I smiled. "Besides, I have to prove to myself that I won't be stopped. That I'm strong."

Patrick frowned, but said nothing else. Larry caught my eye and winked. He'd known me long enough to understand how stubborn I could get. Judy just shook her head and made *tsk, tsk* noises.

In spite of the coffee, my shoulders slumped with exhaustion.

"Let's get you home." Judy stood and cleared coffee cups from the table. "You need rest. Probably should see a doctor, too."

"Right now, I need to see my cats and sleep in my own bed. And I need a shower. I missed my follow-up with Dr. Green for my birdshot-peppered rear end. I'll try to see him tomorrow." I rubbed my eyes. "Who took care of my babies? Please tell me they haven't been alone all this time!"

"I was over there twice a day," Judy said. "They're a bit freaked out with you gone, but they're fine."

"You're the best." My eyes filled with tears. "Thanks."

We stepped outside into a bright, warm morning. The sun had come up while we sat at Bubba's table. I turned my head toward the warmth and sighed. I was safe, for the moment, and surrounded by people who loved and cared about me.

After a bit of debate, it was decided that Judy would drive me home in my car. She'd been at my place when Larry called her, so her car was in my driveway. Patrick had picked her up.

Patrick held me tight once we were all outside. "I worry about you so much. I wish I were taking you home, but I get the logistics issues. Get some rest. I'll call you tomorrow. I love you."

"I love you, too. And I'll be happy to see you again soon, but I need to hibernate for a day."

Judy wanted to stay once she got me home. "You can go on to bed, and I'll hang in the living room."

I sat on the sofa, stroking and hugging my kitties. "I'll be fine. You don't need to babysit me. I'm going to spend a few minutes sitting here petting these squirts, then I'm going to bed."

"Can I make you a sandwich? No idea what's in your fridge, but I'll bet you have peanut butter and jelly."

"*No!*" I shook my head hard. "Sorry. That's all whoever had me locked up fed me. I may never be able to eat a PB&J again." I made a lopsided grin. "I'm actually not hungry right now, anyway."

After Judy left, I poured myself a shot glass of bourbon and tossed it back. It burned my throat, but I hoped it would take the edge off my nerves. I hadn't let anyone see just how shook up I was, though I bet they each knew it anyway.

I took a quick shower, changed into my softest jammies, closed the curtains against the late-morning sun, and crawled into bed. Boggle, Polly, Cooper, Mayfly, and Deke all jumped up and snuggled next to me. I was kitty-stapled into the bed, something I usually loath, but this time it was comforting. I closed my eyes and said a prayer that I wouldn't suffer nightmares. I drifted off with pictures of Mooami's face looming in my mind.

When I opened my eyes, the small gap in the curtains was dark. I'd slept the rest of the day. I sat up and reached for my phone. *Damn. It's gone.* I had to get out tomorrow, or later today—whatever—and get a new one. I had no land line. I couldn't even report my phone as lost.

No one could reach me, which didn't really bother me. But that also meant I couldn't reach anyone else, either, which did worry me. I didn't want to be totally isolated. Not right now.

I shuffled into the kitchen and checked the clock on the microwave, which I usually tried to keep set so it didn't blink all the time. It was almost midnight. I debated going back to bed, but my stomach uttered a loud growl. I dug around in the pantry and found a can of chicken noodle soup. It was expired, but only by six months. I figured it was still edible. The soup was the perfect choice, both nourishing and comforting.

By sun-up, it would be Wednesday. It felt eerie to lose so many days. I hated that I'd slept through Monday and Tuesday. I guess my body needed it. But I'd lost almost a week of my life since I'd been abducted.

I hadn't thought to ask Bubba if he'd lost more cows. All things considered, he might not've been willing to tell me, anyway.

Am I ready to go back on stake-out with the cows? My stomach lurched at the thought, which meant I had to do it. I needed to push past my fear and get back to work.

I left my soup bowl on the breakfast table and returned to bed. I managed to sleep four more hours before my body decided it was done for now.

I started Wednesday morning with a long, steamy shower, using every drop of hot water and turning my skin fuchsia. I scrambled a couple of eggs, figuring the protein would do me good. After some additional kitty time, I headed to the local store for a new phone and to the hardware store for a replacement heavy-duty flashlight. My new phone had a first-rate, built-in camera, which would come in handy.

I knew I'd need to report my gun as stolen, but I couldn't deal with police reports this morning. Instead, I retrieved my Sig 9 mm semi-automatic from my nightstand. I didn't like it as much as my Kahr 380, but it was a perfectly functional weapon.

I drove to the Seton Hospital in Kyle and asked to see Dr. Green.

"You were supposed to come back in seventy-two hours." The woman at the registration desk frowned.

"Yes, I know, but I was…indisposed."

Her frown deepened as she typed into the computer in front of her. "He can see you tomorrow at ten thirty."

I wanted to tell her what had happened, and that I wanted to see the damn doctor right now. I decided it would do no good, and might instigate actions I didn't want to occur. I smiled instead. "Fine."

I was sitting in my car in the Seton parking lot when my new phone beeped with a voicemail. It wasn't a number I recognized, but it was local. I tapped Play and listened.

"Ms. Morgan, this is Linda Favoccia in Lockhart. I got a call from Katherine Fields saying you wanted to talk to me about something important. My apologies for not calling back sooner, but I am interested to hear the important information you say I need to know about my country property."

She left her number and asked me to call her at my convenience. *It's convenient right now.* I dialed and fidgeted through five rings. I got her voicemail. *Damn.*

"Ms. Favoccia, this is Marianna Morgan, the private investigator Katherine Fields spoke to you about. Thank you for contacting me. I do need to talk to you. Please call me as soon as you can."

I headed to Bubba's, frustrated and disappointed. Maybe things would be better when I got back to his cows.

I set my jaw and increased my speed. *I'll solve this damn case, no matter what.* I just hoped discovering the solution didn't involve any more time being drugged and held in a windowless room.

WASHOUT

*It is impossible to live without failing at
something, unless you live so cautiously that
you might as well not lived at all. In which
case, you've failed by default.*
~J. K. Rowling (1965-),
Harvard Commencement Address, 2008

Bubba's voice was stern. "No, dammit. I ain't lettin' you go back there again. Every time you go, somethin' bad happens."

I gave him the same smile I'd learned to give my mother when I was a kid and she'd said I couldn't do something. "But Bubba, I've got to do this. You know that. I'll be fine."

"Ain't no guarantee you'll be fine. I done lost another cow. I don't wanna lose you, too."

I winced at the loss of another cow. I didn't like the idea that came to me, but it seemed my only solution. "Come with me then. We can watch for the alien light together."

He narrowed his eyes and said nothing for several seconds. "Allrighty then. I'll agree to that. Let me get my shotgun." He headed to the back of his house.

"I'm going outside to talk to the calf," I called. "Is it a boy or girl?"

"Bull."

The calf had doubled in size in the few days since I'd seen him. He was no longer wobbly-legged, but still huddled timidly against his mama's side. She lowered her head and mooed at me. Probably the bovine equivalent of, *You keep away from my baby.*

I mooed and made silly arm waves at the calf. He was curious and finally approached the fence where I stood. Mama let him come, but followed close behind. I squatted down and reached through the fence so I could pet his nose. It was soft as silk.

"I'm going to stop whatever's happening to your family. I promise." The calf licked my hand and mooed. Mama finally had enough, and she stomped her hoof. The calf immediately scurried back to her side.

I heard scuffing behind me and stood. Bubba grinned from ear to ear. "They can be mighty cute when they're little."

I nodded. "They sure can. Now let's go protect the rest of them. Maybe tonight's the night we'll figure it out."

After retrieving my flashlight, Sig 9 mm gun, and pillow from the trunk of my car, I climbed onto the Gator beside Bubba and we took off. We had to hunt for the cows, but found them near a large man-made, earthen tank toward the east side of the property. I hadn't been in this area before. The cows had always been farther west.

There were almost no mesquites, but there were a dozen scattered live oaks, much taller and with broader canopies. Parking beneath one would somewhat block our view of the sky, but it would also help obscure us from whatever might arrive from there.

We debated where to park and wait and finally chose the acorn-strewn ground beneath a good-sized oak beside the pond's crescent-shaped earthen dam. We'd easily see things flying above the nearby cows. We settled in and chatted softly while waiting for dark.

"You really don't remember nothin'?" Bubba's voice was filled with frustration.

I shook my head. "Not much. Like I said before, based on what little I saw, it was some kind of medical facility. No idea what goes on there. Whatever they did to me was done while I was drugged."

"What'd the doctor say?"

"I can't see him until tomorrow."

"Marianna! You should've asked for another doc."

"I know. But I feel fine. Far as I can tell they didn't do any permanent damage."

"*Far as you can tell.* That ain't necessarily what's fact."

He had me there. A twinge of fear clenched my stomach, but I fought it down. "I'll ask Dr. Green tomorrow to give me a full once-over. Okay?"

"Gonna have to be, I guess." He shifted on the Gator's seat. "What's really goin' on at the hippies' place? What'd you find when you got shot?"

I closed my eyes and sighed. *I guess it's time to come clean.* I told him about the pot farm.

"Dammit. I'm calling the cops tomorrow. I don't want no damn drug dealers next to me."

"Please don't, Bubba. They know more than they're telling. Give me a few more days. I know G.J. will talk to me. I need to get him alone."

"Aw, hell. Okay. I guess a few more days ain't gonna do no harm."

We talked about odds and ends for another half hour until darkness finally descended. While we waited, the cows wandered into a tree line on the far side of the tank.

"Dang. Do we stay or move?" Bubba asked.

"We better stay. If the...aliens...are going to show up, it'll be soon. Firing up the Gator might scare them off."

"Yeah. Guess you're right."

We grew quiet, anticipating what might happen next.

When the mysterious lights in the sky finally blinked on, sure enough, they were on the far side of the tree line, where the cows had relocated, so we couldn't get a good view.

"Well dammitall." Bubba spat off to the side. "I was afraid that'd happen."

I grabbed my flashlight and hopped from the Gator. "It's not far, come on."

Even from a distance, I could see the cows forming up single-file beneath it. Bubba and I hadn't gone a dozen paces when we heard yelling in the distance, from the direction of the hippies' land.

"Hey! Come here!"

I winced, recognizing G.J.'s voice. What was he doing out in the middle of the night. *Is he trying to help me find the UFOs?* I hadn't meant to inspire him with what I said while he and I were alone. *He might mess up everything.*

Sure enough, the light blinked out.

"I said come here." G.J. yelled again.

There was a brief moment of total silence, not even the cows made any noise, then a vehicle engine started up and rapidly receded into the distance. Whoever had been there chose to leave in a hurry rather than talk to G.J.

"Shit." I wished I was a spitter, because hocking one into the dirt would've been an appropriate addition to my verbal response.

"Who the hell was that?" Bubba asked.

I wasn't sure if he meant who was in the vehicle, or who'd been yelling. I answered as best I could. "That was G.J. yelling. He's the more simple-minded one of the hippies. I don't know who was in the vehicle, but I'd bet money it was the same people I heard the night I was shot. I wondered if they were involved with the pot farm, and the timing of them and the light in the sky was more than coincidence. But I'm now sure the two are related. If aliens are involved, they're in cahoots with people. Bad people."

"Don't know why G.J. had to butt in, but ain't nothin' else gonna happen tonight." Bubba shook his head. "Might as well pack it in."

I hated to admit it, but Bubba was right. We climbed into the Gator and returned to his house.

"You wanna come in for a drink or a cuppa?" Bubba asked.

I shook my head. "Been a long day. I'm heading home. We'll try again tomorrow, and the next day, and the next if we have to. Don't worry."

"I don't trust folks very easily, but you're one stand-up girl." Bubba grinned and nodded.

I didn't even take offense at his calling me a girl. I smiled back. "Thanks."

I'd just turned from Bubba's place onto the Ranch Road, planning on heading straight home, when a wild idea formed in my brain. I took the turn toward the hippies' place, hoping to catch G.J. still out and about and away from the trailers. It was a long shot, but couldn't hurt.

I pulled to the side of the road just passed their gate and shut off my car. As quietly as possible, I unlatched the gate and eased through. I was glad I was wearing my Stealthy-PI-Mode clothes. Being dressed all in black would help hide me as I sneaked down their driveway. I kept to the brush on the far side of the driveway from the trailers, and crouched low as I passed the cul-de-sac parking area.

All three of the single-wides were dark. I was almost on the other side of the clearing when a dog started up with a throaty, menacing bark. I guess Bruiser heard, smelled, or spotted me. Or all three. I froze and crouched even lower.

The center trailer's porch light came on and the door opened. Someone switched on a flashlight and swept it over the area. I tucked my hands under my arms and ducked my head. After a minute, the light switched off.

"Shut the hell up, you stupid dog," Earl yelled. Bruiser wisely shut up. Earl slammed his door and the porch went dark.

I waited a few minutes, then resumed creeping. I was approaching where Bubba and the hippies' land intersected when I saw G.J.'s silhouette. At least I hoped it was him. He didn't seem like the type to shoot first and ask questions later, but I took no chances.

I stayed in my squatted position and called into the darkness. "G.J., it's Marianna Morgan. I heard you yelling at those men awhile ago. Can we talk?"

"Marianna? What the heck are ya' doin' out here in the middle of the night? I can't see you."

I stood and walked toward him. "Bubba and I were watching his cows. The light came back, and we heard you yelling at someone. Then the light went out. What happened?"

"I thought I'd see if the men Bengy and Earl let come on the land are really in cahoots with the aliens. I didn't want you to get hurt again on account of us doin' business with bad folks." G.J. shuffled his feet in the rocky ground.

As upset as I'd been at G.J.'s blowing our chance to find out what was going on, his reason touched my heart. "That's really sweet. From what we could hear, they took off instead of talking to you."

"Yeah. Cowards. I wanted ta ask 'em if they helped them aliens take you."

"They probably wouldn't have told you. They'd have just lied."

"Prob'ly. But I still wanted ta ask."

"Can you tell me anything else about who they are or what they're doing?"

Even in the light of the waning moon, I could see G.J.'s brow furrow in concentration. "I think they're helpin' the aliens."

I nodded. "That may be. But who are they, and what are they doing when they come here?"

"Dunno. Bengy and Earl don't tell me nothin' about them folks." G.J. sniffled. "I'm sorry I ruined your chance to catch 'em."

Is he crying? Bless his heart. Maybe he can still help. I patted his arm. "You didn't ruin things. Heck, if you hadn't yelled, I wouldn't be here talking to you right now. Tell you what. Maybe you can help where no one else can."

"Really?" G.J. did a little shuffle dance. Of joy, I presumed.

"Can you get me their names?"

The shuffle abruptly stopped. "I... Earl would... Bengy might..." his voice trailed off with a hiccup.

In spite of how nice Bengy and Earl had been when I showed up at their place after my abduction, I understood G.J.'s reluctance. "Okay, how about the license plate and description of their vehicle? Can you get me that?"

The shuffling resumed. "You betcha! I can do that without Bengy or Earl every knowin'! And I already seen it's a white van."

"That's great." I fished a card from my back pocket and held it out. "Here's my card. Call me when you learn anything else."

"I'll do that. I promise." G.J. gave me a lung-crushing bear hug.

I hugged him in return. "It's okay. I know you're doing what you can to help. And I really do appreciate it."

"I best get back," G.J. said. "They's probably asleep, but if not, they might find out I'm not there."

We walked without talking back to the clearing. I gave G.J. a quick peck on the cheek, then moved into the brush along the driveway. He cut across the cul-de-sac and slipped into the righthand trailer. This time, Bruiser didn't bark at either of us.

I thought about everything as I drove home. It was almost midnight, and my body sagged with fatigue. *Sure has been a helluva few days. I need a break in this case bad.*

While sitting at a red light, I glanced at my phone. Dammit, I'd missed another call from Linda Favoccia. At least she'd left another message. I'd also missed calls from Patrick, Judy, and Larry. I'd forgotten all about putting my phone on silent. Considering how many calls I'd missed, that was a good thing. I switched the ringer back on, then pressed the Voicemail button.

Larry and Judy wanted to know how I felt. Patrick did, too, but also included another plea to give up the case. I'd deal with those three later. It was Linda's call that interested me at the moment.

"Ms. Morgan, this is Linda Favoccia again. We seem to be playing phone tag. I can meet you at ten tomorrow morning, if you have time. That's Thursday. I'm leaving this message on Wednesday. Let me know."

I glanced at the timestamp. Linda must be a night owl—she'd called at eleven-fifteen, not that long ago. I debated what to do, and decided to go for it. Smart people put their phone on silent or leave it in another room before going to bed. I pressed Call Back and waited. She answered on the third ring.

"Hello."

"Ms. Favoccia, this is Marianna Morgan. I hope you don't mind my calling so late. I just got your voicemail, and I saw that you called not long ago."

"No, it's fine. So would you like to meet?"

"Yes, please. Tell me where and I'll be there."

"Harvey's Restaurant. They have good breakfasts and coffee. Ten o'clock okay?"

"Ten is fine. I'll be there. Thank you." I didn't remember until I disconnected the call that my appointment with Dr. Green was ten-thirty. *Looks like I'll be standing the doctor up again.*

RELATIONSHIPS

Intimate relationships cannot substitute for a life plan. But to have any meaning or viability at all, a life plan must include intimate relationships. ~Harriet Lerner (1944-)

Although I wasn't in the mood for chitchat, I returned Patrick, Larry, and Judy's calls before heading to Lockhart Thursday morning. Judy was teaching a dive class. Her store manager said she'd tell her I called. Larry was in a briefing, so I lucked out there, too. Unfortunately, Patrick answered on the first ring. After the usual *how are you feeling* questions, he got to the point.

"I wish you'd give up this case. I can't stand worrying so much about you." His voice was edgy.

"Then don't."

"Don't be snarky. I love you and don't want anything to happen to you."

I sighed. "I know. And I love you, too. But this is what I do for a living. Sometimes it's dangerous. Not usually, though." This garnered a *hrmph* from Patrick. I continued, "No, really. Most of my cases are way more boring than dangerous. I spend a lot of time in courthouse basements looking through archives and public records. I just seem to have met you during a particularly rough round."

"You got that right."

"Look, I agreed to take Bubba with me when I do cow reconnaissance. Okay?"

"So you'll let that old rancher go, but not me?"

A flash of anger shot through me. "Stop it. Don't get that way. He's my client. It's his property. And his cows."

"I'm sorry." Patrick's voice softened. "Please stay safe. That's all I ask."

"I promise I'll do my best. Gotta go." I'd planned to drive because the weather forecast predicted rain, but Patrick's call had made me edgy and frustrated. *I hope Patrick isn't becoming controlling or overbearing.* I changed into my riding boots, grabbed my jacket and helmet, and headed south on Pancho Villa. Time on my motorcycle would help me relax and shake off my anger.

Arriving a few minutes early at Harvey's gave me a chance to pick where we sat. I chose a booth in the back corner of the room. A young Hispanic man approached as I sat. "Welcome to Harvey's. Breakfast? Coffee?"

I smiled. "Yes, please. To both. And someone's joining me."

He retrieved the coffee pot and a second menu. He was pouring my cup when the door opened. "Morning, Linda," he said.

I looked toward the door and waved. A middle-aged woman with long, flowing grey hair had just entered. She approached the booth.

"Morning, Jack." She turned to me and held out her hand. "You must be Ms. Morgan."

I shook her hand. "Yes, I am. But please call me Marianna."

She slid into the booth opposite me and we took a minute to exchange pleasantries and place our orders. When Jack walked away, Linda's expression grew serious. "So what's this all about? What information is it you're needing?"

"Do you know Mr..." *Oh no. I could only remember his last name.* "Mr. Taylor? Bubba? Lives off Ranch Road 672."

"Nope. I bought that land last year as an investment. Haven't been out there since I leased it."

"He's my current client." I gave her a brief summary of his case, without getting into aliens. Instead, I made it sound like we suspected rustlers were at work.

Linda shook her head. "Who'da thunk cattle rustling would be going on in this day and age. So why do you have questions for me about this? How's my land involved?"

"I have reason to suspect that whoever's involved in the cattle... incidents, is using your land as an access point. Some type of sub-lease agreement as far as I can tell."

"Not after today they won't. I'll tell my tenants that no one is allowed on the property except them and their specific guests. No sub-leases."

I took a sip of coffee. "There's more. I don't think your tenants are involved other than maybe being paid for access, but I'd like to run background checks on them, just to be on the safe side. Could you give me any personal information? Even last names would help."

Linda frowned. "You're for sure a licensed private investigator?"

"Yes. I'm sorry, I should've provided this as soon as you sat down." I fished in my purse and handed her my laminated PI license. She glanced at the photo on the license before handing it back.

"Okay, so you're legit. Do you really think my tenants are involved in illegal activities?"

Of course they are. They're growing an acre or more of pot. I wasn't about to tell her that. I needed access to G.J., and once the pot field came to light, all bets were off. But I didn't want to lie. That might bite me in the ass later. So I hedged. "I can't say what they're doing or not doing for sure. But I try to be a thorough investigator, and background checks are on my always-do-this checklist." I smiled as sincerely as possible.

Linda nodded. "That makes good sense." She signaled to Jack.

He approached the table. "Need more coffee?"

"Always. But could I have a piece of paper and a pen?" Linda pointed to the order pad tucked in his waistband.

"Sure thing." He tore off a couple of the pages and retrieved a pen from the checkout counter.

Linda consulted the contacts on her phone, then wrote on the paper and slid it across the table to me.

Earl Haden

Winifred Polkson

Gareth Blappit, Jr.

I couldn't help but giggle.

"What?" Linda asked.

"No wonder Bengy and G.J. go by nicknames."

Linda laughed. "Guess I don't blame them either."

"How did you meet them? Did you know them before you leased to them? Or did they simply respond to an ad or something?"

"Earl's a cousin, although we were never close. But I heard through family he was looking for some land to live on and didn't have the money himself to buy anything. Seemed a good investment opportunity to me. Lockhart is growing. I figured I could buy now, let Earl and his friends live on it for a few years and cover my mortgage payment, and sell later when development reaches that far east of town."

I nodded. "Sounds like a win-win. They seem like okay people."

"So you've already talked to them?"

"A couple of times. The first time, Bengy took me to the back of the property to search for one of the missing cows. Another was when I was abduc…fell and went unconscious. I was afraid to go all the way back to Bubba's house, so I walked to the trio's trailers instead." *Oh shit, I hope she didn't catch my slip up.*

She obviously did. She narrowed her eyes and pursed her lips. "Were you about to say abducted?"

Damn. What can I say? I shrugged. "Yes, but I wasn't really. I had weird visions, or dreams, or whatever while I was unconscious."

She stared for a beat. "Why'd you go unconscious?"

"I don't know. I haven't felt well. Maybe I'm coming down with a bug."

Her look said it all. *She thinks I'm full of shit.*

I pointed to my cheek, which was once again smooth and clear. "I even ended up with cactus needles in my cheek."

She squinted at my face and frowned. I wasn't helping myself out. Time to get back on subject. "Anyway, G.J. gave me water and kept an eye on me while Earl and Bengy went for Bubba. They were very helpful."

"But you really think they're involved in some cattle rustling ring?"

"Not really. I just want to err on the side of caution."

Linda sighed. "Fair enough." She slid from the booth just as Jack approached with our food. "It may all be moot after I talk to them anyway, if that's how your rustlers are getting to Bubba's herd. I'm heading there. Right now." She turned to Jack. "Can you pack mine to go? And put hers on my tab."

Jack set my plate in front of me and scurried back to the kitchen. While she waited, Linda turned back to me. "I'm sorry. I need to go."

I nodded. "I understand." *She thinks I'm nuts.* "Thank you for breakfast." I probably wouldn't be able to eat it. My stomach was queasy and churning. *I hope I didn't just screw up everything.* I spent fifteen minutes pushing my eggs and hash browns around on my plate before giving up.

I tossed another couple of bucks on the table as a tip and left. I climbed onto Pancho Villa and headed toward Austin. What I wanted was to ride west, toward the winding roads and rolling hills of the Texas Hill Country. Maybe stop at the Blue Bonnet Cafe in Marble Falls for some of their famous pie. Their chocolate ice box pie always made me feel better.

Instead, I returned to my office in Austin to search for the hippies' names in the Electronic Records Archival Service. What I found made it worth foregoing pie. I jotted down the pertinent facts:

Winifred " Bengy" Polkson:

Age: 61

Marital Status: Divorced

Education:

Bachelors in Computer Science

Masters in Biochemistry

PhD in Photonics and Nanoscience

Occupation: Systems Design, Software Development

Employment (10 year history):

DataPoint Corporation, San Antonio, TX

Data Sorcery Systems, San Jose, CA

MicroTechGen Corporation, Austin, TX

Employment Status: Retired

Earl Haden:

Age: 63

Marital Status: Widowed

Education: Associates in Electrical
Engineering

Occupation: HVAC service representative

Employment (10 year history):

Aircom Solutions, Austin, TX

Haden HVAC Systems, Austin, TX

Employment Status: Inactive/Unknown

Gareth "G.J." Blappit, Jr.

Age: 63

Marital Status: Single

Education: High School GED

Occupation: General Laborer

Employment (10 year history):

Mousely Medical Testing, Austin, TX

Haden HVAC Systems, Austin, TX

Employment Status: Unemployed

I stared at the information I'd uncovered, trying to decide if it meant anything related to the case. It seemed pretty obvious that G.J. and Earl knew each other from Earl's HVAC company. But how had either of them known Bengy?

I don't like loose ends, and this case had enough to weave a blanket. I needed to brainstorm, and my best storm-buddy was Judy. I hadn't heard back, so I called her again. Her store manager apologized for forgetting to tell Judy I'd called, then promised she'd get her that instant.

"I thought you didn't care." Judy laughed. "But Rosalie told me you called this morning. Sorry I missed it. What's up?"

"I need your brain."

"You know I'm always up for a good session of Two Heads Are Better Than One. When? Where are you?"

"I'm at my office, but my butt feels better. It might be fourth Thursday instead of our usual third Thursday, but how about the Oasis? I need some wind in my hair. And we missed last week, anyway."

"And bugs on your teeth. Or at least your helmet. How about an hour?"

"I'll be there." I closed up my office and headed west. It was mid afternoon, and the sun wouldn't set for several hours, so we'd probably be gone before the traditional sunset celebration.

As corny as it was, Judy and I still enjoyed the Oasis's long time celebration of each day's sunset by ringing bells and banging gongs, accompanied by patrons stomping their feet just as the sun set over the west side of Lake Travis. Today, though, I was looking more for insight about the case than I was to reveling in a gorgeous sunset and building-shaking public spectacle.

Judy was already on the fourth level, our favorite, thanks to the adorable waiter, Chuck. At around twenty, the blond-haired, turquoise-eyed young man was definitely too young for either of us, but that didn't stop our flirting and dreaming.

I sat down and put my helmet and jacket on the empty chair beside me. I'd just straightened up when Chuck walked over.

"Hello ladies." He grinned as he set two frosty frozen margaritas, a basket of chips, and a bowl of spicy salsa on our table. "You're here early today."

Before I could stop myself, I batted my eyes. When I realized what I was doing, I froze them open in what probably looked like a deer-in-the-headlights stare. "Got exciting things going on."

Chuck winked, patted my shoulder, and moved on to another table. I could feel my hot cheeks, knew they were bright red.

"You're hopeless." Judy laughed and tossed a chip at me. It flew over the side rail and down the cliff, a future snack for some lucky critter. "So what's up?"

We munched on chips and slurped our margaritas while I filled Judy in on my almost-breakfast with Linda and my new knowledge about the hippies. I pulled out my notes and put them on the table between us, holding them down with the salsa bowl.

Judy studied the information. "So Bengy is retired. That explains how she could be living in the middle of nowhere with no visible means of support."

"Well, except for the large pot field." I grinned and waggled my eyebrows.

Judy laughed. "G.J.'s listed as unemployed, but Earl's company status is unknown. Has he closed the company or just taken a leave?"

"Good question. Maybe his business wasn't doing so good, and he's unofficially closed it down."

"Why not just close the business and remove it from tax records?"

"Maybe he owes money." I shrugged. "Maybe he doesn't want creditors to know he's no longer bringing anything in. Stringing them along, so to speak."

"Plausible. That could explain the pot farm." Judy nodded, then frowned. "But what's any of this have to do with Bubba's cows?"

I sighed. "If I knew the answer to that, this case would be close to being solved. I'm missing something big."

"Yeah, like whatever that is that's hanging out in the air over Bubba's cows."

"Cows! Oh crap! I told Bubba we'd go out again tonight." I stood and picked up my helmet and jacket. "Will you cover my tab today? I'll pay next time. I've got to go home, feed the cats, and change into more appropriate clothing before I head south."

Judy waved. "Sure thing. Go babysit some cows." Her expression turned serious. "But you be careful. This hasn't been the safest case for you."

"I know." I nodded. "I'll be careful. Besides, Bubba will be with me. What could go wrong?"

HAVING A FIT

What is this? It's music to get a brain seizure
by. ~Ozzy Osbourne (1948-)

By the time I'd finished washing a couple loads of laundry, cleaning my kitchen, and scrubbing toilets, it was early evening when I headed to Bubba's.

"Figured you'd changed your mind," Bubba said after I'd parked my bike and pulled off my helmet. He was relaxing in a weathered, wooden rocking chair on his porch.

The air felt chilly for a change. October was finally showing signs of wresting summer from the area.

"No. Sorry. I was brainstorming with a friend."

"Come up with anything?"

"More questions than answers, I'm afraid." I decided not to tell him I'd learned more about the neighbors. That would remind him of the pot field.

"We doin' this?" He stood and pushed the rocker against the wall. I'd seen my grandmother do the same thing when I was a little girl and asked her why.

"Cuz then the wind can't bang it around," she'd said.

I smiled at the memory. It also made me more determined than ever to solve this mystery and stop Bubba's cows from dying. Grandma Grace would be proud.

"You bet we're doing this." I grabbed the flashlight and my gun from Pancho Villa's left saddlebag. I'd squashed my pillow into the right bag but opted to leave it there. The pillow would remind Bubba of my injured backside. He'd probably give me hell for missing another doctor's appointment. I could hide any squirming and whining over the movement and noise of the Gator.

"Before we set up for the night, please take me to the latest cow that died. I assume you left it...her there?"

Bubba sighed. "Yeah. I left her. She's not far from the tank where we parked last night."

Once again, we climbed onto the Gator and headed for the back fields. Bubba stopped a few feet from the latest victim of the mysterious lights. The carcass was behind the earthen tank's dam.

Just like the others, this Hereford's head was missing. And just like the others, severed with the same surgical precision.

I wanted to cry, but instead gritted my teeth. "We'll figure this out, Bubba. I promise." *At least thanks to G.J.'s yelling, another cow hadn't died last night.*

Bubba nodded and turned the Gator away from the cow. After a bit of hunting, we found the rest of the herd near the ditch. I'd spent so much time by this ditch I was really glad something—or someone—had dragged off the cow that'd died there. I'm sure the original two carcasses were beyond pungent at this point.

It was close to dark, but still too early for the light show. We chatted about motorcycles as a way to pass the time. Bubba'd been a dedicated Harley rider back in his younger days.

"Used ta belong to the Hogs of Texas Motorcycle Club. Guess I still am, since I never officially quit. Ain't seen none of them HOTMOC guys in a decade." He stared off into the distance, lost in his own memories.

"I belong to the Hill Country Cruisers. Every Saturday morning at nine the group meets for breakfast at the Blue Bonnet Cafe in Marble Falls. After that, we all decide which direction to ride. Spend the next few hours cruising through the hill country."

Bubba chuckled. "Bet those shocks compress to the bottom after one o' them big ol' Blue Bonnet breakfasts. Sounds like fun."

"My shocks sure do." I grinned. "And it *is* fun. I try not to miss it." *Except when I'm abducted.* I shook my head to clear those thoughts before they took over. "You could still ride. You're in good shape. And you're still sharp as a tack."

He shook his head. "Nah. Got my cows now. Too busy."

I laughed, then briefly slapped my hand over my mouth to shut myself up. "Bubba you know that's crap. Your cows would be fine while you go off on a day ride."

He didn't speak for almost a minute. "Yeah. Maybe."

I patted his arm. "You should think about it. There's nothing like riding around the Texas Hill Country." I subconsciously touched the long scar on my leg. *Most of the time.*

Bubba sighed. "Ya got that right. Sometimes I do miss those rides."

We grew quiet as dark descended, surrounding us with the awakening sounds of the night—crickets, toads, owls, and unidentifiable rustlings in the brush. The night noises grew louder as the half moon rose, but there was nothing unnatural among them. We'd almost given up when we heard the hum. I felt Bubba's arm tense next to me, and he sucked in a breath.

"Showtime," I whispered.

Bubba nodded. Remained silent.

I grabbed my flashlight and hopped off the Gator, shoving the light into my waistband. Bubba climbed off his side, and together we ran toward the hum.

I didn't want to turn on my flashlight until I had something to point it at, so we clambered through the underbrush and cactus as quickly as we could. Thorns and needles poked through my jeans.

Gonna take months for my torn up legs to heal after all this.

The overhead light wasn't on yet, but we knew it was only a matter of seconds. I wanted to be beneath it when it came on. I had no doubt Bubba did, too.

I couldn't tell exactly where the hum was coming from, but I figured it was heading for the cows, so I used their white faces as destination guides.

When the light flooded the area, we were almost directly beneath it. I grabbed for my flashlight. In my haste, I dropped the damn thing. I bent to pick it up and…

"Marianna? Marianna?"

I opened my eyes to find Bubba's face looming just inches above mine.

"What's going on? Where am I? What happened?" My head reeled with questions. It also just reeled, I realized when I tried to sit up.

Bubba put his arm around my shoulders. "Let me help you."

My head cleared enough to notice I was sitting on the ground. The cows were a dozen feet away. Mooami was closest. When I sat up she actually stepped closer. I thought she looked worried. Bubba sure did.

I ran my hand through my hair, removing a collection of twigs and leaves, and repeated my most important question, "What happened?"

"Just as the light showed up, you dropped your flashlight. Then you had a fit."

"What do you mean, I *had a fit?*" I shook my head, trying to clear the remaining fog from my brain.

"When ya bent over, ya just kept goin'. Crumpled to the ground like an empty sack o' deer corn."

"You mean I fainted?"

"Yes. No. Well, not really." He looked toward the cows and shook his head, as if looking for some help answering my question.

Even in the dim light, I could see he was trembling. It was clear he was having a hard time with whatever had happened. I touched his arm. "It's okay. I'm fine now. What happened?"

"You had some kinda fit." He repeated. "You was kickin' and thrashin' and makin' weird noises, like growls or moans or somethin'."

That left me speechless. I sat for a moment, processing what he'd said. "You're sure?"

Bubba glared at me, a deep frown distorting his face. "I ain't blind. And I ain't stupid."

"I'm sorry, Bubba. It's just that I've never had seizures before. I don't know what could've caused it."

"You never had seizures *before* you was abducted. I'll bet them aliens did somethin' to ya'. To your brain."

A chill ran down my spine, ending in a quivering puddle in my intestines. My backside clenched, just in case.

I shook my head hard. "No. No, no, no. First, we don't know it was aliens. I *do* know that people were involved. I heard their voices the night I was taken. Might be *only* people involved."

"And might not be, too." Bubba's voice was barely a whisper.

As preposterous as his statement was, it was true. I had no idea where I'd been or who'd been there with me on the other side of that solid, knobless door, for the three days I was gone. All I knew was that people took me. But who—or what—else had been there? My intestines quivered again.

"How long did the light stay on after I collap...fell? What happened?"

"Prob'ly only twenty or thirty seconds. Cows had just barely got all lined up. Hadn't started their singin' yet."

"And when the light went off, what happened?"

"Cows just wandered off again and started grazing. Couple of 'em laid down. You got real still. Wasn't even sure you was alive."

I started shaking, either from the chilly night or my own fear. I didn't want to guess which, because I was afraid of the answer.

Glancing around, I asked, "Where's the Gator?"

"Back in the bushes where we left it." Bubba frowned. "You don't remember?"

I blinked to clear my thoughts. Then realized my thoughts ended at Bubba's house, before we even got on the Gator. "No, I don't. My last memory is deciding to leave my pillow behind." *Oh, damn, I hadn't meant for him to know that.*

"That was a coupla hours ago." Bubba shook his head. "You don't remember us coming back here? Talkin' about motorcycles? Eatin' big breakfasts at the Blue Bonnet Cafe?" He narrowed his eyes. "Pillow?" Thankfully, he opted not to pursue the issue.

"No, I don't remember. Everything is blank." I shivered again. "Help me stand. Let's get back to your place."

We didn't speak until we were sitting on opposite sides of Bubba's kitchen table. A large glass of bourbon on the rocks sat in front of each of us.

"How ya feelin' now?" Bubba looked ready to cry.

I straightened my shoulders and smiled wide. "I'm great. Not even dizzy. Maybe I was just dehydrated or didn't eat enough."

Bubba shot me a caustic look. "I might believe that if I hadn't seen the way you was thrashin' around on the ground. That ain't hunger. Not to mention your memory loss."

I involuntarily shivered for what felt like the hundredth time. "Bubba, I just can't let myself think that aliens had me up in some spaceship. The experience is already scary enough."

Bubba nodded and took a swallow of bourbon. "I know. But ya gotta look at all the possibilities. You're the PI. You know that."

He's right. Whether I want to consider it or not, it might be true. Shut up, brain. Right now! I shook my head and took my own healthy gulp of bourbon. "I don't know what they did, and I don't even know who or what *they* are, but I didn't ever find any signs they'd done experiments or anything."

Anal probes wouldn't show. Shut UP brain!

"What'd the doctor say when you went there?" Bubba asked.

I winced. "I didn't make it. I ended up with a conflicting appointment."

"Dammitall, Marianna. You said you'd go. Somethin' bad might be wrong."

"I know." I sighed. "I'm sorry. I was following a lead on your case, and Linda wanted to meet me at almost the same time as my doctor's appointment."

"Linda who? You didn't say nothin' earlier about no Linda."

I sighed again. "I should've told you, but I didn't want to get you riled up again about the hippies. Linda Favoccia owns the land they're living on. She gave me their last names so I could do background checks."

"And did you tell her about their damn pot farm?"

"No."

"Marianna!"

"Dammit, Bubba, I want to solve your case. I know at least Bengy and Earl are somehow involved. But if they're arrested or hauled off because of some damn pot, I'll lose my chance to find out what their involvement is."

This time it was Bubba who sighed. "Okay. But you *will* tell her, right? Or call the cops yourself? Or let me call 'em?"

"I promise. I won't let that part go. I'm just not ready for it yet."

"Fair 'nuff. So what'd ya learn about those three?"

"Not much." I filled Bubba in on the details I'd learned. I concluded with, "So I know G.J. worked for Earl, and that Earl is Linda's cousin, but that's pretty much it for hard facts. Still, it gives me more data points."

"What's next?"

"I'm going to talk to G.J. again. He said he'd get me the make, model, and license of the van driven by whoever Earl and Bengy are letting onto the property. I'm pretty sure after that things will bust wide open."

"Sure do hope so. I'm tired of losin' cows. And that heifer and bull calf are ready to go back with the rest of the herd, but I ain't ready to do it. Plus, I don't want nuthin' else to happen to you, either."

"I also don't want anything to happen to me. And can't say I blame you about the cows. How many have you lost so far?"

"Five, counting the one we looked at by the tank." His shoulders slumped. "It ain't even about the money no more, although that hurts, too. They's dyin' for no good reason."

"No good reason we can figure. Someone, or something, thinks it's a good reason, or they'd have quit by now. I'm hoping that the men who are coming onto Linda's land will be able to answer that big question—*why*."

"Gonna be a cold day in hell before I think anything they might say is actually a good reason."

"I'm with you on that." I downed the last of my bourbon, stood, and stretched. "It's after midnight. I'm heading out. I'll be down tomorrow to talk to G.J."

"Oh, no, you ain't. I watched you have some kind of a fit. You rode your bike down here. It's pitch dark on these back roads, and there ain't even a full moon to help. And now you've been drinkin'. You're stayin' right here."

"But Bubba, I've got nothing with me." If I'd been in my car, I'd've had my Trusty Spy Kit, which included a change of clothes and a toothbrush. But I'd really needed to spend some time on Pancho Villa. Riding my motorcycle was part of what kept me sane. Mostly sane. Whatever.

"I'll give ya' one of my old undershirts. It's nice and clean and soft. And every time I go to the dentist, he gives me a coupla new toothbrushes. I know I got at least one ain't never been opened."

"But what about my cats?"

"What about 'em. Do they have no food or water?"

"Well, yes, they do, but it's only dry food. And they don't know where I am." That sounded lame even to me. I knew the house would be safe, thanks to the alarm system I'd installed after a bad break-in a few months earlier. I knew the cats would be fine, too. Just pissed by the time I got home. But Bubba was right. Driving home at one in the morning under the circumstances was a bad idea.

I sighed. "Okay. But I've got to head out early."

"Fine by me. I'm up by five."

I couldn't help but laugh. "Not *that* early. I was thinking more like seven, since it's already so late."

"I'll have coffee waitin' for ya whatever time you hit the kitchen."

I followed Bubba down the hall. He opened the door to his guest room and I stepped in. The room was painted soft lavender. The four-poster, antique bed was covered with a white chenille bedspread decorated with red roses the size of dinner plates.

"Bubba this is adorable."

"My wife, Bessie, bless her soul, did this a decade ago. Never have felt a need to change it."

I hadn't ever asked Bubba about his family. I didn't even know he'd been married. I kissed his cheek.

"It's a beautiful reminder of her, I'm sure. Just looking at this room, I can see she must have been a lovely lady."

Bubba nodded and smiled. "That she was. Still miss her every day." His smile faded. "I'm almost glad she's gone, though. All this alien stuff and dyin' cows woulda broke her heart."

I nodded, but said nothing. No words I might choose would be adequate.

He turned. "Let me get ya that shirt and toothbrush."

"Oh! I just remembered." I headed to the hall and the back door.

"What?" Bubba asked. "Where ya goin'?"

"I have my pillow. Brought it in case I wanted something soft to sit on. Be right back."

Twenty minutes later I lay in the dark, covers pulled to my chin. My brain spun, thoughts swishing around like a washing machine. Probably because I was sleeping in a client's home, my thoughts turned to different clients I'd had.

I always ended up with some level of attachment to my longer-lasting cases. I still kept in touch with Stephen Davidson, who'd hired me a few months ago to find his sister. But that was a casual friendship.

Bubba felt different to me. Fatherly. Or grandfatherly. While I'd developed some level of friendship with Stephen, I was growing to truly love the old man who was sleeping down the hall. *I will not let him down. Even if it turns out to be aliens, and they did something scary to me, I'll see this through to the end.*

The thought of aliens again sent a cold slash through my innards. I lay for a long time in the dark before exhaustion finally sent me into a restless sleep.

CHANGING FOCUS

*The whole problem with the world is that fools
and fanatics are always so certain of
themselves, but wiser people so full of doubts.
~Bertrand Russell (1872-1970)*

I woke up disoriented and shivering after a horrific nightmare involving green, fifties-era aliens and scary, whirring examination tools. My heart pounded in my ears. I lay still for several minutes, moving my eyes from one pretty little room decor item to another — dried flower wreath on the left wall, painting of a windmill surrounded by bluebonnets on the right wall, framed needlepoint of cardinals on the wall opposite my feet.

The sight of Bubba's wife's decorating calmed me down and brought me back to normalcy. Or as close as I was going to get these days. At least I knew where I was, and that it was Friday morning.

I eased out of bed and padded to the door. Opening it a crack, I peeked down the hall. The sound of a radio drifted my way, probably from Bubba in the kitchen. There was no clock in the guest room, and I'd left my phone on Bubba's kitchen table. I had no idea what time it was.

I stepped quietly through the door and slipped into the bathroom. After cleaning up and redressing in yesterday's clothes, I joined Bubba in the kitchen. He sat at the table, an empty coffee cup to his right.

The clock above the stove showed it was already almost eight, much later than I'd thought. I'd planned to be home by now, and I hadn't even had any coffee yet.

"Good mornin', Marianna." Bubba grinned and winked. "This what you call an early start?"

My cheeks turned warm, but I smiled. "Guess your wife's lovely room made me feel comfortable and safe, especially under the circumstances. I sure could use some coffee."

Bubba stood, grabbed the coffee pot and a mug, and returned to the table. He filled the mug for me and refilled his own. When he sat, he added, "Hope you slept okay. Not dizzy or nuthin' this mornin'? Wondered all night if I shoulda' taken you to the ER."

I sat and took a big swallow of the molasses-thick coffee before speaking. "I'll admit I had a few nightmares off and on, but I feel good." I smiled and drank more coffee. "The ER would've been a waste of money for me and a waste of time for both of us. I'm fine."

"What's your plan today?" Bubba narrowed his eyes. "Besides going to the doctor, that is."

I smiled. "I will go to the doctor. I promised I would, and I meant it. Not sure what else I'll do today. Guess I'll be back tonight so we can try again with the cows."

"Nuh-unh, let's take the night off. We ain't goin' back out with the cows until you let me know what the doctor said, and I know fer sure you're okay."

"But…"

"No buts." Bubba shook his head. "I'd rather lose another cow than have somethin' happen to you."

"Oh, Bubba, I don't want you to lose any more cows at all." I sighed. "I'll see the doctor and call you with his report. If he gives me the all clear, will you change your mind?"

"We'll see." Bubba frowned. "Ain't like watchin' em all night's doin' any good anyways."

"I know." I sighed. "Four times I've tried to catch whatever that thing is, and four times I've failed. I like to think I'm a good private investigator, but this case is giving me pause."

Bubba slapped his hand on the table, making me jump a foot.

"You stop that line o' thinkin' right now. You're workin' hard for me. I know that. And it ain't like you're wastin' your time back there. You was abducted, shot, interrupted by G.J., and dropped onto the ground in some kinda fit. Those ain't your fault."

"Thanks, Bubba." I smiled, then reached over and squeezed his hand. "I'm going to change tacks. I know I can learn more if I spend some time dealing with Bengy and Earl's roles in this. I'm going to push harder on G.J. to get me some information. And I might need to stake out their driveway, see who's coming in late at night."

"Sounds pretty good. You sure it's safe, bein' on their land late at night? You was already shot once over there."

Long as I stay away from the booby traps in their pot field. "I can park a ways away and walk in. And I can hide in the nearby brush. I'll stay a long way from their pot field. I'll be fine." *I should've done this a week ago. I've been so focused on watching the cows that I quit thinking of other ideas. Every good PI knows that tunnel vision is the number one killer to solving cases.* I shook my head in frustration at myself.

"What?" Bubba asked.

I repeated aloud what I'd just been telling myself.

Bubba waved a dismissive hand. "Glad you was over here. You got to see what's really goin' on with the cows and how they's behavin'. Even if it's been pretty dangerous for you on this side of the barbed wire fence."

I nodded. "I'll be careful. But there's nothing else I can really learn from watching the cows singing and dancing. Well, stomping in sync."

Before he'd let me head for home, Bubba insisted on feeding me scrambled eggs, biscuits and gravy, and sausage. It was the biggest breakfast I'd had in a long time. Also the tastiest. I insisted on washing the dishes before gathering my pillow, helmet, and jacket for my ride home.

I stepped onto the front porch, followed closely by Bubba. "You be careful goin' home." He waggled his finger at me.

"I will."

"And you go straight to the doctor in Kyle."

"I will."

"Okay, then. I guess that's all I can ask."

I gave Bubba a hug. "Thanks for caring so much. I'll let you know as soon as I learn something." I stuffed the feather pillow in my left saddlebag donned my helmet and jacket before straddling Pancho Villa. "Thanks for breakfast," I called just before firing up the bike's engine. Bubba waved as I headed down his driveway.

I hadn't told Bubba of my plans, which was not to go straight home — or to the doctor. I had at least one stop to make first.

When I reached the highway, instead of turning right toward Austin, I cut left and headed for Lockhart's Courthouse Square. According to the courthouse clock tower, it was almost nine. I hoped Chisholm Trail Stables Antiques was already open, or would open soon. I wanted to talk to Katherine.

I circled the courthouse and parked on the side street near Katherine's store. Removing my helmet so I could see better, I pulled my phone from my pocket and texted Judy.

Hey girl, please go feed my furbabies. I'll call later. Still in Lockhart.

I'd call when I got back to Cedar Park, but I didn't want to take the time right now to chat. I pocketed my phone, and was climbing off Pancho, when Katherine's OPEN light blinked on. I draped my jacket over the motorcycle's seat, hung my helmet off a handlebar, and entered the store.

Katherine looked up at the sound of the bell when I opened the door. She smiled. "You're back. Marilyn, wasn't it? No, Marianna."

"You're right. It's Marianna." I laughed. "You're good."

"Good with names, at least. Not much else." Katherine hooted with laughter. "You wanted to talk to Linda Favoccia. She ever call you?"

"She sure did, thanks to you. That's why I came in. To say thank you."

"You get what you need?" Katherine waved at the coffee pot. "Want some coffee?"

"Yes and yes, thanks." I took the styrofoam cup she offered and sipped. "Linda gave me just what I was looking for. I was able to do complete background checks on all her tenants. Still not sure where the information will lead me, but I know I'm headed in the right direction."

"Good. Good." Katherine narrowed her eyes at me. "What else did you come in for?"

I laughed hard enough I almost dropped my coffee. "I see why you're such a good business owner. You don't miss much."

"I try not to miss anything."

I bit my lip, debating how much to divulge. She'd been straight up with me, though, so she deserved as much of an update as I could tell her without violating any confidences. I told her about my abduction and even about my collapsing the previous night.

Her eyes grew bigger and bigger as I talked. When I finished, she shook her head.

"Holy hell, Marianna. You should call the cops."

"And tell them what? That I might have been abducted by aliens? That maybe people are involved? That cows are dropping dead for no apparent reason? They'll think I'm nuts." I sighed. "Maybe I am."

"I'm a good judge of people, and you are *not* nuts."

"Thanks. And you know, I did overhear a conversation the other day. I'm not the only one who's seen and heard things around here. Do you know a Sarah Ann or a Lucas?"

Katherine's forehead furrowed in thought. "I've met Sarah Ann Graves. Owns a local flower shop. Not sure who Lucas is. Maybe her husband or son."

"No idea." I shrugged. "But Sarah Ann was talking about Lucas seeing lights and hearing weird sounds. Maybe I should talk to him. Where's the flower shop?"

"Longhorn Lupine Flowers and Gifts. Other side of the square."

I grinned. "Sure is easy to get around in a small town. Everything's so close."

Katherine nodded. "Sure is. She doesn't open until ten, but you can hang around here if you like." She winked. "Bet I've got a few things you might be interested in."

"I'll bet you do, but today I'm on Pancho Villa."

"Who?"

"My motorcycle. Can't carry much."

"We'll see." Katherine waved for me to follow. "Come look at the jewelry I just got in.

Forty-five minutes and two hundred dollars later, I shoved half a dozen gorgeous necklaces, three bracelets, and a funky purse into my saddlebags. Thankfully, the purse was squashy, or I'd have been in trouble making everything fit. I debated walking to the flower shop—it was only two blocks—but with my gun in my saddlebag it made sense to keep my motorcycle close by.

Turns out Sarah Ann's flower shop was next door to the cafe where Judy and I had overheard Sarah Ann talking about Lucas. When I pushed open the door, the smell of fresh flowers and greenery made me smile. *I wonder if you stop noticing how good everything smells when you work in a place like this?*

"Welcome to Longhorn Lupine Flowers and Gifts. How can I help you?" The woman behind the counter wasn't Sarah Ann, but she seemed about the same age. Perhaps they were business partners.

I joined her at the chest-high laminate counter. "Hi. I'm hoping to talk to Sarah Ann, if she's around."

I saw the woman bristle ever so slightly. I guess I'd offended her by brushing off her offer to help.

"I'd be more than happy to help," she said.

"I'm very appreciative." I leaned toward her and lowered my voice. "It's about Lucas."

That had the desired effect. Her eyes grew big and her mouth twitched. "Oh! She's in the back. May I tell her your name?"

"Thank you. Please tell her I'm Marianna Morgan. We spoke a few days ago in the Market Street Eatery."

The woman raised an eyebrow, then pivoted and hurried down the hall and out of sight. She returned in less than a minute, followed closely by Sarah Ann.

"Can I help you?" No recognition showed on the woman's face.

I smiled. "We met briefly the other day at the Market Street Eatery. I was a bit rude when I interrupted you and your friend Becky while you were talking. My name's Marianna Morgan."

"I vaguely remember." Sarah Ann still showed little interest. "And?"

"You were talking about Lucas and how he'd seen, um..." I hesitated, debating how to proceed under the curious gaze of Sarah

Ann's business partner. Or maybe employee. "About Lucas hunting at night and running across some unexpected lights."

Sarah Ann's eyes grew big with recognition. "Now I remember you." She sounded more accusing than friendly.

In addition to her tone, I noted she didn't ask why I was standing in her store. *I'd best tread lightly. I'll go for the Lost-Puppy-Effect.* "Please, I need your help. Is there someplace we can talk for a few minutes? I won't take much of your time."

Sarah Ann looked me up and down a couple of times. "Fine. Follow me." She turned and headed back the direction she'd come from.

I hurried around the counter and followed. We entered a small office at the back end of the long, narrow building. Sarah Ann waited at the threshold for me to enter, then closed the door, circled a small desk, and sat down.

She waved toward a faded orange plastic chair. "Please have a seat and tell me why you're here."

LUCAS

*Words fall upon the facts like soft snow,
blurring the outline and covering up all the
details. ~George Orwell (1903-1950),
<u>Politics and the English Language</u>, 1946*

I took a deep breath, considering which approach would be best. *Tell her about my case? Keep it more casual, as if I'm just curious?*

Some people are more forthcoming if they think they're helping you with a big problem. Others don't want to get involved in official stuff, but they'll open up on a gossipy level.

I had about two seconds to decide which Sarah Ann was. I knew it probably all depended on her relationship with Lucas. I had to start there. "Is Lucas a relative of yours?"

"He's my son. Why?" Sarah Ann narrowed her eyes.

"I was just curious. I didn't mean to pry." Based on this tidbit, I opted for the official story. *I hope she sees visions of glory and front page headlines for her son.* "I'm a private investigator working on a case for a local man. He's having trouble with—"

"What man?" Her tone was brusque and terse.

I smiled as sweetly as I could. "His name is William Taylor—."

"Bubba? That old coot? What the hell does he want with a PI?" The venom in the words was unmistakable.

Her hostility baffled me. I was going to have to use all my charm, especially since I didn't know what was wrong. Maybe Bubba owed her money. Unlikely, from what I knew of him. Maybe she'd messed up an order. Or maybe it was something someone who wasn't from a small town — such as me — would think was totally petty.

I took a quick glance around her office, looking for guidance. In addition to three photos of Lucas, her desk and walls also featured half a dozen photos of her posing with several different dogs and cats. An animal rights magazine sat on the corner of her desk. *She's an animal lover. Maybe switching the focus to the cows will help ease whatever her anger is about.*

"Yes, I'm talking about Bubba." I nodded. "Something's killing his cows, and each time has been after some mysterious light and sound has appeared over his ranch. I'm trying to find out what's going on so his cows stop dying. Especially the new mama and her bull calf."

It worked.

"I'm sorry to hear that." Sarah Ann's voice softened and her eyes misted. "Gentle creatures. Haven't eaten one in a decade."

"I've gotten to know Bubba's herd over the last couple of weeks. I never knew cows had such distinct personalities. I named my favorite Mooami because she has a red splotch on her nose in the shape of Florida. I don't want her, or any more of them, to die. I'm doing everything I can to stop the deaths."

My comment about Mooami was the final ice breaker. Sarah Ann laughed out loud.

"Mooami! I love it." She nodded and smiled. "I'm glad you care about the cows." She leaned back, her body language relaxing. "I'm sorry I called Bubba an old coot. What happened between us was a long time ago. Water under the bridge and all that."

"I understand," I said, even though I didn't.

"So how can I help?"

"I'd like to talk to Lucas. You said he'd also seen the mysterious alien object. I've had a heckuva a time determining what it is. I hoped Lucas's experience might help. And…" I paused, debating whether to continue, but I had to if I wanted to break this case. "And I need to know if he was on Bubba's land or somewhere else when he saw it."

"He doesn't trespass." Sarah Ann's body language shifted back to the standoffish.

"No, no, that's not why I need to know." I waved my hand dismissively. "If he was elsewhere, there may be more than one of these things out there. If he accidentally ended up on Bubba's land while chasing a hog, then we probably saw the same one. It would be easier to figure out what's happening to Bubba's cows." Bringing the cows back up seemed smart. And it worked. Again.

Sarah Ann's relaxed posture returned. She shook her head. "I hate that he kills hogs, because they're another of God's creatures, but I know they don't belong here, and they're decimating the populations of native wild animals."

"I can understand that." I nodded in sympathy. "We humans sure can mess up the natural balance of things. Then we have to try to go back and fix it. At least Lucas is doing his part to help get things back right again."

"That he is." Sarah Ann smiled with pride, then picked up her cell phone, pressed buttons, and put it to her ear. After a short pause, she said, "Lucas dear, can you come to the shop? No, I don't need deliveries. There's someone here I'd like you to meet. No, not like that. She has some questions for you. No, you're not in trouble. Okay, see you soon."

Just how old is this son? She talked to him like he's eleven or twelve.

Sarah Ann disconnected and returned her phone to the desk. "We live around the corner. He'll be here in ten minutes, soon as he dresses. Would you like some coffee?"

I was pretty wired from all the coffee I'd already had, but didn't want to offend. "Yes, thanks, if you're having some."

"Yes, I am. Be right back."

Sarah Ann had just returned with two ceramic mugs of steaming, black coffee when a young man who looked to be in his mid or late twenties opened the door and sauntered in.

"Hey, Mom. So what's this about?"

Pointing my direction, Sarah Ann said, "This is Ms. Morgan. She's a private investigator. She has an interesting story to tell you."

Lucas stroked his small chin patch and leaned his butt against the front of his Mom's desk. His legs were inches from where I sat and his head loomed over me. I had no idea if this was intentionally dominating or just a casual posture on his part. I flashed him an innocent and disarming grin.

"I overheard your Mom talking about the lights you saw not long ago. I hoped —"

"I'm not crazy." Lucas stood and paced across the room. "Is that why you called me here, Mom? To embarrass me in front of someone?"

"No, dear. Please, hear Ms. Morgan out."

Lucas frowned, but returned to his perched position. This time it felt dominating. His posture was stiff. He radiated anger.

I stared straight into his eyes. "If you're crazy, then so am I, because I've seen it, too. Several times. Always over Bubba's ranch."

Lucas glanced back at his mother, who still sat behind the desk and behind where he leaned. She nodded, but said nothing.

"Okay, so what about it?" Lucas shrugged and refocused his gaze on me.

"Every time it appears over Bubba's ranch, one of his cows dies. He's lost five, and one was pregnant." I heard Sarah Ann gasp. I paused for emphasis, then continued, "I'm trying to figure out what's going on. To stop the deaths. Please. Tell me if you were on

Bubba's ranch at the time. I really hope you were, so I know there's only one of these things out there."

Lucas stared without speaking for several seconds, then his shoulders slumped. "Yeah. I'd been on the ranch next door to Bubba's, hunting for…rabbits." He paused.

I bit the inside of my cheek to keep from smirking. I had no doubt his *rabbits* were the same seven-pointed leafy type I'd actually seen when I told the emergency room staff I'd been hunting rabbits.

"So what happened?" I prompted.

"Well, when this weird light came on up in the sky, I headed that way to see what it was. Even had a good flashlight with me."

I felt my pulse quicken in hope that I was going to learn something new.

"I climbed the fence, then had to walk a ways until I found a bunch of cows that were, I dunno what to call it…singing, I guess. And sort of dancing. I couldn't see what was making the light, even when I pointed my flashlight at it, because it was above the trees. Kind of pissed me off. So I headed back to the other ranch, but by the time I got there, the light had gone out. After that, I headed back to my car."

My heart sank. He didn't know any more than I did.

"Did you catch a glimpse of it? Did you see anything else?"

Lucas's gaze shifted to his mother then back to me. "No. Nope. Nothing else."

He was clearly hiding something. Was it just that he was probably helping himself to some of Bengy, Earl, and G.J.'s pot? Or was there something else?

"Did you see anyone? Or any other vehicles?"

Lucas stared at me before answering. "At nearly midnight in the middle of a field? 'Course not." I couldn't read his expression. He'd make a good poker player.

"I was just wondering—" Before I could finish my sentence, Sarah Ann stood.

"Anything else? Looks like my boy's told you all he knows."

I took the hint and stood, too. "No. Lucas, I really appreciate your coming up here to see me." I held out my hand, which he shook with a firm grip. I pulled a card from my back pocket. He took it and glanced at it before sticking it in his own pocket. "Please call me if you think of anything else. I hate that cows are dying. I want to do whatever I can to stop that."

"Yeah, I'll do that." Lucas avoided my eyes. Another indication he was holding back. But I'd get nothing else today, especially in front of his mom. I wished I had some way to get his phone number, but I was drawing a blank.

"Thanks again to both of you." I made my way to the sidewalk. As I turned toward Pancho Villa, a thought came to me. Lucas didn't know I was on a bike. And wearing my helmet and leather jacket would help disguise me.

I quickly donned my safety gear and rode Pancho around the corner, but with a view of the flower shop's front door. I parked and waited. Sure enough, within a couple of minutes, Lucas exited the store. Climbing into a white Ford Festiva, he backed from his parking spot, drove one block, and turned the corner on the other side of the courthouse square.

I had to squint, but I was able to just make out the license plate: YPL-240, which I decided would stand for *Young Pot Lover 420*. I'd be able to remember the backwards numbers because of that joke about 4:20 being the time to smoke pot, thanks to the Grateful Dead's habit of having their pot-fueled meetings at 4:20 in the afternoon. Or so I'd read once in a magazine.

Even if I couldn't remember that the real number was 240, there were only so many combinations of the three numbers. I was counting on my brain to figure it out if and when the time came.

As soon as Lucas turned the second corner and disappeared from sight, I fired up Pancho Villa and followed. I turned the same corner. He was still ahead of me. After a couple more blocks he turned again. When I reached that corner, I saw him pull into a driveway. I rode past to get a look at the house. It was small, asbestos-sided, and painted tan with forest green fake shutters on the windows. A pole with a *Come and Take It* flag at the top dominated the front yard.

I didn't need the address. As long as I knew the street, I'd have no trouble finding this house again. I accelerated two blocks before slowing and looking at the street sign. Lucas and Sarah Ann lived on Marydale. Close enough to marijuana I'd have no trouble remembering it, either.

I debated what to do next. Checking my phone, I saw a single letter response from Judy to the text I'd sent earlier about feeding my cats:

K

Since my furbabies' breakfast needs were covered, I could dawdle in Lockhart a bit longer. I retraced the route to Bubba's, but turned off before his road. I needed to see if I could talk to G.J. Maybe Bengy and Earl were off on errands.

When I pulled up to the hippies' gate, my shoulders immediately slumped. A large chain and padlock secured the gate to the post.

Maybe they're traveling — making deliveries of their latest harvest.

I leaned Pancho on his kickstand so I could check the lock. It was hefty and strong. I turned it over. A tag on the back said:

    Lock ID 86 — Property of Caldwell County
    Sheriff's Office.

Damn. I bet Linda had somehow discovered and reported the pot farm. What the hell was I going to do now?

CLOSE ENCOUNTERS

The only thing that scares me more than space
aliens is the idea that there aren't any space
aliens. We can't be the best that creation has
to offer. I pray we're not all there is.
If so, we're in big trouble.
~Ellen DeGeneres (1958-)

The minute I stepped through my door at home I was accosted by five cats who wanted to be sure I knew they were not happy about being abandoned the night before. They wound around my ankles, meowing at full volume.

For some reason, their yowls reminded me I'd forgotten to stop by Dr. Green's like I'd promised Bubba. *Dammit. Well, I'm not going back there now.* Not only was it forty miles from Cedar Park to Kyle, I needed to curl up alone at home for a bit. *I'll stop there the next time I head to Lockhart.*

The last twenty four hours had been frustrating and nerve-wracking. It was nice to feel appreciated and missed, even if by cats. Before I showered and changed, I poured a stiff bourbon, then curled up on the sofa, where I spent an hour giving and receiving much-needed affection. And getting slightly tipsy.

While I rubbed bellies, scratched ears, and sipped bourbon, I thought about my next move. Lucas had been little help, but I wasn't discounting cornering him again without his mom's protective presence. *What about the hippies? Have I lost my chance to connect with G.J.? Would he talk to me if I tracked him down in jail? Probably not. They probably blame me for their arrests. I guess it was partly my fault. I didn't tell Linda about the pot, but I was the reason she'd gone there.*

What were my other options? I'd lost my window of opportunity on the one I should have done sooner — I should have snuck onto the hippies' land and waited for that damn van to show up. I wouldn't have confronted whoever arrived, at least not in the middle of the night while all alone, but I'd have gotten the clues I needed — license plate and vehicle description — to find out who was behind all of this. Of course, G.J. had promised to get that information, but now it was too late to get it from him, too.

Dammit, I blew it. I'd let my attachment to the cows themselves, and my fear of how Bubba and Patrick would react to my sneaking onto the hippies' land — again — keep me from pursuing the case like I should have.

That would not happen again.

I was two thirds through my second drink when my cell phone chimed. I sighed at the caller ID — it was Patrick. We'd been in a bit of a rough patch since he'd suggested I take him along to Bubba's or drop the case entirely. But I couldn't keep avoiding him. One way or another, we had to figure things out.

"Hey, Heinz, how ya' doin'?" I answered with a smile. He might not be able to see it, but I was betting he could hear it in my voice.

"How's my best PI?" He laughed, then his voice softened. "I've missed you, Crash. Marianna."

"Just got home. Been doing more on the case. I missed you, too."

"How's it coming along? Any big breaks?"

I hesitated. Did I want to tell him I was stuck? Would that reinforce his apparent opinion that I was in over my head with this case? What about the... fainting spell I'd had?

Either he's your boyfriend and you trust him, or he's not, Marianna. Tell him the truth.

"Frankly, this case has me stumped." I updated him on everything, including what had happened the night before.

I heard Patrick suck in his breath. "I know you don't want to hear it, but I'm worried about you. What if something happened to you, or was done to you, while you were abducted? What if there are, um... outside forces involved?"

I could guess, by the tone of his voice, what he meant by *outside forces.* "You really think aliens are involved with my case?"

"What do you think?"

"Don't pull your cop questioning method on me, Patrick. Don't avoid my question by asking one of your own."

He laughed. "Okay, maybe I am. But this is such a weird case, and the evidence points to the potential for aliens. Don't you think?"

I wanted to argue that the evidence did no such thing, but a tiny doubt nagged at me, although I wasn't going to admit that to Patrick. "No, I don't necessarily think that." *Maybe the aliens brainwashed me while they had me. Shut UP brain.* "The idea of alien visits around the Austin area is laughable. More people would have seen them."

"Maybe more have."

"You can't be serious." I snorted bourbon out my nose, making my eyes water.

"Let's find out."

I rolled my eyes at the cats. "How?"

"There's an Alien Encounter Meetup in Austin. They meet the third Friday of every month, which just happens to be tonight."

"An... What?" Did I really want to meet a bunch of *Close Encounter* loonies? A bunch of nuts just waiting to regale everyone with tales of their abductions and anal probe experiments? *Maybe I'm one of them. Shut UP brain.*

"Look, you said so yourself. You're stuck. Maybe talking to others who've had experiences, or have seen things, will help point you firmly in one direction or another. Can't hurt, can it?"

It might. I'm not sure I want to know where I fit into this little alien puzzle. But Patrick was right about one thing — I was stuck. Watching cows dance and sing was getting me nowhere. "Okay, let's go check out this Meetup bunch. But if anyone starts making sculptures out of mashed potatoes, I'm out of there."

"Huh?" After a few seconds Patrick laughed. "Oh! I remember. From that movie *Close Encounters*. Yeah, right. I'll be right behind you."

"Where do these, um, enthusiasts meet?" I opted not to say *loonies.*

"In the back room at Moonshine Grill."

I couldn't help it, I laughed out loud. "I'm sorry. The name is just too funny of a coincidence."

Patrick laughed, too. "I'll pick you up at six. We'll get there by seven. Dinner meeting starts at seven-fifteen."

I felt guilty at the way I'd been avoiding Patrick. And if I was honest with myself, I was a little lonely, too. "Come over at four. We can have our own close encounter."

"Ooo, close encountering sounds good."

I took a nap, then a long, hot shower. Patrick showed up at five til four, bottle of Bulleit, my favorite bourbon, in hand. He made us each a smooth Manhattan. Relaxed and slightly buzzed, we spent an hour encountering under the covers in a variety of ways. I had to shower again, but it was worth it. Patrick joined me in the shower, almost making us late in heading to Austin.

We parked as close as we could get to Moonshine Grill and hiked the three blocks. Patrick had wisely checked in via the online Meetup page, so they had our names on the list. I hadn't even thought of that.

We soon found ourselves in the restaurant's small back meeting room, crowded in with twenty-three other people. I was shocked. I don't know what I'd expected, but that number was not it. More like five. Six, tops.

We sat at long tables arranged in a U around a central, small table, where I assumed the Meetup leaders or organizers would sit. I was pleased that we weren't immediately accosted by regulars, although a couple of people did smile and nod in our direction.

Patrick leaned close. "I know that guy."

"Which guy?"

"The one in the cheesy tweed coat and horn rimmed glasses. Looks like a caricature of a college professor from the eighties."

I giggled, then caught myself when a couple of nearby attendees glared at me. "From where?"

"I don't remember." Patrick shook his head. "It'll come to me."

Not much happened while the wait staff took everyone's order. That chore done, a man and woman crossed the room and sat at the central table.

The woman wore a simple, maroon, shift dress. Her black-dyed hair was cut in a short bob. The grey-haired man wore a navy suit, white shirt, and red tie. They looked like they were here to lead a marketing seminar, not a meeting about aliens.

The woman tapped her fork on her water glass for attention. "Good evening." She glanced around the room at the attendees. "I'm Betty Weiner. Thank you for joining us this evening."

"And I'm Charlie Hill," the man said. "We know most of you, but since we've got some new faces tonight, let's take a minute and go around the room to introduce ourselves. Please tell us your name and give a quick explanation of what brought you to us. There's a good crowd tonight, so keep is short, please."

I wanted to bolt right then and there. I didn't want to say anything about why I was there. *What should I say? Should I talk about being abducted? Should I mention dancing and singing cows? Maybe I should just admit I'm a PI on a weird case.* I tensed, causing Patrick to pat my leg and whisper, "It'll be okay."

Most of those in attendance simply believed they'd seen a UFO. Only a couple of folks insisted they'd been abducted. That eased my mind somewhat. *At least I'm not in a room full of loonies. Hopefully. Except me. I might be a loony. Shut UP brain.*

I was lucky that Patrick's turn came before mine. He smiled and nodded around the room. "Hi. I'm Patrick O'Meara. I'm a deputy with the Williamson County Sheriff's Department. I haven't had any personal encounters, but patrolling out in the country, I've had quite a few calls from rural residents who said they've seen and heard things. I thought maybe I could learn more from this group about what those reports mean."

Is he lying? Has he really had a bunch of county reports? He's sure never mentioned it. We'll talk later, he can bet on it. I smiled at him, but I'm sure he could tell the corners of my mouth were twitching from the forced nature of it.

Patrick smiled back, but there was concern in his eyes. Maybe fear.

Oh, crap, my turn. I took a deep breath. "Hi. I'm Marianna Morgan. I..." I froze. Patrick patted my leg again. I took another breath. "I'm a private investigator, and I'm on a case right now that could possibly have... My client thinks... I saw..." I gave up, shrugged, and stared at my lap. They could make of it whatever they wanted. *I'm not normally this shy or awkward. What the hell is wrong with me?*

Betty spoke up. "It's okay, Marianna. Lots of us have a hard time articulating what we've seen or experienced."

At that moment the door opened and Lucas Graves walked in. "Sorry I'm late. Is it too late to join in?"

Charlie waved toward an empty seat on the far side of the room. "Not at all. Glad you're here."

As Lucas turned toward the empty chair, he caught sight of me and blanched. I smiled and winked. *At least I won't have to hunt him down. Now I'm glad I came.*

I learned nothing new from Lucas's introduction. He told the same story he'd told me in front of his mom. I'd probably have to get him alone before he'd open up.

The food arrived just as the introductions ended. We ate as Betty and Charlie conducted the meeting. They went over the upcoming calendar, including plans for a couple of field trips to areas where activity was supposed to be high. None were near Lockhart. Then they dropped one big bombshell that made the whole evening worth it.

Charlie stood, tapping the table to quiet the soft titter that had begun during the calendar report. "In the last month, we've received an anonymous email about several cow heads showing up in a local dumpster."

I whipped my head toward Charlie so fast it made me briefly dizzy. *Cow heads? Bubba's cow heads? Duh, how many other cow heads would you think might be floating around Austin?*

Charlie tapped the table again, since I wasn't the only one who'd reacted to his first statement. "They were somewhat decomposed by the time they were found, but the attached photos clearly showed what look like surgical incisions. Even the neck removal was a clean, straight line."

Questions flew from every direction.

"Who put them there?"

"Where are the heads now?"

"Can we see them?"

"Did the aliens take them?"

"Who sent them?"

Charlie waved for silence. "We can't answer most of your questions yet."

Betty remained seated but joined in, "We're trying to find out more about the sender. The heads themselves were turned over to the police for possible cruelty charges, but of course our concerns are in a much different direction."

"One more thing." Charlie sat before continuing. "The heads were hollow."

"What do you mean hollow?" Patrick piped up.

Charlie hesitated. "The brain was removed."

A rumble of shocked voices ran through the room.

"We'll update you as we learn more." Betty smiled and waved her hands in a *calm down* manner. "We promise. Either via email or at the next meeting."

"Let's move on." Charlie shuffled through a small stack of papers. "We received an inquiry from the *Austin Chronicle* for an interview. I called yesterday and—"

I tuned Charlie out and glanced at Lucas. He was staring right at me with eyes as big as saucers. I tipped my head toward the door, and he nodded.

Leaning toward Patrick, I whispered. "I'll be back." I wasn't sure if he noticed that Lucas had just left, too. I didn't care. Lucas and I needed to talk, alone.

STRANGE RELATIONS

Relationships of trust depend on our
willingness to look not only to our own
interests, but also the interests of others.
~Peter Farquharson

I found Lucas hovering outside the meeting room. The main restaurant was noisy, so we moved to the parking lot.

Lucas was close to hyperventilating and stroking his chin patch like he wanted to rub it off. I put my hand on his arm. "Take it easy. Slow down your breathing or you'll pass out."

I stood as patiently as possible—a feat under the current circumstances—until Lucas's breathing returned to near-normal. "What's wrong? You know more than you told me at your Mom's flower shop, don't you?"

Lucas nodded and took a long, slow breath. When he exhaled, instead of answering my question, he asked his own, "Those are Bubba's cows, aren't they? The ones you said were dying every time the light showed up."

"Maybe." I shrugged, then sighed. "Yeah, probably. I obviously can't say for sure, but I'd be surprised if there are rampant decapitated cow heads around Austin."

"What's this mean? What's going on?" Lucas's breathing grew rapid again. This time he tugged on his chin patch.

I wanted to slap his hand away, but instead I said, "It probably means there are no aliens." *It also probably means I was in Austin during my own abduction.*

Lucas shook his head with force. "You don't know that."

No, I don't, but I have got to believe it or I'll go nuts. "Why would aliens leave cow heads in Austin dumpsters? Why not out in the country? Why dump them at all? Just eject 'em into space?"

"Yeah. Maybe." Lucas looked doubtful. "This has me totally freaked out. Whatever's going on at Bubba's? I want to help."

I didn't want this man's help any more than I wanted Patrick's, but at least Lucas had a vested interest other than sack time with me —he'd seen the same things I had.

Before I could come up with some way for him to help, he blurted, "I've got an idea. The night I was in the field next to Bubba's, I was sure I saw a white van."

I nodded. "Is that what you were hiding when we talked in front of your mom?"

Lucas stared at the asphalt. "Yeah."

"Why didn't you want to say anything?"

"Mom worries enough about my being out hunting alone. If she thought I'd stumbled onto some bad guys, she'd pitch a fit."

Not to mention your raiding a pot field. "Okay. So what about them?"

"Maybe we can watch for them to come back. Please trust me. I really do want to help."

"Not possible. The hippies were arrested sometime earlier today. Their place is chained up with a sheriff's department padlock. That means whoever was using the land is locked out, too."

"Arrested? Why?" Lucas briefly stroked his chin patch. "And how do you know it was earlier today?"

"Someone turned them in for growing pot. You know, the pot field you were visiting the night you crossed onto Bubba's property." I didn't tell Lucas I knew it was Friday morning because Bubba and I saw the light again Thursday night, which meant whoever was involved still had access to the hippies' land.

"What pot field?" Lucas did his best to look innocent, but once again his hand drifted to his tiny *beardlet*. I realized his hand went there when he was agitated or lying.

I gave him The Look and he dropped his gaze and shuffled his feet.

"Yeah, all right." He sounded like a child caught stealing cookies before dinner. "But those guys' trailers are still there. And there might be clues in one of them."

"You want to sneak onto government-barricaded property and break into private residences?" *Not that I hadn't thought of doing that myself.*

"Um..."

I shook my head. "Lucas you're, what, twenty-two or twenty-three? You're an adult. That's a felony."

"I'm twenty-four."

"Okay, it's still a felony. Look, give me your number. I'll find some way you can help."

"Aw, you just want to blow me off."

I smiled. "Of course not. You'll just have to trust me." *Actually, yes I do, but I'll see if I can come up with something he can do.*

I added his number to my phone's contacts. I was about to ask him why he was in his mid twenties and still living at home, allowing his mother to treat him like he was twelve, when the restaurant's door opened and Patrick hurried out.

"You were gone too long to be in the bathroom. What's going on?" His voice was coarse, his eyebrows furrowed.

"I'm sorry." I made what I hoped was a contrite face. "I kind of freaked when they talked about the cow heads. I needed some air. So I came outside. Lucas ended up joining me." *It's sort of true.*

To his credit, Lucas backed me up. Maybe he was looking for Brownie points, trying to get on my good side, so I'd let him help.

Lucas nodded vigorously. "I saw Marianna head out, and I really wanted to ask her about the cow heads. She'd probably have come back in if I hadn't started talking to her. But we're both pretty sure they're from Bubba's cows."

I didn't need Patrick to be jealous or upset that I'd snuck out. "I didn't mean to worry you. Between the cow heads and Lucas staring at me, I really did need air."

Patrick stared back and forth between us, then turned to Lucas. "So your name is Lucas?"

Lucas extended his hand and flashed a big smile. "I'm Lucas Graves. Nice to meetcha."

Patrick hesitated, then shook hands. "Patrick O'Meara. Same to you." He turned to me. "Why was he staring at you? How do you know each other?"

"Remember earlier when I told you about overhearing Sarah Ann talking about her son, who'd also seen the light? Well this is him." I waved toward Lucas. "In fact, we were just talking this morning."

"I told Ms. Morgan about crossing onto Bubba's land while I was…hunting hogs. I saw the light and how the cows were acting."

I smiled. "I know your mom introduced me as Ms. Morgan, but please call me Marianna. I feel old enough these past couple days."

"Yes ma'am." Lucas nodded.

I decided not to ask him not to call me *ma'am* either. I was raised in the south so I knew he really was being polite, not making any statements about my age.

"I do remember you telling me about that." Patrick cocked his head. "So, Lucas, you saw this alien ship Marianna's convinced is killing Bubba's cows?"

"I never said I thought—" I began

Lucas once again jumped to my rescue. Or maybe to Patrick's rescue, since I probably looked like I was ready to kill him. "Whatever it is, I saw it, too. She's not making it up."

I raised my chin. "And neither of us are making up the fact that Bubba's cow heads have ended up in a dumpster."

"Minus their brains," Lucas added.

"Sorry," Patrick said. "I didn't mean to make you mad. I don't know any other way to refer to the…whatever, than calling it an alien ship."

I narrowed my eyes but said nothing.

"Is the meeting still on? Should we go back in?" Lucas glanced toward the door.

"Was kind of wrapping up when I headed this way, but you have to at least pay for your dinner. I paid for ours before coming to find Marianna."

"Oh, okay." Lucas glanced at me, before returning to the restaurant.

Uh-oh, here it comes. But what came out of Patrick's mouth was as far from what I expected as possible.

"I remembered where I know the eighties professor looking guy from. It took a few minutes after he introduced himself, but the name finally got the neurons firing."

"That's great. Who is he?"

"Name's James Carter. He's a field investigator with the FBI. We met in a profiling workshop last spring. Chatted several times over the long weekend."

"What the hell is he doing here? Is the FBI involved with alien investigations?" I cocked my head in confusion.

"Those are very good questions. Here he comes. Let's find out."

James Carter stepped from the restaurant into the cool October evening. He glanced our way but showed no signs of recognition. Patrick waved his direction.

"Hey James. James Carter."

He squinted at Patrick in the dim light and grinned. "Patrick? How the hell are ya'?"

The two men crossed the short gap, meeting in the middle with extended hands. I gave them a minute to exchange greetings, then walked up beside them.

Patrick put his arm around my waist. "This is Marianna Morgan. She's a private investigator."

"It's nice to meet you, Agent Carter." I smiled and extended my hand.

Carter shook hands. "Call me James." He said nothing else.

After an awkward silence, I took matters into my own hands. "What brings the FBI out with the alien enthusiasts?"

Even in the dim light I could see Carter's face darken in a deep blush. He uttered a nervous chuckle. "Guess Patrick already mentioned that we attended a profiling seminar together."

"He did mention that." I debated how to vaguely ask again what he was doing at the meeting, then opted for the direct approach instead. "So is the FBI profiling aliens these days?" I winked in an attempt to lessen the tension that hung in the air, although I couldn't figure out why James seemed so nervous.

James shifted his gaze to somewhere over my left shoulder. "Actually, I'm no longer with the Bureau."

"They lost a good man. Are you a civilian now?" Patrick asked.

"No." James's hands fidgeted in his pockets. "I'm with… I really can't talk about it. I never expected to run into someone I know. Please don't mention this to anyone."

"Sure, James, no problem." Patrick smiled, but it didn't spread to his eyes.

"Sorry, but I've got to go. It was nice seeing you again. And nice meeting you, Ms. Morgan." He hurried across the parking lot and disappeared into the street.

His answers and behavior left me wondering for a while. I'd eventually have to find out, if for no other reason than it'd help my sanity. Or maybe not. That would depend on who he was actually working for. *Does whatever government group he worked for now take this aliens-in-the-area thing seriously? I don't want to think about the ramifications of that. Or is James here on his own? If so, why? Why expose himself, which apparently he felt he'd done.*

Once Patrick and I were alone in the car, I asked, "What do you think he was doing there? And who do you think he works for now? Is the government involved in researching local aliens?"

"I wondered the same thing."

I'd gone to the stupid meeting to convince myself that aliens weren't real and the very idea of them having anything to do with Bubba's cows was ludicrous.

Now here I was knowing that—probably—Bubba's brainless cow heads were mysteriously showing up in dumpsters and somehow the government was involved with the local alien hunters. This evening had not gone as planned *at all*.

Even after Patrick and I had a final tumble, I lay in the dark unable to sleep. I was ready to double down on Bubba's case. It was going to take some illegal actions on my part. I hoped they'd be worth it in the long run.

NIGHT MOVES

How would it be if we discovered that aliens
only stopped by earth to let their kids take a
leak? ~Jay Leno (1950-)

I planned to spend Saturday night searching through the hippies'
trailers, but Saturday morning was bright and clear, and I badly
needed riding time with friends. Plus, I could almost hear the
Country Breakfast Special calling my name all the way from the
Blue Bonnet Cafe in Marble Falls, an hour west of home.

I'd woken up late, thanks to our additional romp in the sheets
after Patrick and I got home, so I hurriedly fed the cats, took a
lightning-fast shower, downed only one quick cup of coffee, and
grabbed my riding gear. At least the cooler fall weather made the
boots, leather jacket, and helmet more comfortable.

Most of the members of the Hill Country Cruisers lived in Austin
and surrounding areas to the south. Instead of crossing town and
meeting everyone at the southern rendezvous point, I almost
always chose to head to Marble Falls via the northern route from
Cedar Park.

In spite of my bad accident along this route a few months ago, I
still loved the ride. It was forty miles of lovely winding road, and I

enjoyed cruising alone before hooking up with fifty or sixty other riders.

Every Saturday, except in truly horrendous weather, whoever was available met for breakfast at the Blue Bonnet Cafe at 8:30, then picked a scenic route around the Hill Country. We'd cruise together, usually ending up someplace for another meal before parting ways and heading home.

I reached the cafe at 8:45 — a little late — so the parking lot was full. Mixed among the pickups and cars were at least forty motorcycles, most sharing two and three to a parking space. I squeezed into a space next to a Harley I knew belonged to Chuckie and a Yamaha I didn't recognize. I found Chuckie, Chuck, and Chuck's wife Lynn crammed into a booth.

"Hey, Marianna! Slide on in." Chuckie moved toward the inside, pulling his jacket and helmet with him. I piled my own gear on top of his and sat. I barely fit, and part of my butt cheek was hanging off the bench, but none of that mattered. I was with friends.

We spent an hour guzzling strong coffee and downing massive plates of authentic southern breakfast fare while we caught up on our various escapades.

"What's your latest case?" Chuck asked. Since he was a retired PI, he was always interested in my quirky cases.

I filled him in as much as I could, leaving out names and details to protect Bubba's privacy. I didn't mention my abduction, or recent fit or spell or seizure or…whatever the hell it had been.

"Cows? *Dead* cows?" Lynn nearly choked on her coffee. "You get some wild ones, Marianna."

"Yeah, aliens is pretty out there." Chuckie laughed then made an "Ooooo-eeeeee-ooooo" sound.

I suffered some more ribbing over my unique case before we all found ourselves back in the parking lot deciding where to ride. We finally chose the Devil's Backbone, part of a four-hundred mile state road that follows the top of a limestone ridge along the Balcones Fault.

The Backbone's expansive rolling hills and curvy road is peppered with ghost stories and apparitions of Spanish monks, Native Americans, Confederate soldiers, and others. It was one of my favorite routes, so I enthusiastically agreed it was the best choice for the day.

We cruised our way along the more-or-less loop around the Hill Country, stopping now and then for a quick butt-break or potty stop. We ended after three hours at the Devil's Backbone Tavern near Canyon Lake, where we all toasted a good day with cold beer and old-fashioned burgers.

I couldn't have asked for a better day. When we hugged in the caliche parking lot, I felt revived and refreshed and ready to face my next challenge, which would come in a few hours. Stuffed from the huge breakfast and mid-day burger, I waddled to my bike and headed for home.

It was mid-afternoon, and Lockhart was closer than Cedar Park, but I didn't want to leave my cats abandoned again, and it was too early for my evening plans. Plus, my butt was sore, thanks to the bird shot wounds. They were healing nicely, but I'd been on a stiff, vibrating motorcycle seat for several hours. Besides spending time with the cats, I needed to get off my sore rear end.

Once home, I stripped off my riding gear and jeans, popped some ibuprofen, and crawled into bed. I napped for three hours, surrounded by cats, who were thrilled I'd joined them for their traditional, late-afternoon snooze.

At dusk, I showered, ate a tuna sandwich, and donned my riding gear. I'd rather have driven Pickle Toy to the hippies' place, but it would be harder to hide a bright red Mustang than a much smaller, royal blue Suzuki motorcycle. So I straddled the seat, gritted my teeth for a minute while I shifted my rear into as comfortable a position as possible, and rode south.

I was lucky that the county hadn't recently mowed along the road leading to the hippies' driveway. The head-high Johnson grass made it easy to conceal Pancho. I just hoped when I returned the grass also hadn't provided easy access for critters to nest in any of the bike's nooks and crannies. Last thing I needed was a rattler or copperhead deciding my warm motorcycle looked like a comfy *hidey hole*.

To be on the safe side, instead of hanging my helmet and jacket on the bike, I took them with me. I didn't want a scorpion or brown recluse spider taking up residence. I also fastened my Sig 9 mm semi-automatic's holster to my waist and tucked a pair of latex gloves in my pocket.

Climbing over the metal pipe gate would have been easier without my safety gear, but I managed without falling off or getting hung up. I moved up the driveway, using only the pale moonlight to see. It was unlikely anyone would notice a flashlight, but I didn't want to take any chances.

When I reached the circular parking area, I paused to look and listen. There wasn't a sound other than night critters buzzing, humming, and croaking from the nearby trees and scrub. No barking came from Bruiser's cage, so I assumed he wasn't there. I moved closer, just to be sure. Poor guy—he'd likely been taken to the local animal shelter.

The white pickup was still there, since the hippies hadn't needed their own transportation when the sheriff's deputies showed up. They'd been provided with a free, taxpayer-funded ride to the local lock-up. I made a mental note to find out where they were. Maybe G.J. would still talk to me. I doubted Bengy or Earl would. I didn't want to think about what they might have to say to me.

All three single-wide trailers were dark, which is what I expected. I'd have been surprised, in fact, if any lights had been left on. The electricity probably hadn't been disconnected yet, since the three residents had only been jailed a couple of days. I headed first for Bengy's trailer, set my riding gear on her small porch, then tried the door. Locked. I shuffled in my pocket for the lock pick I'd bought through the back door of an Austin locksmith shop a couple of years earlier. It looked like a narrow screwdriver with a slightly mangled tip, but it worked like a charm.

Picking the simple lock on the trailer door was embarrassingly easy — no security whatsoever. Once inside, I decided I was far enough off the road that lights wouldn't show, so I closed the door then flipped the switches on the wall. The open living room and kitchen area came to life.

I took a minute to look around before moving away from the door. There was no sign of struggle. In fact, the place was neat and clean and smelled of lemon cleaner. It vaguely looked familiar, since the last time I'd been inside was the morning after my abductors released me. I hadn't exactly been at my best.

Bengy's taste in furniture seemed to run toward the Ikea pressed-wood style, but everything was well-coordinated and stylishly arranged. She'd even hung a few pictures on the walls. The pictures themselves were the generic kind of art you might also find at Ikea or even Target, but it coordinated well with the furniture.

I detected the faint odor of rotting food, so I crossed first into the kitchen. Sure enough, the trash had been left behind. I'd have loved to take it with me when I left, knowing if Bengy ever got back here she'd appreciate it, but I didn't dare. Besides, the likelihood of Bengy living here again was slim to none. That thought made me sad. She'd been kind to me after my ordeal.

I pulled the gloves from my pocket and spent the next hour carefully searching her home, ensuring that I left everything looking untouched and unchanged. I didn't find any clues that might lead me to whoever was using the property, but I did find a folder in a small file cabinet in her home office/junk room that reminded me she was Dr. Winifred "Bengy" Polkson.

I'd forgotten she had a PhD in Photonics and Nanoscience. It'd been a while since I'd searched their names in ERAS. Why would someone with such a background retire at sixty one? I wasn't really up on that whole field of science, but I'd read enough to know it was a new field that was just starting to take off. Bengy was too young for Social Security, and most small companies, even successful tech companies, didn't offer retirement benefits. Those days were long gone.

Had Bengy retired for some other reason? Was she ill? She sure didn't seem that way. Was she really making enough money three-way splitting the proceeds from selling pot to justify giving up on a career she'd probably worked a decade to get a PhD for? None of this made sense.

I went through every paper in the inch-thick file. Most were old end-of-year earnings summaries from MicroTechGen, the last place she worked before retiring. The summaries provided her social security number, which would come in handy for researching more about her. They also included her previous address, a prominent street in one of Austin's most expensive neighborhoods.

She'd been making over two-hundred-thousand a year. Maybe she'd just saved enough to cover the costs of living the rural, hippie lifestyle. I still had no inkling why she'd want to abandon her PhD life for trailers and caliche roads.

One paper near the back of the folder finally offered a tantalizing hint. She'd been investigated and reprimanded for potentially removing proprietary equipment and software from the company. No proof was ever found, so no official legal action was taken, but the letter made it clear the higher-ups were convinced she'd had something to do with the missing items.

Maybe she'd been forced out, or maybe she'd chosen to leave, either out of embarrassment or to avoid further investigation and potential prosecution.

I wonder what was missing. The paperwork wasn't specific, other than stating the items were proprietary and leading-edge technology.

Not that the missing items had anything to do with my case, but it did provide a possible motive for why Bengy was living in the country with two scruffy dudes and an acre of pot. I used my cell phone to snap pics of the incriminating paperwork, then took one last look around to make sure I'd put everything back exactly as I'd found it. I slipped out, turning off lights and locking the door as I went.

Moving on to Earl's trailer, I found it just as easy to enter as Bengy's had been. In my mind, the layout was the same, so I took a step in before flipping on the light, only to have my shin meet something hard. Hissing in pain, I reached for the switch and discovered I'd walked into a box of what looked like vehicle parts. I assumed they were for the truck, since that was apparently their only vehicle. Although Bengie had mentioned Earl having a motorcycle. *I wonder where it is?*

I paused to rub my shin, then eased around the box and began my search. Earl's place wasn't nearly as neat and tidy. It smelled of old grease and stale cigarettes. His furniture was what I'd call Available Cheap at Goodwill. It wasn't beat up or tattered, but it spanned styles from the seventies to contemporary, and all of it showed some wear.

Earl's trailer offered up fewer clues, although I did find a couple of old birthday cards—reminders that he was Linda Favoccia's cousin—and probably the reason the hippies were able to live here in the first place. I was about to give up when a ratty, commercial-sized checkbook caught my eye. It was wedged under a small television in Earl's bedroom.

I guess since Earl had set his HVAC business aside, he didn't need the checkbook for anything but elevating his TV. Easing it from beneath the old-style television, I flipped through the check registers. They spanned a period from two to three years ago. The last check was for $1229.38, made out to a wholesale landscape supply house in Austin. The register note said *irrigation parts and pump*, odd for an HVAC guy.

I smiled. I bet if I wandered back to the pot field I'd find a nice pump-driven drip irrigation system, ensuring the crop got plenty of water. Was the pot even still there? Eventually it would be burned, but I had no idea how quickly that was done. Maybe immediately. Maybe not until after a trial or sentencing. Too bad I wasn't much of a user. It just made me drowsy. I preferred a good bourbon on the rocks.

Tucked in a plastic zipper pouch in the checkbook was a list of deposits and a few folded papers. Curious, I pulled them out and flipped through them. The folded papers were tax exempt forms where Earl had done business at a non-profit that didn't want to pay any taxes for parts. The forms themselves were pretty generic, but they did include Earl's social security number and TACLA license number as an HVAC specialist.

Most of the deposits were from small businesses around Austin, paying for HVAC services. One bundle of deposits that was paper-clipped together caught my eye. All were for repair services at MicroTechGen, the same place Bengy had worked. I finally had my connection, or at least the beginnings of it. I didn't know how Earl and Bengy had met, but I now knew where.

But what had drawn a blue-collar repairman with an Associates degree and a scientist with a PhD to each other in the first place? Proximity wasn't enough. Something else was going on. Maybe Earl was spiriting the proprietary equipment out of the building for Bengy. I was extrapolating like crazy, but it was plausible. He could carry supply and parts boxes, tool boxes, and bags of *garbage* out with no one batting an eye.

I'd have to think on it for a while, but I'd see if I could come up with some way to verify my hunch. G.J. had worked for Earl. He was probably just a gopher, but that also meant he was likely the one who carried items in and out, including potentially heavy boxes that should have been empty as they left the building, or garbage that went into the back of the truck instead of the dumpster.

My desire to track down G.J. was now even stronger. I had to find some way to convince him to talk to me. He was just simple-minded enough that he might not blame me for their arrest. Then again, his very simplicity might lead him to the most obvious conclusion. Me.

I used my cell phone camera to take pictures of the tax exemption forms, various deposits, and the check for the irrigation parts. I had no idea if I'd need that information again, but this was probably my only chance to get it. I was careful not to tidy up Earl's place more than it'd been when I invaded.

Search completed, I turned off the trailer lights and stepped onto his porch and froze. Something big rustled in the nearby bushes.

CAUGHT IN THE ACT

Getting caught is the mother of invention.
~Robert Byrne (1930-2016)

I stood still for a few seconds, listening to the sounds of the night. I'm just being paranoid. It was probably a raccoon. I moved toward the top step.

"Who's there?" A male voice called from the left edge of the parking area.

I dropped to a crouch as fast as if someone had knocked my legs from beneath me and eased my gun from it's holster.

"Who's there?" The voice came again. Whoever it was stepped into the clearing.

The half moon barely offered any help, but the voice was familiar. *Damn, where do I know that voice from? Who is it?* I didn't dare call out without knowing who waited an easy shot's distance away.

"I said who's there?" This time the man tried to pitch his voice lower, as if whoever spoke was trying to make himself sound bigger. Or meaner. *Oh! Or older.*

I was now pretty sure I knew who it was. I took a chance. "Lucas? Is that you?"

"Who wants to know?"

I almost laughed at the give-away response. Instead, I remained crouched. After all, I didn't really know him very well.

"It's Marianna, Lucas. Marianna Morgan."

This time Lucas crossed toward me. He had something in his right hand, but it didn't look like a gun. Whatever it was, he moved his hand behind his back to hide it.

Lucas's voice was a cross between angry and whiny. "What are you doing here? I thought you said searching here was a felony. You told me not to do it."

I stood and holstered my gun. "I did tell you that. And it is a felony. But it's my investigation, so I'm taking the chance. What are *you* doing here?"

"Me?" Um…" Lucas shifted back and forth on his feet. "I'm… I just wanted…"

"Are you stealing pot?" This time I did laugh. "You snuck onto their place to steal pot?"

"Well, yeah, but I was too late. Cops already cut down the whole field." Lucas's voice turned petulant. "They'll just end up destroying it. Big waste of some prime stuff. These guys know how to grow first class turf."

"Then what's that behind your back?"

Lucas waved a bag in the air before stuffing into his coat pocket. "Managed to find a few stray leaves. Not gonna be the best smokin', but it's free."

"Whatever, Lucas." I shook my head. "But you should go."

"Are you leaving, too?"

I glanced at G.J.'s trailer. "Not just yet."

"I saw you come out of the middle trailer, so I guess you already searched it. And your coat and helmet are on the stoop of the far trailer. You still hoping to search this one on the right? Is that why you're staying?"

"I just have things I still need to do."

"Like what besides searching trailers?"

I changed the subject. "By the way, where'd you park? How long have you been here?"

"'Bout an hour and a half. I parked a mile up the county road and hiked down. Didn't want to park too close. What about you?"

"I hid my bike in the weeds along the road. Not too far from the gate."

"You're on a motorcycle? What kind?"

Relieved at the change of subject, I said, "Suzuki Bandit."

"Nice."

"Look, Lucas, you really should go on now."

"Nah, I'd rather stay and help you search for clues. I saw them aliens, too. And if these guys have anything to do with it, I want to know. Besides, you promised."

I guess I had promised. But there was no way I was going to let Lucas help me search G.J.'s trailer. That was just all kinds of wrong. He might break or disturb something. If I did get caught, he'd be implicated, too, even if I'd just asked him to stand guard. He might end up being a witness for the prosecution to save his own skin. Even good friends had sold each other out, and Lucas and I barely knew each other. I was already taking a big chance just talking to him.

I had no choice. I had to leave, too. Whether or not I got another opportunity to come back was anyone's guess. But for now, my searching was over. At least I'd learned a few things. I hadn't learned what I'd hoped for—the names or other information about the mysterious men using the property—and I had no clue if the information I'd found would prove useful.

I shrugged. "Ya know what, I'm calling it a night. It was pretty much a waste of time anyway. I'll walk out with you."

Lucas's shoulders drooped. "You just don't want me around."

"It's a felony, Lucas. I don't want either of us to get into trouble. And I didn't find anything worth writing home about. I'll have to find some other way to pursue my case."

"Isn't there some way I can help? Please?"

I sighed. "Tell you what. I knew that Earl had a motorcycle, but I sure don't see it. Any idea where it might be?"

"Oh I can help ya' there!" Lucas grinned big. "It's behind that center trailer. Come on, I'll show you."

He took off around the right side of the trailer and disappeared. I hurried after him. Sure enough, a recent-model Harley Fat Boy was parked under a small shed behind Earl's trailer. I took my pen light from my pocket and circled the beautiful bike. The gas tank was custom airbrushed with an elaborate desert and rattlesnake design.

I whistled softly. "This is no cheap ride. Probably cost at least fifteen thousand dollars."

Lucas nodded. "Or more. I got a friend does custom airbrushing. He gets thousands for some of his designs." He paused. "So is this a clue?"

"Maybe." I shrugged. "Not sure how Earl could afford this as an unemployed HVAC guy."

"Well…" Lucas snorted "They were selling pot. Lots of it."

"You're right, but they were also splitting it three ways."

"Oh, yeah. Still might be a lot of money."

"It might at that. Thanks, Lucas. You really did help."

"I did? Cool!"

"C'mon. Let's go. Nothing else to learn here." I walked back toward the driveway. Lucas hurried after.

I retrieved my riding gear from Bengy's porch, crossed the parking area, and turned down the driveway. I heard Lucas's shoes crunching on the caliche gravel as he followed close behind me.

"What're you gonna do now?" Lucas asked. "Anything else I can help with?"

For a brief moment, I wanted to respond with a melodramatic *I work alone.* But Lucas didn't need me being sarcastic with him. His desire was sincere. I had no idea how freaked out he might actually be about the cows, but it clearly bothered him. So instead, I shook my head. "I don't even know what my next move will be. If I do think of something you can help with, though, I promise I'll call."

"Don't forget."

"I won't."

Lucas hurried past me and all but leaped over the gate, then reached back to give me a hand. I held my riding gear out to him, which made it easier for me to climb the gate's slippery metal pipes. We walked together to where I'd hidden Pancho, and Lucas helped me untangle the bike from the weeds and roll it onto the road.

I shook my head. "My bike's been here for an hour, and it's already choked with weeds. How's that happen?"

Lucas laughed. "I've had that same thing happen to me. It's like that old movie where alien plants take over the earth."

Lucas's mention of aliens caused my stomach to flutter. In spite of mounting evidence to the contrary, a part of my brain still wondered if aliens were involved.

Circling the bike with my flashlight, I checked to be sure there wasn't something living tucked under the seat or one of the fenders. I shooed off a couple of brown and black striped wolf spiders, but found nothing else.

I donned my leather jacket, but hung my helmet on the handlebar before turning to Lucas. "You be sure to take it easy going home. I know you just live up the road in Lockhart, but don't get stopped with *turf* in your car."

Lucas nodded. "Thanks for caring. I'll be careful. I'm more worried about Mama than the local cops. They might arrest me, but she'd kill me if she found my stash."

I laughed. "Sounds like a pretty good mom. She's just looking out for you."

"Yeah, I know." He gave me a quick hug then trotted off into the dark.

I pulled on my helmet and straddled the bike. *Dammit. I really wanted to search G.J.'s trailer, although the likelihood of it holding any useful clues is pretty slim.*

I already knew G.J. didn't know who Bengy and Earl had made a deal with. He'd been clear about that, and I'd never gotten the impression he was lying. He'd even agreed to watch and get the license plate number for me.

I briefly considered going back to his trailer, then frowned and shook my head. Lucas might be out there in the dark, making sure I actually left. If I tried to go back, he'd probably follow. Or it might make him mad and he'd call it in. I doubted it, but I'd learned the hard way that sometimes I can trust too much.

Straddling the bike, I fired up the engine, glad there weren't other houses nearby to hear or see. My foray had proved disappointing, but it wasn't a total waste. I'd take what I could get wherever I could get it. I wasn't going to let limited information slow me down.

One way or another, Marianna, you're going to figure this out. You're going to learn the truth about the aliens and the men who might or might not be helping them.

SMALL BUT SMART CLUES

Nanotechnology is manufacturing with atoms.
~William Powell (1975-2011)

My phone rang at six am Sunday morning. I knew it was either a dire emergency or Bubba. It was Bubba. To him it was probably halfway to lunchtime.

"You okay?" I could hear the concern in his voice and felt a pang of guilt for not having called him on Saturday.

I rubbed my eyes and sat up. "I sure am. I'm sorry I didn't call yesterday. I spent a good part of the day with the Hill Country Cruisers. I needed to step back. Change tacks."

"And did you change 'em?"

I didn't want to tell him I'd been breaking and entering, or that I'd attended an alien enthusiasts meeting, but wanted him to know I'd come up with new information. I fudged. "I did some digging around and found out more about the hippies. I'm still trying to figure their part in all of this. I'm going to my office today to do some more research on ERAS."

"Ear-ass? What's that?"

I giggled. "E. R. A. S. It's the massive database search program I subscribe to as a private investigator. You have to have particular certifications and licenses to be allowed access. Now that I've got more details on the hippies, I'm going to dig deeper." *And I'm going to check out that former FBI agent, James Carter.*

"When ya comin' back down?"

Does Bubba sound lonely?

"Soon. I don't think cow-sitting is doing any good. I want to track things from the other side, so to speak." A thought occurred to me—*if those guys can't get onto the hippies's place, they can't be doing whatever they're doing.* "Have you seen or heard anything in the last couple of days? Any more cow deaths?"

"Nope. All quiet on the western front. Any idea why?"

"Maybe." I padded into the kitchen as I talked so I could start coffee. The cats almost tripped me three times. Guess they wanted breakfast, too. "The hippies have been arrested and hauled off. There's a sheriff's lock on their gate."

"How do you know this?" Bubba's voice turned sulky. "You didn't tell me. When were you there?"

I sighed. Bubba seemed to view me more like a daughter than an investigator he'd hired. I'd do my best not to make him feel ignored or left out, but I still needed to keep our relationship professional. "I ran a couple of errands in Lockhart after I left your place on Friday. Before heading north, I stopped by their place again, hoping to talk to G.J., but they were gone, and the gate was padlocked."

"Oh. Well. I still wish you'da told me earlier."

"I'm sorry, Bubba. I haven't forgotten about you. I guess fainting on Thursday night freaked me out a little more than I realized. I kind of needed to regroup for a day or two."

This time Bubba sighed. "I guess I can surely understand that. What'd the doc say?"

I winced. And decided to lie. I pinched my own arm as I spoke, reminiscent of my mother's response when she'd caught me in a lie. "He wasn't in. I'm supposed to go back Monday morning."

What sounded like growling came through the phone into my ear. "Dammit, Marianna."

"I know, I know. But I feel fine. Honest. I'd have gone to the emergency room if I felt even the slightest twitch."

"Well…all right, I guess. But I ain't happy about it."

Bubba's concern touched my heart. He really did remind me of my own grandfather, who'd passed away a few years ago. "Let me finish my research on the hippies" *and the no-longer-FBI dude* "and I'll come down and we can talk about everything I've learned. Maybe together we can weave the clues into a recognizable pattern."

"I'd like that. You keep in touch."

After Saturday's huge breakfast, I opted for oatmeal and a piece of wheat toast, then dressed and drove to the office. It was a gorgeous day, and I wanted to be on Pancho, but my butt was sore from the long ride through the Hill Country. Pickle Toy was much more comfortable.

I found an envelope from Jason taped to my office door. Inside was a check for the last job I'd done for him and some specs for research on a new client. It looked like Jason had been hired by a local contractor to investigate claims of permanent disability being made by one of his former employees. This one might require some surveillance. I'd have to find time to squeeze it in—I did my best to never turn down Jason's jobs. They weren't big, but they were steady and lucrative.

I watered my palm plant, which was looking perkier than it had in a while. Circling my desk, I flipped on my ERAS computer and sat. While it went through its lengthy verification process, I opened my laptop and downloaded the pictures I'd taken with my cell phone while rummaging through Bengy and Earl's trailers. I printed out all the images and separated out what I wanted to search first.

ERAS beeped, indicating I was now connected and online. Time to see what I could find. The somewhat clunky interface to the ERAS database took time to maneuver, but the wealth of information that could be discovered was impressive.

I started with Bengy. I'd already gotten her basic information when I searched using her full name. This time, I had her social security number and even her employee number at MicroTechGen.

Okay, ERAS, show me your magic. I typed the numbers and hit Enter. A comprehensive list of almost twenty file names scrolled down my screen. Most were variations on what I'd already learned, along with previous addresses, previous and current vehicle registrations, family members, etc. Nothing really leaped out at me, at least until…

Woah, what's this? I leaned in and squinted, as if that would make what I was reading easier to comprehend.

Thanks to the letter of reprimand I'd found in Bengy's trailer, I knew she'd been investigated for allegedly stealing proprietary software and equipment from MicroTechGen. I'd assumed she'd chosen to retire after that, but I had no way to know. Now I did.

Before me displayed a police blotter report in the Austin newspaper about the incident. Bengy hadn't been the only one accused. The report listed Dr. Phil Walters and Dr. Wayne Briden as suspects along with Bengy, or more precisely, Dr. Winifred Polkson.

Phil was an Engineer/Scientist in the company's Research and Development division. Wayne was a Nanofabrication Research and Technology Scientist in the same division. Bengy was listed in the police report as a Magneto-Thermal Neurostimulation Scientist, also in R&D.

All three had been officially questioned by police during an investigation into the alleged thefts from the company. None were charged.

I sat back and rubbed my eyes. Just reading these titles made my brain hurt. Searching for that job title on its own might help me get a better sense of what those people did. The search results produced several descriptions. It appeared that title wasn't a specific career, more a research category for a person with the right set of degrees. I printed out one National Institute of Health project of the same title to add to Bubba's file, along with the police blotter report.

As soon as the printer finished, I grabbed the paper and read the NIH description three more times. It seemed important. It felt important in my gut.

> The research focuses on magneto-thermal targeted neurostimulation and -silencing of circuits in the rodent brain to investigate decision making and gambling. It encompasses nanotechnology, physics, neuroscience and animal behavior experiments.

Gambling? Decision making? I could see the NIH studying these things, but what was MicroTechGen doing? I didn't see them studying gambling, but they likely weren't just studying how to help Alzheimer's sufferers, either. Whatever it was, it probably involved animal experiments. Rodents. Or rabbits. Or…cows?

I shook my head. *It's not likely MicroTechGen has anything to do with Bubba's cows, especially since Bengy, Wayne, and Phil are no longer there.*

Would those three really have jeopardized six-figure salaries and cutting edge research to steal a few secrets? And what about Bubba's cows? How did they tie in? I certainly had no way of knowing anything about Wayne or Phil, but Bengy didn't strike me as the type to throw everything away.

Then again, she *had* resigned. And she was living in the country with two ne'er do wells. Not to mention growing pot. *Okay, maybe I don't know her at all, but she's always come across as a pretty stable, non-*

impulsive person. It seemed the more I researched, the more confusing the facts became.

I returned to the main search menu and entered Earl Haden's name and all the identification numbers I'd come up with for him. His details were much less intriguing than Bengy's, but I did glean some new information.

Earl had five liens filed against him for non-payment to subcontractors and suppliers. He'd also been sued twice. One was when he'd repaired the HVAC system at an exotic orchid nursery. The suit alleged Earl had used defective, rebuilt parts, which caused the unit to fail over the long New Years weekend. The business claimed to have lost thousands in orchids through frost damage.

The other suit was by one of the largest hotels in the area. One week after Earl serviced their main HVAC system, it had a massive failure, requiring total replacement. What made it worse was the failure occurred during the city's annual South By Southwest music festival. The hotel was forced—at considerable expense claimed the suit—to relocate several hundred guests and to even provide them with cars because their replacement hotel locations were much farther away.

Both lawsuits were still pending.

No wonder Earl had quietly stopped working and moved to the country. But why hadn't he just filed bankruptcy? If he'd done that, the lawsuits would have been withdrawn. There had to be a reason why he'd not taken that option. Of course, it could be as simple as being raised with a mindset that bankruptcy was always wrong, but I didn't think so.

I wished I'd made it into G.J.'s trailer, too. I had no new information on him, so additional ERAS searches were pointless.

I used my laptop to do some regular browser searches for MicroTechGen. I didn't have enough information on them to bother with ERAS, especially since I was charged by the search.

It didn't matter. There was plenty in the public domain. The company had been founded three years earlier by a group of scientists who wanted to explore alternative approaches to dealing with Alzheimers. Their vision was to use nanotechnology to stimulate some areas of the brain while suppressing others. Their belief was that tiny but smart artificial particles would be much less destructive to the patient than the powerful drugs many were now taking.

I wasn't sure that implanting smart chips in the brain was actually less destructive than drugs, but it was definitely a novel approach. And I had to admire the corporation's mission statement —*harnessing nanotechnology, the science of the infinitely small, in products that have a big impact on health.*

After a couple of hours of searching, I had a lot of information that seemed to have no connection. Or little connection. I felt like I was putting together a jigsaw puzzle without the benefit of the picture on the box lid. Since I didn't have the assistance of tiny—but smart—chips to help me figure it out, I decided it was time for reinforcements. Besides, I was ever the optimist when it came to brainstorming as a way to lead to new insights. I texted both Larry and Judy.

> *Drinks and dinner at La Mancha? Need y'all's brains.*

My best friends had never failed me before. Let's hope they wouldn't fail me now.

Judy responded first. Our exchange was short and sweet:

> *Sure. What time?*
>
> *Forty five minutes. I'm at my office.*
>
> *I'll beat you there. I'll get a booth.*
>
> *Thanks. See you soon.*

Larry's response followed shortly thereafter and was typical of my oldest friend:

> *Hey Cutie. You buying?*
>
> *If I have to.*
>
> *What a gal. I'll cancel my date with the mayor's daughter.*
>
> *I'm touched. Judy's getting a booth.*

The three of us spent the first half hour catching up and ordering appetizers and Mexican martinis—tarter and yummier than margaritas. Judy and I sat opposite Larry, who manspread across his entire side of the booth.

"Hope you don't do that on the subway." Judy rolled her eyes.

"Do what?" Larry blinked in innocent response.

I smirked. "Take up every available inch of space."

"Of course not." Larry grinned. "We don't have a subway."

Judy leaned in. "Okay, so what's all this about? What's going on now?"

"And you'll have to catch me up. Haven't talked to you in a couple of days," Larry added.

I spent fifteen minutes filling them in on everything, ending with the search results that prompted me to text them.

"Why wouldn't he file bankruptcy?" Judy asked.

"That's the top question in my mind at the moment. Well, that and what really went on at MicroTechGen."

Larry frowned. "You mean, did those three really steal stuff?"

"Yeah." I nodded. "And if so, why? Plus, what happened to the stuff? Did they sell it? To who?"

"And where are Briden and Walters?" Larry added.

"Another good question." I shrugged.

"I can see why you're frustrated." Judy shook her head. "What's next?"

"I need to talk to G.J." I turned to Larry. "I try not to ask for too many insider favors, but can you help me find out where he's locked up and maybe get me in to see him?"

"Might be tricky, since you're not related or a legal representative, but I'll see what I can do." Larry shrugged. "You really think he'll tell you anything?"

"I thought you said he wasn't involved with whoever's coming onto the land," Judy added.

I sighed. "I still don't think he's directly involved. But he might have had suspicions if Earl really was helping spirit things out of the company. And it's possible G.J. managed to get the license plate of the vehicle. At this point, anything will help. All I know is that it's a van, and even that small detail came from G.J."

"So he's seen it?" Larry asked.

"From the night he was yelling at the guys so he could talk to them. Blew my and Bubba's chance at catching the light that night, but at least it narrowed down the type of vehicle."

"Take what you can get, huh?" Judy laughed.

I nodded. "At this point, pretty much."

Our plates and martini shakers were empty, our stomachs were full, and my brain was fuzzy and dull. It was time to head for home. When the server brought the check, I grabbed it and handed it back to him, along with my credit card. "Use mine. It's all on me."

"You got it!" The young man grinned as he took my card and walked away.

"I didn't mean that, you know." Larry looked sheepish.

"I know." I patted both his and Judy's hands. "But I do appreciate y'all's help."

"We didn't do much," Judy said.

I shrugged. "You did enough. You got me to relax and laugh. Haven't done enough of that lately. And who knows? Maybe some of what we've talked about here will end up pointing in the right direction."

As we walked outside, Larry said. "I'll call you tomorrow morning. You should be able to get in to see G.J. in the afternoon. It may be a drug case, but it's pot, not meth, and the Caldwell County jail is in the same building as the Sheriff's office. Sheriff Law and I are old friends.

"Wait." Judy laughed. "The Caldwell County Sheriff is named Law?"

"Yep, Ronny. Ronald Law."

"Let's hope this Law is on my side." I grinned. "And let's hope G.J. has some news for me. At this point, I'll take whatever he can offer."

We three old friends hugged and headed our opposite directions. Today had been productive, but not enough. I needed more. Tomorrow, I'd head early to Lockhart. I'd stop by Bubba's and update him and maybe even try to catch up with Lucas. I wanted to be in the vicinity when Larry called. I was counting on getting into that jail.

WIN SOME, LOSE SOME

*No one that ever lived has ever had enough
power, prestige, or knowledge to overcome the
basic condition of all life — you win some and
you lose some. ~Ken Keyes (1921-1995)*

I spent the morning reading over Jason's latest case request. The client, Happy Holden, was one of the many general contractors who had popped up to take advantage of Austin's boom. There was still more construction jobs than there were contractors to handle them.

One of Happy's younger employees claimed to have permanent pain and severe movement limitations after falling off a ladder on a job site. If the employee was that badly hurt, Happy's insurance might have to pay decades worth of potential lost income. If the employee was faking, or at least exaggerating, Happy would face no such obligation. He could even choose to sue for fraud.

Pain claims are tricky to fight. There are no scientific methods to quantify pain, so it's often the injured person's word as to how badly they hurt. If a case went before a jury, it usually boiled down to how pathetic the injured person seemed on the witness stand. A faking, but poor-little-me person could get hundreds of thousands from a jury, while a truly damaged, but less-likable, person might get little to nothing.

That's where I came in.

I'd helped Jason several times in the past with insurance fraud cases like this. In front of lawyers, doctors, and a jury they limped and winced, but out on their own, they played soccer, gardened, or even, in one case, went sky-diving.

Happy's former employee, twenty-two-year-old Clyde Macker, lived in far south Austin. *Perfect! I can swing by his place on my way to Lockhart. Even if I don't see him, I can get the lay of the land and determine the best way to surveil him.*

By nine, I'd finished all my morning chores. I fidgeted, anxious to get on the road. At least I could kill two birds with one stone—start on Jason's case, then get my butt to Lockhart to visit G.J. I was grabbing my riding gear when it occurred to me to check the weather. A fifty percent chance of rain squashed my motorcycle plans. Sighing, I hung my jacket back up and headed for Pickle Toy.

All looked quiet. One elderly woman pulled weeds in a flower bed. A younger woman jogged behind a three-wheeled stroller. A small dog ran beside her.

Not seeing much activity didn't mean there weren't dozens of prying eyes just waiting to spot me slow-cruising through the neighborhood. I called APD dispatch to let them know I was going to be doing surveillance. That way, if some do-gooder called the cops on me for stalking, the dispatcher would know not to send the cops.

I decided to employ my Survey-Girl persona. Pulling to the curb a few houses down from Clyde's address, I grabbed a clipboard and generic survey forms from the back seat and stuck the employee photo of Clyde under the forms. I pulled a lanyard over my head with an official-looking photo badge hooked to the end. Most people never read the badges. If you were wearing one, and it had your picture on it, they assumed it was valid. I set my phone to camera mode so I could snap pictures fast if the opportunity arose, and climbed out of the car.

The house where I'd parked looked unoccupied — closed curtains, unkempt yard, leaf-covered porch. I wanted to look official, though, so I walked to the porch and rang the bell. After a few minutes, I made a point to look like I was making notes on the clipboard, then moved to the next house, two houses from Clyde's.

A harried looking woman holding a crying baby answered the door. Twin toddlers peeked from behind her legs. Both toddlers had unruly mops of curly brown hair and their synchronized thumb sucking partially blocked their faces. I couldn't tell if the little ones were boys, girls, or one of each.

I smiled at the woman and began my false pitch. "Good morning! I can see you're busy so I'll be very quick. Would you mind answering just a few short questions?"

"What's this about?" The woman frowned and made shushing noises to the baby.

"I'm with a market research firm that was asked to check on services that might be needed in this area. Is there a particular store or business you'd like to see closer to your neighborhood?"

"Yeah, a good daycare."

I made a note on the form. "Thanks! Anything else?"

"How about a nail salon. If I had a place to leave the kids for a while, I could pamper myself now and then."

"What a great idea." I made another note then looked up with a big grin. "Just one last question. Would you be interested in any new eating establishments, and if so, what kind of food would you prefer?" I could have left after two questions, but I figured more questions seemed more authentic for a market researcher.

She paused, looked down at the toddlers, then sighed. "At this point in my life, I guess a burger place that has one of those giant kid's habitrail playscapes would be best."

I nodded and made another note. "I'll let you go. Thanks so much for your help." I turned to leave, then turned back, seemingly as an afterthought. "By the way, it'd save me time if I could skip houses where no one is home. Can you tell me anything about the next two or three houses? Is anyone at them?"

"Loretta lives in the house next door. She looks ancient, probably in her late eighties. Not sure she'll be interested in any new stores. She almost never leaves the house."

Nodding in understanding, I said nothing.

"House next to hers is usually empty during the day. Young married couple. Renters. Mindy works for a bank and Clyde…well, he was working for a construction company but…"

I waited a beat for her to continue. When she didn't, I prompted her. "But what?"

She glanced sideways, as if worried about eavesdroppers. "He said he was hurt, but he's pretty active, if you ask me."

I raised an eyebrow. "I see. So is he at home?"

"I doubt it. He spends a lot of time at the court."

"The court? Which court?"

The woman shifted the still-crying baby to her other hip. "The basketball court by the high school."

"Oh! Well, thanks for telling me. I won't bother stopping at that house."

"You're welcome. I gotta go feed the baby now."

"Of course. You've been very helpful." I didn't really want to ring Loretta's doorbell, I wanted to go check out the basketball court, but in case the new mother was watching me through her living room window, I dutifully walked next door, pressed the doorbell, and waited.

It felt forever before the door opened a crack and a tiny, shrunken woman peeked out.

"Yes?"

Repeating my fake introduction, I then asked my first question. Loretta looked me up and down then said, "Honey I haven't left the house in six months. I don't care what they put in this neighborhood." She closed the door without another word, and I heard a chain lock slide into place.

Great! I can get out of here now.

Once in the car, I mapped the location of the basketball court. It was only half a mile away. I drove that direction.

I pulled to the curb beside the court, grabbed Jason's file photo of Clyde, and rolled down my window. A dozen boys and young men ran around the court. Sure enough, Clyde was one of them.

In case someone was watching, I held my phone as if I was reading email or surfing social media and covertly snapped several pictures, both distance and zoomed. I took two minutes of video for extra measure. Jason would be pleased with the pictorial evidence. This was going to be the shortest evidence gathering I'd ever done for him.

I'd love to see Clyde's face when he's confronted with proof that his pain and injury are clearly not as severe as he claimed. But for now, I have other fish to fry, or at least cows to save.

Gathering evidence against Clyde's claim had gone quickly, so I arrived in Lockhart earlier than planned. I turned toward Chisholm Trail Stables Antiques. Maybe Katherine would have news to share.

Katherine had taken a rare day off, so I was back in my car within five minutes. I sighed in disappointment. *What the hell am I going to do to kill time? Come on Larry, call me already!*

I was backing out, planning to just drive around and get the lay of the land or maybe drive by Lucas's house, when my cell phone rang. I made squealy noises when I glanced at the caller ID—it was Larry.

"Hi! Hope you have good news for me. Am I going to jail?"

He laughed a full belly laugh, rare for my deep-thinking friend. "You are indeed. Be at the Caldwell County Sheriff's Office at twelve-thirty." He paused. "That's only twenty minutes. Can you make it?"

"I'm already in Lockhart. I can make it. Thanks! I owe you another dinner."

"I'll take it. Oh, and ask for John Rogers. Donny's in the field, but he arranged for John to take you back to G.J. See you later, Cutie."

My cell phone's map showed the location of the Sheriff's office as a few blocks away. I was ten minutes early, but better that than late. The small lobby area housed a row of battered, wooden chairs with orange vinyl padding lining the wall by the entrance. On the opposite wall was a large map of Caldwell County, stapled in place. To the right of the map was a bulletproof-glass window and a solid door with a small peephole. A petite blonde woman sat at a desk behind the window.

When I approached, she pressed an intercom button and leaned toward a small microphone. "May I help you?"

"My name's Marianna Morgan. I'm here to see John Rogers."

"I'll let him know you're here. Please have a seat."

I perched on the edge of the nearest chair and waited. After five minutes, the door to the right of the window clicked open. A tall man with short brown hair and mustache, and wearing a neatly pressed deputy's uniform smiled and nodded. "Ms. Morgan? Please follow me."

He stepped back so I could pass into the hallway. We walked a hundred feet down the long hall, and Rogers used his key to unlock the last door on the left.

He waved me into the small visitation room, which was divided in half by a plexiglass wall. On both sides was a chair, small table, and old-fashioned phone handset. "I'll get Blappit. You wait here. You'll have five minutes. I hope that's enough."

"I'm sure it'll be fine. Thank you." My slacks caught a snag on the old wooden chair. *Damn, these were my best pair.*

Within a few minutes, the door opposite the plexiglass opened, and Rogers escorted a forlorn-looking G.J. into the room. My unwitting informant stared at his feet.

Rogers tapped his watch. I nodded in understanding. Rogers nodded in return and left.

G.J. looked up and broke into a big grin. He hurried to the chair and grabbed the handset. I lifted mine just in time to catch his words tumbling out. "Marianna! Sure didn't expect to see you here. How'd you find me?"

"I went by your ranch and saw the gate chained with a Sheriff's Office padlock. This is the only jail in the county so figured you'd be here. Tell me what happened."

"Someone turned us in for growing pot. A dozen cops showed up. Three stayed with us, asking questions. They cuffed us. The rest went back to the field. Didn't see what they did but heard 'em talking on their radios. They cut down every last plant and bagged it all up. Probably took 'em all day. I don't know for sure, since they put us in the back of one of the cars and drove us here. I was scared as a pig at a barbecue."

He glanced down at his hands then looked into my eyes. "I hope it wasn't you. Bengy and Earl said it was. The whole ride here they cussed about you. I told 'em I didn't think you'd do that. They told me to shut up. So I did. It wasn't you, was it?"

I shook my head. "No G.J., it wasn't me." *It was, sort of partly my fault, since I told Linda Favoccia about the men using her property to access Bubba's land. But I didn't tell her about the pot. Somehow she figured that out on her own.* "I'm sorry y'all are in trouble. I'll help if I can."

"You will? Aw, thanks! But...how can you help?"

I have no idea. "I have a lawyer friend in Austin. I'll ask him for suggestions. Maybe there's something he can do." It was a long shot, but I'd certainly be on Jason's good side after my morning's discovery about — and photos of — Clyde.

"That'd be great. I sure don't wanna go to prison."

"I can understand that." I doubted there was anything Jason could do to keep G.J., Earl, and Bengy out of prison. But G.J. looked pitiful enough without my telling him that. Besides, he was a sweet man, I'd do what I could.

"So how're you doin?" G.J. asked. "You figger out yet about them cows?"

"No, I haven't. That's one reason I'm here. You said you'd try to get the make, model, and license plate number of the van that's coming onto your place. Did you have any luck?"

"Sure did!" G.J. beamed. "It's a Chevy Cargo van. One of those kind that has no windows — 'cept for the windshield and door windows, of course."

"That's great, G.J. Did you get the license number?"

G.J. nodded. "Even wrote it down."

"Good for you. Where is it? Do you have it here?"

"Nah, them cops wouldn't let us bring nothin' with us. It's in my trailer, though. On the kitchen counter."

"But I don't have a key." I sure didn't want anyone, especially the trusting G.J., to know I'd already been in the other two trailers.

"I ain't got one here, but there's a key hidden under the butt can on the top step."

"Thanks, G.J. I'll be sure to put the key back, and I'll take care not to mess with any of your things."

After a brief, awkward silence, I realized I was in a prime position to quiz G.J. about his time working for Earl's HVAC company. "Tell me about your job for Earl. What did you do?"

G.J. spent a couple of minutes telling me about his responsibilities — carting and providing tools, opening and unpacking boxes, and dragging ducting around in attics and crawl spaces. Sounded like all the jobs Earl didn't want to do, but G.J. was clearly proud. The more he talked, the straighter he sat up. By the time he was done, his back was military-attention straight.

"That's a lot of responsibility." I smiled. "Isn't that how y'all met Bengy? Working on the AC at MicroTechGen?"

"Sure was! She was nice to me. Brought me Cokes and chips every day we was there."

"That was kind of her. When y'all finished the repair work, did you haul out all the boxes the parts were in?"

"Just like always. Earl always said clean up was one of my most important jobs. Didn't want no unhappy customers cuz we left a mess."

I nodded. "My mother would agree. Clean up is important." I paused, knowing I needed to be careful how I asked the next questions. "Was anything different about that cleanup? Were the boxes any different?"

"Different how?" G.J.'s brow furrowed in confusion.

"Taped back up. Or heavy. Just…different."

G.J. chewed his lower lip. "Now that ya mention it, suma them boxes was taped shut. And heavy. Almost dropped one of 'em. I asked Earl about it, and he said they was full of the old parts. Bengy'd asked him to haul 'em off to recycling. But we usually throw old parts in a big plastic tub. And we never did go to recycling. Least I never did. Maybe Earl went alone, cuz the boxes disappeared."

My heart pounded with excitement. I was leaning in to ask how many taped boxes there were, and how big they were, when the door behind me opened and John stepped in.

"Sorry, Ms. Morgan. Time's up. I've given you all the time I can. Even gave you a few extra minutes."

I sighed and held the phone to my chest. "I understand. I truly appreciate your letting me come here at all." I turned to G.J. and again lifted the phone to my face. "G.J., it was good to see you. I'll talk to my lawyer friend and let you know what he says. You take care of yourself. And try not to worry."

G.J. nodded but didn't speak. I noticed his eyes were glistening wet and his Adam's apple shook. *Poor guy. I hope Jason can help him.*

I spent a few minutes sitting in the Sheriff's Office parking lot, leaving a long, detailed message for Jason about G.J. and the other two pot farmers. He might not be able to help, but Jason was a stand-up guy. He'd at least look into it.

Once I left the Sheriff's Office, I made a bee line for the hippies' place. I didn't care if it was broad daylight. I wanted that license plate number. This time, I followed Lucas's actions and parked far up the county road, near another gate, then hiked back down to the hippies' driveway.

Aw, crap.

The chain that the Sheriff's lock had securely held across the gate was cut and tossed in the weeds on the edge of the driveway. Fresh tire tracks marked the caliche dust. Someone had entered the land, and they'd been in a vehicle with a wide track — like a van. Probably a white van. With no windows.

No matter how much I wanted that license plate number, I didn't dare enter the land right now. I had no idea if the bad guys were there. I'd taken a chance the other night, but the worst that might have happened was getting arrested for breaking and entering. I was absolutely sure if the bad guys caught me the result would be much worse.

I trudged back to my car, muttering every cuss word I knew. I still had no idea if aliens were involved in this mess, but I was sure the men in that van were.

This is bad. Not only do I not have that damn license plate number, it means the bad guys are back at it, whatever IT might be. And that means more of Bubba's cows are likely going to die.

GOTCHA!

The beginning of knowledge is the discovery
of something we do not understand.
~Frank Herbert (1920-1986)

I drove straight to Bubba's from the Sheriff's Office. I didn't even take time to call first. I needed to update him on everything and figure out our next move. Luckily, he was home. Or at least his old truck was there. I pulled in beside it. He stepped out onto his porch as I exited my car.

"Well, hiya." Bubba nodded. "Come on in. I just made a fresh pot of coffee."

Wired up from the day as I was, Bubba's campfire-strength coffee was probably not a good idea, but I didn't want to be rude. "Sure, Bubba. Sounds good."

We took our usual seats at his kitchen table. Bubba downed half his cup before asking, "So, tell me what's up."

I filled him in on my research into the hippies. *I probably shouldn't call them that anymore, based on their former careers, but I just can't help myself.* I didn't tell Bubba about spending time working on Jason's case. I knew the older man well enough at this point to figure it'd probably hurt his feelings that I wasn't focused solely on his cows.

I took a swallow of the strong, bitter coffee and barely managed to avoid coughing. "How's things around here?"

"I lost Mr. T last night." Bubba frowned and stared down at his coffee.

"Your bull?"

Bubba nodded. "Rode the Gator back there this morning to check on everyone. You'd said the hippies were gone and their gate was locked up, so figured it was finally safe to release the cow and calf back into the herd. Also figured I'd check first. Glad I did."

"Oh, Bubba, I'm so sorry." I knew Bubba only had the one bull. And replacing him would be expensive. At least for now, there'd be no more expectant cows or newborn calves to end up in danger. "I stopped by on the way here. Someone cut the chain on the hippies' gate. Don't know when that happened. Last time I was by there was Friday, and the chain and lock were in place."

Bubba slammed his fist on the table, making me jump a foot. "Dammit. This's gotta stop."

"I agree. That's why I'm going to the back of your property again tonight."

"What for?" Bubba shook his head. "To watch that alien light come back? To watch more cows die?"

I reached across the table and squeezed Bubba's rough, weathered hand. "No. I'm going over the fence and waiting for that white van to show up. And I'm going armed."

Bubba looked up into my eyes. "That's too dangerous."

I shook my head. "I'm trained. And I'm smart. I'll be fine." I let go of his hand and leaned back.

"I ain't sayin' you ain't smart, but trained or not, seems to me you've had more than one thing happen to you back there." Bubba narrowed his eyes and frowned.

"Not this time. I'm tired of not solving this case. And I'm sick of your losing cows. And your bull. This stops. Now."

"I'll go with you."

"No, you won't. I can't worry about you and do my job at the same time. I need to cross that fence and find a good hiding spot. I can be sneakier if I'm alone. Plus I need to focus while I wait. And I can't do that if you're on the other side of the fence, potentially in harm's way."

After a long minute, Bubba nodded. "I guess I gotta trust you. It's why I hired you in the first place. I gotta believe you're a girl who knows what she's doin'."

I refrained from commenting about being called *girl*. I knew Bubba's heart was in the right place. He was just from another generation.

Standing, I glanced at the clock. It was mid afternoon. I didn't want to sit in Bubba's kitchen for the next four or five hours waiting for dark. "I'm going to run home and load up some additional gear. I'll be back at dusk." I circled the table and kissed Bubba on the cheek. "I'll figure this out for you. I promise."

My mind raced as I drove north. Whoever had cut the chain seemed to definitely be involved. I was betting good money it was the men in that white van. I'd also bet Earl and Bengy were involved, too. I just wasn't sure how. Yet. And I'd bet even more money humans were the *only* ones involved. There were no aliens.

I stopped at my office on the way north, where I downloaded the pictures I took of Clyde playing basketball. I sent them, along with a brief report and invoice, to Jason. Then I added everything I knew to Bubba's case file, including the entire research history I'd done on Earl, Bengy, and G.J. My last action before heading home was to update the running invoice I had for Bubba. Much as I adored the man, I couldn't afford to work pro bono. I fudged a bit on my time, though, rounding everything down, and including only time when I was directly working on his case. And fully conscious.

I spent a couple of hours at home, preparing for the evening. In addition to the usual contents of my Trusty Spy Kit, I added military-grade, night vision binoculars and two additional flashlights, including a red-filtered one I could use without screwing up my night vision. I wanted to be sure I could see everything that was going on, and get a good look at who was involved.

I changed into my all black Stealthy-PI-Mode clothes, fed the cats, and headed south again. I arrived back at Bubba's just as dusk settled in.

"You sure you don't want me with ya?" Bubba asked as soon as I stepped from my car.

"Not this time. I want to be able to respond quick and change tacks if I need to." I smiled at the older man. "I'd worry too much about you to take any chances." I pulled my canvas bag from the trunk and dropped it with a thud at my feet. "I'm armed and well prepared. I'll be fine."

Bubba frowned, but nodded. "Well okay, then. But I ain't goin' ta bed until you're back here safe and sound."

"Fair enough." I lugged the bag to the Gator and plopped it onto the passenger seat. I climbed on and waved. "I'll see you later. Hopefully, with a lot more information than I have right now."

I parked the Gator at the now-familiar ditch next to the fence. Bubba's remaining cows grazed nearby. A few were bedded down but stood when I got off the Gator. They watched intently as I rooted around in the canvas bag. Mooami took a few steps my direction and mooed.

"Hey, Mooami." I nodded at the cow, but took a step back, still unsure how much I could trust the behavior of an eight hundred pound animal.

I unloaded the three flashlights, my gun, and my night vision binoculars. I strapped or slung all of my equipment around various parts of my body and walked to Bubba's property line.

Shining my big light up and down the simple barbed wire and wood post fence, I searched for a place to hide. The road on the hippies' land ran parallel about twenty feet in from the fence. I couldn't hide on Bubba's side of the fence, the undergrowth was too sparse. I'd have to hide somewhere on the hippies' land.

I climbed over the fence and scanned the area. The closest hiding spot was the row of cedars that edged the former pot field. They were a good hundred feet from the road, farther away than I liked but it would have to do.

I took a minute to tuck in among the scrubby trees with all my gear easily accessible and nothing showing, especially highly reflective lenses on various devices. I settled in and waited.

After three hours of frustrating boredom, not to mention leg cramps from squatting, I gave up. I'd just stood up when I heard the van's engine and saw headlights in the distance, coming up the rutted road. I quickly dropped again to a squat, wincing at the pain in my legs. Tomorrow, I'd probably feel like I'd run a marathon.

The van pulled to a stop forty or so feet from where the ditch was located. The engine cut off and two men exited, one from each door of the cab. They moved to the back and I heard a creaking hinge.

Grabbing my night vision binoculars, I focused on the back of the van. The doors were open, blocking my view.

Dammit!

I duck-walked down behind the line of cedars, moving parallel to the van, until I had a better view of the men and what they were doing. For a few minutes, they fussed with something inside the van. Then the man who was closer to me turned and I got a clear view. In his hands was a large, four-rotor drone.

Gotcha! It's not aliens! I grinned into the dark. *I never really believed there were aliens involved, but it's nice to see proof that it's just humans.*

The man who held the drone raised it as the other man manipulated a hand-held controller. The drone climbed into the air and headed over the fence toward Bubba's cows.

Oh, shit. But there was nothing I could do to protect the cows without giving myself away, a dangerous prospect out here, all alone, armed or not. Especially since these were probably the same two guys who had abducted me.

Instead of trying to follow and stop the drone, I needed to find out more about these men. I might now know that the *alien ship* was actually a drone, but I still had no clue what was really going on.

I slipped back through the cedars until I was in my original hiding spot. The two men were out of sight behind the back of the vehicle. I abandoned my protective cover and scurried like a crab across the clearing until I was crouched in front of the van. I used my red-filtered light to see the license plate. It was BV1-H437, which followed the new seven-character format, a product of the state's rapid growth.

For some reason, seven characters was harder for me to make up acronyms and phrases for, and none came to mind. It'd be hard to remember the plate without an acronym. I snapped a quick picture using the low-light setting on my cell phone camera, then extinguished my small light. No point in taking too many chances.

Slipping to the driver's side, I cupped my hands around my eyes and peeked in through the window. There was a laptop tucked between the two seats. *I'd give my eyeteeth to get my hands on that.*

I reached for the door handle then froze. *Stupid! You open that door and the dome light will come on. May as well jump up and down and wave your arms at these two.*

I shook my head at my close call. In my jubilation at finding that these two seemed to be behind everything, I almost put myself in serious danger. They'd already done who-knew-what to me when they had me locked up. No telling what they'd do if they caught me again.

I slipped down the driver's side of the van toward the rear as far as I dared, hoping to overhear what the guys were saying. Even as close as I was, their voices were low and muffled. After a minute, they grew loud enough to hear, although I still didn't understand what they were talking about:

"Stupid thing's not working now."

"Try channel 23. It's got the update."

"Yeah, okay."

"Hopefully that one big problem's gone."

"That'd be good."

Their voices dropped again, but I stayed put anyway, hoping to get a chance to hear more. Sure enough, after another couple of minutes, their voices again grew loud:

"Dammit, the transmitter's gone all wonky."

"Let's swap it for the old one."

"Is it in the back?"

"No, it's shoved in the driver's door pocket."

"What the heck's it doing there?"

"I was gonna take it back into the lab. Good thing I didn't. Bring Fanny and I'll get the transmitter."

Oh crap! They're heading my way. There was no time to make it all the way back to the cedar trees. I'd have to make a break for Bubba's fence. I scurried around the front of the van as I heard their crunching footsteps circling from the back.

Hunching as low as I could, I ran for the fence. I hoped my black clothing, near pitch blackness thanks to the overcast skies, and temporary night blindness of the men when the cab's dome light came on, would keep me concealed as I crossed the twenty feet between the van and the fence.

When I reached the fence, I scrambled over without pausing for footing, biting my tongue in pain as a metal barb on the barbed wire fence pierced my right palm. My heart was pounding so loud in my ears, I probably couldn't have heard the guys if they'd seen me and started yelling.

I crouched in the ditch, safely back on Bubba's side of the fence. That's when my brain kicked in. *Fanny? They named their drone? Who are these guys? And what are they doing?* I'd find out, just not this particular night.

It took several minutes for my breathing and heart rate to settle down. More or less back to normal, I moved toward the cows, which were grazing and generally hanging out nearby.

I was within half a dozen feet of Mooami when the hum and light both started up again. I now knew the source, but apparently that didn't matter. Suddenly, my head swam and my knees buckled. The last thing I saw as I fell was Mooami falling, too.

No! Not Mooami. Then everything went black.

REMEMBER

*One must have a good memory to be able to
keep the promises one makes.*
~Friedrich Nietzsche (1844-1900)

I came to when my butt started tingling, then I quickly realized it was my cell phone vibrating in my back pocket. Leaves showered from my hair as I shook my head and sat up. My brain was fuzzy. Blinking and shaking my head hard again helped a little, but not much.

It took several tugs to wrestle the phone from my jeans, The caller ID displayed Bubba's name. I also saw it was 2:30 am. "Hey, Bubba." I tried to make my voice sound normal, but it came out a bit squeaky and thin.

"What the hell is goin' on? Why aren't you back? What's wrong? Do I need to ride the mower back there? Are you okay?"

The stream of rapid-fire questions helped drive up my alertness level. "I'm fine, Bubba. Just...um, well I—"

"Did you have another fit?" I could hear the worry in Bubba's voice. "Just hang on. I'm comin' back there for ya'."

"No, please, don't do that." I struggled unsteadily to my feet. "I'm okay now. Really." *I hope I'm not lying.* "Let me gather up my things, and I'll head your way."

After a long pause, Bubba responded. "Well...okay. But if you ain't here in thirty minutes I'm comin'."

"Deal."

I stowed the phone back in my pocket and bent for my flashlight, which rested on the ground next to where I'd been laying. That's when I noticed a cow on her side a few feet behind me. I shined the light and saw a Florida-shaped red spot on the cow's white face.

"Mooami? Mooami! Please don't be dead." *What happened?* Easing slowly toward the large animal, I reached out and gave her a quick goodbye pat on the side. *Aw, she's still warm. Bless her heart.*

I was tired of Bubba's cows dying — any of them — but to lose Mooami especially hurt. Before Bubba hired me, I knew nothing about cows. I still knew very little, but I did know that I'd grown attached to the big red cow with the white face and red Florida on her nose.

Between seeing her dead, and still feeling shaky from my recent seizure — at least that's what I assumed happened to me — my emotions got the better of me, and I burst into tears. I let myself have a minute or two of emotional release, then wiped my eyes and straightened my shoulders. Falling apart wasn't going to help me with this case. And it wasn't going to prevent more cows from dying. I glanced again at Mooami, and noticed a slight rise and fall of her side. *She's not dead!*

I moved my hand around her side until I could feel her heart. It beat slowly, but I didn't know what normal was for a cow. *At least she's alive.*

Having no idea how to wake up a cow, I used both hands to shove her like a rolled up rug I wanted to move across a room. After half a dozen, two-handed shoves, her legs started flailing, as if her feet were looking for purchase, even though she was on her side.

I backed out of the way. Several cows approached her as she struggled, so I moved even farther away and stood next to a big oak tree. It took several minutes, but she finally raised her head, tucked her legs, and rolled herself onto her stomach. She shook her head, simultaneously snorted and farted, and clambered slowly to her feet. Her head hung low, and she seemed unsteady, but at least she was fully upright now.

"You'll be all right, Mooami." I moved toward her until I was in her field of vision. She stared straight into my eyes. "I'm going to solve this. So you don't die. And so your buddies don't, either."

She mooed low and slow, as if in response.

I shook my own head to clear it and walked slowly to the Gator. When I glanced at my Trusty Spy Kit, still on the passenger seat, a cold fear washed through me. The last memory I had was pulling gear out of that bag and climbing over Bubba's fence onto the hippies' land. Then…blank. At least until I woke up on the ground next to Mooami.

It's hard to describe the fear you get when you realize there's a hole in your mind. It hadn't happened to me since college and my occasional nights of extreme partying. Now it'd happened twice in short order. And both times, I'd been back here with the cows.

Last time, Bubba was with me, and he was convinced the light that caused the cows to sing and dance was what triggered my seizure. And very likely, that seizure also caused my memory loss both times, too. I'd gone to school with a boy who suffered terrible epileptic seizures. His memories were Swiss cheese, filled with gaps and holes. I didn't want to be like him, with so many lost memories.

I looked at my phone. It'd been over half an hour since Bubba had called, and I said I'd be right there. Quickly shoving my gun and flashlights back into the bag on the seat behind me, I turned on the noisy Gator and floored it back toward Bubba's house. Of course, flooring a thirteen horsepower utility vehicle isn't exactly all that much. It took ten minutes to get back to Bubba's house.

He was standing on the porch, shotgun in hand, when I pulled up. "I was gettin' ready to come after you. Where ya been? I been nervous as a cat in a room full a rockin' chairs."

I climbed the porch and stood in front of the older man. The fear and worry was deeply etched on his face. Between his expression and my recent experience and emotional outburst—which I'd never tell him about—I couldn't help myself. I grabbed him in a hug as if he were my own grandfather. He hugged me back so hard I could barely breath. It felt wonderful and comforting.

"Come on in." His voice was husky with emotion, and he quickly swiped at the corners of his eyes. "I'll getcha a drink. Want coffee or bourbon?"

"Bourbon."

"Okay, but then you're stayin' the night again. You already look like hell. Addin' booze to the mix ain't gonna do nothin' but lower my confidence you'd get home safe."

I wasn't actually that excited about going home alone, anyway. "Fair enough." I followed Bubba into the house. He stowed his shotgun in the corner by the door and headed to the kitchen.

Sitting at Bubba's table made me feel safe and homey. I sometimes grew close to clients, and I still kept in touch with a few, but Bubba felt special. I couldn't put my finger on it, but he seemed a combination of my Grandaddy Jack, my dad, and every caring old man I'd ever seen in a movie.

I sat in silence as he filled Texas tea-sized glasses with straight bourbon and ice. He sat opposite me and slid my glass across the old formica table. I nodded, picked it up, and downed a quarter of the tall glass. My throat burned from the potent whiskey, but it felt good and oddly comforting. If I didn't solve this case soon, I might come to enjoy this odd comfort a bit too much.

"So, tell me what happened." Bubba reached across the table and patted my hand.

"I don't know. That's the problem. I assume the same thing happened as last time, when we were together. The light must have come back and triggered another seizure."

"What do you mean *must have come back*? You didn't see it?"

"No." I took another big gulp of bourbon. "Actually, I don't know. I might have. My last memory is parking the Gator and heading onto the hippies' land, or at least climbing your fence onto their rutted road that parallels the fence."

"Aw, hell, Marianna. I knew I shoulda gone with you. Dammit, you coulda really been hurt." His face paled. "Or you coulda been abducted again."

My intestines did a little dance and my butt cheeks clenched. "I know. And that scares me." I shook my head. "But I'm more mad than scared. I might have seen or heard something, but I can't remember." I slammed my fist on the table, causing Bubba to jump. "Dammit! I finally might've made good progress. I might've solved the whole damn case. But it's all gone."

Bubba patted my hand again. "Maybe you'll remember. I got faith in you. And you sure are workin' your tail off."

"Aw, thank you." Tears welled in my eyes, probably a combination of Bubba's kind words, the booze, lack of sleep, and my own fears. I cleared my throat and chugged the last of my bourbon. I wasn't going to let myself cry again.

"Want more?" Bubba waved at my empty glass.

I'm going to pay for this tomorrow. "Since you're making me stay overnight anyway, why not." *Maybe the booze will break through my memory loss. Or at least make me not care for a little while.*

After he topped off our glasses and sat, I said, "I do have some good news. When I woke up, Mooami was down, and—"

"I thought you said you had good news!"

"I do! She wasn't dead. I thought she was dead, but she was just out, like I'd been. I shoved on her until she woke up. That's what took so long. I waited until she was on her feet and looking reasonably normal."

"Well, that's sure good ta hear. Maybe I won't lose no more cows, even if that light keeps showin' up."

"I hope so. What I can't figure is, what's changed? Why did every appearance of the light before tonight kill a cow, yet this time only knocked Mooami out?" I shook my head. "Aargh! I might even have already figured that out, except now I can't remember."

"Come on." Bubba stood. "Enough of your pity party. You'll get it. But now, it's damn near dawn. Time for you to get some sleep. You look as wrung out as I feel."

I followed Bubba down the hall to the same guest room I'd occupied only a few days ago. "See you in the morning. Well, later this morning, I guess."

"You sleep as late as you like," he said.

"What about you?"

"Critters don't like me to sleep late. They like their schedule."

"I'll get up when you do."

Bubba stared at me for a beat, then laughed. "Critters don't care what YOUR schedule is. And I'm bettin' between your brain fit and the booze, your brain ain't gonna be ready to rise and shine at six."

I grinned. "You're probably right."

"Get some rest. I already put an old nightshirt on your bed."

"But you didn't know I was going to stay the night."

"Yes I did. Soon as you weren't back here 'fore midnight."

I gave Bubba another quick hug and retired to *my* bedroom. In spite of the booze fog and late hour, I found myself edgy and agitated. I paced circles in the small room.

What happened to me tonight?

What did I see?

Did I figure out what was going on?

Have cows really stopped dying?

If so, why? What's changed?

WHY CAN'T I REMEMBER?

Sleep finally came, but it was restless and filled with nightmares. I was being chased around a white van by ugly, pale aliens. They held some type of device in their hands. In the dream, I believed it was for medical experiments. During my escape, I scrambled over Bubba's barbed-wire fence, piercing my hand.

This last image caused me to start awake, and I bolted upright, panting in the dim room. My heart raced. Light seeped around the edges of the curtain, but I had no idea what time it was.

I turned on the beside lamp and looked at the palm of my hand. An ugly red wound sat almost dead center. A quick memory flashed across my brain: Two men, holding something large and metallic, approaching the rear of a white van while I hid at the front. Me, waiting until they circled the van, hurrying to cross back into Bubba's field, piercing my palm on the fence as I scrambled over it.

I remember! I saw the van. I saw two men. But what were they holding?

I grabbed my phone. It was just after nine. When I set the phone down, another flash of memory hit. Snatching the phone back up, I tapped the photos icon. The last image was the closeup of a license plate. *I got the license plate of the van!*

Excitement sent me jumping from bed onto the cool, hardwood floor. I did a little jig before hurrying to the door. Opening it a crack, I could hear Bubba rattling around in the kitchen. I quickly dressed, made a brief potty stop, and joined Bubba.

He turned as I entered. "Mornin, sunshine. I betcha want coffee."

It wasn't until Bubba spoke that I realized just how hungover I was. My head pounded and my vision shimmered like I was underwater. "Coffee sounds about the most perfect thing I can imagine right now."

I sat at the table in an attempt to hide my unsteadiness. But Bubba was no fool. He grinned. "I see you and that bourbon haven't completely parted company yet."

"Apparently not." I rubbed my eyes and sipped the dark, strong coffee Bubba placed in front of me. "How long have you been up?"

"Got up late, almost six thirty. Animals wasn't happy. But they're all fed now."

"How do you look so perky and alert?"

"My military training still kicks in when I need to push on through, no matter what."

"Maybe I should join. I could use some of that."

"Can't help ya there. But want some breakfast? I got bacon and fresh eggs. Gathered 'em myself."

My stomach lurched. "That's really sweet, but I don't think that's a good idea right now. I'll grab something later."

"What are you gonna do now? What's your next step?"

"I'm going to follow a clue."

"Clue? What clue?"

I smiled. "I had a nightmare, but it caused me to remember seeing the van. And I'd taken a picture of its license plate. I might not remember everything that happened, but I've at least got that. I can trace it to the owners. We'll finally know who these guys are."

"That's great news."

I downed the last of my coffee and stood. "It definitely is. That's why I'm going to head north now. I'll stop at my office first. This is the best clue I've had in a while, and I don't want to postpone finding out all I can."

"You'll call me?"

I turned from the door and nodded. "You'll be the first person to know what I learn." *I hope I have something worth calling for. Guess I'll find out soon.*

WALLED OUT

Sometimes being pushed to the wall gives you
the momentum necessary to get over it!
~Peter de Jager

Sometimes when facing big challenges, it's the little things that make a difference. For me at the moment it was the traffic, or lack thereof. The Wednesday morning commuter traffic had settled down by the time I reached Austin, so I pulled into the parking lot of the Winchester Office Complex in record time. I opted to avoid the molasses-slow elevator and bounded up the steps two at a time to my office on the second floor. I didn't even care that my head pounded in sync with my steps.

For once, there was no envelope from Jason on my door, but it meant I could focus all of my attention on Bubba's case. Of course, that also meant Bubba was my only source of income at the moment. I'd met a couple of private investigators who'd milk a case just to get as much revenue as possible out of it, but I'd never considered doing that, especially not to Bubba. I wanted to wrap this case up as fast as possible. He deserved it. So did his cows.

With that in mind, I crossed my office almost at a trot. I didn't even take the time to water my potted palm. Instead, I circled my desk, flipped on my Electronic Records Archival Service computer, and sat. While the computer booted up, I retrieved the photo of the license plate from my phone.

As soon as the ERAS system beeped its readiness, I entered the license plate in the Search field, and stared at the spinning *in process* icon. My mind wandered, so when the computer beeped in completion, I jumped. I hadn't realized how tightly wound I was until that moment.

I leaned in and read the results displayed on the screen:

> License: BV1-H437
>
> Make: Chevrolet
>
> Model: Express Cargo Van
>
> Color: White with grey interior
>
> Year: 2002
>
> Registration Address:
>
> Ballerton's Motorcycle Seats
>
> 936 St. Elmo Road, Austin, TX 78744
>
> Registrar: Thomas Ballerton

The last couple of lines hit my eyeballs like a laser beam. *Ballerton? I know those guys. What the heck?*

Pancho Villa's custom seat came from them. So had the custom seat on Max, my previous motorcycle.

What's their van doing on the hippies' land? Do the two men I remembered seeing last night work for Ballerton's? If not, what were they doing with the van?

I glanced at the closeup photo on my phone to be sure I'd entered the right plate number. Confused as I was, at least an acronym for the license plate finally came to me: *Ballerton Van One Holds For*... Well, I'd worry about the 3 and 7 another day. For now, remembering five-sevenths of the license would be good enough to recognize the vehicle if I saw it again, like parked outside of Ballerton's.

I really needed to go home and check on my cats, but I needed to follow up on this even more. I hit the second speed dial number on my phone. Judy answered on the first ring.

"Hey, stranger! Seems like I haven't talked to you in ages. I miss you. What's up?"

"I miss you, too. Let's get together later. But right now I need a favor. I just hit on a big lead on the case, and — "

"You need me to go feed the cats." Judy laughed as she finished my sentence.

"Sometimes we sound like an old married couple." I laughed, too. "Yeah, I do. Please. I'll fill you in on everything later. Promise."

"Consider it done. But please be careful."

"I promise that, too."

I disconnected the call and shut down my computer, grabbed my purse and keys, and headed out.

Ballerton's warehouse was in far south Austin, where most wholesale supply and small manufacturing buildings were located. I'd never actually been to the Ballerton location. I'd ordered my custom seats through Zabor's, my favorite Austin motorcycle shop. I probably could have saved money buying direct, but Bob Zabor was a hard working, honest, stand-up guy. He'd been the only one I trusted with Max, my Yamaha Maxim, after my accident. Tossing him a little profit on gear seemed the right thing to do.

I pulled into the pothole-filled lot shared by the two warehouses on either side. The warehouse on the left was the corrugated steel, block-sized Deluxe Tasty Food Supply company. On the right was the slightly smaller, concrete Ballerton building. I parked my still-shiny, vintage Mustang in the only empty slot, next to a beat-up green and bondo-grey Ford Mustang. I prayed to the horse gods that Pickle Toy wouldn't get any ideas from the car next to it.

Ballerton's small lobby area was neat and clean, the linoleum floor shiny but yellowed, thanks to a decade or more of wax. As soon as I entered, I heard an engine rev. Looking around, I realized it was the door open sound, thanks to a customized sensor beam. I was still studying the door when a young man spoke from behind the counter.

"Good morning. How can I help you?" He smiled and ran his hand through his shoulder length, dirty-blond hair, then scratched at a tiny soul patch on his chin. It was so pale I might not have even noticed had he not touched it.

Good question. I have no idea. There was no way I could tell Counter Boy what I was really after. I hesitated for a moment, trying to think of the best approach. Nothing came to mind. CB stared at me, waiting for a response. I'd have to wing it.

"Good morning. I…"

I glanced around the room while I wracked my brain for the best response. The lobby was small. A half dozen chairs that looked like dining room rejects were scattered around. On the center of the left wall was a door marked RESTROOM, flanked by generic motorcycle posters. In addition to the glass entry door, the wall behind me included a bookshelf filled with supply catalogs and riding magazines.

On the wall behind the counter was a door marked EMPLOYEES ONLY. Most of the six-foot counter was bare except for a sparse-leafed ivy that needed adopting by someone who'd pay more attention to it. Another door was centered on the right wall. I lucked out—THOMAS BALLERTON was painted in black, block letters on it.

I smiled at Counter Boy. "Is Thomas here today?"

"Do you have an appointment?"

Damn. "No. We used to ride together." I was probably lying, but it was at least possible we'd been on the same road at the same time.

"Oh, well, he's, like, not here, anyway. Had to go to San Antonio for some supplies or something."

Damn. Again. I needed another excuse to find out as much as I could. I shrugged and smiled. "That's okay. I've bought your gorgeous custom seats in the past. I loved the seat y'all made for Max, my Yamaha Maxim. Thought I'd look into getting one for Pancho Villa. I was going to ask his advice."

"Pancho Villa?" The young man I now thought of as CB cocked his head like a confused dog.

I laughed. "Sorry. My current bike's a royal-blue Suzuki Bandit. I always name my motorcycles. This one's Pancho Villa."

"Oh wow, man, I love Suzis." CB moved to round the corner of the counter. "Cool name for yours! Is it outside?"

Good thing I'm not actually on Pancho today. If this guy saw my bike he'd discover it already has a custom Ballerton seat. "Sorry, but no. I was driving through town and just kind of thought of stopping."

CB's face fell. "Oh, well, that's too bad. Anyway, so, like, what did you have in mind? Maybe I can help."

What I have in mind is to see what's through the door behind you, but I can't tell you that. "Max's seat was totally custom, but my budget's tighter this time." I gestured to the EMPLOYEES ONLY door. "Do you have any off-the-shelf styles in stock? Maybe I could look at some of them and find one I like."

"Sorry. But, like, I'm not supposed to take customers into the shipping area." CB shrugged.

"Shipping area?"

"Yeah." There's no longer a showroom. We only have seats we've received that are ready to ship out to whoever, like, ordered them."

"Received?" I was confused. "Isn't this Ballerton's manufacturing location?"

Counter Boy nodded. "We used to make everything here. Even had a nice showroom." He tipped his head toward the door with Thomas Ballerton's name on it. "It's Tommy's office now."

"Used to?" My spirits fell.

"Yeah, man, like it's cheaper to get everything from China now. All that other was before my time, but I heard it was totally awesome. Big ol' cutters, sewing machines, and stuffers. Whole back of the building was manufacturing. All we do now is receive 'em, inspect 'em, and ship 'em back out."

"Then why are you here? Why have a sales counter?"

CB shrugged. "Counter's from back in the day. I'm here cuz we receive and ship boxes off and on all day." He grinned wide enough to eat a banana sideways. "Tommy trusts me to run the whole place!"

"That's great for you." I smiled and gestured again toward the door. "So what's back there, then?"

"Nothin', I guess. Stays locked up tight."

I decided to implement Rosie, my Regular-Blue-Collar-Girl persona, so I pulled it out of my mental costume closet and put it on. I hadn't used it for a couple of months. It usually worked with sales and counter clerk types, especially the more simple-minded ones. The young man behind the counter seemed to qualify.

I bit my lip and cocked my head, but refrained from taking the next step of twirling a lock of hair. "Please show me what's in shipping. Maybe I'll get some ideas." I accentuated my native-Texan drawl.

"Sorry, no can do." He shook his head, sending his hair flying like an old string mop.

I opted to add the hair-lock twirl. "But Tommy knows me."

"Yeah? Then why'd you call him Thomas?" The young man squinted. "Only his stuck-up wife calls him that."

I took a more direct chance. "That's what we call him in the Hill Country Cruisers Motorcycle Club."

"No it ain't." Counter Boy countered verbally. "He rides with the Texas Rattlesnake Riders."

Well, that chance was a big flop. I could feel my cheeks grow warm and knew I was blushing bright red.

CB's face turned hard. "Look, lady. Firstly, don't try to play no silly head games on me. I seen 'em all. Secondly, uh, second, Tommy founded the Snakes. He ain't been part of the Cruisers for a decade. Why're you lyin'? What's up with that? What's your thing?"

I was probably screwed at this point. May as well investigate outside on my own. I shrugged. "Just wanted to look, that's all. Don't get all freaked out." In my best Offended-Girl manner, I whirled and stomped out. The engine rev door sound made a nice overture for my dramatic exit.

As soon as I was through the front door, I hurried around the corner on the opposite side of the building from the shared parking lot. I hoped CB didn't notice I turned left outside the door instead of right, but I didn't want any Deluxe Tasty Food Supply employee's able to watch my movements. I walked quickly down the eight-foot wide, gravel easement between the windowless Ballerton building wall and a concrete drainage ditch.

Maybe the van was parked out back.

SNEAKING AROUND

We shall not cease from exploration,
and the end of all our exploring
will be to arrive where we started
and know the place for the first time.
~T. S. Eliot (1888-1965),
Little Gidding, from Four Quartets

I was halfway down the building when I heard Counter Boy's voice. He must have come outside.

I hope he's not looking for me, checking to make sure I left. I ducked behind an AC unit that was a few feet farther down the wall and waited. I didn't dare try to peek, both fearing I'd be seen and that my shifting weight would cause my feet to crunch on the gravel.

Barely breathing, I strained to hear. Counter Boy was talking on his cell phone. I could only hear a few words, but he was making a deal to buy something from someone named Tony.

His voice grew louder. "Yeah, okay, man, like I'll see ya' at the gig on Saturday."

Maybe he'll go back inside now.

After a few seconds of silence, I heard a click that sounded like one of those old-fashioned, flip-top, metal lighters. Then I smelled it. Either CB was smudging the outside of the building with sage sticks, or he was smoking a joint. *That's probably what he was making a deal to buy, too. I should introduce him to that flower lady's son, Lucas. They'd probably get along great.*

I winced as a leg cramp started in my right calf. I leaned left, causing my right foot to shift on the gravel and make a loud crunch. I froze again. Tears of pain from the cramp welled in my eyes. I blinked them away and gritted my teeth. *Great! What now?*

I glanced around. The ditch prevented any sideways movement, even without CB's presence. The back of the building was only ten feet away, but I was afraid I'd make noise trying to traverse even that small distance.

Before I could think of anything else, I heard CB on the phone again. *I don't care who he's talking to. Now's my chance!*

I squat-walked in slow motion to the corner, keeping the AC unit between me and CB. As soon as I rounded the corner, I stood and rubbed hard on the persistent leg cramp.

The back wall was also windowless, but included a truck-sized roll-up, metal door and a human-sized, solid door with a large padlock on it. A small, paved lot allowed for larger trucks to back to the roll-up door. A driveway in need of repaving crossed from the lot to the next street over, squeezing between two more warehouses whose entrances faced the other street. The Ballerton's loading/unloading lot itself was currently empty—no van in sight.

I'm wasting my time. Might as well move on. I crossed the paved lot behind the building and started up the side adjacent to the shared parking lot. Then a thought hit me hard enough to cause me to miss a step and almost trip. *I didn't hear the revving engine door sound when CB came out. Maybe he won't hear me going in. Do I dare? Oh, hell yeah. Larry doesn't occasionally call me Stupid PI for nothing.*

I hurried up the side of the building to the entrance, and opened the door just barely enough to squeeze through. I hoped it would close quickly and muffle the sound of the engine rev to outside ears, just in case.

I crossed the room, circled the counter, and passed through the EMPLOYEES ONLY door. The space wasn't nearly as big as I'd expected — perhaps twenty by forty. The walls were lined with metal shelving, and two other shelves spanned the center of the room. Custom seats in every shape and size were arranged side-by-side on the shelves next to the walls. The center shelves were filled with stacks of flattened boxes as well as bins of tape, styrofoam peanuts, and shipping labels. Between the two shelves on the back wall was a metal door with a small window in the upper center.

Maybe Counter Boy was right about the back half of the building being empty, but I badly wanted to see what was on the other side of that door. Was it really unused space?

I approached the door and was unsurprised to find it locked, although the size and sturdiness of the deadbolt gave me pause. *What's back there?*

I was especially disappointed to discover the small window was covered with cardboard. *Dang, a girl can't get a break.*

I frowned at the cardboard in frustration, then saw a small tear in the lower left corner. Cupping my hands on the glass, I squinted into the darkness beyond. It was hard to see, but one small light at the far end showed one thing — it wasn't one big warehouse. There was a central hall with closed doors on either side. None of those had windows. at least based on my limited view.

Staring into the darkness through the tiny tear might not reveal how the space was being used, but it indicated one thing: the room was not empty and just used to store stuff. Something was back there.

The sound of an engine revving shot through me like a cattle prod. *Oh crap! Counter Boy's back!*

If I was lucky, he wouldn't come back here. I could wait until the end of day and break out if I had to. Not the best plan, but nothing else came immediately to mind.

I hurried across the room and stood to the side of the main door, so if he opened it I'd be behind it, out of CB's view. From my location, I heard him talking to someone. I pressed my ear to the thin wall that separated me from the lobby.

This is NOT my lucky day. A delivery man must have followed CB back inside. The exchange was short, but long enough to shift me into mild panic mode.

"How many boxes?" CB asked.

"Just these three."

"Aw, like, then just leave 'em on the counter. I'll carry them to the back."

"You're the boss. Sign here."

The engine rev sound came again as the delivery guy left. CB was alone. And probably headed my way any moment. I saw the doorknob start to turn and bolted for the far end of the center shelves, hoping the bins and stacks of supply boxes would hide me.

CB was whistling a tune I didn't recognize as he entered the room. It was ghastly, probably some contemporary hip hop song, but it helped me follow his movements.

I could barely see him through the gaps in the supplies as I peered through the length of the center shelves. He carried one large box and crossed the room on the left side of the center shelves. I moved along their right side, keeping tabs on CB, who was busy grunting and shoving the box onto one shelf against the left wall.

I suddenly noticed CB had propped open the door to the lobby, probably so he could easily retrieve the other two boxes. *Maybe my luck is changing.*

I crouched and ran for the door, but barely circled the counter before I heard the whistling grow louder, indicating CB was returning for the next box. I dove for the floor on the front side of the counter, laying as flat as possible so my reflection wouldn't show in the glass entry doors.

I heard Counter Boy grab the next box and retreat again to the back room. It was now or never. I ran for the door and winced as the engine rev noise signaled my escape. I sprinted as fast as I could to the parking lot, but before I could reach my car I heard CB's voice from behind me.

Aw crap, I'm caught! Then I realized he was yelling at someone on his phone. I swung around a large, beat-up dumpster occupying two parking spaces just a few feet to my right.

I could no longer see the young man, but his voice carried just fine. "I don't give a damn. I need it on Saturday!"

Two female employees from the food supply warehouse walked past me, headed to their cars. They paused, glanced toward CB, then turned to stare at me.

I made prayer hands and mouthed "Please!"

Probably assuming I was trying to escape an abusive boyfriend or drug dealer, they nodded and moved on. One of the women glanced briefly back in my direction, but continued walking.

They climbed into adjacent cars, backed out, and drove off. Through all of this, CB ranted on the phone. Thank goodness he hadn't seen the women staring at me.

After a couple more minutes of CB's yelling, all went silent. I had no way of knowing if he'd gone back inside. I'd best wait a little longer. While I waited, my focus shifted to the dumpster.

It reeked so bad, my gag reflex kicked in. *What's that smell? I want to know which restaurants the Deluxe Tasty Food Supply folks deliver to, because I never, ever want to eat at one of them after smelling this.*

The last thing I needed was to start barfing, so I followed the advice of every crime show I'd ever seen—I breathed through my mouth to reduce the attack on my sensitive nose.

Please, for the love of all that's tasty, Counter Boy, go back inside now.

I took a chance and peeked around the dumpster. The sidewalk in front of Ballerton's was empty. I hurried to my car.

The minute I was safely inside, I cranked the engine and turned the AC fan up to full blast. I breathed deeply two or three times, trying to clear my lungs of the stench coming from the dumpster.

But I needed to get out of there before CB came outside for another smoke or phone call. Avoiding squealing my tires, I hauled Pickle Toy—and my own sorry ass—out of the parking lot and turned toward the interstate.

I need to know what's in that back warehouse area. And I need to know what's up with that white van. Is Ballerton really involved?

I found that hard to believe. Maybe he'd sold the van and the new owner hadn't changed the registration. Maybe it was stolen and Ballerton hadn't noticed yet.

I doubted it was stolen. It'd been showing up at the hippies' place for a couple of weeks, plenty long enough for even the most inattentive owner to realize it was gone.

But where is it? And who were the two men I'd seen? Not that I actually remembered seeing them, except while dreaming. What were the men holding between them in my dream? For that matter, was that flash of supposed memory I dreamed even true? And how does any of this relate to Ballerton's Motorcycle Seats or Thomas Ballerton?

I sighed and shook my head. *I wish I knew what had really happened.*

It'd been a long time since I'd been this frustrated. I was used to hitting dead ends in cases. Happened all the time. But to know I'd seen something that now eluded me was enough to drive me bonkers.

I beat my hands on the steering wheel. *DAMMIT I NEED TO REMEMBER WHAT I SAW.*

Since I had no solution for recovering my memory gap, I had to find another way to keep moving forward. My best bet at the moment was to stake out the building to see if the white van showed up. I wasn't ready to do another breaking and entering. I'd pushed my luck inside the Ballerton building enough for a bit. Perhaps a brainstorming session with Judy would uncover a way for me to talk to Thomas Ballerton about his van without raising his suspicions.

As I drove north, my mind reeled. Thanks to my seizure-induced memory loss, I had way more questions than answers about the previous night. I felt like I was back at square one. Hitting nothing but dead ends at Ballerton's hadn't helped, but stopping there at least revealed two things—it was a real business with a real product, just as it had been for more than a decade. But because manufacturing was no longer done there, Ballerton's Motorcycle Seats was using less than half of the building's space. So who was using the rest? And for what?

I need to find that white van.

THUNDERBOLT AND LIGHTNING

*Times of general calamity and confusion
create great minds. The purest ore is produced
from the hottest furnace, and the brightest
thunderbolt is elicited from the darkest storms.*
~Charles Caleb Colton (1780-1832)

Aunt Louise, my sweet, cross-dressing uncle, called as I headed
north. My old car wasn't equipped with Bluetooth, so to comply
with the handsfree law, I put my phone on speaker and put it in my
lap. I had to practically yell for Aunt Louise to hear me.

"What's going on? Where are you?" Her voice was harsh and
clipped.

I wasn't used to such terse communication from the man I'd
always thought of as my aunt. "I'm... I'm heading home from
Bubba's. The case I'm working on right now."

Aunt Louise's voice softened. "Are you all right? I had another
vision. A terrible one."

"Yes, Aunt Louise, I'm fine. Honest." *No way I'm telling her about
my seizures.* "I'm sorry you had a terrible vision, but I really am
okay." *More or less.*

"Please be extra careful. You're in danger."

"I always try to be careful. What was this vision that upset you so much? How am I in danger?"

"I heard thunderbolts. And I saw lightning."

Before I could stop myself I blurted, "That's very, very frightening." I did manage to avoid adding, "Galileo, Galileo."

I didn't want to hurt her feelings, although she might not have gotten the Queen song reference, anyway. "Well, if the vision is weather-related, the forecast for the next week is overcast and chilly, but not rain or storms. A thunderstorm would be odd for October."

"I doubt it's weather-related, Luv. But I can't say what it does mean. Sometimes visions are vague and indeterminate."

But all of your visions are that way. "I understand. I'll be extra vigilant. I promise."

"Thank you. Please call me every day for the next week."

That seemed a bit on the extreme side, but I dearly loved Aunt Louise, and it wouldn't take any time at all to touch base, especially if I texted. So I made a counter offer. "I'm back and forth in my car a lot right now, and it's hard to talk on my phone. How about if I text you every morning and evening. Eight or eight-thirty."

"Twice a day would be wonderful." Aunt Louise laughed. "You youngsters and your texting. But okay. I accept."

I refrained from reminding Aunt Louise I was almost thirty-five. She was in her sixties, so I guess to her I counted as a youngster.

"Done and done. I'll start tonight." I set an alarm on my phone so I wouldn't forget.

The first thing I did when I got home was snuggle and play with the cats. Next, I drank two large glasses of water, trying to get my body over the last throes of its hangover. Finally, I called Judy and gave her a quick update. Tasks accomplished, I crawled into bed for a nap.

True to my word, I texted Aunt Louise before heading south that evening. She responded with another plea for me to be careful.

I reached south Austin just after nine-thirty. The thin sliver of a moon left the night dark and brooding. I slowly cruised down the street where the Ballerton's back entrance driveway came out. I debated the merits of parking in the pool of light provided by the widely spaced streetlights versus parking in the stealth-benefiting darkness in between. I opted for the security of a street light, figuring no one was around the warehouse district this time of night to watch where I went. Someone cruising through might be interested in a nice, vintage Mustang parked in near-darkness, though.

I was dressed in my usual Stealthy-PI-Mode black clothing, this time topped with a black peacoat for warmth against the chilly October air. Every pocket of the coat held something from my Trusty Spy Kit: flashlight, handgun, cell phone, even a small can of mace to use if I was confronted and didn't want to shoot anyone.

My soft-soled shoes made almost no sound as I walked up the long driveway and paused at the edge of the parking area. The lot was empty. An ancient mercury-vapor security light provided a well-lit circle for both the employee door and the roll-up door. The rest of the lot was shrouded in shadows.

I turned left and tucked into some unkempt, dying red tip photinia shrubs at the far corner of the lot. The only sound breaking the quiet was water gurgling in the concrete ditch to my left. Shrubville wasn't the best place to hide, but unless someone looked directly at me, expecting to see someone, I'd be safe and undiscovered.

I'd been crouched behind the bushes for over an hour when I saw headlights heading up the driveway. *Awfully late to be after something stored in the warehouse.*

Of course, I hadn't believed Counter Boy when he'd said that's all the warehouse was used for. It was a good bet that whoever was approaching had more in mind than rooting through boxes of unused items.

The van parked in front of the smaller door. Two men exited the vehicle. I assumed it was the same two I'd seen on the hippies' land. Based on the license plate, it was definitely the same van. That experience felt like ancient history at this point, but it was only the previous night. I shook my head in the darkness.

The men circled the van and opened the rear door, which emitted a loud squeak. Even from across the parking lot, I could hear the men grunting as they leaned in, apparently wrestling with something. When they stood up, they held a large four-rotor drone between them

An inadvertent "Ah!" escaped my lips. I immediately clamped my hand over my mouth. My eyes felt as big as saucers. I hoped the men wouldn't be able to see them in the darkness. The van's driver glanced around but must have decided the noise came from a night bird or animal, because he turned back to the passenger, shrugged, and said something too low for me to hear.

I breathed a sigh of relief, both because I hadn't been discovered, and because I now knew what I'd seen the night before — the memory that had been blanked out by my seizure.

A drone makes total sense! It was never aliens. Not that I ever really believed that. My cheeks grew warm with my denial. If I was honest, I'd admit that a small part of me thought it *might* be aliens.

The men wrestled the large drone to the back door and managed to get the thing and themselves inside. The door swung shut in slow motion, thanks to the automatic closer. It finally finished with a loud click.

I stayed still for another ten minutes before approaching the van. I didn't dare open the back door, having heard it squeak when the men opened it. Moving to the passenger door, I tried the handle. I'd expected it to be locked, but I still sighed in frustration.

I dug my lock pick from my pocket and worked it around in the old van's door lock. After a minute, I felt the lock release. I eased the door open and crawled inside.

Aunt Louise would kill me if she knew what I'm doing. So would Larry. Heck, so would everyone I know. But it couldn't be helped. I had to find out everything I could while I had a chance. I opened the glovebox, but the light was burned out. Pulling a penlight from my left coat pocket, I illuminated the contents.

Most of the items in the glovebox were gas and fast food receipts, a handful of small tools, a few tattered pages from the owner's manual, and…BINGO! The Proof of Insurance form.

I smoothed the wrinkled form out on the driver's seat and shined my light across it. I would've given my eyeteeth if the name on the insurance form was anyone other than Thomas Ballerton, but that sadly was not the case. Whoever these guys were, not only was Ballerton letting them borrow his van, he was still paying for the insurance.

I used my cell phone camera to take pictures of the insurance form and several of the gas receipts. No idea if either would prove helpful, but I was here now, and getting my hands on these again later would be tough.

Returning my phone to my coat pocket, I shimmied through the gap between the passenger and driver seats into the van's cavernous back end. There was no back seat. The space held half a dozen shoebox-sized cardboard boxes, a large cantilever toolbox, and a three-ring binder shoved partway under the driver's seat.

I decided to start with the binder. Inside were schematics that made no sense to me, but I could tell they were detailed and professional. I took a picture of each of the dozen pages. I doubted the toolbox would provide any clues, but to be thorough, I popped the latches and unfolded both sides of the lid to reveal the multiple trays inside.

Nothing specific jumped out at me, but the overall contents were strange. The majority of the trays were crammed with hand tools, which wasn't unusual for a toolbox, but the tools looked appropriately sized for working on jewelry, not typical workshop projects. Also included were two volt meters, a small Dremel rotary tool with a dozen different tips, and a soldering iron.

I turned my attention to the cardboard boxes. Each small box contained items for the drone: a dozen plastic propellors, tons of batteries, light bulbs, bunches of wires, tiny circuit boards, and various sized connectors.

I guess it made sense, seeing as how they were in the middle of nowhere when they were messing with Bubba's cows. Their behavior might be thoroughly reprehensible, but I gave them kudos for being well-equipped and prepared for pretty much anything.

I shifted my position, and my legs pushed against a small moving blanket. I'd assumed that was all it was, but I discovered a tough, watertight, Pelican case beneath it. This raised my eyebrows. Pelican cases were built to Department of Defense standards and were used by the military, law enforcement, fire safety, and even the entertainment industry to protect expensive cameras and sensitive electronics equipment.

I unsnapped the latches and lifted the heavy lid. Tucked inside a small cut-out in the case's otherwise solid foam lining was some type of device. I pulled it out and turned it over, studying it from all sides. It was smooth black plastic, and about the size of a walkie talkie or portable radio. There was a tiny switch on one corner, but nothing else. No buttons. No dials. No nothing. It was clearly high tech, but I couldn't begin to guess what it was.

Still, I took a picture of it. As I put away my phone, I glanced at the time and uttered a short, "Oh!" I'd been crawling around inside the van for half an hour and was probably deep into pushing-my-luck territory at this point.

Time to blow this joint. I quickly shoved the device back into its box and snapped it shut.

It would be easier to slip out the back of the vehicle, but I couldn't take a chance on the squeaky door alerting the men inside the warehouse. So I took the long way, clambering once again through the gap between the seats.

Scrambling around the confines of the van made me feel like I'd run an obstacle course. I paused for a quick rest on the passenger seat, then decided to root around under the seats to see if there was anything else worth noting. My hand found only one item, but it caused me to shudder. It was a map of Caldwell County, with Bubba's ranch circled in red marker.

Who the hell are these guys? What are they doing? Why did they decide to target Bubba? And his cows?

I was deep in my musing when movement caught the corner of my eye.

Crap! OH CRAP OH CRAP OH CRAP!

The warehouse door was opening. I tossed the map on the floor and jerked on the door handle, shoving it open and hitting the pavement just as the two men exited the building.

"Hey! Who are you? What the hell are you doing in our van?" one of the men yelled.

"It's her! Wait! Get back here!" the other one yelled.

I took off at breakneck speed down the driveway toward Pickle Toy. Unlike in the movies, I didn't look back over my shoulder to see how close they were, but I could hear footsteps pounding the pavement behind me.

"Keep after her. I'm going back for the van," one of them said.

A cold dread shot through me, causing a shudder that almost made me trip. I hunkered down and pulled out all the stops, glad that most of the time I ran up the stairs to my office instead of lazily taking the elevator.

Hitting the end of the driveway, I turned right and bolted for my car. *Damn I wish I'd parked in the dark. Now this jerk's gonna get a clear view of my car.*

I fumbled my key from my pocket and immediately dropped it. *Shit!*

I did a quick stumble, trying to grab the key without coming to a full stop. My clumsiness cost me precious seconds. As I stood, I chanced a quick glance behind me.

SHIT! He was closing in. That lit a new fire in me and I reached my car in seconds, pressing the unlock button as I rounded the driver's side. In one quick move, I opened the door, dove inside, shoved the key in the ignition, and fired her up. I'd never been happier to hear Pickle Toy's throaty, gas-guzzling V8 engine.

Shifting into drive and punching it, I fishtailed and burned rubber. I glanced in the rearview mirror and saw the white van turn from the driveway onto the street. It stopped long enough for the man who'd been on foot to jump inside, then it did its own fishtail as the driver gunned it.

My escape options in this area were limited. Most of these streets were in poor shape and peppered with stop signs, sharp turns, and even dead ends. I had to get out of the warehouse district. My best bet was to reach Interstate 35 and floor the Mustang. I doubted a beat up old van with bad rear-end traction could keep up on the highway.

I took a wrong turn and found myself on a dead end. An involuntary "Ahhhh!" escaped my lips. I hit reverse, whipped back, shifted again to drive, and floored it.

There was barely room on the street, and I scraped bumpers with the van as I passed. The squealing of metal on metal seemed deafening, but it might have been the screaming in my brain.

I turned the next corner and checked the rearview mirror again. The van was again in hot pursuit. Just two more blocks and I could turn onto the access road to 35. It took forever, like those hallways in horror movies that keep getting longer as the victim runs to escape.

When I reached the T at the end of the road, I immediately turned right and shot toward freedom. But traffic was heavy, even that time of night. I found myself trapped behind a long haul eighteen-wheeler and sandwiched on the left by an SUV and on the right by a guardrail. The van managed to catch up, thanks to those rare, unexplainable, gaps in otherwise heavy traffic.

I'll call the cops and tell them I'm being pursued.

I fumbled for my phone, but in my stressed-out state, it slipped from my grip and slid under the seat.

Dammit!

A screaming pain suddenly shot through my head like lightning. My vision flashed bright then blurred. *Oh, ouch! What's happening?*

Pickle Toy veered left. I jerked the wheel just inches before hitting the SUV. My Mustang lurched right and hit the guardrail. Even the car's heavy weight wasn't enough stability. The seatbelt locked hard as I flipped. The thundering noise of metal crumpling against asphalt pounded through me as I lost consciousness.

OCCIPITAL RIDGE

If you hear it, darling, then it's there.
~Freddie Mercury (on the meaning of
Bohemian Rhapsody) (1946-1991)

I woke up disoriented and confused. It took a minute to realize I was in a hospital. Blinking rapidly to clear my head and focus my eyes, I saw several doctors and nurses, and I could hear lots of activity outside the thin curtain that was pulled closed around my bed.

"Where am I?" My voice was barely above a whisper, but the doctor standing nearby, making notes on a laptop as he studied monitors, heard anyway.

"Ah, you're awake. I'm Doctor Welch. You're in the ER at Seton Hospital in Kyle."

"Again?"

Dr. Welch raised his eyebrows but didn't pursue my question. "You were in a car accident last night. Can you tell me your name?"

"You don't know?"

The doctor smiled. "We just want make sure you do. It's to gauge your temporal stability."

I didn't really understand *temporal stability*, but I nodded. "Marianna Morgan."

"That's fine." The doctor nodded. "We've completed our preliminary exam. You have no broken bones or detectable internal organ damage. The neuromorphic chip in your brainstem is undisturbed."

"The what in my where?" I tried to sit up, but Dr Welch gently pushed me back down.

"Easy, now. The chip that's implanted at the back of your neck, where your Cerebellum connects to the spinal cord."

"I don't have anything implanted in my brain." A wave of panic and fear flushed through me.

"You're sure it wasn't inserted by a doctor at some point?" Dr. Welch frowned.

"I'm totally sure. Get it out of me. Please!" By now I was panting.

"Easy, now." Dr. Welch repeated. He pulled the curtain aside and called, "Nurse get Surgery Room One ready."

When I woke up again, I found I was now in a room. Larry, Patrick, Judy, Bubba, and even Aunt Louise were in a semi-circle around the foot of my bed.

"What are y'all doing here?" I tried to raise my hand and point at them, but a tangle of tubes and sensors restricted my movement. "For that matter, what am I doing here?"

"You don't remember?" Aunt Louise asked.

"You were in a car accident last night." Judy dabbed at her eyes.

"Oh, that's right." I nodded. "I remember a doctor talking to me in the ER."

Larry shook his head. "I'm afraid your Mustang is totaled."

"And you ain't lookin' too good, neither." Bubba's voice hitched as he spoke.

"Guess that explains why everything hurts." The control box was tucked beneath my left hand, so I pressed the button and raised myself from flat to a reclined-sitting position. I felt like I'd been run over by a Mack truck. Maybe I had.

"Pickle Toy's gone? Aw, damn." Tears streamed down my face. "What time is it? What day is it?"

"It's almost noon on Thursday," Aunt Louise said.

Judy stepped forward and used her tissue to wipe my cheeks. "What can you remember?"

I frowned in concentration. "I was at the Ballerton's warehouse. The guys pulled up in the white van and took something out of the back. Next thing I remember is talking to the doctor in the ER about…I'm not sure what."

"You went to Ballerton's alone?" Patrick's tone had a scolding edge to it.

"Yes." I glared at him. "I was doing my job."

"Took something? What was it?" Larry asked.

I will NOT forget again, dammit. I closed my eyes and searched through my fuzzy brain. "A drone! Bubba, they've been using a drone on your cows."

"Well I'll swanee." Bubba shook his head. "Never woulda guessed that. Course I ain't up on all that new technologic stuff. Did see one news story about drones, though."

"A drone?" Patrick asked. "You're sure?"

I shot him a look at the same time I saw Larry raise his eyebrows. "Yes, dammit, I'm sure. I know what a drone is." I turned to Aunt Louise. "Hey, Aunty, what are you doing here?"

"You didn't text me this morning like you promised. I called Larry."

"And I called Judy, Patrick, and Bubba." Larry added. "None of them had heard from you, either."

Judy patted my arm. "I ran over to check on you, but it was obvious you hadn't been home all night. So I called Larry back. Oh, and I also fed your kitties."

"And I tracked you down through the accident report." Larry sighed.

Aunt Louise shook her head. "You shouldn't have gone there alone. Not after my warning."

"But I didn't have a problem there." Of course, I couldn't be sure. I remembered seeing the drone, but not much after that. Patrick repeated pretty much what I was thinking.

"You don't remember everything, so you can't be sure."

I shrugged. "Yeah, okay, but where was my accident? Not at Ballerton's."

"No, it was on Interstate 35 a few miles south of the warehouse district. Witnesses said you seemed to lose control of your car. You went into a guardrail and flipped."

"Oh! Oh, my." *No wonder I hurt so bad.* "Do they know what caused the accident?"

"I might." A voice from the doorway caused my friends to all spin at once. They parted as a doctor carrying what looked like a urine specimen cup approached the foot of my bed. "Hello, Ms. Morgan. I'm Doctor Welch. Do you remember our conversation in the ER? We removed this from near your brainstem."

"Barely." I squinted to see what he held. "What is that?

The doctor circled to the opposite side of the bed from where Judy stood and held the cup out. I took it in a shaky hand.

"What is this?" It looked like a burnt grain of rice with an inch of wire thinner than a hair snaking out one end.

"It's the neuromorphic chip we removed from near your brainstem. You said no doctor had inserted it, so we have no idea what it was doing."

"No. No doctor put that in." My eyes felt big as saucers. "It was in my neck?" I only vaguely remembered our earlier conversation.

Dr. Welch nodded.

"But why didn't I feel it? I shampoo. I rub my neck. Shouldn't I have felt it?" The array of monitors I was connected to all started beeping faster.

"Take it easy." Dr. Welch grabbed my wrist and felt my pulse. "It was subcutaneous—about half an inch under your skin—and very carefully lined up with the occipital ridge, which masked the object."

"Occipital ridge?" Judy asked.

I shook my head. "I don't know what that is, either."

The doctor released my wrist. "The occipital bone is a trapezoidal cranial dermal bone, and is the main bone of the occiput. It's..." He glanced around the room. I imagine my eyes were as glazed as everyone else's. He smiled. "It's at the back of the head, where the base of the skull meets the spine. It feels to the touch like an upside-down V."

"Someone was messing around near my spine?" My mouth fell open. I quickly snapped it shut.

"What is that thang?" Bubba asked.

The doctor turned to the elderly man and smiled. "Neuromorphic implants are technological devices that connect directly to a biological subject's brain—usually placed on the surface of the brain, or attached to the brain's cortex, as this one was."

"That weren't much help." Bubba frowned, his voice a quiet mumble.

"What on earth?" Aunt Louise's voice was more baritone than usual, causing Dr. Welch's eyebrows to do a little dance. "What would it be doing in my niece's brain?"

Dr. Welch shrugged. "They're used for many indications. Most common is sensory substitution, such as to compensate for visual or hearing loss."

"But she sees and hears just fine." Larry waved toward me. "At least when she's not being stubborn."

I stuck out my tongue but also nodded in agreement. "Yeah. So what's this thing doing in my brain?"

"I'm afraid I cannot answer that." Dr. Welch shook his head. "Unless you know who inserted it, we'll likely never know what purpose it served."

The realization hit me like a baseball bat to the ear. "Those damn van guys."

"Van Goghs?" Dr. Welch cocked his head.

I couldn't help but laugh, probably as much out of stress as anything. "No. Sorry. I'm a private investigator on a case where I've been tracking two men. It's a long story, but their using nano chips makes perfect sense."

"The cows!" Judy's hand shot to her mouth.

"Cows?" Dr. Welch's head listed even farther.

"Is that why they been killin' my cows and cuttin' off their heads?" Bubba stepped forward. "Do my cows have these damn *new-row-morf* things in them, too?"

Dr. Welch's head jerked toward Bubba. "Someone's decapitating your cows? I don't understand."

"Neither did I, until you handed me this specimen cup." I moved it to within a few inches of my eyes. I needed something that provided magnification, but got as close a look as possible under the circumstances. There were no markings anywhere on its smooth, oblong casing, so I doubted it was mass manufactured. *What the hell are those guys doing?*

The doctor reached for the cup, but I pulled it away. "I need to keep this."

Dr. Welch shook his head. "No. It needs to go to pathology for examination."

"Nope. It came out of me. It's mine. And I'm keeping it."

The doctor stared with narrowed eyes, then sighed. "I'll need to fill out some paperwork on the item and have you sign it."

"Not a problem." I tucked the cup by my side beneath the sheets, just in case the doctor tried to do a snatch-and-grab.

Dr. Welch removed his stethoscope from around his neck. "Now I need to do a quick checkup on you."

"Before I'm released?" I grinned like a kid at Christmas.

"Not likely. Nurse?" The doctor waved toward the door and a nurse came in, pushing a rolling cart that included a laptop and various other medical devices. She shooed my friends out and closed the door.

After a head to toe check of everything that moved, pulsed, pumped, or acted as input or output for my body, Dr. Welch stood straight and folded his arms over his chest.

"I'm recommending you stay in observation for thirty-six hours. I don't see any residual damage from that neural implant, and your accident injuries are mostly contusions and a few lacerations, but some things take time to show up. The problem with a head injury is a possible slow sub-dural hematoma. We need to watch for that."

"Aw, damn." I sighed. "Okay, I guess. Can my friends come back in?"

The nurse, who'd been busy typing and shuffling papers, smiled as she handed me a clipboard. "Shortly. But sign here first, please."

"What is this? You aren't releasing me. So what am I signing?"

"I am releasing the neuromorphic chip to your custody," Dr. Welch said.

"Oh. Thanks."I scrawled my signature across the bottom and asked again. "Can my friends come back in now?"

"I'll send your friends in as I leave." The nurse's voice was soft, her expression sympathetic. She patted my arm. "Don't worry. You'll be just fine."

"But what about that thing from my brain?" I didn't want to admit how freaked out I was, but the nurse could obviously tell anyway.

"I wish I could answer your question, but at least you seem unaffected. You're alert, all your parts work, and you seem pretty darned smart." She smiled. "Whatever it is, it doesn't seem to have done any permanent damage."

I guess that was comforting. Sort of.

The nurse put away the various testing and torture devices and opened the door to leave. My friends streamed back in. They and the nurse did a little shuffle dance as everyone tried to maneuver through the door at the same time.

Five concerned faces stared at me, then everyone started asking questions at the same time. I held up my hand.

"Doc says I have to stay. He wants me for thirty-six hours."

Everyone started talking again, slightly louder and more high-pitched.

This time Dr. Welch held up his hand. "We see no immediate cause for concern. This is precautionary." He turned to me. "And I want you back in five days for a follow-up, just to be safe. I'll have scheduling contact you. Please have someone make a note of the appointment, in case any memory issues develop."

"I'll do it." Bubba pointed at me. "And this time no excuses. No missing appointments. If'n you'd gone to that doc who treated your birdshot, you might've found that *new-row-morf* thing a lot sooner."

He had me there, although that doctor had been looking at my butt, not my head. I could sometimes act like an ass, but the doctor was unlikely to get the two body parts confused.

Rather than argue, I smiled. "Okay, Bubba. I promise."

"We believe Ms. Morgan has no serious injuries, thanks to her seatbelt, air bag deployment, and the fact that she may have been unconscious when the car flipped—she didn't stiffen up or grip the steering wheel. Keeping her for observation is erring on the safe side because of the potential for head injury."

"Probably because of the damn implant, too." I pursed my lips. "Isn't it?"

"It's a huge unknown, but it doesn't hurt to be cautious about any serious car accident. And don't be concerned if you develop black eyes today. Those will be the result of the airbag, not a developing head injury." Dr. Welch smiled. He gave me a little wave as he left.

"Thunderbolt and lightning." Aunt Louise's voice was barely audible.

"What's Queen have to do with this?" Larry asked.

I fell into a giggle fit for a couple of minutes. "Sorry for laughing Aunt Louise. Nothing, Larry. It was one of my aunt's visions."

"Oh, I see." Patrick's expression made it clear he didn't see at all.

"She heard a thunderbolt and saw lightning in her vision. I guess my accident fulfilled both."

Patrick still looked confused.

Larry rolled his eyes. "You know, *Bohemian Rhapsody*?"

Patrick shrugged. "I guess I wasn't really a Queen fan."

An impromptu, mostly accurate and semi-on-key, a capella performance of the song broke out in the room. By the time we were done, I was laughing and feeling better. Until Judy spoke up.

"What about that chip from your head?" Judy pointed at the specimen cup I'd placed on the side table while the doctor examined me.

I picked up the cup and lightly shook it. "I need to find someone who can look at it. I don't even know where to start."

"Maybe I do." Larry frowned in concentration. "I knew a woman at the University of Texas. She was in the Computer Science department. Helped us on a case. I'll see if she can help, soon as I remember her name."

"Thanks." I stared at the neural chip in its cup, lost in thought.

Patrick eased up beside me and brushed a lock of tangled hair off my forehead. "Sorry for how I came across. I worry about you. What do you think was going on? And how'd that get in you in the first place?"

A cold chill washed through me. "I'd bet big money they put it in while they had me. When I was abducted. So it's been in me for a while."

"That's pretty creepy," Larry said.

"Yeah." I nodded. "It might explain the seizures I had. Both times, I was with Bubba's cows, and the guys and their drone were nearby."

"That figures." Larry patted my foot through the sheets. "Do you think those guys, or that chip, had something to do with the accident, too?"

"Probably, but I may never know."

"So what are they doing?" Bubba asked. "What's the chip for? What's been going on with my cows?"

"I don't know. That's why I need someone else to look at this thing."

"I'll follow up this afternoon." Larry glanced at me. "Would you trust me with the chip?"

"I…" Could I trust anyone with something that had been inside my brain, perhaps controlling me? Causing seizures? "I guess I'll have to. But I'm not comfortable letting this thing out of my sight." I reluctantly handed the cup to Larry.

"I promise I'll take good care of it. And I'll be sure to keep track of it at all times." He uncapped the specimen cup and tipped the tiny device into the palm of his hand. He took his phone out of his pocket with his other hand and snapped half a dozen pictures of the rice-grain-sized implant.

I watched but said nothing. *I hope Larry's right and it'll be okay. That's the only clue I've got to what's been going on, even if I don't know the details yet.*

I'd refrained up to that point, but I finally felt the back of my neck. There was a quarter-sized, shaved spot and what felt like a couple of stitches. It was sore to the touch but otherwise didn't hurt. Another chill ran down my spine. *What are they up to? Who are chips like mine destined for? I don't think cows singing and dancing are the ultimate goal.*

A wave of exhaustion washed over me. "I love each of you dearly, but I think I need to crash for a bit. No pun intended."

Everyone took a turn giving me a hug and kiss before filing out. Once alone, I thought about my next move. *Dammit, I don't want to be trapped here for two days. I've got to talk the doctor into letting me go home earlier. I'm too close to solving the case now to languish in a bed.*

As I drifted off, a memory pulsed through me. I'd been inside that van. But what had I learned or discovered?

AGAINST MEDICAL ADVICE

I owe my success to having listened
respectfully to the very best advice, and then
going away and doing the exact opposite.
~G. K. Chesterton (1874-1936)

I slept for the next fourteen hours, except for being interrupted every hour by a nurse who took my vital signs. That wouldn't have been so bad, but he also insisted on asking questions. Three questions each time: what's your name, where are you, what is the date.

I grumbled to the nurse when he woke me at three am. "Isn't rest important after an injury?"

He tucked the blood pressure cuff back into his pocket, gently untangled my IV drip tube from around my hand, and patted my shoulder. "Sorry about that, but we have to check your temporal stability. We need to ensure there's no swelling or bleeding in your brain."

Dr Welch stopped by around nine Friday morning, although he didn't stay long and mostly talked to the nurse who'd been constantly pestering me.

Larry, Patrick, and Judy showed up just before noon. I was sipping on grape juice and eating meat loaf and mashed potatoes. For hospital food, it wasn't bad.

I was glad Bubba and Aunt Louise hadn't returned. I didn't have to pretend as much with my three friends about how upset and stressed I really was.

"Look at you!" Judy smiled. "You seem more alert and clear-headed."

Larry nodded. "Hospitals agree with you."

"Ha!" I grimaced. "I've had approximately five hours sleep in the last fourteen hours, thanks to hourly pestering by my nurse."

"Look at it this way." Patrick winked. "It shows how much they care."

I rolled my eyes. "Yeah, I guess so. But I can't believe the doc wants to keep me here another day. I feel fine."

Larry smirked. "Yeah, right."

"Okay, maybe I AM a bit sore, but I want to go home. Y'all need to help me escape."

Patrick shook his head. "Maybe you should do what the doctor says."

"Following orders would be a new thing for you." Judy grinned. "Maybe give it a try."

I stuck out my tongue. "Why? I've always done fine ignoring orders." Before anyone could object, I pressed the Nurse Call button. When the day nurse came in, I smiled, but my voice was firm. "Please, I want to go home this afternoon. What do I need to do? Can you help make that happen?"

"I don't think that's a good idea." Concern etched Patrick's face.

"What he said." The nurse bobbed her head Patrick's direction.

"It's an excellent idea. I feel fine. I'm bruised and sore, but I can deal with that."

The nurse shook her head and sighed. "I have to contact Dr. Welch."

Fiddling with the bandage covering my IV needle reminded me of the chip and Larry's promise. "Speaking of things stuck under my skin, what's up with my neural—um neuromorphic—chip? Where is it?"

"I rooted around through my files as soon as I got back to the office and found her name. Dr. Barbara Ramsey. She asked me to bring the chip right over. So she's now got it in her lab at the university."

I involuntarily shuddered. "Can you trust her? Can I?"

"It'll be okay." Larry smiled. "She wants to know as bad as you do what this thing does and why it was inside you."

"I doubt that."

"Maybe not *quite* as bad," Judy countered, "but I'm sure she's motivated. By scientific curiosity, if nothing else."

I pursed my lips and held my tongue. I didn't want to be someone's scientific curiosity, but I did want answers.

Twenty minutes later, the nurse returned, followed by Dr. Welch.

"I hear you want to be released early." Dr. Welch crossed his arms over his chest.

I nodded and smiled. "Yes, please. I feel fine other than being sore, and I really want to go home. I have cats there. And my own comfy bed. And my favorite pillow and fuzzy slippers."

Dr. Welch shook his head. "I still think you should stay another day, but I'll sign an AMA if you'll agree to choose someone to do your neural evaluation every hour until noon tomorrow."

"Agreed." I grinned. "But what will they actually do? And what's an AMA?"

"Same questions we've asked you every hour for the past day," the nurse explained. "It's important to make sure you don't develop any cognitive problems, which could indicate a serious condition."

"*I'll* do it," Judy said. "I can even stay with her if it'll help."

"That would be an excellent idea." Dr. Welch nodded, but his mouth was a straight, unhappy line. "And an AMA is an Against Medical Advice form. It means you are leaving the hospital against my explicit advice and counsel. I can't keep you here, even though I think you shculd stay."

Judy raised her hand in a *scout's honor* move. "I promise to get her back in here, or call for an ambulance, if anything looks at all questionable."

"Fair enough." Dr. Welch turned to the nurse. "Please see to her paperwork and arrange for a wheelchair."

"Yes, doctor."

Dr. Welch turned back to me and smiled. "And Ms. Morgan, I'd like you to keep me posted on that neuromorphic chip. Both from a medical perspective and my own curiosity, I'd like to know what you learn."

"I promise." I smiled and nodded.

He left with a final wave. My friends and I chatted as we waited for the nurse, although I was restless and had a hard time following the conversation. I wanted to go home. The nurse finally returned after half an hour and handed me a clipboard. "Sign here, please."

I scrawled my signature across the bottom and handed it back.

She set th∋ form on the bed and shooed everyone out of the room. "I need to remove her IV and monitors. You can come back in when I'm done."

All unplugging and de-attaching completed, the nurse opened the door and my friends streamed in. The nurse pushed the last of the monitors out of the way against the wall. "I'll grab a wheelchair. You go ahead and get dressed."

I looked around the room. "I have no idea where my clothes are, or even if they're still wearable."

"On the shelf under your bed," the nurse said over her shoulder as she left the room.

Larry and Patrick shrugged and followed her back out. Judy closed the door and helped me dress. Stiff and sore as I was, it took close to five minutes to get me properly attired.

"Where's my phone? Please tell me it didn't get lost again."

Judy checked the bottom of the bag that had held my clothes. "Your purse is in here, but no phone."

"Dammit." I sighed. "What about my gun?"

"Where was it?"

"Last I remember, it was snapped into my right coat pocket." I waved toward my peacoat, which was hanging on a hook outside the small bathroom.

Judy retrieved the coat and searched through the pockets. "Flashlight. Chapstick. Sorry, no gun!"

"Aw, crap." The last thing I needed right now was to have to report another lost or stolen weapon. And Larry and Patrick hated it when I lost my gun.

"Is the pocket open? Did it fall out somewhere?"

Judy shook her head. "Nope. Pocket flap is snapped closed."

"Damn." I pressed the call button on my control. The nurse who responded looked about sixteen and had a sweet smile and an expression untarnished by years of watching pain and death. "Hi. How can I help you?"

I returned her smile. "I hope you can. I'm a private investigator, and my gun was in my coat pocket when I had my accident. The pocket is snapped closed, so I'm hoping someone in the emergency room or the nurse's station on this floor removed it."

The nurse's eyes grew big, but she nodded. "Let me see what I can find out. Maybe it's at hospital security."

When the young nurse opened the door to leave, both men, and my day nurse, returned. The nurse pushed a wheelchair big enough for a gorilla.

"Do you need help getting into the chair?" the nurse asked.

I shook my head. "No, but I can't go yet."

"Excuse me?" The nurse frowned.

"They're looking for my gun."

"You lost another gun?" Patrick pursed his lips.

"No, I didn't lose my gun. The hospital took it." *At least I hope the hospital took it.*

Before anyone else could chew me out, the young nurse returned, followed closely by a woman wearing a uniform that said *Hospital Security* above the breast pocket. The security woman carried an evidence bag as if it contained a poisonous snake. The young nurse held a clipboard.

"I'll take that." Larry held out his hand for the gun.

The security woman looked at me. I nodded. "He's a detective with the Austin Police Department and an old friend." She handed the bag over and retreated to the door.

"Please sign this property release form." The nurse handed me the clipboard. After I signed, she and the security woman both left.

Gun safely back in my — well, Larry's — possession, my little procession of friends followed my wheelchair through the hospital and out to the entrance. Everyone hurried to the parking lot to retrieve their cars. I was bundled into Larry's SUV, because it had the most leg room, and we all headed north.

PHOTO EVIDENCE

A photograph is a secret about a secret. The
more it tells you the less you know.
~Diane Arbus (1923-1971)

I stared at my hands as Larry drove. Neither of us spoke for several minutes. A radio station played softly in the background.

I reached over and turned down the radio's volume. "Did the doctor say how long?"

"Which doctor? How long for what?"

"The doc at the university. How long before she knows something."

Larry shook his head. "But she promised to start on it as soon as I left yesterday. She was actually pretty excited about the opportunity to figure out what it was.

"Okay." I sighed. *Dammit I'm not going to let this get to me this much. I will not cry or fall apart.* I gritted my teeth and set my jaw. "I need to find out where they took Pickle Toy. I sure hope my phone is in it."

"Let me see what I can do." Larry punched a button on his SUV's digital display. "Call headquarters."

After a short conversation, it was determined that my car was in the city's main impound. A small bag of possessions had been collected and was being held in Austin PD's headquarters in downtown Austin.

"Let's go get my phone." I grabbed Larry's arm. "Please?"

"Nope. You're going home. Soon as you're settled, I'll come back downtown and get your stuff. I'll even bring it back to you today."

"But—"

"No buts." Larry shook his head.

Once we reached my house, everyone got busy making the house safe enough for a total invalid.

"Guys, I'm fine. I'm just sore. No need to go to all this trouble." My protestations fell on deaf ears.

Patrick paused in shoving an end table against the wall. "And what if you develop a neurologic issue and you faint?"

Both men continued right on with padding corners, shifting around furniture, and removing area rugs that I might slip on.

Judy finally ran the men off after half an hour.

"Sheesh." I shook my head and curled up on the sofa.

"At least they care." Judy laughed.

"Yeah, that's true." As annoyed as I'd been at their redecorating, it was also a nice feeling knowing I had friends who cared and worried that much.

"First things first. What's your name? Where are you? What day is it?"

"Really?"

"I promised the doc. So out with it."

I sighed. "Marianna Morgan. My home in Cedar Park. Friday, and the longest damn day of my life."

Judy laughed. "Good enough. Now go rest. I'm running home to get some things."

"You're really staying tonight?"

"You bet I am. Now, shoo."

I expected to be restless, but the minute I climbed into bed I was out like a light.

Judy shook me awake me when she returned just over an hour later.

Grumbling loudly, I rolled over. "What?"

"Time for your test. What's your name? Where are you? What's the date?"

"I just wanna sleep." I tried to roll back over, but Judy grabbed my shoulder.

"Not until you answer. I take my promises seriously."

"That's true. No one can say you aren't loyal and honorable." I sighed, then answered. "Marianna Morgan. My bed, where I'm trying to get some damn sleep. I have no idea, but it hasn't been long enough since I've laid down, so I'm assuming it's still Friday."

Judy patted my shoulder. "Go back to sleep."

She did this to me every hour for the next four hours, when voices from the other room woke me and I gave up and climbed out of bed. I shuffled down the hall and found Larry and Judy drinking beers at my kitchen table.

"I want one!"

"Hmmmm." Judy's mouth twitched sideways. "Not sure that's a good idea."

I put my hands on my hips. "But doc didn't say no."

Judy narrowed her eyes. "First, prove you're okay. What's your name? Where are you? What day is it?"

I laughed, but answered the questions.

"Fine, but only one. And only a light beer." Larry retrieved a bottle of pale brew, opened it, and handed it over as I joined them at the table.

"What are y'all talking about?"

"Not much of anything." Judy shrugged.

She looked guilty to me, but I didn't say anything.

Larry fished in his pocket. "Here."

"My phone!" I eagerly grabbed it and flipped it into the photo library. "Look! I've got lots of pictures from inside the van."

"You got in their van while they were there?" Larry glared. "Are you kidding me?"

"Did they catch you?" Judy asked.

"Were you fleeing when you had your accident?" Larry added.

"I don't know. But at least I've got lots of evidence, some of which might help solve this damn case."

I downloaded all the photos and printed them out. The three of us studied each page, trying to make sense of what it meant.

"Looks like the insurance form and gas receipts won't help." Judy frowned.

"Not as much as I wish. But it does show me that Ballerton is at least connected enough to let these guys use the van while still covering the costs himself."

"Good point." Larry shuffled the other pages. "Lots of drone-related stuff. Enough parts to open a drone store."

"Yeah. Guess they wanted to be prepared for anything."

"What's that?" Judy pointed to a picture of a small rectangular box.

I picked it up and studied it. A brief flash of memory popped into my head. "This was in that Pelican box." I pointed to another print. "Very well protected. I can't tell what it does, though."

"May I?" Judy reached for the photo. "Looks like it has one small switch."

"Hang on." I hurried to the bathroom and returned with a magnifying glass. "You're right. It's a simple on/off type switch. No other markings that I can see."

"Print me out another copy." Larry stood. "I'll take it to Dr. Ramsey. Maybe it's related to the neuromorphic chip."

After Larry left, with a promise to call as soon as he'd talked to Dr. Ramsey, Judy and I retired to the living room and the comfort of overstuffed furniture and fluffy cats scattered around.

We chatted for a while, but I was restless. I'd finally caught up on sleep, and the evidence spread on printer paper across my kitchen table had me distracted.

I glanced at the time on my phone. Just after eight. It would be fully dark outside. October nights came early.

"I can see you fidgeting over there." Judy frowned. "Do you feel all right? Are you in pain? What's up?"

"I'm fine."

"I can see that you're not. Time to answer the questions." Judy asked me the same three questions she'd been asking all day. I answered, only half paying attention.

"It's not Saturday." Judy stood and sat on the arm of the sofa so she could feel my forehead.

Biting my lip, I debated telling Judy about my idea. But I had no choice. At the moment she thought something was physically wrong with me. Plus, she was watching me like a hawk, not to mention that my car was totaled.

"I want to go to Ballerton's. I want to see what's in his office."

"You said there's that guy there every day. What'd you call him?"

"Counter Boy. And I mean tonight. Now."

"Are you crazy?" Judy put her hand to her chest.

"Maybe. But please, Judy. I can't just sit here." I gave her my best pouty look. "I'm so close to solving this case. If you don't want to go, you can stay here. I'll call a cab."

"Like hell you will!" Judy stood. "Fine. I know you. If I don't go, you WILL go without me. Let me change. Got anything appropriate? I don't think my pink *Scuba Maui* T-shirt will fit the bill."

I tried to bound off the sofa, but my stiff, sore body balked. I stood slowly, still wincing at the pain movement caused.

"I see that." Judy frowned.

"I'm just sore. I'd be this same sore if I'd started going back to the gym."

Judy shot me a piercing look. "Don't even."

Thirty minutes later, we were both dressed in black clothes and heading south in Judy's car.

"I've never worn Stealthy-PI-Mode clothes before." Judy laughed, then frowned and shook her head. "I can't believe I let you talk me into this."

I'd known her a long time—the twitch at the corner of her lip meant she was a little excited about what we were doing, no matter what she said.

As if reading my mind, she asked. "So what are we doing?"

"We're going to slip into the Ballerton building and see what we can find."

"In other words, we're going to do some breaking and entering."

"Well…yeah."

Judy shook her head. "Some day, when we're be old and feeble, we'll be laughing at the exploits of our youth…sort of youth. I just hope I look back on tonight from the comfort of a nursing home, and not a jail cell."

"You and me both." I shrugged. "Take the next exit. We're almost there."

THE KEY TO IT ALL

*If we knew what it was we were doing, it
would not be called research, would it?
~Albert Einstein (1879-1955)*

"Where should I park?" Judy asked when we reached Ballerton's warehouse. Ballerton's might be closed for the night, but from the number of cars in the shared parking lot, the Deluxe Tasty Food Supply company operated late shifts.

I pointed to the lot. "There. Near the back. The shadows are thicker, and because the streetlights barely reach."

I opened the passenger door, but Judy shook her head. "Unh uh. Not until you answer the questions."

"What questions?"

Judy rolled her eyes. "THOSE questions. Come on. Name, location, date."

"Now?" I sighed.

"Especially now. If we're going to do something stupid, I want to be sure it's your usual level of crazy and not because your brain's scrambled."

"Fair enough." I sat up straight and put my hands flat on my lap, imagining I was at my old desk from my grade school years. "My name is Marianna Morgan. The date is Friday, two days after the two jerks caused me to total my car. The location is the Ballerton warehouse, where I hope to finally find out what those same jerks have been up to and to solve this case."

Judy laughed. "Close enough."

We exited the car and Judy looked around. "How are we going to get in without being seen?"

I grinned. "We aren't going to worry about it. We're going to do the *High Anxiety* thing."

"The what?"

"There's a scene from that old Mel Brooks movie. He and Madeline Kahn are fugitives and have to make it through airport security. She's afraid of being seen, but he says that you have to be loud and annoying, because then people ignore you. So they staged a big fight about some trivial family issue, and everyone turned away and ignored them, including security."

Judy narrowed her eyes. "So we're going to be loud and annoying?"

"Okay, we're not going to be exactly like *High Anxiety*, but we are going to just walk to the door like we belong there. Anyone driving by will see us all confident and self-assured and assume we have every right to do what we're doing."

"If you say so." Judy shrugged. "Lead on, Macduff."

I squared my shoulders, and strode—with more confidence than I felt—to Ballerton's front entrance. Judy shadowed close behind.

When we stopped at the door, she whispered, "Now what? We don't exactly have a key."

"Close enough." I held up my lock pick. "I can make it look like I'm fumbling with my key."

"Yeesh. Some day you're going to get us arrested."

I grinned. "But hopefully not today." I inserted the pick and worked on the lock. Just as I felt the final pin give, the pick broke off in my hand. "Aw, dammit!"

"What?" Judy's voice sounded a touch panicked.

"Don't worry. Nothing too serious. My lock pick broke. But I got the door open. You stay out here while I go in and look around."

"Oh, hell no." Judy shook her head.

I put my hands on my hips. "Look, I shouldn't have even made you bring me. I'm not going to get you arrested or hurt."

"First, you didn't make me bring you." Judy pointed at me.

I flashed her *the look.*

"Well, okay, maybe you were a bit…persuasive, but I still could have said no. And second, there's no way I'm letting you go in there alone. We're in this together."

I hugged my friend. "I don't know what I'd do without you. Thanks."

We entered the dark lobby so close together we'd probably have cast a single shadow.

"Where do you want to start?" Judy looked around the dim space.

I sighed. "I want to start in the back warehouse area, where the guys took the drone, but now I have no lock pick. So let's start in the office and search for a key."

"Do we turn on the lights?" Judy whispered.

I shook my head. "Probably best not to push our luck." I closed the entry door after one final glance at the lock with my broken pick stuck inside, then turned right and shuffled across the dark room, mindful of the scattered chairs I'd seen on my last visit.

When I reached the door with Ballerton's name printed on it, I was pleased when the knob easily turned and the door clicked open.

"Jackpot!" I grinned at Judy. I might have been able to kick or force it, since it looked like a hollow-core, interior door, and the doorknob sported a simple twist-lock, but was glad I didn't have to, especially in my post-crash, battered state.

After closing the door behind us, I turned on my red penlight and shined it around. Luckily, the room had no windows.

"Looks like we can use the lights in here." I flipped the switch and we both blinked and squinted as our eyes adjusted to the sudden fluorescent onslaught.

I waved toward a four-drawer file cabinet on the far wall. "You look through the files, and I'll search the desk."

"What are we looking for?"

"A warehouse key, of course, but also anything that ties Thomas Ballerton to the two men and that van."

We searched for ten minutes, only the sound of shuffling papers and drawers opening and closing broke the silence.

Judy stood and kicked the bottom file drawer closed. "That's it. I got nothing."

I held up a blue pressboard report folder I'd just found in the bottom left drawer. "Check this out." I flipped the folder open on Ballerton's desk.

We almost bumped heads as we leaned in for a closer look.

"Is that what I think it is?" Judy asked.

My heart rate quickened with excitement. "Yep. It's a lease agreement for the back half of the building. Lessees are Dr. Phil Walters and Dr. Wayne Briden." I shook my head. "I know those names, but I can't remember from where."

"It'll come to you."

I used my phone to take pictures of the three-page agreement. "I'll look them up later, if I don't remember before then."

Judy straightened up. "Think about it while I run to the bathroom. Where is it?"

"Across the lobby, but do you really have to go to the bathroom now?"

Judy shrugged and opened the door. "All this sneaking around has me nervous, and my digestive system doesn't like it when I'm nervous."

"Okay, but be careful. There's chairs scattered around the lobby." I waved my hand toward the desk. "I have one last drawer to search, anyway. If the warehouse key isn't in there, I don't know what to do."

As soon as Judy left, I turned my focus to the cluttered contents of the bottom right drawer. My disappointment was palpable as I rooted through the pens, paperclips, Post-it notes, scissors, and other office miscellanea. I was about to give up when my hand felt a small, metal box at the back of the drawer. I pulled it out and opened it, then squealed. The box was full of keys, all neatly labeled with paper key tags. And sure enough, one said: WAREHOUSE.

A shuffling sound from the lobby registered just as I pocketed the key. "Judy?"

The shuffling grew louder. I stood, pulling my gun from its holster on my waist. I eased around the desk, turned off the light, and placed my ear to the door. I could hear muffled voices, but could tell nothing other than one was female, the other male. *Who's out there with Judy?*

Before I could react, the door jerked open and Judy was shoved in. She landed against me, and we both fell back. I cracked my hip hard on the corner of Ballerton's desk. Judy rolled sideways and went down with a grunt. Then silence.

Fresh pain shot through my already bruised body. My eyes teared up. My head spun. I gripped the desk to keep from falling. A figure loomed before me, but I couldn't focus clearly enough to see any features.

"Who are you?" I panted the words, thanks to the searing pain from my hip. I forced my breathing to slow so I wouldn't faint.

"Who the hell are YOU?" The man stepped forward and shoved me with his left hand. The dim light filtering through the lobby from the street was enough to show his right hand held a gun. I fell on top of Judy, who uttered another grunt. I couldn't tell if she was conscious or if the sound was simply from air escaping her unconscious body.

I gritted my teeth from the pain. *Is my hip broken?* I was afraid to move. I turned and looked at the silhouette, wishing I'd left the office light on.

As if reading my mind, the man switched the lights back on. "Get up. Now." He pointed the gun at my head.

Do I dare get up? What if I can't? I had no choice but to try. I flailed like a turtle on its back then rolled sideways and used the desk to awkwardly pull myself to my feet. I bent to retrieve my gun, but the man kicked it away.

He pointed at a rickety-looking, wooden chair by the file cabinet Judy had searched. "You. Sit."

I hobbled to the chair and sat, all the while scanning the room for anything that would help me fight back. I also took a minute to study the man. He look to be in his late forties with a bit of spread around his middle. His hair was salt and pepper. He wasn't much taller than me, maybe five eight.

I glanced again at Judy. Her face was toward me, away from the man. Her eyes were closed, her slow breathing indicating she was probably unconscious. I hoped she was safer that way.

Why the hell did I make her come? Stupid. Stupid. Stupid. I pleaded to the universe, *Please don't let anything else happen to her.*

My eyes finally adjusted to the bright light, and I turned toward the man, who stood staring at me with piercing eyes.

"We haven't done anything to you. Just let us leave." I doubted it would work, but it was worth a shot.

"Fat chance. Why'd you come back here, anyway?"

Back here? So he must be one of the men I watched carry a drone through the back door. And then they followed me as I drove away. I looked at Judy again. This time, her eyes were open.

She winked at me but didn't move.

Oh thank the gods that she's okay. I didn't dare wink back, because the guy with the gun was looking straight at me.

He stepped toward me, skirting around Judy's legs, but she kicked out. The man tripped. He fell to the left. His gun flew right. I dove for the gun, yelping from pain in the process. But I got it. The pain didn't matter.

I pointed the gun at the prone man, who was moaning and holding his head. Blood trickled from a gash on his left temple where he'd hit his head on a bookcase as he fell.

"Don't even think of moving." I almost spat the words. "I'm pissed, and I hurt. I might even be pre-menstrual. Do not mess with me."

Judy sat up, rubbing her head. "Are you okay?"

"I don't know. My hip may be broken." I had to ignore the waves of pain. At least for now. "How are you?"

Judy slowly stood. "I think I'm fine. No harm done other than maybe a bruise or two that'll show up later."

I smiled. "Best news I've heard lately. Can you give me a hand? There's duct tape in the bottom right drawer. Let's get him into a chair and tape him up. Roll Ballerton's desk chair around here. The one this guy made me sit in isn't sturdy enough."

Judy bound the man's hands while he was still on the ground, then we dragged him to the chair. Good thing Judy was strong from years of scuba diving and gym classes. My hip was barely supporting my own weight, let alone the weight of a full-grown man. But Judy managed to wrestle him alone into the rolling chair while I did my best to hold it still. We used the rest of the tape to bind him to the chair.

I retrieved my gun from under Ballerton's desk and handed the man's gun to Judy. We stood on either side of him. I pointed my gun and Judy pointed his. It was overkill, but it definitely got his attention.

"What do you want? Why did you come back here?" He tried to sound angry, but I could hear the fear in his voice.

"Back here?" Judy looked at me, her head cocked.

I nodded. "This is one of the men I watched the other night. Before my accident." Checking the photos I took of the lease agreement, I continued, "So, are you Dr. Phil Walters or Dr. Wayne Briden?"

He started at the mention of the names. "Who told you? How do you know us?"

"First, answer her question." Judy waved the gun. She seemed to be enjoying this.

The man's shoulders slumped. "I'm Walters."

I nodded. "Okay, Walters, what are you doing here?"

"I lease space from my uncle. I have every right to be here." He glared. "What are YOU doing here?"

So Thomas Ballerton is the uncle. No wonder he loaned them a van and even payed the insurance. "What have you been doing with that drone? Why are you killing Bubba's cows? And what about me? Did you put that thing in my brain?"

"I...we..." Walters shook his head. "I'm not answering. You can call the cops or do whatever you want." His mouth twisted into a smirk. "I don't believe either of you will shoot me. I don't even think you'll call the cops. Especially since you two are the ones who did the breaking and entering."

Damn. He has a point. I need to remember where else I know his name from.

"So what do you want to do with him?" Judy asked.

"Roll him out."

"What?" Judy cocked her head.

I grinned. "He's going to go with us to the warehouse. We'll all see what's back there together. He's conveniently tied to a rolling chair."

Judy uttered a nervous laugh. "You lead. I'll push."

We were crossing the lobby when someone else barged through the entry door. Oblivious to the pain in my hip, I spun, gun leveled and ready to fire.

"Whoa! Wait! Don't shoot." Larry's baritone voice boomed.

"Larry? What the heck are you doing here?" I holstered my gun and limped toward him.

"Judy called. And what's wrong with you?"

"I fell. Well, was pushed." I turned to Judy. "You called Larry?"

She bit her lip and nodded. "When I went to the bathroom. I was worried about us getting into trouble. I'm sorry."

"It's okay." I smiled. "I know you were nervous. I shouldn't have talked you into coming."

Larry looked around. "She said y'all had broken into Ballerton's. I didn't want to believe her, but here we all are."

"I had to know the truth." I shrugged. "I couldn't wait."

Larry pointed toward Walters, who'd sat silently, shoulders slumped, in the rolling chair. "Who the hell is that?"

"That is Dr. Phil Walters. He's one of the two men who've been using a drone on Bubba's cows." I blanched. "And me."

"Let me loose. You can't do anything to me." Walters' voice shook as he spoke. He might be some type of doctor, but he apparently wasn't a brave one.

"Not a chance, buddy." Larry grinned at me. "I'm impressed that you two got him into this position. What's your plan?"

"We're going to search the back of the building." I pointed to the door behind the counter. "Through that storage area. I want to see what's back there besides the drone Walters and his partner carted in the other night."

"I'll text Patrick. Tell him what we're doing." Larry pulled his phone from his pocket.

"Patrick's here, too?" My mouth fell open. "Where is he?"

Larry made a twisted grin. "He wouldn't come inside. Said if he was caught cooperating with a breaking and entering, he could be kicked off the force. Or worse."

"Good grief." I rolled my eyes. "But I see it didn't stop you."

"I've known you longer. We've been through more crap together." Larry winked. "Or maybe I'm just braver."

"Or more reckless." Judy laughed.

"Anyway, where is Patrick?" I asked.

"He said he was going to walk the building perimeter and make sure everything else was safe and secure."

"Okay then. Let's go." I limped across the room.

"You okay? You said you were pushed." Larry turned and glared at Walters.

"Ballerton's desk and I had a little encounter." I shrugged. "The desk won. I'll be okay."

"You always say that." Larry shook his head. "Once in a while it's actually true."

We circled the counter, maneuvered around the center shelves in the storage area, and paused at the door to the warehouse.

"Don't ask for my help." Sarcasm and stress wove through the captive doctor's words.

I held up the key. "Don't worry. I don't need it."

Walters frowned, and his eyes shifted as if looking for an escape.

I inserted the key and pushed the door open with much less bravado than I felt. What I felt was a cold dread. *Do I really want to know what's back here? Maybe not, but I owe it to Bubba. And his cows.*

BEHIND CLOSED DOORS

*When in doubt, have two guys come through
the door with guns.*
~Raymond Chandler (1888-1959)

"You gonna just stand there?" Larry's words, and a poke in the back, urged me forward.

Why am I so nervous? I'm finally going to solve this case. But inside, my nerves were crawling. *What else am I going to learn?*

I pulled my gun from its holster and motioned Larry to do the same. "Better safe than sorry."

Larry narrowed his eyes at me, then nodded. "Yeah."

Larry and I moved into the dark hallway, followed by Judy and her chair-bound captive.

I reached through the door and felt along the wall on both sides, then turned to Dr. Walters. "Where's the light switch?"

When he didn't answer, I continued, "Fine. I've got a flashlight, but Judy doesn't. If she runs your knees into walls a bunch of times, don't blame us."

Walters sighed. "Up high. On the right. My uncle's contractor was well over six feet tall. Liked things at *his* eye level."

I found the switch where Walters said. The entire warehouse ceiling lit up like a landing strip. "Guess they needed plenty of light when this was a manufacturing area."

"Yeah." Larry nodded.

The hallway, now bathed in light, had three doors on each side, with the door to the back parking lot at the far end.

"What are we looking for?" Judy waved toward the hallway. "Which door do we choose first?"

"Walters, you want to tell us?" I cocked my head and waited. He lowered his eyes and looked at the floor. I shrugged. "Guess we search every room in order, then."

Larry stepped around me and tried the first door on the right. It was locked. He solved that problem with one swift, hard kick. I scurried into the room. It was dark, thanks to an eight foot ceiling blocking the bright overhead lighting from the warehouse ceiling, twenty feet above us.

I switched on the light, illuminating a typical small office. Wood desk, rolling chair, and credenza with office supplies on the shelves and a printer centered on top.

I shrugged at Larry and holstered my gun. "Looks safe for now." He nodded and holstered his, too. We both studied the office more closely.

There was a scattering of personal elements around the room—a framed photo of a man, woman, and toddler on the credenza; a stained coffee mug that said *World's Greatest Dad* on the desk; a framed certificate on the wall.

I approached the certificate. It was a proclamation from the CEO of MicroTechGen, thanking Dr. Wayne Briden for his scientific contribution toward product development in the Nanofabrication Research and Technology division of the company.

I stepped back, head spinning in confusion. Where did I know that company name from? And Briden's and Walters' names?

Remembering held the key to everything, but try as I might, I couldn't pull up the memory.

I hope whatever these guys did to me hasn't left permanent brain damage. I just hope the memory will come to me. Maybe I need to let it go and not try to force it. I returned to the hallway and tried the door on the opposite side. It was also locked.

Before Larry could kick it in, Dr. Walters spoke up. "Please don't break my door. There's a key ring in my right pants pocket."

Judy fished around, apologizing for getting a bit familiar before finally retrieving the keys. She handed them to Larry.

Larry handed them to me. "You do the honors."

I unlocked the door and switched on the light. It was an almost identical office to Briden's, except the picture on the desk was of Walters alone on a fishing trip. And instead of a certificate on the wall, there was a framed group photo.

Crossing the room, I studied the photo. It clearly showed a group of professionals in some type of medical or scientific capacity. Everyone was wearing white lab coats. In the background was a two-story, brick building. I could only see the tops of a few letters, barely visible above everyone's heads, but it clearly said MicroTechGen.

So both Briden and Walters had worked for MicroTechGen. Who else did I know? The memory was stirring stronger. One face in the photo caught my attention and the memory rushed back with enough force to almost knock me down.

I spun, hurried back to the hallway, and pointed at Walters. "Bengy! You worked with Bengy."

"Who?" Walters looked sincerely confused.

I closed my eyes and forced the rest of the memory. "Dr. Winifred Polkson." I opened my eyes. "That's where you all met. That's why you had access to the hippies' land."

"The whosits' land?" Dr. Walters huffed. "Lady, I don't know what you are talking about. This has gone far enough. You better—"

Judy jerked on the chair, which startled Walters into shutting up.

Larry stepped in front of Walters and leaned down until he was inches from the man's face. He spoke each word slowly and distinctly. The resulting effect sounded as menacing as he likely intended. "I'd suggest you listen to Marianna and answer her questions."

Walters nodded, his eyes big.

Larry turned to me, bowed slightly, and made an *after you* gesture.

I stepped closer. "You, Bengy, and Briden all worked for MicroTechGen. Until a scandal where you were investigated for stealing proprietary technology."

"We—"

I held up my hand and continued. "The company was investigating the dynamics of decision-making and gambling, and how to use neuro…" I stumbled on the word, pausing to remember the National Institute of Health study I'd read and reread. "Magneto-thermal neurostimulation. You were experimenting on rat brains with neuromorphic chips to help control everything from decision-making to gambling addiction."

"They didn't see the potential." Walters shook his head, his voice barely a whisper. "They were blind to the possibilities."

"Possibilities?" Judy asked.

I nodded. "Those three pushed for more. When the company wouldn't go along, they started stealing proprietary technology. Somebody in the company grew suspicious and started the investigation I read about. No charges were filed, but Bengy chose to retire. Apparently you and Dr. Briden didn't stay either."

"They found nothing." Walters' voice was haughty, but fear caused the last word to hitch.

"That's because poor, innocent G.J. carried things out for you every time he and Earl had a service call there, which I'll bet you three managed to ensure was pretty often. Instead of HVAC garbage and used parts, G.J. carried out your bits and pieces. No one ever suspected the AC repair guys, and especially not G.J. and his simple mind."

"So what about the hippies?" Larry asked.

"And the cows?" Judy added.

I shrugged. "I don't know what order things happened in. Did the two doctors choose Bubba's particular herd of cows first, then look for the best way to access them? Or did Bengy, Earl, and G.J move onto Earl's cousin's land, then help look for nearby cows? Regardless, conveniently next door to the hippies—as I guess I'll always think of them—was Bubba's ranch and his Hereford cows. And equally convenient, no other nearby neighbors."

"Either way, they started experimenting on Bubba's cows." Judy frowned.

I nodded. "At least Walters and Briden did. I don't think Bengy had more to do with it than giving them access. But I'm sure she knew what they were doing. They might have even consulted with her. After all, she's got her own PhD in nanoscience."

"It was—" Before Walters could continue, the door at the far end of the hall banged open.

Everyone jerked their attention to the commotion. Patrick stumbled in from the back parking lot, his arm gripped by another man, who had a gun shoved against Patrick's side.

"Patrick!" I tried to run toward him, but Larry grabbed my arm.

"Don't." He shook his head. "That other dude's got a gun."

"So do we," I hissed.

"Don't start a shootout." Larry whispered. "It's too confined. Judy has no training. Wait."

I stood, frozen in place, as the two men approached.

"I'm sorry, Marianna." Patrick shook his head "He came out of nowhere and attacked me from behind. Whacked me on the head with something. Probably his gun. Knocked me out for a few minutes."

"It's okay. He probably hid in the same shrubs where I did."

"What the hell?" the man with the gun said, pointing at Walters. "Why are you taped up?" He waved the gun at Judy. "You cut him loose right now."

"I...I don't have any scissors." Judy's voice and hands both shook.

The man rolled his eyes and stepped toward Judy, dragging Patrick with him. "Give me the gun." She reluctantly handed over Briden's gun and stepped back, head bowed. He pocketed Briden's gun, but kept his own pointed at Judy's head as he looked at me and Larry. "Both of yours, too. On the floor at Walters' feet."

I briefly debated going for mine and shooting him, but the likelihood was that he'd shoot Judy before I had time to fire. I glanced at Larry. His eyes were narrowed, and I knew he was having the same internal debate I'd had. He glanced at me, and I shook my head. He sighed and nodded.

We both did as ordered, laying our guns at the foot of the rolling chair. The man kicked them down the hall. They slid through the open door into the storage area, stopping under the center shelves I'd hidden behind—what seemed like a year ago.

Pointing the gun our direction, the man said, "All three of you, against the wall. Hands nice and loose at your sides."

I glanced at Judy, who was visibly shaking, and stepped against the wall. Both men hesitated.

"NOW!"

Their faces full of fury, Larry and Patrick took positions on either side of me.

The man nodded and fished a knife from his pocket. His gun wavered as he dug around in his pants. Larry made a move forward and the guy jerked to attention, gun again pointed at Judy's head. "Don't."

Larry stepped back.

I could see Larry's hands clenching and unclenching. I had no doubt he was debating something brave, stupid, or both. I caught his eye again, and again shook my head. We'd find a way, but now wasn't it.

"You're Dr. Wayne Briden." It wasn't a question. I already knew. He was much taller and slimmer than Briden, probably six feet, with greying hair and scruffy beard. Even with the grey hair, I'd still guess him at mid forties.

Briden continued removing Walters' bindings. "So?"

"So…you two have been killing Bubba's cows for weeks now. And you kidnapped me. Then you inserted something in the back of my brain. Why?"

Walters stood, rubbing his wrists, which had sticky bits of tape residue on them. "You wouldn't understand."

"Try us." Patrick leaned casually against the wall, but his eyes shifted and his jaw pulsed. He was looking for options, too.

Briden ignored Patrick's statement. He pointed his gun at Judy and grabbed her upper arm. She winced at the tight squeeze. "Let's go."

Briden handed Walters' gun back to him. He promptly pointed it at me. "What are we going to do with them?" Walters asked. "We can't shoot them. We can't let them go."

"Well…in the movies they tie them up." Briden nodded his head toward Larry. "Like this guy did to you."

Larry smirked. "I got here late. The women took care of your friend."

Patrick chuckled, drawing glares from Walters and Briden.

I sensed the two doctors were out of their league. They were scientists, perhaps brilliant ones, but they weren't thugs. They spent their days looking at microcircuits. I'd bet the most active they got was messing around with the drone. We could use that to our advantage. I tried to catch Patrick's or Larry's eye, but both were staring at the other men.

Walters and Briden exchanged a look and Walters grinned. "I have the perfect idea. We've talked about needing more detailed trials."

"You're right." Briden nodded. "And here are four who all but fell into our laps."

"What do you mean? What trials?" Judy's voice shook with fear.

Walters pulled his keys from the doorknob of his office, then waved his gun at me. "This way everyone. Next door down on your right."

Briden led the way with Judy clutched beside him. She looked stiff with fear. He almost had to drag her.

The doctors were outnumbered, but they had the guns. Maybe we should have done more not to give up our own guns, but we were all keenly aware of our responsibility to Judy.

We reluctantly followed Briden. Walters took up the rear, tossing the keys to Briden when we reached the door. Briden unlocked it and the two men pushed us into the room.

EXPERIMENTS AND RESEARCH

Our observation of nature must be diligent,
our reflection profound, and our experiments
exact. We rarely see these three means
combined; and for this reason, creative
geniuses are not common.
~Denis Diderot (1713-1784)

As soon as Walters turned on the lights, I knew where I was, and the realization sent a wave of abject fear through my body. I grabbed Larry's arm to keep from crumpling to the floor.

I felt Larry's bicep tense in my grasp. "You okay?" I could hear the concern in his voice.

"Yes. No. I don't know." I took a couple of deep breaths to steady myself, released Larry's arm, and did my best to study the room with detached curiosity.

In the center of the room was a steel surgical table with a bright spotlight directly overhead. Against one wall was a row of tall, metal cabinets with their doors closed. On the opposite wall was a large, commercial freezer.

The freezer's thrum-thrum sound pulsed through my brain. *That's the sound I heard coming from behind me when I woke up lying on this very table after my abduction. I was afraid I'd fall off if I moved while my feet and arms were bound.*

Fear turned to fury. I ignored the pain in my hip and spun, launching into a diatribe. "You had me here. This is where you inserted that…that…thing in my brain."

Both men stared, mouths agape and eyes wide. "You weren't supposed to remember," Walters stammered.

"But I do." With a primal scream of absolute rage, I lunged at him like a football tackle, hitting him square in the chest. His gun flew across the room, banging against one of the cabinets. He fell back against the table, grunted, and slid to the floor. I jumped on top of him and pounded him on the chest, yelling "How dare you!" over and over.

Larry took advantage of the chaos and dove for Briden. The two men went down in a heap on the floor. Only Larry stood back up. Briden was out cold.

Patrick ran to me and pulled me off of Walters. "Easy now. Don't kill him. It'll be okay. He'll get what's coming to him."

Judy hurried over and stood beside me. "Don't faint. You look like a diver about to have an embolism."

"My hip." The rush of anger and adrenalin had briefly dulled the pain, but it now returned with a vengeance.

Larry disappeared then quickly returned with the rolling chair from the hallway. "Here, sit." He, Judy, and Patrick eased me into it.

Walters lay on the floor, moaning. Briden lay a few feet away, silent, but starting to stir.

While I calmed myself down and caught my breath, Larry and Patrick rooted through the cabinets, the only things I'd been able to see through my loose blindfold when I'd been the doctors' captive. And guinea pig.

Patrick found a roll of gauze wrap, which he and Judy used to bind the men to opposite sides of the surgical table's pedestal base.

Larry kept rooting around. "Look what I found." He handed me a large specimen cup. In it was a good two or three dozen neuromorphic chips like the one that Dr. Welch had removed from me.

I stared at the small chips. They looked like black rice grains. Rolling my chair over to where the doctors sat on the floor, I glared at each in turn. I shook the capped cup like a rattle. "What were you doing? What's the purpose of these chips?"

Both men stared down. Neither spoke. Their bravado gone.

"I think I can answer that." Judy held up a binder she'd found in one cabinet. She opened it and read the title. *A non-linear regression and deterministic analysis of in situ data sets involving the in vivo implantation of neurologic behavior modification hardware in the medulla oblangata of* Bos taurus *as an anamorphic similogue for the human warfighter: Findings and challenges of electrically-induced realtime behaviour modification* (Walters et Briden)."

"What the hell does that mean?" I kicked Walden's foot. "Answer me now. In English."

Walden's mumble was too low to hear.

"ANSWER ME!" I stood, clenching and unclenching my fists. The throbbing in my hip exponentially increased my anger with each movement.

"It means we were researching cows' brains as a test to see if the chips could control combat behavior and response in soldiers."

"You were going to put these in our soldiers' brains?" Judy's mouth gaped open.

"You wanted to create robot soldiers?" Larry's voice had that brittle edge I recognized as a sign he was about to lose it. I didn't care. These guys needed a good ass-kicking, and I was in no shape to do it myself. But Larry, to his credit, I guess, stayed still. Only the veins in his neck and temples belied his inner rage.

"No, not robots." Briden's voice was haughty. "Just more efficient. More synchronized."

"Damn dancing cows." I shook my head.

"Huh?" Patrick asked.

"Remember, that's what they were doing out there every night. Getting all the cows to moo and stomp their feet in sync was a test to see if they could force soldiers into synchronized behavior against their will."

"Mindless killing machines." Larry shook his head. "No worries about combat training or teaching them to follow orders. Just plug a chip in their brains and control them all with one joystick."

"But cows died, didn't they?" Judy's eyes were huge, her mouth gaped open.

"Yes." I sat back down to give my exhausted and battered body a break. I'd moved around enough I was sure the hip wasn't broken, but it was badly bruised, and my actions were probably making things worse I swiveled to face Walters. "You killed a cow every time. Except Mooami."

"Mooami?" Briden asked. "What the hell is a Mooami?"

"She's not a *what*." Now *my* voice was brittle. "She's a cow. And she's the only one of Bubba's cows that lived after she fell unconscious."

Larry stepped toward the men. "Why? What changed?"

Walters shrugged. "Every test trial was different. We refined. Improved. Upgraded."

"How'd you even get the chips into the cows in the first place?" Patrick asked.

"With this. I'll bet." Judy pulled something from another of the cabinets and held it up. It looked like a cross between a blow dart gun and a pistol."

Walters nodded, his pride at their accomplishments seemingly overtook his fear at his current predicament. "We were very good with the drone. We could position the chip-deployer directly over any cow we chose."

"Is that what you did to me?" My mouth fell open. "You shot me in the back of the neck?"

Briden actually rolled his eyes. It took all my willpower not to kick him in the face. "Of course not. We had you here in our lab. We made a micro-incision and inserted the chip. You weren't actually harmed."

"Not harmed? NOT HARMED!" I jumped to my feet again, gritting my teeth against my hip pain. "You kept me for days, yet I barely remember a thing. How many times did you turn on that chip? How many times did you make me stomp my feet and do what you wanted?" I plopped back down, shoulders slumped. In a near-whisper, I added, "At least you didn't cut off my head."

"You mean like the cows?" Judy asked.

I nodded.

"What about the cows? What do you mean cut off your head?" Patrick asked.

"I told you about that. These two cut off all the heads of the cows that died." I shook my head. "And left the rest of the poor cows to rot in the field."

"Oh, yeah, that's right." Patrick nodded. "The dumpster heads."

"So what about the heads?" Larry turned to Patrick. "Dumpster heads?"

A sudden chill washed through me like a tidal wave. I looked at the freezer against the wall, then at the surgical table. "No. Oh, no. Tell me you didn't put me on the same table where you dissected cow heads."

Both men bit their lips and stared at the far wall.

I limp-stomped to the freezer and jerked it open. Staring out at me was the head of Mr. T, Bubba's one and only bull. I may—mostly —be a tough girl, but that was the final straw on a couple of days that had drained me of all resources. I felt my legs buckle and my vision blur. Before I actually fell, Patrick was behind me with his hands under my arms.

"Woah! Easy now." He guided me around the table. "Let's get you back into the chair."

I put my head between my knees until the lightheadedness passed, then sat up. "It's pretty obvious you were removing Bubba's cows' heads to see what damage your chips were doing to their brains. Then you tossed the brainless heads in a dumpster. Patrick and I learned that a week ago at the Austin Alien Encounter Meetup." I felt the blood drain from my head again. "You were leaving them in the dumpster next to this building, weren't you?"

Briden nodded.

"I noticed it seemed extra ripe when I hid behind it the other day."

"Hid behind it? Why?" Patrick frowned.

"Never mind." I shook my head at Patrick, then returned my attention to the men. "How did you get such clean, surgical cuts?"

When the men didn't answer, Larry said, "Want me to rip everything out of these cabinets, looking for the answer?"

Walters sighed. "We used a prototype, hand-held laser cutter."

"Hand-held laser powerful enough to cut through bone?" Patrick shook his head. "What could possibly go wrong?"

"How did you know that damn chip wouldn't kill Marianna or give her brain damage?" Larry glared down at the doctors.

Walters bit his lip and said nothing.

"We were pretty sure it'd be okay." Briden's voice had a whiney tone. "It was our newest design."

I smirked. "The arrogance of scientists. Read an article about it a couple months ago."

"We knew what we were doing." Walters raised his chin.

I pointed to the freezer. "Tell that to Mr. T. Or all the cows that had no names."

"Why didn't you just propose the idea to the military?" Patrick shook his head in confusion. "Why all this cloak and dagger? Why kidnap Marianna?"

Briden shrugged. "We talked to them, but they weren't interested without a proof of concept. That's what we were working on."

"We weren't trying to hurt anyone. Not even your client's cows. And certainly not you." Walters looked up at me with pleading eyes. "We were just trying to... Hey, what's that?"

"What?" Briden and Larry asked simultaneously.

"Under the table. There." Walters used his chin to point, since his hands were bound.

Patrick squatted down to see what Walters meant. "Well, look here." He held up a small black square about half the size of a book of matches.

"What is that?" Judy squinted and frowned.

Larry answered what I was thinking. "It's a listening device." He laughed and slapped the table, causing Walters and Briden to jump. "Y'all are being bugged."

"How dare someone spy on us!" Briden clipped the words in anger.

I laughed so hard I got a side cramp. "What's good for the goose, assholes. You can dish out your covert crap, but you can't take it."

"Who could have put that there?" Walters asked no one in particular. "We always kept this room locked."

"Well, Thomas Ballerton had a key." I shrugged. "That's how we got back here."

"He wouldn't have done this." Briden's voice shook slightly, clearly disconcerted at the discovery.

Patrick pocketed the bug. "Whoever it was probably knows everything, including what you did to Marianna."

"That's right." Larry nodded. "So when we take you two in for questioning, I'd suggest you leave any mention of Marianna and Judy's breaking and entering out of your statements. Perhaps you invited them to meet you here. How's that sound?"

"So you're taking them in?" Judy set the chip-deployment gun on the table and circled to stare down at the two men.

"I'm off duty, but I'll call it in." Larry waggled his phone.

"Wait." I held up my hand. "My broken lock pick is still in the door."

"Not for long." Patrick smiled. "I'll take care of that."

"You?" I raised my eyebrows. "Tamper with a scene? You wouldn't even come inside earlier."

Patrick hung his head. "Yeah, I know. But I'm not going to let you get arrested. You've been through enough." He kissed my cheek and headed for the hallway.

He was back within a few minutes. "Pick is in my pocket. Front door is locked."

"Thanks." I smiled.

Before Patrick could cross the room to where I sat, six men suddenly burst in. All wore identical dark grey suits. All had large handguns. None looked friendly. The biggest of the bunch pointed his gun our direction. "Nobody move."

"Who the hell are you?" Patrick straightened his shoulders and squared his jaw.

"Never mind." One of the men crossed to Briden and Walters. "You two are coming with us."

"Not so fast." Larry held up his hand. "I'm a detective with the Austin Police Department. These men are under arrest."

One of the suited men cracked a smile that lasted just seconds. "Not today, Detective Morrow."

Larry stepped forward. "How do you know my name? I want to see some ID."

A different suited man moved toward Larry. "We know all of your names. We aren't obligated to show you ID. You're illegally on this property."

Patrick joined Larry. "You have no right to do this. I'm also in law enforcement. I'm a deputy with the Williamson County Sheriff's Department. These men are in our custody."

The suited man who had held back by the door stepped forward. "I don't think so, Patrick."

Patrick's mouth fell open. "Jack? What are you doing here? What's going on?"

"Who the hell is Jack?" Larry asked.

"He used to be FBI." Patrick shook his head. "We ran into him at the Alien Encounter Meetup. He wouldn't say what he's been doing since leaving the FBI. Guess now I know why."

"Please, Jack." I hoped sweetness and politeness might work. "Tell me who y'all are. These men kidnapped me. They implanted something in my brain. They experimented on my clients' cows. They killed some of them."

Jack walked over and squatted next to me. His voice was soft. "We know all that, but I can't answer your questions. I will tell you that I'm sorry about you and the cows. We couldn't do anything sooner."

I narrowed my eyes. "Couldn't, or wouldn't?"

He straightened up before he answered. The softness was gone from his voice. "I'll take that." He grabbed the specimen cup containing the neuromorphic chips from my hand. I'd almost forgotten I was still holding it. He then turned to Patrick. "Sorry Patrick, I need the bug back."

"I don't know what happened to it." Patrick pursed his lips.

"Want us to search all your pockets?" One of the other men stepped toward Patrick.

Patrick sighed, reached into his pants pocket, and handed the bug to Jack, who put it in his own pocket, then pointed to Walters and Briden. "And the cutter? Where's it located?"

Briden, facing the floor in defeat, mumbled, "Second cabinet from the left."

Another of the men retrieved the laser cutter from the cabinet, then grabbed the chip-deployer gun and the binder Judy'd placed on the exam table.

"Let's go." The man who had cut Walters and Briden loose stood and straightened his jacket.

Briden and Walters were each joined by one of the men, holding guns in the two doctors' backs. The doctors eyes were large, their faces white with fear. Neither spoke as they were escorted out.

Two of the remaining men took up positions on either side of the door. Jack and one of the other men held out their hands. "We'll take your guns," Jack said.

None of us moved. The man standing next to Jack spoke, his tone cold and hard. "All of them. Now."

We complied, handing over our own guns as well as the guns we'd taken from Briden and Walters.

Jack and his cohort who'd collected the guns left without another word. After they were gone, one of the men who'd guarded the door spoke. "I'd suggest you four leave now. Take nothing. Touch nothing. None of this concerns you. And tell no one. Understand?"

"Doesn't concern—" Before I could finish, Larry squeezed my arm and shook his head. I had to bite my lip to remain quiet.

"We understand." Judy's voice was barely above a whisper.

None of us said another word for a full minute after the men and the doctors left.

"What the hell just happened?" Judy's voice cracked.

I shook my head. "I'm assuming that's who's been monitoring the doctors' progress."

"But who is it?" Patrick frowned. "What the hell is Jack a part of?"

Larry shrugged. "Some kind of feds. Maybe military. Or a black project. We'll probably never know."

I stood and glanced around the room. "At least I should be safe now. So should Bubba's cows. No more experiments on any of us."

"I sure hope not." Patrick put his arm around my waist. "C'mon. Time to get out of here."

Larry nodded. "We should go out the back. Don't want to attract any more attention tonight."

We moved together down the hall. As we passed the last door on the left I froze. Everyone stopped with me.

"What is it?" Judy squeezed my hand."What's wrong?"

I couldn't speak. I stared at the small sliding panel cut into the bottom of the regular door.

Patrick reached out, but I grabbed his arm. "Don't open it. Please."

He nodded and dropped his hand.

I might never remember what had happened to me while I was captive here and at the mercy of the doctors' experiments, but part of me recognized that small sliding panel. It was where a little rolling dolly had delivered food, water, and a bucket of some type. I didn't want to ever see the inside of that room again.

"Let's go." I forced myself to look away. "Time to get my life back. Time to move on. Time to get the hell out of here."

INTO THE SUNSET

This is the time to put all bad memories
behind you and look forward into the New
Year with nothing but good things to come.
~Nishan Panwar (1989-)

I spent the weekend curled up on the sofa with ice on my ever-purpling hip. I did my best to move as little as possible. The cats did their best to walk across it half a dozen times a day. Each.

I called Bubba to fill him in. At first, he didn't believe me. When I finally convinced him I was telling the truth, and the six men in suits really had shown up, he grew worried. "You sure it's all over? The gubment, or whoever they was, won't keep at it, or let them two doctors start up again?"

I wasn't completely sure, but I was pretty confident. "Your cows are going to be fine now. You can have your vet remove the chips or just leave them there. With no device to activate them, they can't control your cows ever again." And for all I knew, the *gubment* agents had already removed the chips, or soon would. Bubba would likely never know.

"Allrighty, Marianna. You get down here to see me soon as you're able."

"I promise. Tell Mooami I said hi."

I heard Bubba chuckling as he hung up.

The rest of the weekend was filled with kitty cuddles and calls from Judy, Larry, and Patrick, all making sure I was okay. One of them must have contacted Aunt Louise, because she phoned Saturday evening. After reassuring her I was going to be just fine, I had to ask, "You haven't had anymore visions about me, have you?"

"No, dear. The spirits are quiet this week."

Thank goodness. I'm not sure I could take any more dire warnings.

Since I still had no car, first thing Monday morning Judy took me to see Dr. Welch. When he walked into the exam room at the hospital, his first question was, "How's your head?"

"My head is doing great." I laughed. "And Judy followed your instructions about the three questions so thoroughly I was ready to throttle her."

He winked at Judy. "Good for you." Pulling his pen light from his shirt pocket, he continued, "Let's check your pupils." He waved the light back and forth across my eyes, then stowed the light back in his pocket. He felt around on my neck. "Looks like you're good to go."

"Can you look at my hip?" I asked.

"Your hip?" Dr. Welch frowned. "I'm not an orthopedist. Besides, what happened to your hip?"

"I fell against a desk." I saw the look that crossed his face and quickly added, "It had nothing to do with my head. Someone shoved me, and I fell backwards."

Dr. Welch raised his eyebrows, but thankfully didn't ask about the shove. "Let's have a look. I'll have a nurse bring a gown."

Within minutes, my jeans were folded on the chair in the corner of the small room and I was wearing a paper gown that I tore twice while putting it on. I lay on my good side on the table. In spite of my best efforts, memories of that other metal table kept creeping into my head.

Dr. Welch poked and prodded on the hip. I gritted my teeth against the onslaught.

"It's definitely badly bruised, but doesn't appear broken."

I'd already guessed that much, but it was nice to get confirmation.

"Should I be doing, or not doing, anything special?" I asked.

"Just generally take it easy." Dr. Welch crossed his arms. "No big marathons, don't go bungee jumping or rock climbing."

I laughed. "No chance of that. I hate jogging. And I'm not big on putting my life on the line." *At least not for sport. Now, when I'm on a case…*

Dr. Welch nodded. "It's going to take a few weeks for all the bruising to go away. I'd still prefer you avoid any nonsteroidal anti-inflammatory medicine like ibuprofen because of your recent head injury. If you have too much pain or discomfort, take some acetaminophen. And if it gets worse, go see an orthopedist."

I thanked the doctor, then hurriedly dressed and joined Judy in the waiting area.

"Too late for breakfast?" she asked.

I glanced at my phone and shook my head. "It's only ten, and I'm starving. All I had this morning was a granola bar. Let's go to Kerbey Lane. After all I've been through, I need some comfort food. Nothing like some nice migas to warm the soul."

"And pad the thighs." Judy laughed. "But sure. Let's go."

Judy offered to take me car hunting, but I still wasn't sure what I wanted. "Rain check. I can ride Pancho Villa for a few days while I decide."

"You okay to ride a motorcycle?" Judy frowned.

"It's sore, but no serious damage."

Judy narrowed her eyes. "What did the doctor say?"

"He didn't say I couldn't." I shrugged. *That's not really a lie.*

"Right. I know that kind of answer from you." Judy shook her head. "You and your fact-dodging answers. Just promise you'll be careful."

"I promise."

Kerbey Lane wasn't crowded, and we spent a leisurely hour eating fresh, homestyle food while we chatted about scuba diving. I needed a break from talking about cows, aliens, feds, and all things creepy.

Within minutes after Judy dropped me back home, I'd changed into my riding clothes. I wheeled Pancho out of the garage and looked up at the clear autumn sky. *Lockhart's just an hour down the road. Perfect for a nice afternoon ride.* I hopped on the bike and headed south.

I hadn't intended to go by Ballerton's. I didn't want to meet Ballerton or ever see Counter Boy again, but I still found I'd taken the exit before I could stop myself. For a minute, I thought I'd turned up the wrong street, until I saw the Deluxe Tasty Food Supply sign. I pulled into the parking lot, removed my helmet, and stared.

The Ballerton's Motorcycle Seats sign was gone. I hung my helmet on Pancho's handlebar and walked to the warehouse entrance. I was surprised to find the door unlocked. I could see through the glass door that lobby was empty. All the chairs were gone. I hesitated, then walked inside. Ballerton's office door stood open. It was empty, too.

Circling the counter, I found the storage door open and that room was as barren as the others. The door to the warehouse was also open, but I didn't bother going through it, confident the entire warehouse would also be empty.

A decades-old business had vanished into thin air.

What happened? Where'd Ballerton's go? Did he relocate? This didn't feel like a relocation. It felt like an…evacuation or eviction. It felt wrong. A chill ran down my spine and I hurried back to my bike.

I was fastening my helmet strap when an employee exited Tasty Foods and headed toward the parking lot. I quickly pulled the helmet off and trotted to the young man.

"Hi! Can you tell me where Ballerton's moved?"

His eyes shifted to the building then back to me. They were big as saucers. "Wow. They're gone? Oh, man, like, they were here on Saturday. I worked early shift. Shared a, um, smoke with Taylor."

"Taylor?" I cocked my head. "Oh you mean the guy who worked the counter?"

The young man shrugged. "Yeah, I guess. He handled shipments in and out." He turned back to the building and stared. "Man, like, wow."

"Well, thanks." I returned to Pancho and continued heading south. It took all my concentration to pay attention to the road and keep my mind from wandering to what Ballerton's disappearance really meant.

I checked the time before turning out of the parking lot. It was only 12:30, plenty of time to make an additional stop before heading to Bubba's. When I reached Lockhart, I turned right and pulled up in front of Chisholm Trail Stables Antiques.

I approached the counter where Katherine was leaning over a tray of various jewelry items. "Afternoon, Katherine."

"Well, hello there." Katherine straightened. "How's the cow investigation going?"

"All wrapped up. I guess."

Katherine raised her eyebrows and waited.

I shrugged. "Didn't wrap up like I expected." I told her everything that had happened. She'd been instrumental, and I'd promised to fill her in at the end.

Katherine didn't speak for half a minute after I finished, then she shook her head. "Are all your cases this nutty?"

"Some are, for sure." I laughed. "At least I know Bubba and his cows will be fine, now."

"Hopefully, so will you." Katherine smiled. "Might seem anticlimactic after everything you've been through, but you doing anything for Halloween?"

"That's today?" I shook my head. "I completely forgot. In any case, I'm not much into the whole trick or treating thing. I have no kids, and I live in a neighborhood full of retirees and old people. Probably won't be home by dusk anyway. From here I'm headed to Bubba's. No idea after that."

"Just be safe on the roads. Pickup trucks full of country kids will be out later, heading to town to trick or treat the best neighborhoods."

"Thanks. I will." I pointed to the tray Katherine had been studying. "What's all this?"

"New batch of jewelry. Came from an estate sale. Elderly gentleman passed away."

I leaned toward the case and one piece immediately caught my eye. It was a beautiful bolo tie. The braided cord was black leather. The clasp holding the cord was a silver longhorn. Even though it wasn't a Hereford, I'll bet Bubba wouldn't care. "Please tell me this isn't too expensive."

Katherine narrowed her eyes. "You plan to give this to Bubba?"

I nodded.

She held the tie out. "Then you can have it."

She packaged it in a cotton filled box and handed it over. I hugged her, thanked her half a dozen times, and headed for my next stop.

Bubba must have heard my motorcycle coming up his long driveway, because he was standing on the porch when I pulled up. "Well, hiya." He grinned from ear to ear.

When I reached the top step, he grabbed me in a bear hug. "I was worried about you. I'm glad all this is over. Now I know nothin' else'll happen to you cuz of me." He released me and opened his door. "Come on in for a cuppa. Then I've got somethin' to show you."

We sat for what I hoped wasn't the last time at his kitchen table. As hard as it was to stomach Bubba's sliceable coffee, I didn't want to miss future opportunities. My own grandfather had passed several years ago and I'd truly grown fond of the man who sat across from me.

I reached in my purse and handed him the box from Karen's shop. "I brought you something."

He raised his eyebrows as he took the box. He lifted the lid, then looked up at me with glistening eyes. "You didn't haveta' do this."

"But I wanted to."

He got up, circled the table, and bent to hug me again, even harder this time. "I'll wear this to my next lodge meeting." He wiped his eyes on his sleeve as he returned to his chair.

It was pretty obvious he was flustered, so I changed the subject by giving him a more detailed recap than I'd provided in our phone call, ending with today's discovery — the mysterious disappearance of everything that'd been in Ballerton's warehouse.

The elderly man shook his head. "This sure turned out to be a lot bigger'n just my cows singin' and dancin', didn't it?"

"It sure did." I nodded. "How are your cows?"

Bubba grinned. "Got three new calves, the last progeny from poor ol' Mr. T. Also just this mornin' got me a new bull. Named him Alien."

I snorted coffee, which burned my nose and splattered Bubba's table. "Oh, I'm sorry."

"No matter." Bubba stood, retrieved a sponge from the sink, and cleaned up my mess. "You done?"

I nodded.

He stood. "Follow me. Wanna show ya somethin'."

I followed Bubba out the back door, figuring we were going to check out Alien in the sorting pen. Instead, we walked by the empty pen and stopped at the detached, single-car garage on the far side.

As soon as he raised the wooden garage door, I couldn't help but squeal. "Bubba! You got a motorcycle."

"I shorely did. Been thinkin' about it since we talked that one time about the joy of ridin'. Brought back a lot of memories. Picked this one up on Saturday."

He rolled the bike into the sun and we stood and admired it. "That's a mighty nice Electra Glide." I ran my hand across the Harley's golden-brown fuel tank. "It's beautiful. I love the color."

Bubba laughed. "Perfect for this old fart. Harley calls it Amber Whiskey."

"Have you named it?"

"Didn't use to name my Harley's back in the day, but you namin' your Suzuki Pancho Villa changed my mind. This here marvel of technology is Mother Ship. She's even got a digital display. Big change from what I use ta ride. Just hope my fat ol' fingers don't mess nothin' up."

"I'm sure you'll be fine." I winked at my former-client-turned-friend. "Want to go for a ride?"

"I was hopin' you'd want to." Bubba retrieved his helmet and a leather jacket, both color-matched to the bike of course, and wheeled the bike around to where I'd parked.

Before donning my helmet, I asked, "Where to?"

"You lead. Anyplace is fine with me."

I cocked my head and bit my lip. "Let's head east, toward Bastrop and the piney woods. But first, I'd like to go by the hippies' land one last time, even though I'm sure they're not there."

"I heard they was bein' transferred from our little county jail to some high security federal facility. Seems kinda extreme for nuthin' but pot. Still, probably never comin' back to their old trailers. But sure, if you want to go by there, I'm game."

It only took a few minutes to reach the hippies' gate, which stood wide open. I parked my bike at the edge of the dusty, caliche-gravel driveway. Bubba pulled up beside me. Together we walked to the clearing that served as the three trailers' parking area.

"What the...?" Bubba stopped so abruptly I bumped into him.

"Sorry!" I followed his gaze. The trailers were gone. The dog kennel was gone. Their old truck was gone. The small shed where Earl's motorcycle was stored was gone, as was the motorcycle.

The place looked like a moonscape. The caliche was raked clean, as was the dirt where the trailers had sat. I squinted to narrow my focus. "If you look closely, you can see the remnants of big tire tracks. Bigger than that white van I hunted for so long."

"Gubment." Bubba shook his head and said nothing else.

Out of curiosity, I walked to where Bruiser's kennel had stood. "They even took the dog doo."

"They's definitely up to no good." Bubba shook his head again. "Don't want no evidence." He paused, then continued in a shaky voice. "I wonder if those three folks that lived here really did get transferred to another prison. Or if they's somewheres else, now."

My stomach did a little dance. "That's a good question, but I doubt we'll ever know."

I walked to where G.J.'s trailer had been, then to the former location of Earl's steps, and ended where Bengy's trailer had stood. Not a scrap of paper or even a cigarette butt remained. Turning back to Bubba, I shrugged. "Maybe Linda Favoccia had the property cleaned up. Maybe she's going to sell it."

"You know that ain't likely true." Bubba shook his head.

"I know." I kicked the white gravel in concentration. *This is weird. Did the same people who emptied out Ballerton's really do this, too? Guess I'll never know. At least Bubba's ordeal is over.*

Something big was definitely going on. But unless I wanted to step into the world of government coverups and conspiracies, I'd need to let it go.

As I glanced around one last time, a glint of something where I'd been kicking the dirt caught my eye. I bent to pick it up, then almost dropped it in surprise. I stood and stared at the small object.

"Whatcha got there?" Bubba walked over to see what I held. "What is that?"

"I wish I knew." I turned the five by three inch, silver metal triangle over in my hand. It was the same shape and size as one I'd seen in an online photo a couple of weeks earlier. Part of an article about the cattle mutilations of the sixties and seventies. A shiver ran through me and I looked around, wondering if we were being watched.

I pocketed the triangle. "Let's ride."

Bubba nodded. "Enough strangeness. Let's find some nice, friendly nature to enjoy."

"I couldn't agree more."

We returned to our bikes, donned our helmets, and headed down the highway, done, at least for now, with mysteries and government projects. Or aliens. Or whatever.

Case Closed

ACKNOWLEDGMENTS & THANKS

So many wonderful people helped me research this book. Thanks to the following for their time, patience, and invaluable contributions:

- Robert Wallace Finlay — physician assistant certified PA-C who does remote care in the Aleutians Islands (located on the Alaska peninsula). Robert is also the author of *End of the Chain*, about medical care in the most remote parts of Alaska. When not in Alaska, Robert and his wonder dog Yoda live in Medway, Maine.

- Chuck Foreman — Manager at Chuck Foreman Investigations, as well as founder and former CEO of the non-profit: Center for Search & Investigations (CFSI). CFSI is dedicated to assisting and training families and communities in locating missing children worldwide.

- Chris Yates — LVN and AHA CPR instructor. Chris has been an Army medic and a nurse for over twenty years. She spends her time in the wilds of Vermont with her young son and her sweetheart, spinning fire and learning the Woodchuck Way.

- Captain John M. Roescher — John is a thirty year veteran of the Lockhart Police Department. He began as a patrol officer and worked up the ladder, with most of his career working in the Criminal Investigations Division.

- Karen Phillips — professional graphic designer and world's best cover artist.

- Eric Marsh — husband and best friend since 1989 for his endless patience as I read each chapter aloud to him.

- The members of the Lockhart Writers Group: Tam Francis, Gretchen Rix, Wayne Walther, and Phil McBride. Our four-plus years together has made me a better and more enthusiastic writer.

www.ingramcontent.com/pod-product-compliance
Lightning Source LLC
Chambersburg PA
CBHW022141170626
46807CB00005B/2028